FAIR WINDS OF DECEIT

Jean,

Thanks for foreviwing Marcus on this latest Adventure!

Fair Winds Always!

Bill Wood

14 APR 23

FAIR WINDS

OF

DECEIT

B. R. WADE, JR.

A Wade Publishing Novel

Wade Publishing LLC
1782 Trinity Road
Belington, West Virginia 26250

www.wadepublishing.com

Library of Congress Control Number:
2022922050

ISBN 978-1-7375461-3-9 (paperbound)
ISBN 978-1-7375461-4-6 (e-book)
ISBN 978-1-7375461-5-3 (hardcover)

Printed in the United States of America

Cover design and typesetting by Stewart A. Williams

This is a work of fiction. Space and time have been rearranged to suit the convenience of the book, and with the exception of references to historical figures, any resemblance to persons living or dead is coincidental. Certain long-standing and factual institutions, ships, buildings, military facilities and equipment, vehicles, and public places are mentioned, but the characters involved are wholly imaginary and their interaction with these actual entities is pure fantasy.

This work does include some of the author's recollections of serving in the United States Navy while attending Yeoman A School at NTC Bainbridge, and later serving as a Yeoman to the Naval Investigative Service Office Norfolk. Those recollections have been added to honor all the fantastic men and women he knew and served with at the time.

DEDICATION

This is to honor the few honest people out there.
Life is hard enough without having to filter out deceit.
Your honesty is appreciated more than you will ever know.

ACKNOWLEDGEMENTS

Writing the story is an easy task for me. The plot thickens, the words flow, action happens, and the pages add up fast. But after that, the hard part starts, and I do my best to avoid that level of work! I am in the debt of several people who took on these arduous tasks.

Alice handled the initial punctuation and grammar editing chores efficiently and with great kindness. She also did a beta read of the story and shared her thoughts that led to great improvements.

Louise provided a level of professional editing that massaged rough words into a readable story. Her encouragement from my first novel was a lasting and greatly appreciated gift.

Stewart handled the conversion of Word pages into book format and gave them a very professional look. He also took my rough, boring concept and created a cover that entices the potential readers.

PROLOGUE

THE UNION OF SOVIET SOCIALIST REPUBLICS is most often called the USSR in English-speaking countries, since it is easier and quicker to say than the entire name. In Russian, the country's name is even more of a mouthful. The Russian abbreviation for the name is CCCP, and these were the initials painted on the object of attention at Baikonur Cosmodrome that evening.

A number of men stood around the specially designed launch control room, which was filled with several rows of unique desks containing communication and monitoring equipment. Each desk had a flickering, closed-circuit television screen, most showing the same image: the entire Sputnik 11A59 two-stage rocket.

The day had been spent reviewing the rocket's data—making sure temperatures, electrical circuits, and fuel pressures were primed for a successful launch. The gleaming white rocket with lettered body was the center of attention for all there, and for many in other parts of the country. The men now awaited the call announcing the success of the launch.

To long-term employees, the rocket looked very familiar, with a launch vehicle that was a derivative of the R-7 Semyorka ICBM designed by Sergei Korolev. A couple of TV screens were focused on the nose cone of the rocket, which now contained the package, and not a nuclear weapon.

Several more screens monitored the base of the rocket, including the engine and four boosters strapped to the sides.

The package for this launch was a 22"-diameter shiny silver sphere, which had four straight antennas equally spaced around the center line of the sphere, all pointed to the rear of the satellite. Its weight of 184 pounds came mostly from the batteries needed to power the radio transmitter onboard. This soon-to-be-launched satellite was called Sputnik I. It sounds impressive until you translate it from Russian and find it means *satellite*.

The successful launch, at 10:29 p.m. Moscow time on 4 October, placed the package in an orbit that would track it over the United States several times per day for the next couple of months. Many citizens on ham radios were able to pick up the beep-beep-beep sound transmitted by Sputnik I. Naturally, the government and military constantly monitored the satellite.

This simple satellite launch led to a second one that triggered what became known as the "space race." The Russians were ahead, and the Americans had a lot of catching up to do. And as in any decent poker game, the stakes increased: the Russians sent a dog into orbit. The Americans finally got a satellite in orbit the next year, but Russia again raced ahead by putting the first man, and later the first woman, into orbit.

But the Americans succeeded in the first and second planetary flybys, speeding unmanned craft by Venus and later Mars. Ultimately, the Americans won the race by landing a human on the moon in July 1969, accomplishing the feat several more times over the next few years.

This space race was aided by two other important contests: the race to steal information from each other and the race to capture scientists from the defeated Nazis. While countries had always tried to get info from one another covertly, it had escalated with Russian spies in the Manhattan Project, the effort to create an atomic bomb, in the early 1940s.

Before World War II, Russians had started immigrating to the U.S. to be sleeper cells. Often complete families would blend into the melting pot of America and wait patiently to worm their way into high priority projects to steal data for the Soviet Union.

The race to steal information strengthened when Stalin dropped the Iron Curtain after WWII. Churchill coined the phrase "Iron Curtain" during a speech in the U.S., describing the Soviets' plan to let nothing into or out of the USSR while ceaselessly trying to steal information from everyone else.

Immediately after WWII, the race to capture and utilize German scientists emerged. Fortunately, the United States had a win in this race for key rocket scientists under Operation Overcast, later renamed Operation Paperclip. Former Nazi Party members and leaders were among the group of scientists who, via presidential order, were allowed into the U.S. to work for the government space program. The premier find was Werner Von Braun—a Nazi—but his rocketry knowledge quickly overpowered that flaw.

Over 1,600 German scientists, technicians, and engineers, many from the German V-2 rocket team, were happily moved to the U.S. between 1945 and 1959. Those Germans put the U.S. on a successful path in the space race. At the same time, more than 3,000 were hauled off to the Soviet Union, most without consent, for the same reason.

Information and people are often considered mere commodities when governments decide to best their enemies. It was so then, and it continues today.

I

THE NOON TIME CROWD THAT Thursday was about average for a midweek winter's day. Not quite winter, but a late fall day that felt about the same. The building was nearly empty, with more security guards than visitors. There might have been fifty people on this level of the museum, but they were spread out and the museum was somewhat cluttered, so it was hard to know for sure. None were visible, and this made it a perfect location for two people to meet unnoticed.

The National Museum of American History, nicknamed "America's Attic," is the place to see commonplace items with a great story to tell. In addition, the Attic houses some unique pieces of American history. The pieces stand alone. The commonplace items are shown in the context of their own use or even previous ownership. A baseball is just a baseball until it's the one autographed by the Babe after his last game; Mr. Ruth's signature makes it a special piece of American history.

This building of the Smithsonian complex consists of several floors, with each floor divided into sections, allowing the rare artifacts to be displayed in an organized, educational manner. Pure education would bore the hell out of the average person so entertainment is woven into

4

every display. The curators of the Smithsonian are extreme professionals in mastering this delicate combination.

The World War I display had been set up a couple of years before that late fall day to honor the fiftieth anniversary of the war's end on November 11, 1918. Known as the "War to End All Wars," it was fought mostly on European soil and saw the introduction of chemical warfare, aircraft, submarines, and machine guns. Killing had become easier; by the end of the war, over twenty million were dead and over twenty-one million were wounded.

Sadly, it did not end all wars, as WWII, Korea, and now Indochina had shown. Most of the WWI display would be returned to storage the following winter and replaced with something else that would have its turn before the hundreds of thousands who visited each year.

A man stood studying the exquisite model locked in the glass case. Some military artifacts are too large to display, so the museum has accurate scale models in their places. This particular model allowed people to appreciate a WWI U.S. Navy railway artillery gun—ten feet wide and over one hundred feet long in reality—without requiring that much space. The model, only three feet long, honored the five guns built by the Baldwin Locomotive Company and shipped overseas to fight the dreaded *Boche*, or as Americans said, the Hun. The last surviving railway gun of the five is on display at the U.S. Navy yard in D.C.

As the man studied the model, a shadow fell across the case; another person had stopped to look at the railway gun. No words were spoken and neither party looked at each other, but a small package, slightly smaller than a pack of cigarettes, was passed to the new arrival. A quick glance around verified there were no others in this area. The exchange was fast, conducted along the side of the display case that security cameras would not pick up.

The package safely tucked into a jacket pocket, the new arrival strolled to the next display case and studied the doughboy uniform the mannequin silently wore. It was easy to start humming the George M. Cohan song "Over There" while looking at the brown uniform donned by so many men back in 1917–18. After a reasonable amount of time looking around the displays, the new arrival walked out of the room, through another display area, and out of the museum.

After watching to make sure the new arrival had successfully left, the first man headed downstairs to the railroad display in the basement. All forms of transportation were represented, but the railroad was his favorite. Due to size limitations, there wasn't a huge assortment, but it was better than nothing.

He wandered around, taking in several real steam locomotives alongside other pieces of railroad history. It was always a great place to spend a few minutes and appreciate the U.S. rail system. Perhaps this summer would allow a trip to Steamtown, up north, to see a much larger collection of retired steam locomotives.

On that day, it was also a good place to reflect on his recent actions. One hundred years ago, men had taken a chance—risking fortunes, reputations, and lives, and sometimes losing them—to build a railroad across this nation, connecting the Atlantic and Pacific Oceans. They succeeded, and America became a great nation because of it.

While his actions wouldn't result in something as concrete as a railroad, they would monumentally change the world, just as the telegraph had. His actions would also make monumental additions to his special bank account, but he didn't care about that.

As he studied the telegraph equipment and read how it had revolutionized long-distance communication in the mid-1800s, a few miles away, the new arrival entered the embassy. With the package passed to the person who had ordered the pickup, the new arrival returned to the residential area of the building.

No, the man reflected, it wasn't about the money. The important thing was, like those railroaders a century ago, he was risking it all.

2

DOCTOR FREDERICK MONROE WAS STILL at his desk when the evening clean-up crew came through. Janitor Michael Jefferson was not used to seeing him this late, past 1900, and it startled him to open the door and see him there.

"Sorry to bother you, Doctor Monroe, but is it alright for me to run the vacuum now or should I circle back around?" Michael asked carefully, not to sound too pushy. Seemed the doc was lost in thought or just ignoring him, so he tried again, louder. "Doctor, can I vac now?"

Monroe looked toward the door but didn't focus on Michael. He gave a small smile as he pushed his glasses back up with his left hand, then coughed slightly, more like a throat clearing. "Sure, Michael. Come on in and do what you need to do." Doctor Monroe returned his focus to the folder on the center of his desk.

Michael emptied the trash, dumped the ashtrays, and ran the vacuum all around the office. Doctor Monroe moved back from his desk long enough for Michael to get the area under the desk, where Monroe's chair had created permanent dents in the short-nap carpet. As the janitor did, he noticed the open file had "Top Secret – Rembrandt" stamped in red ink across the top of the page. Michael usually ignored these things, but something about the stamp grabbed his attention; he wasn't sure why.

"Thank you, Doctor. Sorry I had to bother you. Goodnight."

Fred Monroe looked up again at Michael and smiled as he gave a small salute. "You take care, Michael. Thanks for the good work." And he returned his attention to the open file.

He seemed a bit out of it, Michael thought as he headed down the hall to the next office. And he wasn't usually here this late. Maybe he was just getting old, like so many around here. Dr. Monroe was ancient, after all, at least fifty. He was nearly bald and was starting to walk slightly hunched over, with a mild limp. But he still did a good day's work. Like so many in this building. Michael put the doc out of his mind as he opened the door to the next office needing his skills.

Back up the hall, Fred continued to read, finally leaning back in his chair after another hour of study. He placed his hands behind his head and looked around his office. The wall behind his desk was covered with shelving and an actual ton, at least, of research books. The shelves even held some he'd written over the years. The wall to his right was covered with a white board, filled with several colors of ink, showing the details of his latest project. A multicolored flow chart, a list of parameters in green ink, several potential problems in red ink, and their possible solutions in black ink were just some of those details.

The other two walls were covered with plaques—awards and other tokens of recognition received over the decades—and nicely framed photos. Military personnel call this their "I was there" wall. It's a way to brag about their careers while honoring the men and women who played a part in those careers. A few photos showed some of his successful projects, and a few more showed him with various dignitaries who had presented his plaques. But the majority of photos showed Fred as he wished he still was: an active duty officer wearing a uniform identifying him as a captain in the U.S. Navy. Hopefully when all this was over—well, at least when his life was over—he would be remembered that way.

Life isn't fair, he thought for at least the thousandth time. He still worked in the research lab. He still had the same projects. And he still garnered the respect of those working around him. Yet due to a small heart attack several years ago, he was medically retired from the Navy. That had started his depression; he missed wearing the uniform. And he greatly missed the comradery of his fellow officers, especially since his best friend transferred to a new duty station. Oh, some of the old gang got together for drinks and dinner from time to time, but it just wasn't the same since he was officially "on the beach": a Navy term for retirement.

Okay, he thought, *enough wallowing in frustration and pity.* It was time to refocus on the problem with Rembrandt. It was almost working. And with some luck and a bit more thought, he might just know what snafu created the "almost" part. So back to reading, pondering, and rationalizing to overcome the problem. Rembrandt would have its solution soon, he hoped, with just one more thing to work out. *Well, not just one more thing,* he thought with a chuckle.

The next morning, when the rest of the staff arrived for work, they were surprised to find Doctor Monroe's office door standing wide open. Actually, they were shocked. He never left his office door open and never, ever left it unlocked unless he was in there. And he was not in there. He was not in his office, not in the restroom, nor was he in the lab. No hat or coat hung on the rack. No papers were on his desk. After a very serious, thorough search, it was determined without a shadow of a doubt that the doctor was not in the building.

Agents of the Naval Investigative Service (NIS, pronounced *niz*) were called. Their search confirmed the doctor was neither in the office nor the building. They came to a firm conclusion, after searching his home and auto, that the doctor was gone. Nothing was found to cause them to visit the usual options. He probably didn't commit suicide since no body or note was found, unless he'd jumped into the Anacostia River and his body washed away. He probably didn't run off with a lover since no one knew about, or found any evidence of, any relationship he might have had. No signs of a forced kidnapping. Nothing was found. No hints, no clues, no evidence. Nothing. It was as if aliens had used that television space program's technology and beamed him off the planet.

Local police didn't discover any clues. The Federal Bureau of Investigation was called, since the doctor was working on projects of far-reaching national security issues and the possibility of kidnapping hadn't been eliminated. But their investigation equaled that of the NIS and local police: the doctor was gone, and no one had a clue why or how. But everyone knew his white board had been scrubbed clean sometime after 1900 hrs the previous evening. Whatever was on that board was gone forever.

No one noticed that a few files were missing from his office safe.

3

THE THICK FOLIAGE FELT LIKE a heavy, wet blanket. It made it hard to move, and moving was the only thing that could keep them alive. The rain helped by canceling out the noise they were making while moving—if you could call it moving. But the rain made everything slick as elephant snot, and that was not a good thing. Moving could get them back to the rest of the team alive, and that was the primary goal; not getting shot again was a close second.

Marcus looked down at Doc, noticing his face was pale, at least the parts not covered in camo and mud. Though passed out, he was breathing steady, and it looked like the wound in his leg had finally stopped bleeding. Marcus had used his uniform pants leg as part of the bandage for his shoulder. That left shoulder still looked like it was leaking, but with all the rainwater falling on the bandages it was hard to be sure.

The head wound that affected Marcus had finally stopped bleeding. The wound on his side burned like the fires of hell, but at least it, too, had stopped leaking the red stuff of life. They still hurt like hell, and he knew there would be a scar or two or three—damn easy to lose count—but hopefully the bad ones on his skull wouldn't show until he got old and went bald like his father.

Not having more bandages prevented Marcus from applying a proper new dressing to Doc. All he could do was cinch a stack of huge leaves over his old dressing with a belt. Remembering some first aid training that said pressure is good, Marcus thought, *I can do pressure.* And he thought again that they really needed to get back to the team since they had more supplies.

Pulling Doc through the jungle wasn't a good plan and too damn slow, so Marcus shifted his M-16 to the left shoulder. They were out of ammo, but it had been a good rifle and he refused to leave it behind. There was some logic there, he believed, but right then he didn't know what it was and was too tired to argue with himself. So the rifle went with him. The team had more ammo. His mind finished the statement with a plea: *I hope.*

Following that position change, he carefully picked Doc up and hoisted him over the right shoulder. Being a few inches taller and about ten pounds heavier than Doc, carrying him was not a problem. Most of their body fat was gone and their muscles were toned. Marcus chuckled as he realized, *if we just didn't have so many holes in our bodies and could stop all the blood leaks, we would be considered very healthy.*

There was no need to think about whatever germs and other bugs were running through their bodies. Couldn't worry about things he couldn't change right this minute, and he had to focus on Doc. He decided to stop and check his wounds every half hour or so and take a rest at the same time.

Marcus felt pretty much done in, but he remembered Johnny constantly playing his SEAL mind games and saying that for a SEAL, *done in* means you've only used forty percent of your energy. Marcus knew he still had a lot more to use. *Can't let Johnny down, now can I,* kept running through his mind. And he knew he would not fail Doc.

Either the rain covered their noise or the little guys with AK-47s had given up trying to find them. No more bullets were flying by. They just had to keep moving. The early morning light allowed Marcus to check the position of the sunrise and find a couple of landmarks that would briefly appear, at times, through the jungle canopy. With this tiny amount of geographical knowledge, he knew they were heading in the right direction. At least he thought they were heading in the right direction. There was no clue how far they had to go.

Pushing through the undergrowth, he wasn't expecting to find a break in the mess, yet he finally came upon a trail. It wasn't much, just a visible path that had been created by hundreds of feet running along it over time. The width was narrower than his body, so there was still plenty of green stuff slapping at him and Doc as they headed toward the team. Now there was a chance to make some good time, as long as they didn't run into the bad guys.

But Marcus realized that euphoria didn't last long in the jungle. Only ten minutes after finding the trail, they rounded a curve and ran right into a mass of leaves and vines that blocked the way. *Well, crap, that is downright weird.* The vines were on both sides of the trail, and as he turned around, they seemed to be closing in around them. As he pushed against them to try to get through, the vines came alive and started to wrap around the two men. The more Marcus struggled, the tighter they became. The only sound was the rain and Doc moaning as the vines pulled tighter.

Marcus tried to reach his Ka-Bar, which was kept sharp enough to cut through this mess, but it was like someone, or something, was holding his left arm. It would not move. He needed his knife and cried out in frustration, even though it might bring the enemy.

His right arm was holding Doc, who had woken up and started fighting. Then Doc yelled, "Marcus. Marcus. Stop, Marcus!"

"I'm trying to get us through, Doc. Hold on. Hold on, Doc! We'll get there, Doc!" Marcus yelled, though leaves and vines were closing in around his mouth. He could not see anything but green vines and leaves, but kept fighting.

Doc's voice became an octave or two higher as he yelled, "Marcus, stop. Hold on, Marcus. It's okay. Stop, baby."

What the hell is going on here? Doc never calls me "baby," thought Marcus. Then it was night again. The rain had stopped. He no longer felt Doc's weight on his shoulder as he wondered, *did I drop him? Why am I lying down.* The ground was soft, and smooth, and dry. A soft, sweet, gentle voice was pleading for him to wake up. What the hell was going on?

"Where is Doc?" he cried.

Kelly was lying beside Marcus, holding his head against her bare chest. His left arm was under her, and she held his other hand in hers. She sobbed softly as she pleaded with him. "Please, Marcus, come back to me. Please, baby. Wake up!"

As quickly as the vines had appeared, they were gone, and Marcus realized he was in their Alexandria, Virginia townhouse in late October, 1971. It took a few moments to realize the jungle had been another horrible dream. In real life, or rather in his wake state, he was in bed with Kelly, his wife of under two months. *I'm safe*, he thought. There was no one to rescue and no one trying to kill him.

He latched onto Kelly and held her close. Their breathing fell into sync and she slowly rubbed his back. Her warmth and gentle caresses reassured him that all was good. And with that knowledge, he drifted back to sleep.

4

THE SUNLIGHT LEAKING INTO THE bedroom gave it the warm yellow shade of morning. The eastern-facing shades were down, but they were not the blackout kind and admitted the morning glow. On non-workdays like this, the soft light allowed a slower, more gentle rousing from sleep. Too bad it only happened on two out of seven days—if he was lucky and had the weekend off.

As Marcus crossed over from a dream state to wake, flashes of what he'd been dreaming vanished from his mind. He wasn't sure if the dream was good or bad since it vanished so quickly. He did know one thing: it was frustrating, after a night's sleep, to feel more tired than before bed. He rolled over to give Kelly the first hug and kiss of the day, but her spot in the bed was empty. Running his hand over the sheet, he realized it was as cold as ice—she had been up for a while. It took a minute, but Marcus finally remembered what happened last night. Another one of those damn dreams had disrupted their sleep.

The dreams, actually nightmares by any definition, had first started while he was in Saigon's military hospital. The docs there said the dreams were leftovers from the mental trauma suffered in the field. That made sense, since he was reliving some of the same crap that almost killed him. After he got back to the States, the nightmares calmed down, becoming infrequent. Then, with all the fun and games of the CNO's special mission in Norfolk, Virginia earlier that year, Marcus believed his brain became so overloaded with work that the nightmares actually stopped.

Now that the operation was over, and he and Kelly had made it through their wedding, his brain must have found some spare time to dig up those horrible memories. Probably seeing the rest of the SEAL team at the wedding, and the two VIP gents from D.C. whom they'd rescued, helped trigger the dreams. Maybe it was just his guilty conscience driving him crazy.

A hot shower helped clear the fog from his brain. Shaving the face and brushing the teeth were two more steps toward properly starting the day. After a quick dry-off, he wrapped the towel around his waist and headed back to the bedroom to find critical pieces of clothing. Kelly was sitting on the side of the bed holding two mugs of coffee. Her soft blond hair stood out nicely as it lay carefree against the burgundy of her robe.

"I like your outfit, sailor."

"Thank you, Ma'am. I hear it's the latest thing on the Paris runways for secret agents and newlyweds."

"Your coffee mug was just sitting there lonely and empty, so I figured filling it and bringing it up to you would help get you moving. Come join me," she softly said, nodding to a spot on the bed beside her. She passed him his mug as he gently sat there. He leaned over and gave her the first "good morning" kiss. The day doesn't officially start until the kiss happens.

They drank their coffee in silence, enjoying the ability to just sit together, knowing there was nothing demanding their immediate attention. Most of that year had been a hectic affair that finally calmed down after the wedding on 4 September. With his left arm healed and almost back to its original strength from the knife attack earlier that year, Marcus was able to drink his coffee and gently rub Kelly's back at the same time. She reciprocated by running her hand on his towel-covered thigh.

She smiled softly and made something like a purring sound. Marcus was not sure why, but it had a positive effect on certain parts of his body, and the towel was not able to keep things under wraps. Whatever she had planned for this morning would have to wait a while longer as there was a more pressing issue that needed attention.

"I am not going to let your shower go to waste, sailor," she whispered as she stood, untied the belt of her robe, and pushed it back off her bare body. His towel fell to the floor beside her robe.

5

WITH THE BEST PART OF waking up married behind them, they washed each other's backs in the hot shower, dressed for a casual day of household chores, and came downstairs to the kitchen for another cup of coffee. If Marcus guessed correctly, bacon and pancakes were next on the Saturday morning checklist. Nope, he was wrong.

"Ready to talk about last night?" Kelly asked gently, yet with major concern in her voice. She looked down while pouring more coffee in both their mugs, receiving only silence. "Babe, that's the third nightmare you've had since we got back from Rome. At least they waited until we finished our outstanding honeymoon. Your screams might have caused an international incident."

Marcus let out a huge sigh before he could stop it. Such a sigh was usually a sound of frustration, but he was not frustrated, just tired from not enough sleep and too much early morning exercise. "How about we get some pancakes and bacon down first?" he offered with a big smile. "I'm ready to pass out from hunger and will need a couple of eggs to rebuild my strength. Someone used up all of my energy a bit ago."

"Ah, ha, trying to sidetrack me with food, eh? Okay, that works for now, but we really need to get to the root of your issues, Marcus. I know you've told me a lot about last year, but I suspect there is something else that needs to come to the surface. Perhaps it's something you don't think is important."

"Yea, probably. Okay, we'll have a good talk later, but right now, the chef's hat has to take priority over the shrink's couch," he said with as much humor as he could muster. Being married to a professional psychologist had its good and bad points. You knew you were in trouble when she asked "and how does that make you feel?"

Preparing and feasting on breakfast was time well spent; they enjoyed each other's company and chatting about things to get done that day. Laundry, grocery shopping, and minor yard work were high on the list. In addition, fall was in the air, October was one-third over, and it was time to think about Halloween decorating.

One thought led to another as they discussed Halloween and shared memories of costume parties from their pasts. Neither really enjoyed the costume stuff; however, getting together with friends and neighbors, without the stress of costumes, was always fun. They wished there was time to plan a small get-to-know-ya party for the neighbors the following weekend. Lots of interesting décor and food choices came with the ghoul and monster themes, and that might add enough fun to take the stress off socializing. Maybe next year, they decided.

Since Kelly hadn't spent much time in Alexandria, she didn't have many friends here. The couple had come up from Norfolk about a dozen times over the summer but had lived there full time only the last couple of weeks. She needed to meet all the neighbors to hopefully build some strong friendships.

Likewise, it was time for Marcus to meet—or re-meet—many of them, since he'd been gone most of the time he'd owned the place. Looked like Christmas would be the next opportunity; at least they had time to get ready for that.

Their neighborhood was considered well-established, a realtor term for *old*, and was near the politically powerful District of Columbia. Most of the townhouses were owned by government bureaucrats. The Colts' six-unit block dated to just after the end of WWI, but all units had been refurbished in the late 1960s to bring them up to code and modernize them. Marcus purchased his primarily as a place to live, but also as an investment. He figured that, when he transferred to another duty station, he would rent it to another Navy officer.

The townhouses all featured standard red brick construction, a small basement, and three floors topped off with a small attic area under a

Mansard roof. Williamsburg Blue shutters framed each window, and the same color was used on the doors.

When he bought this place, it was a bit much, but now he was growing into it. For a small girl, Kelly took up a lot of space. More than likely it was her huge personality, not her physical size, that was filling their house.

Initially, Marcus hadn't gone overboard decorating, picking just the basics: sofa, end tables, dining room set, bed, etc. He was consistent on style, going with early American-inspired pieces featuring medium dark wood accented with earth-toned fabric. The combination was comfortable and restful.

Over the summer, on their weekend trips up from Norfolk, Kelly added at least one piece of furniture per trip, so it was totally furnished by the time they moved in after the honeymoon. The admiral's daughter, and now lieutenant commander's wife, was properly trained and ready for entertaining.

Kelly's dad, the admiral who sat behind the Pentagon desk belonging to the Chief of Naval Operations (CNO), was the highest-ranking military person in the Navy. He was deputy to the Secretary of the Navy and a member of the Joint Chiefs of Staff. The JCS consisted of the senior ranking members of each branch of the military, and together they provided professional military advice to the Secretary of Defense and the President. People respected his opinions.

The CNO had approved the townhouse, wearing both his hats: one as a father-in-law and the second as a military career guidance counselor for Marcus. With a nod, the admiral had said it was an appropriate size and location, and properly outfitted, befitting a Navy commander (O-5). Marcus was still a lieutenant commander (O-4), but "one must plan ahead a wee bit," the admiral counseled. The O-6, or captain level, would require a larger place, but that would be a few years in the future.

Kelly's mother, Elaine, had spent a lot of time working with Kelly on the wedding registration list in the early summer. Her skills as a senior admiral's spouse ensured that the proper items, i.e. those befitting a senior Navy officer's house, were listed. Because of her efforts and the large number of wedding guests, the house was now decked out properly. Their kitchen was filled with the right accessories all the way down to two styles of shrimp forks.

The Colts were ready to play the political and social games needed to climb the ladder in the military, and Marcus knew Kelly would do a lot to keep him out of trouble on that end.

With all this help, and with the in-laws' approval, the house was ready for entertaining, and he and Kelly would be ready when the time came. But first, one more cup of coffee while he finished the rest of the eggs on his plate.

6

THE MORNING WENT BY FAST; the Colts usually spent Saturdays doing household chores. Kelly did laundry while Marcus, with his trusty yard broom, tried to find the grass in the back yard. It was buried under a half ton of red, yellow, and dull brown leaves. "Hey, it is fall after all," he kept mumbling to himself, realizing that's what leaves do this time of year.

Marcus had wanted a yard with several maple and oak trees, and now he was reaping one of the benefits of having them. At least leaf raking was one of those tasks that took little brain power and let the mind drift off the task at hand. But in his raking stupor, he thought back to his nightmare.

Some of what he remembered had actually happened the previous year, while on a special mission. Doc was real. The wounds were real. Vietnam was very real. Little guys with AK-47s were extremely real. Man-grabbing vines, well, not so much. Although it could feel that way at times, when moving through the foliage of the backcountry. Maybe Kelly could figure out what they represented. It was probably one of those "man's inhumanity to man" things.

Kelly would eventually unlock his mind. As a trained psychologist, she had learned how to get into the deep dark crevices and pull out the info that helped people overcome their problems. Two years before Marcus met her, she had lost her fiancée in 'Nam and decided to focus her life on helping those who came back from that hellhole cope, by training as a psychologist. Everyone returning had to face and conquer their issues. Kelly and Marcus met earlier that year in March, as she was finishing up her master's degree; that meeting had changed his life so much for the better.

And as he pondered, he reminded himself that he was one very lucky guy, and Kelly was just the cherry on top of the delicious sundae that was his life then. Well, that description wasn't really accurate. She was not a decoration—she was the most important thing in his life. Her love and support made him a better person. The next fifty-plus years together should be a fun-filled time.

Marcus also knew he was lucky being in the Navy, and he really enjoyed his job. He was one of the youngest lieutenant commanders in the Navy. His duty station was the Naval Investigative Service (NIS), where he was a special investigator in charge of the Internal Affairs division. His luck had him working out of the headquarters in the Washington Navy Yard, the oldest shore facility in the Navy. The place had lots of history and class, and he loved it there.

Usually Marcus would just tell people he worked in an office in the Navy Yard. Boring paper-pushing tasks and counting paperclips were his forte. But when he had to tell non-Navy people where he worked in more accurate detail, he ended up getting a blank stare followed by a variation of "you do what for whom?" It was easier to explain to civilians that the Navy has a police department: the Shore Patrol (SP) personnel are the beat cops and the NIS agents are the detectives. It was his job in Internal Affairs to keep NIS personnel honest.

If they were really interested, he would get into more detail about the organization of NIS, none of it classified material: Washington, D.C. is the NIS headquarters, where an admiral is in charge. Marcus hung his hat there. Under NISHQ are multiple NISOs, Naval Investigative Service Offices, which coordinate the work in a geographic area, such as the 5th Naval District.

The Navy breaks up the world into districts, with a large Navy base as the headquarters (HQ) for each district. For example, Norfolk, Virginia is the home of the 5th Naval District. It extends from northern Virginia down through much of North Carolina, with multiple ships, Navy and Marine bases, and all units therein assigned to the 5th Naval District. And under each NISO are a number of NISRAs, Naval Investigative

Service Resident Agencies, which house the agents who do the actual investigative work at various locations around the district.

His investigative division, consisting of three other officers, several enlisted personnel, and a few civilians, spent most of the time at the NISRA level weeding out agents who had gone astray. They also spent time making sure that agents who had made tough decisions, like shooting a bad guy, had followed all the rules while doing it. That part of the job did not make them any friends in the agent ranks, but it kept the press and politicians happy when they proved all the proper procedures were followed.

While running the Internal Affairs unit, it seemed another part of his job—one not specified in the job description or organizational chart—involved operations and projects that senior brass thought couldn't be done in the conventional manner. Since he had a track record of success with the unconventional, Marcus would get the call. He had gotten two such assignments so far in the three years he'd been assigned to NIS. The latest unconventional assignment had brought him face to face with Kelly.

The rake continued to move across the lawn, the leaves piled up, and his mind drifted back to earlier that year.

7

NIS USES CONFIDENTIAL INFORMANTS (CIs) to solve cases and get convictions. Late the previous year, NIS CIs started dying in unusual circumstances, some around the Norfolk Naval Base. The brass in D.C. believed someone in NISO or NISRA Norfolk was leaking information about the CIs, and Marcus was placed on temporary duty to work directly for the CNO and stop the problem.

The leaker, killers, and reasons for the killings were all unknowns. The only solid information was a growing number of dead sailors. To keep NIS staff from locking down, Marcus went to Norfolk undercover and joined that NISO as a yeoman. As a low-level enlisted man, he might be ignored while snooping around.

With help from the NISO Norfolk's commanding officer, Captain Humphrey Miller, he created a fake assignment that would get him even closer to the agents. While visiting the captain's house to plan, he met the captain's niece, an adorable Old Dominion University grad student named Kelly. Marcus was knocked off his feet instantly by this beauty.

And almost as fast, it became clear this lovely lady felt the same way and was chasing Marcus with 'forever after' in mind. He was very happy when Kelly caught him three days later. And it was only after she caught him that she mentioned being the daughter of the CNO, his boss's boss. Her uncle, Captain Miller, was married to the CNO's little sister.

Marcus still wasn't sure what she saw in him. Standing six feet tall, he had a slender look due to his weight of 165, though he was athletic. His face was not Hollywood quality, his ears stuck out a bit too much, and he looked younger than he really was. At least his brown hair cooperated when combed. Usually.

As for Kelly, she was every man's dream girl. When he first saw her, it was like meeting a fashion model on her day off, or for sure an actress. She looked like Grace Kelly in *High Society*, but her hair was longer and she was much prettier.

She had a laid-back, easygoing look. Her preferred dress code had her long legs encased in snug blue jeans, dainty feet slipped into white deck shoes, and magnificent bosom hidden by a bulky Old Dominion sweatshirt. Her sand-colored hair was usually pulled back into a ponytail, and that beautiful face with the brightest smile never needed makeup. At around 5'6", she was just the right height for Marcus to kiss her on the top of her head.

Two weeks after their first meeting, they were engaged—when it's right, time is immaterial. Less than six months later, their Norfolk wedding was the social event of the year for Naval Base Norfolk.

And while Kelly and Marcus were romancing, he found time to discover that the leaker was not a member of NIS. The Norfolk police department's lead detective had been friendly with the supervisory special agent in charge of the NISRA under the pretense of sharing information between law enforcement agencies. But Marcus saw a correlation between the timing of their chats and the deaths of the CIs. Sometimes two plus two really did add up to four.

Marcus then found that the logistics center of the naval base was the home of what his team called a "nest of vipers": bad guys heavy into supply theft, drugs, and murder for hire. In hopes of getting closer to the unknown ringleader, Marcus and another agent went to work there undercover as CIs. Except they were not far undercover: under Marcus's orders, the SSA passed the information of their existence to the dirty detective. The trap was properly baited.

The two crazy volunteers thought they had their security covered, between the Shore Patrol, extra NIS agents, and two SEAL teams watching their backs. But within a week, both became targets of the vipers, landing in the hospital. One viper went directly to the morgue, thanks to Marcus's 1911 .45 semi-automatic pistol. Two other vipers were injured:

Marcus shot one, and his SEAL buddies took down the other. It's never good to anger a SEAL.

Eventually, they caught the ringleader and pulled more of his minions off the street. Cold cases were closed and the drug flow on the base slowed greatly. Once his wounds healed, Marcus returned to D.C. to continue as the lead Internal Affairs investigator.

Other than the nightmares, the number of people who had tried to kill him the last couple of years, and too many scars on his twenty-seven-year-old body, he was really a lucky guy.

8

MARCUS REFOCUSED ON FINISHING UP the leaf issue that plagued the back yard. With the leaves raked, he spent a moment looking at the completed job. As he always told his team, savor the small victories when possible; they may not come often.

After returning the rake to its place of honor—hanging on the back wall of the garage, Marcus paused to admire their two vehicles. Kelly's car was a fire engine red, two-door, 1965 Mustang convertible, and Marcus drove a 1965 Plymouth Barracuda. Painted in bright yellow with a black racing stripe, it stood out in the parking lot. But they both needed a good coat of wax before winter set in, he realized.

For now, he was looking forward to spending a few minutes sipping a cold beer and reading Alvin Toffler's book *Future Shock*. Toffler believed that society was undergoing a massive change to a much more complex industrial society. This change would cause stress and leave people disoriented. He popularized the term "information overload," and when Marcus looked at all the data he had to access when working a case, he could see it coming. Marcus knew society always wanted more information, and one day that huge amount would actually bog them down. Yep, information overload was coming, or might already be here.

Walking slowly toward the house, he glanced up at the trees to see how much more they would dump on the yard before winter. They actually looked rather bare; he guessed the big storm the previous week helped clean them out.

Before he got within ten feet of the back door, it opened, and Doc came charging out. "Hey, Marcus, how ya doin'?" he barked.

"Careful, Doc, you are between me and a cold beer. That's a very dangerous place to be, as you well know," Marcus replied with a big smile. "What's up, buddy?" He caught up with Doc at the small porch that sat under the back door, and their handshake quickly changed into a back-slapping hug.

"I think I told you years ago that calculus was the thing that stopped my early college career. It's about to do it again."

"Doc, you told me last year in 'Nam that the nemesis that stopped your college dreams was a stacked blond named Ginger. I recall you saying that you spent too many nights trying to crack her reluctance to your amorous desires rather than cracking your books."

Doc held up his hands, put on his standard *you caught me* smile and shrugged. "Okay, bossman, your damn memory is way too good. But I did have a calculus problem then, and it's back now. Please tell me you have a few minutes to explain a few things to me." His voice dropped as he continued, "Please, sir? I really need your help."

Marcus hated it when Doc got polite and quiet. That meant it was serious. It was especially serious when he called him "sir." In the normal world, the enlisted sailor would be calling all officers by their rank, or at the very least, "sir." But HM1 Donald 'Doc' Stevens fell into a different category.

As one of the few Navy SEALs, Doc put his life on the line the previous year to save Marcus at least twice, and they became closer than brothers in the less than two years they had known each other. They had worked together in 'Nam for a few months on a special assignment before heading back to their own units.

In addition to being a SEAL, Doc was also a hospital corpsman first class. Before joining the Navy eight years ago he was in his third year of college, wanting to be a doctor. But chasing girls and failing calculus put his GPA below the 2–S draft deferment level, so rather than succumbing to the draft and heading into the Army, he joined the Navy and pushed to become a medic. Due to his rating choice, the SEALs recruited him to be one of them.

Doc did not fit the standard image that was conjured up by the term SEAL. He didn't have rippling muscles or a square jaw, or even the body bulk expected. At twenty-nine years of age, he stood 5'10" and weighed in around 160 pounds. His rather common-looking face was topped off with a 1950s flattop haircut. That hair was the first thing you noticed about him.

Second thing you noticed was his sense of humor: Doc always had a comeback. He could lighten the darkest mood and was easy going. But don't let his easygoing persona fool you. He was a fighter who could take down men twice his size. And even though he was a healer, he could harm just as fast. He was a true warrior, a great friend, and a dangerous man to his enemies. He was also uncommonly loyal to his friends, and Marcus was honored to be one. They completely trusted each other.

Earlier that year in Norfolk, Doc and the rest of his SEAL team came back into his life as part of his protection detail while Marcus worked undercover to crack the viper case. After the stab wound from an attempted assassin immobilized Marcus's left arm in a sling for months, Doc was asked by the CNO to be his assistant/driver/medic/bodyguard, allowing Marcus to safely keep working on the case. While Doc would be by his side 24/7 to help drive and change his bandages, his main role was to make sure Marcus didn't do anything stupid that would harm his arm's recovery.

To accomplish that task, Doc was given temporary duty (TAD) orders from the SEAL team to NIS and granted the status of special agent, although he didn't have the qualifications or the training. The brass figured Marcus would keep an eye on him since Doc would always be by his side. He performed very well in the role of an agent, and he started thinking about becoming one full time. Only one problem existed: becoming an agent required a college degree, the one he was again pursuing.

After the vipers were put away, Marcus stayed in Norfolk for physical therapy and to document a new and different way to analyze case data. He taught the method to Doc, and together they wrote the manual. Even though Marcus was completely healed, Doc was able to come back with him to D.C. and work out of the NISHQ. Doc was now using his specific knowledge to train agents on the new technique while getting his degree. Within the year, he hoped to be able to qualify as an agent for real.

9

SEEING DOC ALWAYS MADE MARCUS smile. Even though he'd be talking about calculus for the next hour or so, Doc was worth whatever trouble he caused. As they walked into the kitchen, Marcus asked, "Does Kelly know you're here, Doc?"

"For sure, Marcus. When I think the princess might be in the palace, I always ring the bell."

"Good plan, buddy. Stick with that procedure." As newlyweds, they might have been caught in an embarrassing situation if Doc had just busted in using the key they gave him. Due to their close friendship with Doc, the Colts had given him a key to the house, just in case. One never knew when he might need access in a hurry when they weren't around.

Marcus had not generated Kelly's nickname, though she really looked the regal part. When his SEAL team friends found out that Kelly's dad was the CNO, they nicknamed her "Princess," since the CNO is like royalty to most sailors. As they came into the kitchen via the back door, Kelly strolled in from the living room. Her smile lit up the room. "Doc, you are staying for dinner, right?"

"Babe, we're going up to the office to talk calculus for a while. So, yea, we better plan on him being here for a few hours."

"Super!" Kelly responded with honest enthusiasm and kissed Doc on the cheek. "My big brother is always welcome. You boys behave and hold down the fort while I make a grocery run. Will you be up to fixing crab cakes for dinner?"

"Not a problem. Pick up cabbage and I'll prepare slaw also." Marcus pulled her into his arms. "I think we need Italian bread crumbs, and you'd better grab a couple of bottles of a good German Spatlese Riesling to go with the crab."

"I love a man with a plan!" Kelly replied. "Especially a great food plan."

"Grab two beers, Doc, while I kiss this adorable creature before she darts out the door."

"Got ya covered, boss," Doc said with a grin as he strolled to the refrigerator.

With Kelly on the mission to get the food, Doc and Marcus grabbed some pretzels to go with the beers and climbed the stairs to his office. They discussed his problems with calculus for nearly an hour before Marcus noticed the light bulb click on behind Doc's eyes. He had made an important connection that would probably help him pass the course. The rest of the courses needed for his BA in business management were relatively easy compared to calculus. If all went well, he would graduate with the June class of 1972.

As the tutoring tapered off, they got into discussing the best thing in life: women! In Doc's case, this meant his fiancée. "How's Ann doing, Doc?"

"Adorable as ever, Marcus. It looks like she'll be up for a duty station transfer early next year, and with our upcoming wedding plans, the best news is that it looks like she'll get her transfer to Walter Reed. Her schedule is a mess right now, so it will be a couple weeks before she can get back up here for a weekend break."

"Sorry for your dry spell without hugs and kisses these next few weeks. You and Ann need to plan on staying with us that weekend."

"Well, we love free food, and your place is our favorite bed-and-breakfast, so sure, count on us to be here."

Doc's humor had struck again, and the laughter was contagious. Ann was always fun to have around. Just like Doc, she had saved Marcus's life. Marcus owed her big time.

Doc first met Ann when he was in the hospital room as part of the security team, and she came in to check on Marcus after his surgery. Though she and Marcus were not long-term close friends, she took the

extra step to check on a new friend who was also a patient, and then became an important part of their lives.

With Ann still living in Norfolk and Doc now in D.C., the relationship
was difficult, as with so many on active duty, in all branches of service.
The distance did make the time together much more intense, in a good
way. But it would be great when her transfer came through.

After they settled down from the laughter, Doc got a serious look on
his face and sighed. He shook his head and said, "With Ann moving up
here next year, I need to be looking for a place to rent. Now that's a challenge I do not look forward to handling. Got any suggestions, bossman?"

Marcus sat there trying to decide how much he should say. In his position, he was aware of many plans that had yet to be announced to the staff
and should be kept quiet. But Doc was different. So Marcus let him know
some things. Smiling, he replied, "Doc, this does not leave this room. The
admiral and I were talking about you the other day. He's pleased with the
way you are handling the training. And is very happy with your pursuit
of that degree. While nothing is cast in stone, his plan after you graduate
and get through your agent training is to keep you at HQ for at least another year doing what you're doing now."

"Ugh. You know I want to be out in the field as a regular agent, Marcus.
And with more experience, I could later be a better instructor."

"Yea, in a normal situation, that is true. But you're teaching a totally
new set of methods that you and I perfected. And you already have used
them in the field in Norfolk. Regular field experience would not make
any difference. And looking at the training schedule, it will take about
eighteen months to get all the NISRAs up to speed on the new methods.
After that, you'll probably be sent to a NISRA."

Doc sighed and shook his head. "Guess I should be happy to be here
in D.C. At least I'm working in the same building as you, and we get to
spend some time together. With Ann getting up here, our first year of
marriage will be somewhat settled down."

"Look for the positives, Doc. Remember, unlike military personnel,
agents do not move around a lot. They might get promoted from SA to
SSA and go to a different NISRA, but that isn't frequent. Here's what I
see that could be a good path for you after you complete all that new
training in the next two years. First, you get assigned as an agent to the
Washington NISRA. That would keep you in the area in case your training expertise is needed. Then after a couple of years in the field, you might
move back to HQ as either a trainer or perhaps in Internal Affairs. I can

see you doing well there after what we went through in Norfolk. All that would allow you and Ann to become fairly well settled in the area and provide a great life together."

"Huh. I really hadn't thought about it from that viewpoint. Thanks, Marcus, for getting my thought process going in the right direction. So maybe I should look to buy instead of rent?"

Marcus smiled. "What you should do is have this talk with Ann. Sooner and not later. She might want to get out of the Navy and move back home to Leadville, Colorado and take you with her." He chuckled at the thought of Doc in the small town of Leadville. "You two are a team now and need to work together."

Doc gave an agreeing nod and picked up another pretzel. They both knew it was time to get back to uncovering the secrets of calculus.

10

DINNER WAS A GOOD COMBINATION of great food, good wine, and excellent company from Doc. As they enjoyed the crab, Doc spent a lot of time running wedding thoughts by Kelly. Just like Marcus did with his housing plans, Kelly insisted that Doc share those wedding thoughts with Ann sooner and not later. Marcus saw that Doc was slowly getting the relationship/marriage attitude straight in his mind after too many years of chasing skirts, looking for one-night stands.

They finished the meal, cleaned up the table and kitchen, and moved to the living room for some chat. Kelly was thrilled that Ann would be in town soon, but confided that she was still a bit down that they didn't have time to put together a Halloween party.

"How about we start planning one for next year now, and that'll give us plenty of time to do it right, eh?" Marcus suggested. He threw out the standard Bloody Mary and Virgin Mary drinks. Then caught them off guard by mentioning Iceland's signature beverage, *Brennivin*, which is clear potato mash schnapps flavored with caraway seeds. In Iceland it is called "Black Death" since the drinker wishes he were dead the next morning after drinking too much of it. But it goes really great with the Icelandic snack of dried cod fish called *hardfiskur*.

Kelly and Doc just looked at each other and shrugged. Some days they didn't know what to do with Marcus and his somewhat strange sense of humor.

That planning conversation went on until Doc reached his socializing limit, thanked them for another great dinner, and headed back to the base. He was staying in the BOQ, Bachelor Officer's Quarters, since his pseudo-civilian position at NIS placed him equivalent to a lieutenant level for housing.

After waving Doc goodbye and watching his 'Vette's tail lights fade down the road, Kelly and Marcus retired to their favorite spot, the sofa, to snuggle. They started talking about their neighbors. There wasn't much to say as he barely remembered what he knew about them from living there almost a year ago.

Since knowledge of the locals was limited, they decided to make personal visits to the five other townhouses the next afternoon after worship service. They hoped their plan to introduce themselves and chat a few minutes would give them a chance to become real neighbors.

As they snuggled, they turned the conversation to the status of Kelly's job search. The fact was their financial position meant she didn't need to work to help pay the bills and keep food on the table. But her decision to go into psychology was based on an internal need to help warriors coming home from combat. And that need to help still existed.

Kelly had graduated from Old Dominion with her master's degree in psychology last May. Over the summer, she volunteered her services at the Norfolk Naval Station hospital, while Doc and Marcus wrapped up the cases against the vipers and Marcus completed the physical therapy on his arm. She had the book knowledge and at least some practical experience. All she needed now was a local hospital to realize her great potential and use it.

She had already interviewed with several local hospitals and clinics, but none had shown promise yet. Kelly still hoped to work at Walter Reed, and decided to call Monday to check on the status of things. Marcus felt the squeaky wheel gets the grease, and letting them know she really wanted the job was the quickest way to get it. He suggested a personal visit rather than a simple phone call. Her smile might just break down a few doors.

It was important for him to remember that his lady was extremely independent. She knew what she wanted and had her own method of getting it. She didn't want her father's position as CNO to influence their hiring decisions, so she kept her maiden name quiet. She did emphasize that while the standard military wife frequently moves, her husband's position with NIS would keep him in the immediate area for at least a few more years. As the conversation wound down, she told Marcus she would consider his suggestion of making a visit to Walter Reed.

The events of the day were catching up with them and sleep was calling when the phone rang. Marcus answered on the second ring. "Lieutenant Commander Colt's residence. Colt speaking."

"Mr. Colt, I need your help. This is Carl Freeman, and agents from NISRA Washington have arrested my son, Martin."

"What happened, Carl?"

Carl let out a big sigh. "They're not telling me much, Mr. Colt, just that he is under arrest for drug possession and assault. Can you come down here and figure this out?"

"Carl, tell me where you are. And who is the lead agent?"

"Sorry, Mr. Colt, I'm not thinking straight. This has upset me so much. I'm here at the NISHQ office. SA Tucker has the lead, sir."

"Okay. Sit tight and I'll see you in about thirty minutes."

"I appreciate it, Mr. Colt. Thank you."

Hanging up the phone, he turned to Kelly and shrugged. She smiled and said, "Sounds like you're heading to work. What happened with Carl?"

Marcus gave her all the information he had, which wasn't much, and went upstairs for a quick shirt change and to pick up his weapons. Since it wasn't an official workday, he could get away with wearing civvies for this visit to the office. Like the setup in Norfolk, the NISRA shared building space with headquarters.

As he approached the back door, Kelly stood in his way. She wrapped her arms around him and gave a warm kiss. Then she pulled his head down and whispered in his ear, "Stay safe. Shoot straight. I need you, sailor." It had become her standard goodbye when he left for work.

"Always for you, Princess." That had become his standard reply. With a returned kiss, Marcus stepped out into the night to help Carl.

II

THE DASHBOARD CLOCK OF THE 1965 yellow Barracuda moved the minute hand past the twelve, so it was officially Sunday morning as Marcus approached the gate to the Washington Navy Yard. The drive was easy this time of night, and the lack of traffic allowed him to think about Carl and his family. He was too nice a guy for this type of thing to happen to him.

When Marcus first came onto active duty, Carl was already a fixture in the NISHQ. He'd been working there for several years and was very proficient. Standing right at six feet tall and hitting the scale at around 190 pounds, he was in great shape for a middle-aged man. His short black hair was starting to recede, but his dark coffee-tone skin had few wrinkles. He rarely smiled and his eyes seemed to look deep into your soul. Many found him to be intimidating, but Marcus liked what he saw. Discovering he was a former Marine Master Gunnery Sergeant, Marcus followed the sacred advice given to all young officers: find a good senior NCO and listen to him. With that attitude, they worked well together and soon became friends.

Carl Freeman was a retired Marine who had hung up his uniform about seven years ago. His retirement ceremony happened about six months after his wife died of breast cancer. He had met Katherine right after he graduated from recruit training at Montford Point Camp, a seg-regated part of Camp Lejeune, North Carolina, in early 1944. They mar-ried just before he shipped out to visit several tropical islands in the South Pacific.

It was not a south sea pleasure cruise, since the Japanese army held these islands and wanted to keep them. His time on Saipan and Okinawa was rough. He came home shortly after V-J Day, having spent seventeen months fighting for a country that considered him a second-class citizen. The Victory over Japan celebration found Carl wearing the stripes of a sergeant and several more ribbons on his uniform, including a Silver Star, a Bronze Star, and a Purple Heart. His Purple Heart was affixed with three small gold stars indicating he had been wounded multiple times.

His experiences in the war provided him with the knowledge of sur-vival and fighting that needed to be taught to the recruits. So, with the exception of a visit to Korea in the 1950s, where he fought at the Chosin Reservoir and earned a second Bronze Star, he spent his time in uniform as an instructor, passing his knowledge as a warrior on to the newest Marines. Many Marines survived Vietnam because they listened to Carl.

Peacetime America was good to Carl, even though he still fought racism and the stupidity of segregation. The passing of the Civil Rights Act of 1964 helped get things moving in the right direction, but not fast enough to please everyone. Carl was one of the few who understood that most big things don't happen quickly. He had joined NIS as a civilian less than a year after retiring from the Corps in 1965.

For pay purposes, Carl was a GS-12, which meant he was roughly equivalent to a Navy lieutenant. The comparison to military ranks is in-formally used to delegate responsibilities. And in case he was sent to a remote military base, he would be given quarters equal to those of his matching military rank. The folks in the admin office had him listed as an Intelligence Administrator. But as far as Marcus Colt was concerned, Carl was his executive assistant and a friend.

His only child, Martin, was fifteen at the time of Katherine's passing, and the teenager took her death really hard. His grades dropped, and he started hanging around the wrong crowd. Carl tried to talk him into enlisting in the Corps after he finally graduated from high school, but Martin didn't want anything to do with it. Nor did he want to try any college or trade school. He finally tired of listening to Carl's advice, and had moved out a couple of years ago. Now, at twenty-two, it seemed his goal in life was to hang out with people Carl, and a great many others, considered lowlifes. It weighed heavily on Carl.

The office was quiet, and Carl was just sitting at his desk with a far-away stare. Marcus wasn't sure if Carl even knew he was there. "Talk to me, Gunny. What's going on with Martin?"

"Tucker still won't tell me anything, Mr. Colt. That's why I called you. Maybe you can figure it out."

"Okay, Carl, stay here and I will be back shortly." Marcus turned and headed down the hall to the elevator. NISHQ had the entire second floor of the building. NISO Washington and NISRA Washington shared the first floor. The sound of the elevator got the attention of the two agents working in the NISRA.

SA Ronald J. Tucker had been with NIS just over five years. He'd been an agent with the FBI for two years before that, but got tired of the politics needed to get ahead there. At least that was what he told anyone who asked. There had been a quiet rumor circulating that he left the Bureau due to conflicts with minority staff members. Nothing had come across the desks in Internal Affairs suggesting there were any problems like that at NISRA Washington, though. Marcus had little faith in rumors.

His partner was a young guy, fresh out of training. SA Christopher McCormick, who preferred "Chris," was a graduate of Florida State University with a degree in criminal justice. Growing up, he'd dreamed of joining the Secret Service and protecting the President. But after doing the applications and interviews, there were no openings unless he wanted to join the uniformed division. His dream was not that, so he found out about an opening in NIS and was accepted.

"Hello, Marcus. What causes you to visit the dungeon on an early Sunday morning?" Ron asked.

"Evening, Ron. Just trying to take care of one of our own," Marcus said as he waved at the pair, "Hey, Chris. Doin' okay?"

"Yes, sir, Mr. Colt."

"Ron, what is going on with Martin Freeman? His dad is upstairs and worried sick. Why was he arrested?"

"The young Freeman is not one of us, Marcus. And he is here just for questioning and hasn't yet been arrested. We picked him up on the base, where the SP caught him assaulting a sailor. The sailor is in the hospital. He's expected to recover, but has yet to regain consciousness from one hell of a beating. Freeman had blood on his hands. The SP found him leaning over the sailor"—he picked up the file and read—"a guy named

Larry Masters, a petty officer second class. He is a white guy." He tossed the file back on the desk.

"And what has Martin had to say about it?"

"Nothing that makes sense. Says he came to help Masters when he saw him being beat, but the SP didn't see anyone else around, and no witnesses have come forward."

"What about the drugs? What and how much?"

Tucker laughed. "Nothing worth fighting over, Marcus, that's for sure. A bag of what looks to be marijuana, maybe an ounce if that much, was found beside the victim. It needs to go to the lab for analysis so we can rule out oregano," he said with a big smile.

Marcus picked up the file to give himself a minute to collect his thoughts. Flipping through it, he saw they had collected samples of the blood on Martin's hands, logged in the suspect drugs after pulling prints from the bag, and shot sufficient photos to keep everyone happy. The lab would develop them the following day—make that later that day since it was post-midnight—or worst case, on Monday.

The victim had been in the club prior to the assault. The bartender remembered he was alone for a while, then joined by another man unknown to the bartender. Masters was a regular, but the other guy was not.

"So the drugs could belong to the victim or the unknown assailant. Okay if I talk with Martin, Ron?" Marcus asked. He had the authority to do so anyway, but not overtly stepping on an agent's territory would keep everyone happier. Him being there in the middle of the night was bad enough to ring territorial warning bells in Ron's head, but since it involved the family of one of Marcus's team members, it shouldn't cause too many hard feelings.

"Sure. Chris and I will be watching, if that is acceptable to you."

"Perfect," Marcus said with a smile that resembled one of a shark about to attack. He'd learned that from his new uncle-in-law, the CO of NISO Norfolk. That smile came in handy to throw people off their game; Marcus knew it messed up his mind the first time it was used on him.

12

THE INTERROGATION ROOMS ARE RATHER plain: a metal table bolted to the floor in the center. Two, sometimes three chairs. Sound proofing tiles are on the walls and overhead—a nautical term for a room's ceiling. Lights intentionally positioned to shine onto the suspect's side of the table. And a large mirror on one wall, which everyone knows is a two-way mirror, thereby allowing people to watch and hear what is going on during the interrogation. Everything in the room is done in various shades of gray, but hey: this is the Navy, and gray paint is cheap and easy to get.

Martin was sitting with his hands resting on the table under the watchful eyes of one of the SP petty officers who had apprehended him. Marcus thanked the SP and asked him to step out and wait in the hallway. Martin had his head hanging down and didn't look up at the changing of the guard. The first thing Marcus noticed, aside from his being about two years older than the last time they met, and that his afro hair style was larger, was there were no cuts on his hands. Savage beatings usually inflict damage to the attacker's hands as well as the victim's face and body. *Interesting.*

"Hello, Martin. Remember me?"

He finally looked up and a brief look of recognition came to him, but he shook his head. "No, sir. Are you another agent?"

40

Marcus smiled. "True, I'm an agent. My name is Colt and we met about two years ago at an office cookout—you came with your father. I'm also your father's boss. He's upstairs right now and is very distraught. Can you guess why?"

He snickered and shook his head. "Yea, I bet even I can figure that one out."

"So, tell me, Martin, what happened tonight. Start from when you came on the base and how."

"No matter what my dad or those agents have told you, I ain't a drug user or a gang member. I cleaned up my act about a year ago when I started dating a girl who's in the Navy and stationed here. We spent the day together and I rode back to the base with her."

"Write her name and where we can find her on this pad." Marcus slid a legal pad and pen across the table and Martin started writing.

"I put her barracks phone number down, but I can't remember the exact address. She works at the research center." He pushed the pad back across the table where Marcus could see what he wrote.

"No problem. I think we can find Petty Officer Diana Fletcher with this info. She should be able to confirm what you did today, right?"

"Sure."

"What time did you leave her and how were you going to get back home. And where is home, by the way?"

Martin provided the information, and Marcus jotted it all down on the pad. He knew Ron and Chris were doing the same behind the mirror. And wouldn't be surprised to find Ron already on the phone, asking the SP to pick up Diana and bring her in for questioning.

"And tell me about your problem with the sailor."

"I ain't got a problem with that guy. Someone was beating the crap out of him when I came around the corner. I yelled, the guy on top ran off—couldn't tell anything about him 'cause he had on dark clothes. I ran to help the kid on the ground. His face was bleeding and I checked to see if he was breathing. And then the Shore Patrol dudes were pulling me to my feet and putting on the handcuffs. I tried to tell them I was helping the guy, but no one listened."

Marcus didn't say anything for a minute and just looked at Martin. After a while in this job, faces had become easier to read. Granted, he never hit one hundred percent accuracy with his gut feelings, but he came pretty dang close. Martin had just told the truth, but not the whole truth: there was something he held back.

"Okay, Martin, what are you not telling me. This is the time to lay it all on the table because if I find you lied, or held back something important, that will not go well for you. Talk to me."

Martin just looked down and shook his head. "Same ol' story, man. Black guy hurtin' a white kid is the first reaction. Black guy is automatically guilty and gets arrested. Things don't change."

"I can see where it looks that way right this minute. Attitudes are slow to change in some places. But that is not true here at NIS. You were not arrested, but brought in for questioning. There's a big difference."

"I guess, but it still looks like arrest to me."

Marcus nodded. "I suppose it does. We will check your story based simply on the facts. Skin color does not matter here." With that, Marcus stood, grabbed the legal pad, and left Martin under the watchful eyes of the SP petty officer.

Ron and Chris were heading back to their desks when he exited the interrogation room. Both agents needed the phones: Ron to ask the SP to pick up Diana and Chris to arrange a follow-up with the hospital. Chris found out that Larry Masters was finally awake, but not talking. His jaw was broken in the assault. But he could still write and nod.

"Before you guys head to the hospital, I have a question. Did you notice the lack of damage to Martin's hands?"

Chris shook his head, but Ron nodded. "Yea, I noticed. I planned to check if Freeman was a judo expert or something. Those guys can injure without damaging their hands."

That sounded a bit weak, but it could just be that Ron, like everyone else at this time of day, was tired. Marcus knew he was ready to get horizontal soon.

Ron continued, "I shot a Polaroid of Freeman. We'll run to the hospital and see if Masters can recognize him. If not, then we'll cut him loose. If that is okay with you, Marcus."

"Logical move, Ron. While you guys are gone, I'm going to bring Carl down to be with Martin. Martin is family, just like your wife or children. My gut is telling me he's on the level, and the only thing hinky about his statement is his fear of being accused because he is black. I don't believe that is happening here. Looks like he was just in the wrong place at the wrong time. Or in the right place, since he tried to help Masters."

Chris nodded and Ron said, "I suppose you're right, Marcus, he is family. How about this? Go ahead and cut him loose. No need to stress him or Carl out any more tonight. By the way, thanks for handling that interview, Marcus. Well done." And with that, they both left to interview the victim. Marcus went to the interrogation room, released the SP to return to his duties, and then escorted Martin up to see his father.

Seeing them walk in, Carl stood and gave a partial smile. "You okay, Martin?"

"Sure, Dad." Martin looked down and shrugged.

"Carl, Martin is free to go. No charges have been filed since he was just brought in for questioning. I suspect in about an hour or so, the two agents going to interview the victim will find that Martin is totally clear and was a hero for trying to help the guy. However, he'll need to stay in the area in case there are more questions about the attack. For the rest of tonight, it might be best if he was with you. That okay with you, Martin?"

"Sure. Just glad to get out of this place."

Carl walked over to Marcus and grabbed his hand. "Thanks, Mr. Colt. We appreciate all your help. Don't we, Martin?"

"Yea. Thanks, man. Sorry I don't remember you."

"Not a problem. See ya Monday, Carl."

Marcus headed back to the NISRA area and left a note on Ron's desk asking for a copy of the case file to be on his desk Monday morning. There was something nagging at the back of his mind about this case, but he couldn't make any logical connections yet.

And with that, he headed back to the house. As he shut off the engine in the garage, the dashboard clock in the 'Cuda told him he had maybe four hours of sleep before it was time to face the day. Kelly opened the back door and welcomed him home as a newlywed wife should.

13

THE ALARM CLOCK WAS CRUEL. Marcus needed more sleep, but the electric beast on the nightstand had other plans and kept making an obnoxious buzz. He and Kelly had talked a bit after he got home. That meant there was less sleep than he had expected when shutting down the 'Cuda in the garage. Kelly needed to know what was going on, and Marcus needed to talk it out to help get things straight in his mind. Some say sleep is overrated, but he'd really wanted more.

After the first cup of coffee, Marcus called the office and caught Ron before he headed out to get his own measure of sleep after a long night. He did have good news to share. Martin's girlfriend confirmed all that Martin had said, and the victim said Martin was not the guy who hit him. But no, the sailor did not know who beat him up or why. Ron explained he planned to call Martin later that day to thank him for his cooperation and for helping Larry Masters. Marcus mentioned that a small apology would go a long way, and he agreed. Thanks were passed to Ron as well as a strong suggestion for him to get some rest.

Kelly was unusually quiet, probably due to lack of sleep. "Hope the preacher has a good sermon today," Marcus told her, or both of them might be caught snoozing. At least he got a small chuckle out of her for that. He poured her another cup of coffee and sat smiling at her.

"Guess we need to get moving, sailor. The day is getting away from us," she softly said between sips.

"So true, my darling. Go get your shower and I will have breakfast ready by the time you're done. It's a huevos rancheros kind of morning, *mi esposa.*"

Kelly smiled. "I love it when you call me 'your wife' in any language, but Spanish isn't as sexy as Italian, *il mio amore.* Cook quick, I will be right back, my love." With that, she gave him another kiss and ran up the stairs.

Breakfast prep was mindlessly easy and allowed Marcus to think back on last night's activities. Who beat up Masters, and why, were the two questions nagging around the edges of his mind. It wasn't his case, but when it got Carl upset, it involved him too. He was glad Martin was clear, and it looked like Martin and Carl might just be getting back to a closer relationship. Those were two really good things. He knew he should pull back with a clear conscience since—he told himself again—it was not his case. *But that ain't happening, don't ya know.* The "who" and the "why" were staying on his mind.

True to her word, Kelly came back down faster than he had expected. However, the fantastic gas stove and his minor cooking skills had done their job—breakfast was ready. They ate quietly, smiling at each other between bites, and headed back up to the bedroom to finish getting ready.

They lucked out at worship service. The sermon was really good and kept them both awake. It was a much needed reminder about the obligation Christians have to share the gospel around the world. The preacher, Brother Bob, talked about the challenges the apostles faced spreading the word in a world without fast or safe transportation, and without any fast form of communication. Personal visits and a few letters were the standard. Delivery time for letters was slow, and slow travel was fraught with danger; yet they spread the word about Jesus and it took root.

Service was over and it was time to drive home. Thankfully, Kelly offered to drive the 'Cuda because Marcus really needed the down time to let his mind wander. As Kelly enjoyed the power of the 'Cuda, he closed his eyes and leaned back in the bucket seat.

The book *Future Shock* and its warnings of information overload were in the back of his mind, and the sermon about the challenges of spreading the word of God were in the front. It was driving Marcus nuts trying to figure out how these things tied together. Or if they really did. Probably it was just a case of his tired brain trying to put together things that should not be joined. He pushed it aside and enjoyed the sound of the 'Cuda as Kelly took them home.

But the last few years of experience had shown Marcus that his mind didn't waste time on nonsense. Information overload and communication issues were both important, but neither were nonsense. If something was going round and round inside his head, it was for a good reason, and he needed to pay attention. And sometimes, after wearing himself out thinking about a problem, not paying attention allowed his subconscious to work on the problem with greater skill than his conscious mind.

Lunch was an easy fix, with several leftover crab cakes from last night. They became crab burgers after a short time in a hot skillet. Placed on toasted buns that had been slathered with a homemade remoulade sauce, then topped off with some of the leftover slaw, they provided the Colts with the fuel needed to get through the afternoon.

Kelly wanted to have plenty of time to meet the neighbors, so they finished lunch and clean-up in record time. Ever efficient, Kelly had her notepad and her radiant smile, ready to socialize. Time to make like a normal person for a while.

14

MONDAYS ARE THE DAYS THAT working people usually hate. The fun-filled two-day weekend was over, and it was time to get back to work. But Marcus looked at Mondays as the first day of a possible new adventure. And that was just one of the many reasons people who worked with him thought he was more than a bit strange. He told himself he could live with that.

The coffee was already hot when he arrived an hour plus earlier than usual. The NIS staff was on the ball as always. Early coffee was courtesy of the crew who worked nights in the computer room. He hated to leave Kelly early, but felt there was something that needed to be looked at sooner rather than later. His gut had a great track record, and Kelly understood and supported it. She had seen how his gut feeling helped with the operation in Norfolk. The coffee mug was filled, and he headed down the hall to his office to find whatever was causing the worry.

Carl stood as Marcus entered the outer office of the Internal Affairs division. He had an unusual smile on his typically stoic face.

"As you were, Master Gunny, it's too early for such stuff. How ya doin'?" Marcus asked with a smile.

"Mighty fine, Mr. Colt. You felt the need to get here early today also, I see," Carl responded as he sat back down.

Marcus chuckled. "Guess it's the call of the wild that brings us strange ones in early, Carl. I'll check the radio traffic to see what might be causing me grief. On hopefully a happier note, did things go okay with Martin yesterday?"

"Thanks to you, Mr. Colt, things are much better. We actually talked and realized how much we both need each other. And Martin has changed so much for the better since he met Diana. Did you get a chance to meet her?"

"No, but SA Tucker said he was impressed by her."

"She reminds me of Katherine, sir. She's a real class act and spent the afternoon yesterday at the house. SA Tucker told us he really liked her when he called yesterday afternoon. He also apologized to Martin and thanked him for trying to help that sailor. I think that went a long way. I'm looking forward to getting to know more about her soon."

"How about this. When things settle down with that case, Kelly and I would like to take you, Diana, and Martin out to dinner. I want us to get more acquainted and I want Martin to know we are here for him. Will that work for you?"

Carl's eyes seemed to water up a bit, and he had to clear his throat a couple of times before he said, "Thank you, sir. That would be real nice."

Marcus smiled. "We will make it happen, Carl. But right now, I have a few pounds of incoming messages that need to be read. Unless you know one that should get higher priority?"

"No, sir, I'm still going through the NISO AUTOVON traffic right now. There is a pile of it. So far, it's all more information copies and a few ROIs. I will let you know if I see something strange."

"Thanks, buddy. More chat later." Marcus entered his office, smiling about the code words, usually acronyms, they used around NIS. Such as ROIs. Saying "Roys" is so much easier, and quicker, than saying the official full name, Report of Investigation.

The standard case file handled by NIS consists of a stack of proper paperwork in a very specific order. First, there is a NIR, a Naval Investigative Request that initiates the investigation: when someone asks for one, that starts the ball rolling. Next the file will have at least one, and possibly an infinite number of ROIs, the Report of Investigation, which is just as it sounds: a report about any progress found to date. The final piece of paper in the file, the RUC, is the Referred Upon Closing report that documents what was done with the subject of the investigation, the evidence, etc. *NIR-ROI-ROI-RUC almost sounds like a football cheer; okay, morning chuckle is over.*

Unlike many others, Marcus's office didn't have any windows to the real world. Seemed in the office pecking order, windows were a high priority. With that in mind, he made sure, when he was promoted to lead this division, that members of his team had the offices with windows. He didn't need such things, and if it made one of his people just a little happier, that was a good thing.

But his office did have the one thing he considered critical: a door that closed tight and locked. Internal Affairs cases often involved extremely sensitive details, and privacy was critical. On top of that, Carl performed the same access control that YNMC Bartow did for the CNO. You had to get through Carl before you could get to him. And as much as he respected David Bartow's abilities and level of control, he believed Carl was tougher on access. Marines, even retired versions, are usually tougher than Navy CPOs.

Aside from the door that he loved, his office was nothing special. Standard two-tone gray carpet ran wall-to-wall, with inexpensive wood paneling covering the walls. His "I was there" wall wasn't extensive. It consisted of a couple photos of the IA teams he had been a member of in the past, and the current team. Add to that a photo or two of awards ceremonies, pistol and rifle sharpshooter certificates, and one wedding photo. Then there was his most honored photo, of his two SEAL teams in Vietnam. In that photo, the men lost over there were still alive, and that was very special to him. Aside from these few items were the awards and other plaques he'd received, barely covering part of one wall. But it was a start, and made him happy.

The critical furniture included the fancy office chair with multiple positions, a standard-issue gray metal desk with an addition on the side for his IBM Selectric typewriter, a small TV to check on news broadcasts, and a medium-sized conference table large enough to seat eight, which was more than enough for his team. He thought about getting a dartboard, until he considered the faces which could end up on it: that might cause problems. He did keep a small stereo on the credenza behind the desk so he could have soothing music when working late during the week, and Beach Boys tunes on the weekend.

And it was into this sanctuary that he carried the radio traffic destined for IA. A quick sort showed that the larger stack of messages was simply informational copies. These are sent to NIS not for any action, but as a way for the originator to make sure the i's are dotted and t's crossed. Each one could seem unimportant at first glance, but each was seriously considered. But first, those directed to NIS for action got Marcus's attention. And this short stack showed that the day would be interesting.

The first message had originated in southern California a little over three hours ago, just after midnight California time. The NISRA at Camp Pendleton, a Marine base with an air station, had an agent-involved shooting resulting in the death of one Marine suspect, and worst of all, the deaths of two civilian bystanders who worked on the base. This could be another public relations nightmare, so Marcus's team needed to be on the scene quickly.

At least one member of his team should leave town shortly, but a feeling came over him to send two to California. A yeoman named Dexter, who he'd met at NISO Norfolk had said he had voices in his head giving him warnings about people and situations. It looked like some of Dexter's voices had jumped to Marcus's brain, as he was hearing them say loud and clear: California is potential trouble.

The rest of the short stack was follow-up traffic about ongoing cases. Nothing to cause any immediate concerns, but updating those files would generate a bit more paperwork. Marcus was glad he came in early.

A quick couple of moments on the typewriter generated a brief for Vice Admiral John Chance, his direct boss and commanding officer, i.e. the man in charge of NIS. He dropped the carbon copy of the brief on Carl's desk as he walked past. Then Marcus asked that Carl get on the phone with Andrews Air Force Base and get a Military Airlift Command flight to California for two lined up, ASAP. All Carl did was glance at the brief and nod. He had the need-to-know and, of course, would later file it properly.

Senior Chief Yeoman Victor O'Keef was placing his cover on the coat rack when Marcus entered his office. Getting to see the admiral required getting past Victor. Marcus had always gotten along well with Vic, but after Vic saw the grades Marcus achieved at Yeoman A School as part of an undercover operation in Norfolk, he was impressed, and they became much closer. The crossed quills, the yeoman rating insignia, made Victor consider them nearly blood brothers. He often kidded Marcus that he should put a set of crossed quills under the gold stripes on his sleeve.

"Good morning, Mr. Colt. What brings you in early?"

"Senior Chief, it's just one of those mornings where my gut refused to let me hang around the house, drink coffee, and enjoy Kelly's smile for another hour. Some days I really hate my gut. But the gut won another round, and here is a brief for the admiral as soon as he arrives." Marcus passed him the single sheet of paper.

"I understand your resentment. She does have a lovely smile, sir." Victor grinned while taking the brief. After a quick read, his smile vanished. "Damn, this is not good, sir."

With a chuckle and a touch of friendly sarcasm in his voice, Marcus replied, "Even on an early Monday morning, you are the sharp one, Vic." He gave Vic a small smile as he continued, "Seriously, you are so right—that issue is the stuff PR nightmares are made of. Let me know when the boss arrives. Thanks."

"You got it, Mr. Colt."

15

MARCUS NEEDED ANOTHER CUP OF coffee already. With the coffee mess on the way back to his office, it was an easy decision to duck in for another cup. As he started to leave, one of his team came in to get his cup of "go juice," as some had started to call it.

1stLt Henry Bates, USMC, preferred to be called *Hank*, and Marcus could understand that. Henry didn't convey the toughness that Hank did. And everyone knew Marines are tough, even lawyer versions. Hank had passed the bar exams in both Virginia and Maryland. Lots of intelligence under that short blond hair. Hank smiled as he entered the coffee mess and said, "Well damn, sir, it is hard to impress the boss by arriving early only to find him coming in even earlier. Hope this doesn't mean we have problems?"

"Only one so far and it's in California. We'll cover it in the morning meeting, but I need to run right now. Unless there is something more pressing for you, come to my office after you get your coffee."

"Yes, sir."

As he walked back to the office, the second cup of coffee kicked a few brain cells into higher gear. Marcus needed to change his plans, and soon.

Carl was still on the phone with Andrews when Marcus passed. Marcus quickly scribbled a note telling him to get three seats to Pendleton. He nodded in understanding.

Dropping into the chair behind his desk, Marcus checked the NIS directory and placed a call to the NISRA at Camp Pendleton. Figured someone might be on duty and able to provide more information. He was right.

"NISRA Camp Pendleton. Special Agent Brandt speaking. How may I help you?"

Marcus lucked out again. He had met Charlie Brandt the previous year, when he came back from Vietnam and spent a week in the hospital in southern California before heading back to D.C. Admiral Chance had sent an agent to see if he needed anything, though the admiral really just wanted to make sure he behaved. Charlie, the poor guy, got the assignment.

An agent with over fifteen years of experience, Charlie had come to NIS from an unusual place: the Army's CID, Criminal Investigative Division, where he'd been an agent. He was a damn good CID agent, but did not enjoy being around the Army. His father was a career Navy officer with a distinguished record in WWII, and he felt an obligation to the Navy that had raised him. The Army's loss was the Navy's gain.

Marcus pressed the speakerphone button and leaned forward. "Hello, Charlie. Marcus Colt calling. Just read the radio traffic and see y'all are having a bad day out there. Not much was in the message about the shooting—do you have any more details?"

He heard a noise and looked up to see Hank Bates coming into his office. He pointed to one of the chairs facing his desk; Hank sat and sipped on his coffee.

"Yea, buddy, it is a very bad day around here. SA Patrick Sanderson was involved in a gun battle at the air station with a gunner's mate second class, Leonard Lincoln. Lincoln was caught drinking on duty. His division officer called NIS. When Sanderson arrived, Lincoln just started shooting. No one knew he had a weapon. Sanderson shot and killed him, but in the heat of battle, a couple of his stray rounds took out two civilian workers. You know how it is in a gun fight. They just happened to be in the wrong place at the wrong time, from all indication."

"Does the shooting of Lincoln look justified?"

"Yea, Marcus, it does. Problem is that Lincoln and one of the civilians are both black. The other civilian is Hispanic, so the boss's concern is it might look like our pasty white agent gunned down three minorities without any care or concern. Think 1965 in Los Angeles."

"Ouch. That does make it worse. Anyone talking out loud in that direction?"

"No, sir, and the SSA Howard does not want to hear that kind of talk, hence the vague message to you," Charlie replied. "No one wants a repeat of the 1965 Watts riot here."

"Okay, tell SSA Howard that I'm sending three of my people out today to handle the investigation of the shooting. The lead will be LT Doty. You know the drill—line up the witnesses, dig into the background of the deceased, etc. Keep me in the loop if anything changes. Carl will send you the travel info."

"Can do, Marcus. Thanks for your help, sir. All for now."

As Marcus hung up and picked up his coffee cup, Carl walked in. "Mr. Colt, we have three seats on a TWA flight leaving Dulles at 1300. Connection at LAX to Oceanside. I just need the names to go with the reservations. Nothing out of Andrews would have got there until late Wednesday."

"Excellent work, Carl. Names for the flight will be Bates, Doty, and Neil. Send the travel data to NISRA Pendleton attention SA Brandt." Marcus grinned at Hank's surprised look and asked, "How's your knowledge of Camp Pendleton?"

"Never been there, sir," he said. "But I will adapt."

Carl nodded and returned to his desk to complete the air travel plans. Marcus passed Hank the radio message from NISRA Pendleton.

He read it and looked up. "Do we have any more info on this, sir?"

"Just what you heard on the phone just now. And you heard me tell NISRA Pendleton to line up the witnesses, dig into the background of the victim, etc. We will have a status meeting at 0815. Spread the word. That's all."

"Aye, aye, sir."

Marcus drained his second cup and leaned back for a moment of thought. His mind went to the standard question: what had he forgotten to do so far?

Before he could form the answer, the phone rang and the internal line to the admiral's office lit up. "Colt speaking, sir."

"The boss has arrived, Mr. Colt."

"Thanks, Vic. Remind me later that I owe you another lunch soon," Marcus said as he hung up the phone and stood. Time to get the boss's approval on all the plans he had already set in motion.

16

ON HIS WAY OUT, MARCUS realized he needed yet another cup of coffee. The coffee police would be after him for having three cups before the staff meeting, but it had been a rough morning. He grabbed it and went to see the admiral.

Vic nodded when he entered. "Go right in, Mr. Colt. The admiral is looking forward to your chat, sir." He gave a big grin and pulled his finger across his neck like a knife: a clear indication he thought Marcus was doomed. *Been there before*, Marcus thought. The admiral had a bad tendency to kill the messenger.

He knocked on the open door casing and came to attention. "Morning, Admiral. I hope you have a couple of minutes to spare me, sir."

Vice Admiral John Chance was a true piece of work. His blood was navy blue in color. He had joined the Navy as an enlisted man right before WWII started. He was on the bridge of the aircraft carrier USS Enterprise, cruising around the Hawaiian Islands, when the Japanese attacked Pearl Harbor and started WWII.

He later received a commission as an ensign and finished the war as a lieutenant in charge of operations on a destroyer. After the war, he transitioned to various intelligence billets, where he excelled and ended up at the top of the heap. His position in charge of NIS was his final command.

In three more years he would retire from the service. That would be a great loss to the Navy and a personal loss for Marcus.

Looking at Admiral Chance, it was hard to imagine him being a hard ass, but he was. If you got on his bad side, you would regret it. He stood less than six feet tall and weighed around 180 pounds, but physically larger men had been turned to jelly by his wrath. At first glance, you would think you were meeting Jimmy Cagney when he starred as a Navy officer in *Mr. Roberts*, but Chance was not acting: he was the real thing.

"Colt, you certainly do have a knack for messing up a good Monday morning. Any other disasters you need to add to this brief before we get started? And for crying out loud, at ease and sit your butt down before you dump coffee on your uniform," the admiral bellowed, pointing to a chair in front of his desk while waving the brief Marcus had provided. At least he had half a smile on his standard sour face. Maybe the messenger would survive this meeting.

"Thank you, sir. There are no other issues to add to that disaster list, at least so far. But I can provide more info on the Pendleton case." Marcus laid out the information received from the agent out there. He finished, "Sir, I plan to send LT Doty as the lead on this case. In addition, I will send 1stLt Bates and YN2 Neil with him. Neil was raised in Oceanside, and my gut is telling me his knowledge of the area, and his laid-back surfer attitude, will help keep LT Doty on an even keel. I suspect it might get a bit hairy out there. And Bates, being a Marine, will help smooth ruffled feathers on that Marine base."

The admiral twisted his mouth a bit and took a deep breath before replying, "Logical move, Marcus. Hopefully having a black man lead the investigation will help reduce the cries of a racist cover up. Anything else pressing?"

"Again, not at this time, Admiral, but it is still ..." He stopped before saying *early*. "Admiral, one other thing happened Saturday night, but I cannot see where it is a problem. Just something about it is nagging at me." With that, he provided a quick overview of Martin Freeman's detainment and subsequent release. They kicked the case parameters around for a minute or so, and finally the admiral said he didn't see anything there either.

"I will let you know if I figure out that nagging thing, Admiral. I want to nose around on this but I will do my best not to step on the agents' toes."

The admiral chuckled. "Just try not to cause a public relations night-mare or World War III before lunch."

Marcus could not stop a chuckle from erupting. "Thank you, sir. Now if there is nothing else, I have a lot to get done."

"Carry on, Colt. Keep me in the loop on both of these things."

He got a thumbs up from Vic as he left the admiral to go back to IA. One of the many clocks on the wall indicated it was 0805: the day had officially started.

17

DESKS AND OFFICES WERE FILLED back in the IA area. The IA team was small but extremely competent. The admiral had staffed the operation with good people, and Marcus made sure they kept sharp with additional training between cases.

Carl let him know that the Pendleton reservations were all set. Marcus asked Carl if he had any problem with him mentioning his son's issue over the weekend in the status meeting. He didn't, but asked why.

"Carl, my gut is bugging me about something with this case. Nothing to do with Martin, he's the good guy in this situation. But there is just something I heard or saw that I just can't connect yet. Maybe talking with the team will jog something loose. And get Neil and Howland in the meeting also."

Carl shrugged and smiled. He knew the boss's gut had a good track record, and as long as Martin was clear, he was all behind the plan. Marcus thanked him and headed into his office.

Nothing new had appeared on his desk in the last few minutes, no lights were flashing on the phone, and the admiral had been updated. So with about six whole minutes to call his very own, he parked his butt in the chair and leaned back to finish cup number three of coffee. The first hour and a half of what looked to be a long, painful day had gone by already. His rev-erie was short lived and totally destroyed by a knock on the door casing.

The IA team was ready for the Monday status meeting. Just his luck, they were early for a change, so no moment of quiet. He waved them in and approached the conference table. The two officers included LT Jacob "Jake" Doty, USN, and 1stLt Henry "Hank" Bates, USMC. IA was one officer short since LT Tomlin rotated out in August, and Marcus hoped that slot got filled soon. Carl was a standard feature in all of the meetings since he was Marcus's backup, and running the office required him to be current on all projects. Marcus requested that the morning's meeting include YN2 Bradley Neil and Rita Howland.

YN2 Bradley "Brad" Neil, USN, was a single twenty-four-year-old who stood just under 5'10" and was in slightly above average physical shape. Born in southern California, his short blond hair gave him a surfer look and went well with his laid-back attitude. While he was laid back, he had a keen attention to detail and was always looking for problems before they occurred.

Margarita "Rita" Howland was the senior of the two civilian secretar-ies assigned to the IA division. Rita looked younger than her forty-plus years. Maybe it had something to do with her Hispanic heritage. She was married to a dentist named Frederick and they had two children in their late teens. Her medium-length dark brown hair was usually pulled into a bun. Although she was slightly overweight and wore glasses all the time, she was attractive for two reasons: she was fluent in Cuban Spanish, with a cute Cuban accent, and she was extremely efficient in her job.

And to his surprise, Senior Chief Vic O'Keef asked to join the meeting. He pulled Colt aside to say the admiral wanted him in the loop. It would save time updating the admiral, he said. The meeting now had nearly a full house, with most of the chairs in use. Time to get to work.

"Welcome to Monday morning. Hope you had a great weekend, peo-ple, because this week is starting off rather nasty, and I suspect it will only get worse. It usually does," Marcus said. They went over the status of on-going cases, and then Marcus gave them a rundown on the one hot issue from Pendleton. It didn't take long to share all the info they had thus far. And when you don't have much to go on, you go with what ya got.

"So, knowing all that, here is the plan. LT Doty, 1stLt Bates, and YN2 Neil, you three will be heading to Pendleton this afternoon. Carl has the travel info for you and will be your primary point of contact here. SA Charlie Brandt, a real good local guy, will meet you at the airport. Jake, you will need to maintain a balance between being a hard ass getting to the truth, and a bomb disposal tech walking on race-colored eggshells. This can blow up without notice and you have to work to either clear or hang the agent immediately. And just to be clear, your skin tone was the deciding factor that got you the lead on this case."

Jake didn't react upon hearing that news. As the ringmaster of this circus, Marcus tried to let everyone know what was behind decisions and offered more. "Here is a hard fact, Jake. The people around this table, and the vast majority of people working at NIS, do not give a rat's ass about anyone's skin color."

Marcus paused to let that sink in. "It is rather humorous when you think about it, but here in NIS we deal in absolutes. For us, things are usually black and white or good and bad, and now we have a situation dealing with black and white skin color that is not really a black and white situation to the locals."

"Well phrased, boss," said Jake with a big smile. "I can handle this case, sir, and I am not bothered by the reason I'm being selected. Hell, I was just wondering why I have all the backup? Expecting trouble?"

Marcus continued, "It is due to the issues we face out there. The fools in the media do not believe the Navy or a white man can be impartial when dealing with the parameters of this case." Everyone nodded in agreement. "And there are probably some that cannot, but I do not believe we have that problem here. We deal with facts, but sometimes, such as now, we also have to play the political games."

Marcus paused and took a sip of coffee. "As for your backup, Brad is from the area, so you won't have to spend time with your head stuck in a map. He knows his way around. And Hank will be there to smooth over any ruffled Marine feathers. And both of them will help watch your back. I trust y'all can handle this case properly."

The three nodded their understanding.

"Maybe Brad can lead y'all to a good restaurant in his old neighborhood that serves great local seafood. Jake will pick up the check, of course." Marcus grinned. "You three hang around after this meeting."

Marcus pointed toward Carl and Rita next when he said, "You two need to coordinate new work schedules and duties for a few days while the team is in California. Rita, I want you to handle Carl's morning duties. Okay?" She nodded, indicating it was fine.

With one down and one to go, he continued, "And starting tomorrow, Carl, we need you to shift your day to start at 1400 hours. Will that be a problem?"

"Not a bit, boss. Whatever you need."

"Good," Marcus said. "Then Carl, each day before Rita leaves, get up to speed on the events of the day and if our Pendleton team needs anything early. Then plan on staying until 2200 so you'll be here to support the Pendleton team through their normal day, plus an hour or so. Sorry for the long and mixed up days, but considering the importance of this case, we need you here. I will make it up to you."

Carl chuckled as he rubbed his hands together. "I see a cookout at the Colt residence in my near future." That got a good laugh from everyone as well as several "I'll be there too" comments.

"Okay, before we lose total control—which I really hope Vic will leave out of his update to the admiral—let's wrap this meeting up quickly since I need more coffee." Marcus paused, realizing there was another task that needed to be done. Vic started to raise his hand, but Marcus motioned him to hold a minute.

He then explained what happened with Martin Freeman on Saturday night. Everyone agreed it seemed like a simple case, with Martin the hero, but knowing how the boss's hunches worked, they all agreed to keep an ear open for anything that might be related.

Marcus then looked at Vic. "What do you need to add, Vic?"

He flashed a big grin. "Nothing serious, just the admiral would like a moment of your time. At your convenience, sir."

"Okay, can the admiral hold on for about five minutes?" Marcus asked. "I need to talk with Jake, Hank, and Brad, and their schedule is tight."

Vic nodded his agreement.

"Well then, that's all for now, people. Thanks."

When everyone else had left, Marcus moved back to his desk and pointed to the chairs in front of it. The three men sat and waited. Colt smiled as he gave the orders. "Gentlemen, I want you all in civilian clothing on this trip. Take uniforms, just in case, but suits or sports coats will be the working attire. Perhaps the lack of a Navy uniform on a Marine base will give you an edge. Lord knows we need all the help we can get. Use your NIS badges, Lieutenants. Neil, Carl will shortly have a special set of NIS credentials for you. Avoid using your military IDs, if possible. Stick with *Mr.* instead of the standard military salutations. And I think the brass will allow first names to be used if you feel it works better in the climate you find there."

They chuckled and nodded in agreement. No one had any questions.

"Lieutenants, I know you two understand why you're heading to Camp Pendleton, but I'm not sure Yeoman Neil fully grasps it, right?"

"Not completely, Mr. Colt," responded Yeoman Neil.

"You have two primary tasks, Neil. First and foremost, you are to watch the lieutenants' backs at all times. We're not sure what we'll face out there, but with you and SA Brandt watching out, it all should be fine. Second task is to make sure that the lieutenants don't miss anything. You are sharp, and I've seen your thoroughness—carry it with you to California. And as a bonus for the team, your knowledge of the area will be a great asset by providing one less thing for them to worry about, with you as a designated driver."

"Yes, sir. I will do my best."

"I know you will. Watch and learn from these two guys. And another reason I'm sending you back to your home ground is a bit of a reward. Assuming this case wraps up in a couple of days, these two officers will return immediately to finalize the case paperwork. I order you to hang around out there visiting your folks, surfing, chasing girls, whatever. Just be back here next Wednesday morning."

"I don't know what to say, sir. Thank you, sir."

"Yeoman Neil, you've done a great job around here, and while I can't promote you, I can help get you a bit of R&R not charged as leave. You earned it. Okay, gents, get the hell out of here and go see Carl. He should have your travel orders by now. Keep in touch. Good luck and be careful. Oh, Jake, hold on one."

"Sir?" Jake asked as the other two left the office.

"Yeoman Neil is considering getting out of the Navy when his current enlistment is up in about seven months. I would like to see him join NIS as an agent. In addition to letting him drive you around, give him some tasks that will allow him to see his potential as an agent. He's a good kid."

"I understand, boss. Will do."

Marcus nodded and Jake left to join the others. He took a moment to gather his thoughts and went to see the admiral again.

18

VIC AGAIN GAVE HIS BEST *you are doomed* smile and pointed to the admiral's door. "Go right in, sir, he is expecting you."

Marcus's thoughts as he passed Vic were best not vocalized. He respected his yeoman brother, but some days Vic took too much pleasure from watching Marcus squirm. Or at least trying to get him to squirm. Ergo, Marcus did his best not to let him see him uncomfortable. And because of that, Vic tried even harder. This time, Marcus simply smiled and nodded at him.

Standing at attention and knocking on the door casing again, Marcus was waved in before the admiral pointed to the "hot seat" directly in front of his desk.

"And how may I help the Admiral, sir?" Marcus asked in his best *I know I am in deep doggie doo-doo but I have no idea why* voice.

Admiral Chance chuckled at the visible discomfort. He glanced down at his desk and then back up. "And when did you last talk with your father-in-law?"

Well, that caught him totally off guard. "Sir, not during this past week. Kelly and I were over there for dinner a week ago this past Saturday. No Navy business was discussed then. And nothing since then, why?"

"Our mutual friend called about you a bit ago. Seems he wants you for another special case. Know anything about it?"

Marcus let out a deep sigh and quietly replied, "Oh, hell no, sir. Please tell me the CNO was kidding. I have enough scar tissue."

The admiral laughed. "Sorry, no joke, Marcus. Well, I told him that we were shorthanded in IA right now due to the Pendleton case, and he kindly told me that the good news is that the case is located here in the Navy Yard. No TAD needed, which will allow you to do your normal work and handle a special case. He expects to see us at noon. Just in time to join him for a working lunch, I suppose. You will ride with me—we will leave at 1120 to arrive on time."

"No further details, sir?"

"Never is with that man. He loves the drama and secrecy. See you at 1115 hours. Dismissed."

Marcus nodded and started back to his office. Vic gave another smile, tempting Marcus to respond with a vulgar hand signal. But he resisted temptation and gave him a nod and a thumbs up. The stress demanded yet another stop in the coffee mess for the fourth cup. *Hey, who's counting; definitely not me*, Marcus thought.

With a fresh hot cup in his possession, Marcus returned to the IA area. *No need to worry about what the CNO wants because whatever it is, we'll do it.* But perhaps he would now have a moment to read Ron's file on the Saturday night assault. It had been on his desk earlier, but with the Pendleton problem grabbing all the attention, he had yet to open it. It was only 0910 hrs, so maybe now was the time.

Carl shook his head as Marcus entered the office. It was a standard signal that nothing new had happened since he'd left. He liked it when nothing exciting happened, especially on days like this one. Marcus told him about going to the Pentagon for lunch with the admiral and CNO at 1115 hrs. Carl asked why, and all Marcus could do was shrug and tell him it was about a new and local issue. The closing click of the latch on his office door was a welcome sound; it had been too hectic already that day, and some quiet time was needed.

SA Ron Tucker's file on the Saturday assault was his standard good work; it was complete, at least until Sunday morning when the team headed home, and well detailed. It even included transcripts of the interview Marcus had conducted with Martin Freeman. Larry Masters, the assault victim, was a Radarman Second Class that worked in the Naval Research

Laboratory's liaison office for the Advanced Research Projects Agency. He didn't know why he was attacked. No known enemies. Not a robbery, etc.

SA Chris McCormick included a thorough report on the questioning of Martin's girlfriend, Diana Fletcher. She was a hospital corpsman third class who was also assigned to the Naval Research Laboratory. *Wonder why a research lab needs a corpsman? Interesting.* She did know the victim but hadn't had any social contact with him. Diana had been there for just over a year. She had a clean service record and positive evaluations: a good future in the Navy awaited her.

Tucker and McCormick were most likely at the Naval Research Laboratory right then, interviewing the victim's coworkers and examining his desk. Who knew, there might be a link hidden in one of the desk drawers that might point to something useful, but probably not.

Another quick look in the directory gave him the number for the research lab, and Marcus placed the call. "Good morning, petty officer. This is Lieutenant Commander Colt from NIS. I think I have two NIS special agents still there. If so, please get one of them on the phone," he asked the voice on the end of the line.

A moment later, the quest was answered. "Special Agent Ron Tucker, Mr. Colt. How can I help you?"

"Ron, I just finished reading your report. Excellent work as always. And I took a guess that you might be there. Got a silly question about Diana Fletcher. Why does the research center need a hospital corpsman?"

After a moment of silence on the line, Ron replied with exasperation. "Damned if I know. It does sound strange now that you mention it. I'll look into it and get right back with you, Marcus."

"No panic, Ron. Just put it in your report. Like I said, it's a silly question, but something is nagging at me about this one. By the way, the admiral and I have been invited to lunch with the CNO to discuss a new project, so just leave a copy with Carl if I'm not around."

He laughed. "Glad it's you and not me."

"Thanks, buddy. I'm not looking forward to it. Every time he gives me an assignment, I get more scar tissue. All for now," Marcus said and hung up.

The Naval Research Laboratory name was nagging at the back of his mind. He picked up the phone again, punched the internal line button, and dialed the other civilian secretary assigned to the IA division, Veronica Mays.

This twenty-five-year-old single female had shining, reddish brown hair that flipped up before touching her shoulders, decently proportioned body parts, and a face that melted hearts from any distance. To make matters worse, her sexy, husky voice made it a challenge to focus when talking with her. There were perks for working there, and seeing and listening to Veronica was one, unless you needed to focus on the subject at hand.

"Good morning, Veronica, I need you to check the files for the last couple of years—make it thirty months—and pull anything related to the Naval Research Laboratory," Marcus asked as formally as he could.

"Certainly, sir, I will get them pulled right away. Anything else I can do for you, sir? Anything at all?" she replied in her standard sexy voice.

"No, that's all I need right now. Thank you," he answered with as much strict military decorum as he could muster while trying not to imagine her in the shower.

Marcus reread the file on the Saturday assault and finished the current cup of coffee. Nothing new jumped off the printed pages of the file. Nothing from his memory of the interview with Martin Freeman caused any issues. He'd just have to wait and see what Ron and Chris found.

Only a dozen minutes had gone by when a knock on the door interrupted his contemplation. "Enter," he responded.

Veronica approached the desk. "Sir, while waiting for the computer report on all cases involving the research center, I remembered one from earlier that year while you were TAD in Norfolk. It's still an open case, so I went downstairs and pulled the file."

Marcus thanked her for her excellent memory as he took the file, receiving a warm smile in return. As the office door clicked shut, it blew a hint of Veronica's perfume in his direction. While enjoying that fragrance, he noticed this file was a slim one, from 12 June. A quick look showed why: Doctor Frederick Monroe had simply vanished from his office in the Naval Research Laboratory late that night. There was no indication of a struggle. No body was found. There was no financial trail. NIS, FBI, and local police all failed to find anything related to his disappearance. He was just gone.

The only interesting thing was the code name of a project the doctor was getting ready for testing: *Rembrandt*. His sarcasm streak immediately thought the Navy had no business investing in oil paintings. Or teaching sailors to paint portraits or landscapes.

No other information about the project was in the file. Marcus made note of the project name and that Special Agent Edgar "Ed" Dondridge was the lead agent. A quick call downstairs to NISRA D.C. informed him that Dondridge was out of the office. He left a message for him to call when he returned.

The morning was racing by; time to freshen up, grab his cover, and meet the admiral for the lunch date with the CNO. Marcus told Carl that Dondridge might be calling and that Marcus wanted an update on a case. Marcus passed the file to Carl so he would be up to speed on it and headed down the corridor.

19

MASTER CHIEF YEOMAN DAVID BARTOW and YN2 Lester Cummings stood as Colt and the admiral entered the outer office of the CNO at 1155 hours. Admiral Chance immediately said, "As you were."

David Bartow had a John Wayne look about him that conveyed high intelligence and a massive "do not mess with me" attitude. His uniform was always perfect, his "fruit salad," i.e. the ribbons on his left chest that indicated medals earned and areas served, was immense, and the gold hash marks on his left sleeve, each representing four years of service, added up to twenty-eight years plus. He was a longtime friend of the CNO and ran a tight ship as the CNO's gate keeper. Walking toward the two officers with his hand extended, David said, "Good to see you again, Admiral."

"You, too, David. All going well with you?"

"Yes, sir. But I usually find that seeing this lieutenant commander here means trouble. Good afternoon anyway, Mr. Colt," said Bartow with a grin.

David was a very good friend, and they had a lot of respect for each other. Since he was Kelly's godfather, Marcus thought of him as his god-father-in-law. He'd been helpful with the assignment in Norfolk, and both knew they had each other's backs when the need arrived.

"Always a pleasure to see you too, Master Chief," Marcus said with a smile. "I see Lester is doing a great job keeping you out of trouble. Good to see you, Les."

Lester smiled and nodded an acknowledgment as he reached for the ringing phone. After a short conversation and a sharp "yes, sir" response, Les hung up the phone and announced, "The admiral is ready for you gentlemen. Go right in." He opened the door leading to the admiral.

Keeping military protocol, they marched to the admiral's desk and came to attention. Vice Admiral John Chance barked, "Reporting as ordered, sir."

Admiral William Gallagher was the epitome of a Navy admiral. At six feet and with just a small amount of fat on his body, the thing that caught your eyes immediately was the weathered look of his face. Crow's feet and a permanent tan on aged skin that had seen too many hours on the bridge wing of a naval vessel grabbed your attention first. Then you noticed the receding hairline and the gray that was working toward overcoming the brown in the crew cut hair. The four stars on his collar gleamed with power. He could be the poster boy for the office of the Chief of Naval Operations.

As he stood, Gallagher broke into a chuckle. "Impressive. You may stand at ease, gentlemen." Walking around the desk, he grabbed Chance's hand and pulled him into a brief hug. "Thanks for coming, John, and I think it was a request rather than an order."

"Always happy to be at your service, Bill, no matter how the invitation comes across."

Gallagher chuckled, nodded, and turned to Colt. "Doing okay this morning, Marcus?"

"Yes, sir."

"Good. David, take the lead and let's get some lunch."

The four headed to the cafeteria, and upon arrival, were immediately led into a side room that had a table set for five. Three stewards were at near attention by another door. Standing over to the side was a gentleman in a dark suit. He smiled as he nodded to Marcus and said, "Hello, Marcus, good to see you again so soon."

Marcus chuckled and extended his hand as he walked over to him. "It's a strange world, Jason, seeing you this far from the Old Executive Office Building." Jason laughed and Marcus continued, "I admit I did have trouble believing you're just a paper pusher at the OEOB like you said."

Jason continued smiling as he responded, "And you're not exactly counting paperclips at a musty old office in the Navy Yard either. I suspect we both tend to shy away from describing what we really do in order to avoid uncomfortable questions, right?"

"So very true, neighbor, and with exceptions of wives, I hope we continue to keep our job descriptions on the down low."

Admiral Gallagher seemed to be enjoying the surprise and the verbal sparring as he took over the conversation. "Vice Admiral John Chance, this gentleman is Jason Wright, chief of staff for Representative A. Jackson Allen, who you might recall is chairman of the House Integrated Intelligence Committee. When Mr. Wright came to me this morning to discuss his problem, I found out he is a neighbor of Marcus and Kelly. He saw their wedding photo on my desk. I immediately realized this as one of those win-win situations if we involved Marcus. Hence the need for this meeting."

Chance looked Wright over from top to bottom as he accepted the extended hand. "Well, this should be interesting," he said.

"Admiral, I appreciate you and Marcus being here today. I do believe, based upon the CNO's recommendation, that Marcus is just what we need for our problem."

"And what precisely is your problem, Mr. Wright?" replied Chance with a hint of antagonism in his voice emphasizing the *your*.

Master Chief Bartow immediately jumped in to smooth any ruffled feathers that might be starting. "Gentlemen, let's get started on lunch and get into specifics after the servers have departed."

Lunch was served, consisting of a tomato–basil salad, beef medallions with green peppercorn sauce, baked potato with sour cream and chives, and roasted asparagus with just a hint of garlic. For a few moments, the conversation was set aside while they enjoyed the excellent flavors. The stewards refilled the coffee cups and iced tea glasses and quietly left the room.

Admiral Gallagher started the discussion. "Gentlemen, Jason came to me this morning with his problem, and I hope that the five of us can come up with a workable solution. Jason, lay out the parameters, please."

"Certainly, Admiral. A few months ago, a renowned scientist working in the Washington Navy Yard vanished. We need to find him because of his connection with a top-secret project. And I know …"

"Excuse me, Jason," Marcus interrupted. "Would that scientist be Doctor Frederick Monroe from the Naval Research Laboratory? And the project, *Rembrandt*?"

"How the hell do you know that?" John replied with more than a touch of anger. "Less than two dozen people even know the name of that project."

"Then you need to up the count by at least a dozen, since that project name is included in the NIS file on the doctor's disappearance. I had my secretary pull it this morning due to possible links to another case we have open with a research center staff member." Marcus then laid out the situation with the assault on Saturday night.

He finished with, "And Saturday night's events with the center personnel triggered a gut reaction. It felt like there was something else going on there. So earlier today I asked to see all cases that mentioned the center over the last thirty months. Veronica, one of my secretaries, remembered the missing doctor case and pulled that open file while waiting for the computer to track any others."

"Marcus," the CNO asked, "in what context was the project name used in the file?"

"Sir, it just mentioned in one of the ROIs that there had been a file folder on the doctor's desk, and that name was stamped in red on the top page. Nothing else was included in our file about the project. I have no idea what the FBI included in their documentation, but since they were on scene the day after we were, I suspect the other staff members might have already put that file away. I will ask the FBI for a copy of their case file to verify that."

Jason didn't look happy hearing that news. He gave out a huge sigh and continued where Marcus had interrupted him. "And as I was saying, Marcus is the perfect investigator to help us find the doctor. I initially based my opinion upon the history and recommendation that the admiral provided about this officer."

Marcus snickered at that. "Jason, while we know the CNO is never wrong, my father-in-law has a tendency to fluff up my abilities to make sure people do not believe his daughter married below her station."

Both admirals and David Bartow broke up laughing at that one.

Jason remained extremely focused, continuing, "And now, hearing that he is already one step ahead of us even before knowing about my request, it's obvious he's the one we need."

Marcus realized he was shaking his head as he listened. His first reaction: *what the hell can I do that hasn't already been done*. Then one of Dexter's voices in his head chimed in, and he vocalized it: "Here is the ugly fact, Jason—a few months have passed since he disappeared and no body has been found. My first reaction is a negative one, as I cannot imagine how you expect me to succeed where many other investigators have not. Then it hit me—Rembrandt."

Admiral Chance spoke first. "And what does that have to do with finding the man, Marcus?"

"Glad you asked, John, as I don't follow it either," added the CNO. Jason, looking confused, remained silent. David just showed his usual knowing smile.

"Sirs, we at NIS do not know what Rembrandt is. And I suspect neither do the folks at the FBI. It's just a name. However, I cannot see how we can get any further along without knowing the specifics of that project. Again, since no body has been found, my first gut reaction as I read that file is that it was a kidnapping. And since there have not been any ransom demands, the kidnapping must be due to someone wanting his knowledge. And that knowledge probably has something to do with his latest project—Rembrandt. So care to fill us in?"

Jason bit his lower lip as he took a deep breath. His head was shaking side to side a small amount as he said, "Admiral Gallagher, I need your permission to bring these gentlemen into the tent."

"Granted, Jason. Finding the doctor is more important than keeping two more officers out in the cold. Lay it out for them."

Jason cleared his throat and started, "Monroe has been in charge of developing a system that will tell us more about the location of submarines than the existing SOSUS system. Are you familiar with that?"

Admiral Chance and Colt nodded that they were. SOSUS had been around for years, listening for subs. It's hard for anything to be totally silent, and the system picked up those sounds as the subs moved around. Most subs had been tagged with unique sounds that screamed their name like it was in lights.

Jason continued, "With Monroe's new system, we would be using geosynchronous satellites … do you know what that means?"

"We are still with you, Jason, and understand those are satellites that stay in one place, focusing on a specific spot on the earth," Marcus said while the admiral nodded.

"Okay, these new satellites will use a new version of focused radar to look down into the oceans and thereby locate subs. Monroe was nearly finished developing the radar focusing system needed to make it all work. He kept saying his system would 'paint the oceans,' and there is why we dubbed it with the name Rembrandt. I can go into further detail if needed, but that is the picture in broad strokes, if I can keep in the art theme."

No one said anything for a moment or two as they absorbed the information. The importance of that new system was difficult to classify, but on a scale of one to ten, it would probably be around an eleven. Or at least a ten point five. The Navy needed it. And obviously, many other countries would also love to have it.

"So we have a dozen world powers that hate us and about that many who like us, and they would all love to have this system, or at least know how to work around it. Add to that a handful of evil weapons dealers looking for a big sale, and a dozen or so greedy companies that want the plans to give them an advantage for their proposals. Now our potential suspect list fills several pages," Marcus said.

The CNO nodded. "Now you know why we need you on this, Marcus. Take a week or so and go over all the case data, revisit the important sites, and get your gut churning. Find Monroe."

20

THE DISCUSSION WITH THE CNO and Jason Wright continued for another hour as they dug into more specifics of the Rembrandt system. Jason continued to impress on them the importance of finding Monroe.

Jason returned to the OEOB, and the remaining four went back to the CNO's office. Master Chief Yeoman David Bartow pulled Marcus aside once the admirals went into seclusion to discuss whatever admirals discuss in private: probably their latest golf scores or maybe the quality of that month's Playboy centerfold, like junior officers do. David led him to the admiral's coffee mess and they each grabbed a cup. He looked concerned.

"Okay, David, what's bothering you?"

"It wasn't my place to mention it during the meeting, and Jason seemed to ignore it, but there could be some real nasty people involved in this. Kidnapping and stealing military secrets can be a dangerous thing. Please keep alert and make sure someone is watching your back at all times," David said in a low voice.

"That's my standard plan, David."

"And as with the Norfolk operation, your 'get out of jail free' card is still in effect. And you know the phone numbers where you can call for

75

help at any time. At least I'm closer on this one and can come in shooting if you need me."

Marcus chuckled at that thought and truly felt reassured. He and David spent a lot of time on the pistol range together, and both were expert marksmen with their 1911 .45 ACP pistols. The plan was to never need to pull a weapon—but sometimes the bad guys don't cooperate with that, so they strove to be ready.

And the "get out of jail free" card gave a lowly lieutenant commander a lot more power. It was a standard laminated ID-sized card. On one side was his head shot with no uniform showing, his real name, rank, etc. The power came from the wording on the back.

> Lieutenant Commander Marcus James Colt is working
> directly for, and with the full authority of, the office of the
> Chief of Naval Operations. All requests he may have should
> be considered as coming directly from me and be fulfilled
> without question or delay.
> Signed, William M. Gallagher
> Chief of Naval Operations

In addition to having David as a backup, the Chief of Naval Operations could call on just about any resource the Navy had available, so the backup team could be huge. "I appreciate that," Marcus said. "And I hope I don't need you. But the good news is that you know I will call. Ain't proud, as the sayin' goes."

"Well, we all know you seem to pick up scar tissue when on these CNO-approved assignments. Don't wait too long before calling." David laid a hand on his shoulder, then waited a moment. "So, super investigator, where do you plan to start?"

Marcus took a couple of sips of coffee as he framed the answer. Sad part was he needed more time than he had, so his standard procedure still held true: go with what ya got. "David, I'll start with all the NIS files that referenced the research center over the last thirty months since Rembrandt started a little over two years ago. Perhaps there's a link to Monroe and the beating from last Saturday in there. And I need you to call your buddy at BUPERS to get me a copy of all the service records of the current staff at the center. And include anyone who transferred out since the first of the year."

"Can do, sir, and I suspect you will have them tomorrow."

"What will he have tomorrow, Master Chief?" asked Admiral Chance, who had just walked in behind him.

Marcus handled the response for David. "Admiral, David will provide us the service records of all the research center personnel. I'll go through them after I look at any NIS cases involving the research center."

"Huh," said the admiral. "Then you had better plan on spending twenty-four hours per day for the next week or so reading, since there are over two hundred people in that center."

"Ouch. Oh, well, sleep is so overrated. Perhaps I can find a volunteer or two from the NISRA staff."

"Let's go back to the office and develop a plan, Marcus. We need to put together a task force for this one. David, good to see you again, and thanks for your help," said the admiral as they headed out the door.

The drive back to the NIS office was a quiet one, as both the admiral and Marcus stayed lost in their own thoughts about this case. So many unknowns faced Marcus. He needed more input so he could start to think about this mess. And when input is not offered, it's best to simply ask.

As they pulled into the admiral's reserved parking place, Marcus asked the question foremost on his mind. "Admiral, what is your initial reaction to this case?"

A slight smile crossed his face. "Marcus, my first reaction is that we just heard the old 'Washington Two Step' being played by your neighbor. He's acting like the man went missing yesterday, and we know it's been months. What he didn't say is that the local police, NIS, FBI, and probably even the CIA were not able to find the man, so he is throwing a 'Hail Mary' pass. And he is hoping our super investigator—you—will catch it and thereby be able to pull his fat from the fire."

The admiral chuckled and shook his head. "And this way, we end up looking like the failures if we do not solve the case that the other guys could not. And his boss has probably forgotten others failed months ago. So don't think about the pressure being dumped on you, my boy. Probably just the approval of next year's budget, but don't let that stress you out." Again the admiral gave a small laugh.

"Some days I really hate my job, Admiral," Marcus sighed. "Think I need another day or two off, boss."

"Certainly, take a week off … just as soon as you find Doctor Monroe. Like I said, no performance stress here, Marcus."

"Okay, Admiral. I'll hold you to that week off. Now the question is who do you have in mind for the 'task force' you mentioned to David? Or do I have a free hand in choosing my team?"

Again the admiral chuckled. Marcus was glad someone was finding humor in the mess; there was none he could see. Smiling, the admiral said, "Since the bulk of your IA team is out of town, plan on pulling agents from NISRA Washington and any other NISRAs you might like … including a certain guy on the training team. As I recall, you and Doc pulled off some miracles in Norfolk, so perhaps you two can do it again. This has the highest priority, Marcus, and you can have whomever you want. I'll gently rein you in if I see things getting out of hand."

"Aye, aye, sir. We'll get right on it. I would thank you for this 'honor,' but somehow I think I'll regret that free lunch from my father-in-law."

Again, the admiral laughed. It irritated Marcus. The admiral strolled toward his lair and Marcus to his.

Carl gave a quizzical look as Marcus walked toward his office. He motioned for Carl to join him behind his closed door. As he plopped down in his chair and rubbed his hands over tired eyes, Marcus saw on the side of his desk a tall stack of NIS case files. His gut told him they were the ones related to the research center that he'd requested Veronica to pull. And he noticed a small stack of message forms centered on his desk. He looked at Carl as he took a seat across from Marcus and asked, "Anything critical here, Carl?"

"No, sir, nothing really critical. Kelly thinks dinner out is a good plan for your evening, and your friend, the agent at Camp Pendleton, is heading to the airport to pick up our team. Kelly seemed to be excited but wouldn't share any reason why—perhaps she found a new seafood place. Anything interesting said in the Pentagon luncheon?"

Marcus snickered and gave him a synopsis of the afternoon and his new assignment. He finished it with a question. "And have ya got any miracles in your hip pocket? I really could use a few."

"Damn, Mr. Colt. That is one big mess. And you think it's tied to that attack that Martin stopped on Saturday?"

Marcus shrugged and blew out his cheeks in frustration. Maybe it was desperation. Then he gave himself a mental kick in the butt and got things moving by passing the first edicts: "Okay, before you take off, please call and have the following people here for a meeting at 0900 hours tomorrow. It's a place to start." Marcus gave him a short list of NIS agents who would be members of the new task force. Next challenge was to find a good name for it.

Carl nodded. Marcus stood and said, "See you tomorrow afternoon, Carl, and thanks for handling those calls. I've pegged my fun meter and I'm gone."

21

KELLY OPENED THE DOOR AS Marcus approached. She must have been watching for the garage light to come on, indicating his arrival. It was amazing how great she always looked, but that night she had a greater glow than normal. Carl was right: she was excited about something. But experience had taught him to be patient. It would all come out soon.

"Hi, sailor, good to have you back home. It has been a long, lonely day without you," she whispered. Her smile was kicked up to the left: a "tell" that she was up to something. The extra long and sensual kiss she gave him confirmed that something was up.

"Looking very good, Mrs. Colt. What mischief have you been into today?" he asked as they held each other close. The investigator in him wanted to know what prompted the phone message and her fancy dress, but the husband in him just wanted to hold her close and inhale her wonderful natural fragrance as it mixed with just a small amount of perfume.

"You need to hurry and change. We have reservations for dinner at 1930 and we need to leave in about forty minutes."

"Are we celebrating surviving another Monday?" Marcus joked. A small negative shake of her head was all the answer he got.

"I've got the appropriate attire laid out for you, Marcus," she said, her eyes twinkling. "And if you promise to behave, I'll even help you change."

"With such an offer, how can I refuse, but no guarantees on the behavior thing," he replied with a grin to match hers. As they climbed the stairs to the bedroom, the view of her adorable, shapely rear filled his vision. With that image on his mind, the frustrations and worries of the day slipped away.

Carl was right. Kelly had found a new seafood restaurant for them to try. Best of all, it was also an Italian place: their two culinary loves, mingled. The décor and background music were soft, as was the lighting, augmented with candles stuck in empty wine bottles on each table. Interesting thing was that from their table, they could see a hospital down the street. Walter Reed is a huge facility and projects an impressive image.

And it also kicked off the sadness of too many wounded service men and women. They were special people, now suffering because they gave so much physically and mentally to preserve the freedoms loved in this country. People like them followed Marcus in Vietnam, and they paid that price. He must have held his stare out the window too long.

Kelly placed her hand on his. "Penny for your thoughts, Marcus." Her sweet smile was still there, but her eyes showed major concern. She gently stroked the back of his hand with her fingertips as she waited for the answer.

His face spoke volumes as moisture filled his eyes, and the smile he returned was hesitant. It let her know without words that his thoughts were again back in Southeast Asia over a year ago. "Sorry," he whispered as he covered her hand with his. "Just got lost thinking about the good that comes from war. Hard to imagine that, right? But without the Spanish-American war and the many deaths from yellow fever, Major Walter Reed, U.S. Army, wouldn't have been assigned to determine how the disease was transmitted. His work because of those deaths—discovering the bug bite transmission—has saved millions of lives since then. The spirit of the man and his work became the legacy that is that hospital.

Her smile expanded and seemed to cover her face. Kelly squeezed his hand as she said, "I love the way you are able to find good in just about anything. So many people focus only on the negatives, but you push past the bad to find the positives. You're such a wonderful person."

He gave her his standard shrug and a soft smile.

"And I hope you'll find the positive in my news as I help carry on that legacy. Starting next Tuesday, I'll be working there helping our vets find the good in themselves. I got the job!"

His melancholy quickly turned into happiness as he bolted around the table, pulled Kelly into his arms, and held her tightly. "Babe, that is the most wonderful news and I am so happy for you! Give me all the details and leave nothing out."

As they worked their way through a shared antipasto tray and enjoyed glasses of a nice Chianti Classico from Tuscany, Kelly provided all the details of her day with the doctors and human resource staff at Walter Reed. Watching her bubble over with excitement as she talked about it filled him with pride in her accomplishments, and happiness that she was going to her dream job.

Descriptions of the office area and the staff she'd be joining continued into the second course, as they devoured plates of seasoned scallops on pasta with cream sauce. A glass of Vernaccia, a crisp white wine also from the Tuscany region, complimented the pasta. The excellent quality of the food helped make the evening even more memorable. They finished off the meal with a small glass of limoncello instead of a standard dessert.

Kelly was emotionally drained from sharing so much information so fast. Yet her smile and look of contentment as they strolled slowly back to the 'Cuda assured him that all was well.

"Do you think it's too late to call Mom and Dad to share the good news?" Kelly asked as he closed the driver's door and started the engine.

Marcus glanced at the dashboard clock. "Probably not, but ya might want to wait till I fill ya in on today's events. Your dad invited me and Chance to a working lunch." He grimaced as he said the hard part: "And he needs me for a special assignment."

Kelly's head jerked around to face him. Her usually soft eyes were filled with fire. Marcus held up his hands, indicating a combination of surrender and defense. And before he could continue, Kelly firmly and slowly said, "Your wounds from his last adventure haven't fully healed, Marcus. Please tell me you said 'no' to his request."

"Babe, a lowly lieutenant commander does not say 'no' to the CNO who is also his father-in-law. Besides, the assignment is looking into an important—but very cold—case that happened in the Washington Navy Yard back in June, so no travel needed."

Kelly faced forward again, crossing her arms over her chest as her jaw clenched. That was her *leave me alone because I am not happy* look. Fortunately, it wasn't a look Marcus had seen often. He checked the mirrors and backed the 'Cuda from the parking spot. As they drove to the house, he explained the assignment to the non-responsive and extremely upset beautiful lady.

When Marcus got to the part where he was wondering if the attack stopped by Carl's son was part of the issue, the ice melted, and Kelly turned toward him, asking a few questions. Things became more real, and much more important, when their friends and family were involved. They thought of Carl as both. They bounced ideas and thoughts back and forth until reaching home.

Opening her door and helping her out gave Marcus the opportunity to pull her into his arms. They shared a smile, then a kiss. She leaned back to look up at his face while his arms were still around her waist. Her hands gently stroked his cheeks and she quietly said, "Sorry, sailor."

He shook his head. "No apologies needed, Princess. For the record, my first comment to Chance when he told me about the lunch was something along the lines of me already having too much scar tissue thanks to your dad, so we're on the same train of thought. Problem is … I'm not the engineer of this train."

Laughter started to overcome Marcus. Kelly looked confused, then concerned that he had lost his mind. He offered an explanation: "And that reminds me of an old railroad poem. Something that ends with 'the whistle I can't blow, nor even ring the bell, but let the damn thing jump the track and see who catches hell.' That's how things go in the Navy, and with your father, at times."

That got a giggle out of Kelly. "Now that I truly believe!" she said before planting another kiss on his lips. Her happy spirit had returned. "Let's get inside and call the old coot who's making our lives challenging. Promise I'll be nice—well, maybe."

22

THE COFFEE WAS BREWED; PEOPLE came in and out of the coffee mess as Marcus prepared his first cup. He'd arrived only a few minutes before the official start time of 0800 hrs, not his usual thirty to sixty minutes early. He'd suspected the day might be long and had slept in as much as he could. With Carl on the late shift and three of the IA team in California, the office would be somewhat empty. Well, at least until members of the new task force arrived for the 0900 meeting.

"Good morning, Mr. Colt," Rita said as he walked toward his office. "I've gone through the AUTOVON and radio traffic. Nothing is critical—all info copy stuff. Carl left a note that the team arrived safely in Pendleton. We can expect to see a few ROIs late today. And Senior Chief O'Keef would like a moment of your time."

"Thanks, Rita. Did Carl leave you a note about the new task force?"

"Yes, sir, Mr. Colt, and I've taken the liberty to reserve the smaller conference room down the hall for the next few weeks. Additional phones and portable cork and white boards will be in there shortly, and Veronica will be available for shorthand, filing, etc. She's stocking the room with supplies right now."

"You're wonderful, Rita, thanks! Oh, please check the schedule for the bigger conference room also. If free, put in a tentative reservation, as we might need that extra space. I just don't know what to expect from this mess."

Rita smiled. "Mr. Colt, we all know you better than that. You know."

He laughed. "Well, okay, glad I have you all fooled. Since you have everything under control, I'll be visiting with Vic, so check off that request from your list. And Rita, when we are alone, any chance you could call me Marcus?"

Shaking her head slowly, she gave him "the look" which said "don't be stupid, boss." He smiled and nodded in agreement as he raised his hands in surrender and walked out of the area.

Vic was lost in thought, staring a hole through whatever was on his desk. Marcus was able to walk up to his desk before Vic realized he was not alone.

"Good morning, Senior Chief. I understand you need help changing the ribbon on your typewriter. Technology has come a long way since you were cutting letters into wax tablets when you first enlisted, eh," Marcus said with a big grin.

"Good one, Mr. Colt. Can I get back to you with an appropriate comeback? This memo has me a bit baffled and totally sidetracked," he replied with zero enthusiasm.

"Is that what you needed to see me about, Vic?" Marcus asked in a serious tone.

Vic shook his head and laid the memo face down. "No, sir. What I got for you is that late yesterday Carl asked that I get room reservations for the agents you requested from Norfolk. Special Agents John Driscol and Douglas Knox each have rooms at the VIP quarters. They're driving up now from Norfolk in one vehicle and should be here shortly—have them see me for the details when there is time. The admiral filled me in on the task force. Just let me know whatever else you need."

"Thanks, Vic, we'll be set up in the small conference room. Drop by anytime as fresh eyes are always good. And please let the boss know where we're set up."

"Can do, sir."

As he headed back to his office, Marcus heard chatter in the coffee mess. He looked in and found a reunion happening. Doc Stevens was laughing at something John Driscol had said, and Douglas Knox was shaking his head in resignation.

"Good morning, gentlemen. Nice to see you three together again," Marcus said as he started shaking hands, which turned into hugs.

"What's got us doing an early morning drive, Marcus?" asked Doug.

"Just another fun time requested by the CNO. Get your coffee and find the small conference room. Doc will show you the way after he runs you by Senior Chief O'Keef, Admiral Chance's yeoman, who has your lodging info. I'll be in the conference room shortly. And thanks for making that drive, guys. Having your help for a few days is greatly appreciated," Marcus replied. "Doc, walk with me a moment."

"What's up, Marcus?"

"Yesterday afternoon I had a meeting in the CNO's office with my neighbor, Jason Wright, who I just met day before yesterday."

"What? Why?" Confusion flowed over Doc's face.

Marcus let out a sigh. "Seems he's not just another D.C. paper pusher like he said, but is actually the chief of staff for Representative A. Jackson Allen. Mr. Wright is the reason for today's fun and games. I'll tell ya more later. Just know all this comes from a very high place. Take care of the guys." Doc nodded, and Marcus headed back to his office.

Since it was just a little after 0815, he had time to read the note Carl left on the Pendleton case. Just because the CNO had a special project didn't mean all other work stopped. Hopefully, information coming in later that day would be positive.

The morning was thundering on and the wall clock told him he had just a few minutes to get to the conference room and take control of the circus. Hopefully, all the extra help would allow them to get the job done. Passing through the office area, he saw Veronica was working on something at her desk. She smiled as he approached.

"Good morning, Mr. Colt. I have everything ready to go in the conference room."

Marcus nodded. "Great job as always, Veronica. Please join us as soon as you can. Guess it's time to sound *Boots and Saddles* and go face the team."

That comment received the expected chuckles from both ladies; they'd heard it many times in the past. *Boots and Saddles* is an old Army bugle call telling cavalry troops it was time to move out. An old Army master sergeant named Barney, one of the ROTC instructors Marcus knew at Georgia Tech, told them whenever they were ready to head out for training that it was time to sound *Boots and Saddles*. It seemed right for this adventure.

Rita just smiled and shook her head. "Have fun, boss. I'll call if anything critical happens."

The chatter in the room quieted as Marcus entered and stood at the head of the twelve-seat table. Veronica was efficient, so the table was ready with phones, water pitchers, glasses, pads, and pencils. Everyone waited. He I took a deep breath and said, "Everyone know each other?" All heads nodded. "Okay, take a seat and let's get this thing started, and hopefully over just as quickly. Since I have to bounce in and out from time to time, Doc will be second-in-command and try to keep things flowing. If he and I are both MIA, then John Driscol is stuck with this baton of power." He held up a pencil and got the expected smiles.

Doc, John Driscol, and Chris McCormick grabbed the chairs on his right, and Ron Tucker, Doug Knox, and Ed Dondridge took the seats to his left.

When Veronica arrived, Marcus pointed her towards a chair at the other end of the long table. She understood that she wasn't being banned to the empty end but would need space for her task of documenting their efforts. John and Doug were introduced to her, and with pleasantries out of the way, they got down to work.

"This task force was formed to handle one problem. The problem is simple. A scientist from the Naval Research Center here in the Navy Yard vanished back in June. No trace of him, and no clues on why he is gone. NIS couldn't find him, the local police failed, and so did the FBI. The CNO, after been reminded of the scientist's importance by a chief of staff of a high-level congressman, says we must find this scientist due to his knowledge of radar and its application for submarine detection. That is all classified Top Secret. Since he hasn't been seen since June, finding him may not be simple."

As Marcus paused to take a sip of coffee, there were several moans from the six agents, to go along with the downcast looks and head shaking he was seeing. Getting a high priority case is exciting, but getting one that has little chance of success is not. A five-month-old cold case with no leads and no suspects is one with a small chance of success.

Marcus chuckled. "I'm so glad to see everyone has the same belief in success that I do! However, there might be an opportunity for success if we ignore the obvious things in the files and look for the unusual. To start, I want each of you to read the copy of the original missing person's file, which Veronica will now pass around. Afterwards, Ed will field any questions."

As expected, Veronica was ready and the copies were distributed. Ed gave Marcus a look that translated into "I want to kill you," since it had been his case and it was dead cold. Marcus suspected he thought that made him look bad.

To calm the roughed up feathers, Marcus said, "Ed, I read that file in detail. You did all you could with no evidence. None of us could have done more at the time, but perhaps these other agents will see something and ask a question that kicks off a memory that might be important. It's at least worth a try."

Ed reluctantly nodded in agreement and everyone started reading. Marcus slipped out of the room while the reading was underway and checked back with Rita. Nothing new to report, she said.

He asked her to call Kelly and mention they would be having guests for dinner. "Tell her to plan on at least three and probably seven hungry mouths to feed. A tossed salad, country-style steak, garlic-mashed potatoes, and a green veggie would be a good menu choice. Our favorite Merlot would be the right wine. Dessert will be more wine with a cheese and cracker plate."

Rita chuckled at the dessert choice and said she looked forward to her next dinner with the Colts. Marcus promised her it would happen soon.

He got back to the conference room in time to see the last page of the reports being turned over. There was still too much headshaking, and he needed to kick them into a more positive position. No one had a question for Ed, much to his relief.

"Okay, I doubt any of you were able to solve this case based on that one file. Now, Ron and Chris will give ya a verbal update on a sailor who was attacked this past Saturday night. Gents, you have the floor."

Ron displayed a shocked and disappointed look. "So that's why we're on this case, Mr. Colt? You think there is a connection?"

"Not sure about a connection, Ron, but you and Chris have just spent hours at the research center. That makes you two, and Ed, our experts on the place and some of the staff, in my opinion. And with such little to go on in the original file, I'm grasping at straws here. So, when we add your knowledge derived from this new case to the fact you three are excellent agents, then it's a win-win situation."

Ron nodded his acceptance of the logic and gave a complete analysis of the attack on the sailor, from memory. Again, this case as a standalone did not offer any answers. But it might be a piece of the puzzle.

"Thanks, Ron, well done," Marcus said. "Now let's add some additional information that may or may not be relevant. The brass believes the radar system Doctor Monroe was developing is something foreign governments and weapons dealers would love to get their hands on. With that info, it seems the logical choice is to keep kidnapping on the table."

Doc had been unnaturally quiet during the meeting. Finally he said, "Mr. Colt, are you sure there isn't another clue or two that you're holding back? There isn't enough here to fill out a fu ... freaking single index card!"

"That question brings out three very important points, Doc. Unless the admiral is hanging around, we are all on a first name basis—formality takes too much time. Also, in addition to making sure we have sufficient supplies, Veronica is taking notes of all that is said, so keep your language clean. And as for clues, I don't have any up my sleeves, but we have a lot of files to dig through in hopes of finding some for those index cards. Veronica, please get the case files I asked you to pull."

As she moved the stack of NIS case files to the center of the table, Marcus added, "These twenty-nine cases from the last thirty months are ones that have the research center or staff members involved, for whatever reason. We start there looking for anything ... well, I almost said *weird*, but on second thought, we need to create a set of index cards for each case since we don't know what we're looking for yet."

"Logical first step, Marcus," offered Doug.

"And by late today, or early tomorrow, we'll have copies of the service records for the staff of the research center. I don't expect to see anything weird there, but again, we just might trip over something that needs further investigation."

John asked, "When can we see this doctor's office and house?"

"Probably on Thursday, John. With today used to check the NIS case files, and tomorrow spent going over the personnel files, that is about as soon as we can get there. And since it is such an old case, we're not on a time crunch to preserve evidence there."

They decided to move half the agents to the other conference room and opened the internal door between the two rooms. Veronica took care of getting more phones in place, and passed the word to Rita to lock in both rooms for the foreseeable future.

Lunchtime came quickly, and with everyone knee deep in case analysis, they simply ordered pizza. The afternoon passed as fast as the morning, but eventually every one of the files had been studied by at least two agents, and the corkboards were covered with index cards that noted pieces of evidence, locations, and individuals involved. Each card was checked and double-checked. Yet nothing jumped out as a link to the missing scientist.

Marcus had decided earlier that 1600 hrs was quitting time for this team, especially since two members had left Norfolk before 0600.

"Time to call it a day, people. Unless you have any complaints or other plans, I'd like you all to come to my place for dinner," Marcus announced. That offer receive positive nods and comments. "Doc—John and Doug will need directions to the house. How about you ride with them as a talking map, then later you can help them find the VIP quarters after we eat. That okay with everyone?" No arguments were received.

Marcus locked the conference room doors and the team departed. Before leaving he checked with Carl, who hadn't heard from the Pendleton team. No news is good news, he reasoned. Rita hadn't passed any negatives to him when she left, so while the team had been hidden in the conference room, the world did not end.

A quick call to Kelly confirmed the number and names of the dinner guests. She couldn't contain her excitement about seeing some of their Norfolk friends. Hopefully that would help smooth over her frustration with her dad assigning him to the case.

23

KELLY HAD USED HER ENTERTAINING skills adeptly—her mother had taught her well—and dinner was a great success. It was refreshing to share food and relaxing conversation with friends after a long day of research and study. John and Doug enjoyed updating everyone on the happenings in Norfolk. The group was happy to hear about Kelly's new position at Walter Reed.

After dinner, they sat around the table finishing glasses of wine and chatting about the case. The first discussion was on a name for the task force. The wild suggestions ranged from "TF Impossible" all the way to "TF You're Outta Your Mind," each garnering wine-induced laughter.

When the laughter died down, Kelly's smile kicked up to the left as she said, "Call it 'TF Cold Fog.' It's fitting since we all feel lost in a thick fog and the case is so cold."

"The lady is perfect, as always," said Doug, "and I think that name is spot on."

Agreement was unanimous and they gave her a round of applause. Then Veronica threw out a question that caused the team to quiet down and start thinking differently. "Marcus, is our research center the only one working on that radar development?"

"Not sure. Interesting thought, Veronica. Perhaps Ed can stop by there on his way into the office in the morning and ask the commanding officer. Okay, Ed?"

Ed nodded. "Not a problem, Marcus. You know, while working the missing doctor case, I focused only on the doctor and this local office. Nothing was said at the time about his project being something that might be spread to other offices or one that other governments would want via kidnapping. That info would have changed the parameters."

Everyone agreed. And Veronica's question caused Marcus to call the NIS's computer room crew to request a list of all national cases dealing with Navy research centers, or which mentioned radar development, over the last thirty months. The petty officer on duty let out a huge sigh but promised to have the reports on Carl's desk by daybreak.

A stray thought ran through his mind as he returned to the table. "Ron, did you find out why the research center has a hospital corpsman on staff?"

Doug said, "Well, that does sounds strange."

Ron nodded. "It seems they have three hospital corpsmen on staff. In addition to research, they do a lot of prototype development. And while doing that, the engineers get cuts, soldering iron burns, etc. and need quick attention. At times, they run twenty-four hours a day, so they have enough corpsmen for shift work."

"Okay, that makes sense," Marcus replied. "Makes ya wonder why they didn't use R&D in the name. Unless they want to keep the 'development' part a secret."

John grinned, adding, "Perhaps another question for Ed to tackle tomorrow?"

"Do ya think I need to start a list?" Ed asked with a smile.

Marcus chuckled. "No, just ask the first question and if asked, just tell the CO that we are doing a standard periodic review of all open cold cases. Don't let on that this is a special deal. Ed, with you doing the follow-up, it will seem natural."

Chris had been unusually quiet, but he added an important consideration. "I wanna look over the personnel files really deep before we get over there and start asking a lot of questions. No need to spook anyone who might be involved."

"That's important, Chris," Marcus conceded. "Good plan."

Doc cleared his throat. "And what time do we start in the morning, boss? While this is fun, it is gettin' late."

"Normal 0800 is a good time, Doc. And you're right, this has been fun, but time to call it a night. And we all know you need a lot of beauty sleep."

That got the expected laughter, and after hugging Kelly, everyone headed out. The last to leave was Veronica. She paused by the door, and after thanking them for a great dinner, quietly said, "Marcus, hope I wasn't out of line with my question."

"Not a bit—you gave us a new direction to consider. You have a lot of basic knowledge about what an agent does, and with that knowledge, I believe you bring a fresh perspective to the team. You are not locked into an established methodology. So please, never hesitate to offer a question or comment," Marcus said. "See ya in the morning."

They watched Veronica until she was safely in her car, then closed and locked the door to enjoy a few minutes of quiet. Finishing their wine, they cleaned up the dining room and kitchen, and then went up to bed. As they snuggled together in the darkness, Kelly let out a huge sigh.

"Okay, babe, what's on your mind? I know sleep will not be allowed with all that noise you're making."

"I'm concerned, Marcus," she whispered. "Just be careful with whatever this case brings your way. Promise?"

"Always. Does your intuition tell you anything special about the case? Or any of the team members?"

"Team? No. You've got a great group of talented people who will be watching your back. As for the case, the potential for foreign involvement bothers me. No matter what you think, you're not 007."

"Huh." Marcus quipped, "Perhaps you need to see me in a tux. You would probably change your mind. I'm at least close to a 007, maybe a 006.5."

Kelly giggled. "Move your hand, 006.5. I can't fall asleep with you doing that."

"That's the plan, wife—the honeymoon is far from over."

24

KELLY'S CONCERN LINGERED IN THE back of his mind as Marcus did the special exercises designed to restore the muscles of his damaged left arm, then took a hot shower to start the day. Gut feelings, intuition— whatever you want to call it—could keep you alive. Marcus had been warned; he would keep a watch out for evil.

And while his intuition watched for the bad guys, his gut wondered what the hell happened to the doctor and how the team would ever figure it out with such weak data. Challenges can be fun, but they can also drive ya nuts.

Perhaps I'm locking myself into a preconceived notion, Marcus thought, *but the kidnapping thing keeps coming back to wave a red flag at me.* No obvious suicide parameters were found. Nothing was discovered to point to him running off with a lover. Financial issues were eliminated. And there were no known enemies. Kidnapping by a foreign agent seemed likelier, since they now knew of the important project he was developing. He wished they'd had that info a few months ago.

Kelly told him she had a full day planned. Her work wardrobe needed an upgrade before she joined the Walter Reed staff the following week, so her mother would pick her up after breakfast, and the two ladies would shop until they dropped at a local mall or two. American Express would be happy with her shopping trip.

After a well-balanced breakfast and a superb goodbye kiss from the delightful Kelly, Marcus went out to tilt a few windmills. Don Quixote had nothing on NIS when it came to impossible dreams. Seemed that some weeks, "impossible" was the standard operating procedure. Marcus agreed with, and frequently borrowed, the unofficial slogan of many other units: *the difficult we do immediately; the impossible takes just a little bit longer.*

While waiting at a stoplight, Marcus glanced up to watch a small private jet climb toward its designated altitude after departing National Airport. It was probably carrying a D.C. bureaucrat who thought he needed to be someplace faster than the Average Joe heading out on vacation. And then it hit him that getting a kidnapped scientist out of the country would be easy with a private aircraft. It would be hard to sneak a kidnap victim onto a commercial aircraft. So private aircraft was something else for the team to check out.

Or a ship could have gotten him out of the country. Hiding someone on a freighter would be fairly easy. Ditto for getting them on board. He realized the team needed to see what ships left the area right after the doc vanished. Especially from ports within a few hours drive from D.C., since they could have driven out of the area. Or they could have driven to Canada and flew out of there. Damn, the possibilities kept expanding, and they needed to narrow things. Impossible kept rearing its ugly head.

25

ALL THE CLOCKS PROCLAIMED THE time as 0730, but glancing into the conference rooms, Marcus found everyone already there, going over the personnel files the good chief at BUPERS had dropped off. Seemed everyone was giving one hundred and ten percent on this project already. He caught Doc's attention and beckoned him into the hall.

"Morning, Doc. Hard at it, I see," Marcus quietly said. Doc matched the grin on Marcus's face and nodded.

"Marcus, on the way back to the base last night, we decided 0700 was a better start time. And Ron, Chris, and Veronica had the same thought. Great minds are always following the same path. Didn't think you would mind too much, boss," Doc replied with a chuckle.

Marcus shook his head. "You know y'all are totally crazy, right? Just as well, since it is a requirement to fit in better around here. Anyway, I've got to check to see what's on my desk before I can get back here. Take charge and keep them in line, okay?"

"Aye, aye, sir. You got it, Marcus." Doc returned to the large conference room.

After hitting the coffee mess for the first cup of many, Marcus stopped to get his marching orders from Rita. He knew she'd have the updates from the team in California, as well as knowledge of any other issues that

96

had cropped up overnight. She was still looking through the overnight AUTOVON traffic when he approached her desk.

"Good morning, Chief. As I passed the conference rooms, I noticed everyone is starting early today." She switched to Spanish: "*¿Algun problema para compartir, jefe?*" Rita asked that frequently, always with a single raised eyebrow.

That special facial expression and accent always put Marcus in a better mood. "No problems to share, Rita, at least none that I know about. Looks like the dinner conversation last night got the team even more motivated. And we decided the task force would be named 'Cold Fog,' so update whatever files and records were anxiously awaiting that name."

Rita smiled. "Nice name. It makes me think of being lost in a fog."

"You broke the code on that one," Marcus said with a laugh. "Find anything interesting in the morning traffic?" He noticed she had two piles of messages, which meant not all fell into the "for your information" category.

"Couple of things will make you smile a bit more. Carl left a note that two of our boys will be returning to D.C. late tonight. No problems in Pendleton, and our favorite yeoman is happily on his special home-based assignment," she said, smiling. "But I'm not sure how you're going to feel about this one." She handed him a copy of personnel orders from BUPERS. "Sorry you didn't get your way."

Marcus scanned the orders. An ensign who was finishing up NIS agent training that week would fill the open slot in the IA division. He had been pushing for a seasoned civilian agent to be assigned to that position, thinking the field experience would be an asset, but the slot called for a junior Navy officer. Now one had been assigned.

"As the seasoned and scarred leader of this circus, I'm always happy to have new people come on board. Guess we need to make sure the empty office is cleaned and stocked with supplies by next Monday. And pull her service record, please," he said with a big grin that helped hide his frustration.

"Already done, boss. I'll make sure the intro package is up to date and on the desk, ready for the ensign to absorb on day one. Anything else?"

"Nope. As always, you have it all covered, and again you're a step ahead of me. You or Carl should be in charge of this division."

Rita moved her head slowly from side to side. "You're the reason we are so damn good at what we do, boss. None of us could replace you, and frankly, none of us want that horrible job. So stay healthy and keep doin' what you do."

"Yes, ma'am, I'll work on that." He went into his office for a minute of quiet before heading back to the conference room. With another sip of coffee in his system, he jotted down his thoughts about the use of private aircraft or cargo ships for getting a kidnapped doctor out of the country. Part of him wondered why even consider it, since it had been four months. Memories fade and paperwork gets lost. But it was another rock to look under, and that was part of the job.

He had just finished a list of things to consider in case it was a kidnapping when the intercom line buzzed. "Yes, Rita?"

"Ed Dondridge is on line two for you."

"Thanks," Marcus replied as he pushed the lit button. "This is Colt."

"Mr. Colt, we have a problem," he said quietly.

Since Ed was being formal, Marcus suspected he was in an area with the commanding officer of the research center, or at least one of his staff, listening to his side of the conversation. So he kicked up the formality a notch when he asked, "And what is that problem, Special Agent?"

"Sir, the CO here is reluctant to discuss anything about the doctor's project without written authority and wants to talk to my commanding officer. How shall I proceed?"

The day had just started going downhill, and Marcus had yet to finish one cup of coffee. "Tell him I'll be over shortly. Meet me outside the center in about ten minutes. Leaving now." He hung up, drained the cup, and grabbed his cover from the rack. "Rita, I'm heading over to the research center. Hope I won't be gone long."

She nodded her understanding and gave him a wink. "Be nice, boss." Obviously she'd been listening to the conversation and knew of his tendency to not appreciate stonewalling with any of the cases.

26

ED WAS STANDING ON THE sidewalk as Marcus walked up. His shrug expressed his feelings. Marcus offered a shrug back. "Hey, Ed. Who's the CO and what is his attitude?"

"*She's* new, Marcus. She just came on board in late August from an XO slot in the research center in San Diego. Name is Jennifer Collier. She's a newly minted captain, and just seems to want to strictly follow all the rules. Said she didn't know much about the missing doctor, or at least claims not to know. She is friendly, in a professional sort of way."

Marcus smiled at the description. Anyone getting promoted to captain and getting a commanding officer slot understands they now have a lot of weight on the shoulders—more so for women. And no one wants to make mistakes. Mistakes like talking about a secret project without authorization. Older skippers would realize that a NIS investigation grants more leeway with access. He said, "Okay, Special Agent, let's go play 'good cop–good cop' and see if we can get the info we need. Lead on!"

The yeoman in the outer office stood when they walked in and pointed to the closed door. "Go right in, sirs, the captain is waiting for you," he offered.

Marcus knocked, waited until he heard "enter," then marched to a position six feet in front of her desk. Ed followed a few paces behind as he came to attention and said, "Lieutenant Commander Colt, reporting as ordered."

"At ease, Mr. Colt, Agent Dondridge. I appreciate your quick response to my request. Sorry if you thought my request was an order. Care for some coffee?" She stood and walked around her desk with her hand extended.

They sized each other up as they shook hands. She had to look up, since Colt was a few inches taller. But that didn't deter the authoritative look she had; it gave off a firm "I am in command here" attitude. Her brown eyes complimented her medium brown hair, which was pulled back into a tight bun at the base of her neck. The minimal makeup she wore allowed her natural beauty to show. While not magazine-cover beautiful, the CO fell into the cuter-than-average category. Marcus held his focus on her eyes so she would not think he was checking out her body.

"Thank you, Captain, coffee would be nice. It has been a challenging morning already," he chuckled as they took the chairs she pointed out. She called out to the yeoman and placed the order. He must have anticipated her request as he carried in a serving tray almost immediately. He poured three cups and departed, closing the door behind him.

She smiled slightly as she asked, "And why do I think my lack of response to your agent has complicated your morning, Mr. Colt?"

Marcus finished stirring his coffee and took a small sip. It gave him time to properly frame a diplomatic response. "Interrupted perhaps, Captain, but not complicated. It has saved me from potential paper cuts and eye strain while reading too many old dusty NIS case files relating to every Naval Research Laboratory problem over the last few years."

Her chuckle seemed friendlier than her attitude when they first arrived. She said as she nodded toward Ed, "While waiting for your arrival, I checked into the issue with the missing doctor that he mentioned. Since it was months before I arrived, I had not yet been made aware of the situation. But I am still not going to talk about his project without authorization."

"Understood, Captain. Perhaps this will help." Marcus pulled out his "get out of jail free" card.

She studied both sides and passed it back. "I suppose I should call the CNO's office to verify this."

"If it will make you feel better about talking to us, please do so. Master Chief David Bartow runs the admiral's office and is read in on this assignment in case Admiral Gallagher is not available. Just know that the

CNO himself asked me to find the doctor over lunch on Monday. And to do that, we immediately need to know if the work on Rembrandt was isolated here, or if it was being worked on in other locations. And the faster we know that, the quicker we can narrow our search parameters, and the less time we'll waste looking at every old case file," Marcus said somewhat sternly. "Fewer paper cuts, also," he added with a lighter attitude.

Collier's face got a stern contemplative look for a few seconds, then her smile returned. "Mr. Colt, give me a few minutes and I will have the location information for you. I'll be right back."

As she left the office, Ed and Marcus shrugged again. At least they had time to finish their coffee while they waited. Marcus noticed her diploma hanging on the wall; MIT did not pass out those electrical engineering degrees to just anyone. Collier was a serious scientist as well as a Navy officer.

It was a short wait, as Captain Collier came back faster than expected and took her seat. She sipped her coffee and did not offer any more information.

"Captain, how involved are you with Rembrandt? And did you know Doctor Frederick Monroe?" Marcus asked.

She looked up at the overhead and puckered her lips. Her gaze returned to Marcus, after a quick glance at Ed. "I know the highlights of the project, but I never worked with that doctor. You might want to track down the previous CO, Captain Peters—he might have more info."

Interesting, Marcus thought, but he kept silent and gave a quick nod. *That didn't sound totally truthful. Why do I think she knows more about Monroe.*

A quizzical look came to her face. "Am I permitted to ask you a few questions, Mr. Colt, while we wait?"

"Ask away, Captain. But don't be upset if we cannot answer all of them."

"I see. Okay, why is an internal affair division doing this investigation? That implies a problem with the agents who conducted the initial investigation, correct?"

Marcus nodded. "In a normal world that would be true, but not in this case. SA Dondridge here was the lead agent on the case when the doctor vanished. No improprieties have been suggested about his work and none should be assumed. He's assigned to this team due to his knowledge of both your operation and the old case. In reality, our IA division should be named Internal Affairs and Special and Weird Projects. We get the cases that need special attention for whatever reason. This is the third one I've worked in less than two years."

"Okay," she said. "Why did you leave the SEALs to join NIS?"

It was now time for Marcus to take a slow breath as he formulated his answer. After a moment, he replied, "I have been with NIS since joining the Navy. A special project last year, also assigned personally by the CNO, saw me working with two SEAL teams. Their efforts saw to it that I could wear the Trident."

"That seems highly irregular. What was that project?"

"Sorry, that is still classified. Next question?"

Collier tucked that information away and rapidly hit them with her next question. "And what else will this office need to provide you?"

"Ed, you want to handle that one?"

"Sure. Captain, in a day or so, several of us will be here to look over the doctor's office and most of the building. We have agents from Norfolk working this case, and their fresh eyes might find something we initially missed. And while I doubt the office has been untouched, if there is anything from that office placed in storage, we will need to look at that too."

Both agents noticed Collier rubbing her left hand. Perhaps that was a nervous tick or a stress indicator. She looked between the two, then asked, "Is that all?"

"No, ma'am," Marcus said. "We will be interviewing your personnel who have knowledge of the doctor or the project after we finish going over all the file data. We will try not to interrupt your operation as we do so."

Before she could respond, her yeoman knocked on the door casing and said, "Captain, I have that information you requested." He handed the folder to the captain and left.

Captain Collier glanced at the report and passed it to Colt. "Is that enough for now, Mr. Colt?"

The report included locations, descriptions of the tasks assigned, and the names of the primary staff working on Rembrandt. "Thank you, Captain. This will be a big help. Now if there is nothing else, we will head back to our office, ma'am."

"I suppose I should say 'dismissed' or 'carry on,' but to compensate for my abruptness earlier, I'll just thank you for your time, gentlemen, say 'good day' and wish you luck with your investigation."

As he stood to leave, another thought hit Marcus. He turned back to the captain and asked, "Captain, do you have any thoughts as to why one of your petty officers was beaten on Saturday night?"

Her smile tightened. "I thought it was the job of your office to determine that, Mr. Colt."

"Very true, and we're working on it, but I find it amazing how quickly scuttlebutt gets around a unit, even one as big as this. And more often than not, such rumors have a lot of truth in them," Marcus said. "Heard anything?"

"Nothing has reached my office, but I'll keep my ears open," she said as she walked them to the door. "Know that this office is always open to you and your team. Call me anytime, Mr. Colt, and I do mean anytime. I'm in the BOQ for now, so I can be here or your office in a few minutes if need be." She shook their hands and handed Marcus her card. It had her BOQ number written on the back.

27

GETTING BACK TO THE TEAM at a little after 0830, Ed and Marcus shared their information about the new skipper and the report she provided. Veronica made everyone copies of the report and passed them around. Doug went to work pulling out the case files for the locations that shared the Rembrandt project, and Chris started looking for personnel files mentioned.

As the team started digging and sorting, Marcus rapped on the table with his knuckles to redirect their attention. "First off, thanks for getting an early start. You have my permission to work as long as you like, but just don't burn out." That got the expected laughs. "And I know the admiral will want an update if I bump into him, so do we have anything positive to report?"

John Driscol shook his head. Doc shrugged as he replied, "Marcus, it could be said we have eliminated the obvious and have started to focus on the unknown."

Marcus sighed. "So we have nothing. Good news it is just the start of the second day, so miracles are not expected until the second week. Continue pulling and studying related files and I will return shortly. I need to do a bit of my primary job for a few minutes."

When he'd looked at the report in Collier's office, Marcus noticed that the research center in San Diego was involved with Rembrandt. And since it was almost 0600 hrs in California, he made a quick decision and needed to act.

Rita provided the phone number for the visiting VIPs lodging at Camp Pendleton, and he placed the call. The phone was answered on the fifth ring by a familiar and somewhat grouchy voice. "Hello?"

"And a very pleasant 'good morning' to you, Jake. This is your 0600 wakeup call from the NISHQ offices of your fearless leader. Got a minute?"

Sounding more awake and a touch more pleasant, Jake answered, "Of course, sir. How are things in Foggy Bottom this wonderful morning, sir?"

"Your sarcasm is noted and greatly appreciated, Jake. Actually, it's a bit of a mess here. On Monday afternoon, the CNO assigned us the cold case of the missing scientist from the Naval Research Laboratory. Carl left a note that you were heading back today. Y'all get a 'well done' on clearing up a possible disaster. But I need ya to head down to San Diego instead."

Jake let out a sigh, "Your wish is always our command, boss. But we sent Neil home last night. He was so happy I hate to call him back."

Marcus chuckled. "Understand. No need to rain on his parade just yet. I'll talk with the SSA Paul Doubleday about having Charlie continue to be with you and Hank. Will that work for you?"

"Fine, Marcus. We really like Brandt and I think he can tolerate us for another day or so. What do you need down there?"

It only took a few minutes to fill him in on the highlights of the case and the concern that other centers working on Rembrandt might have problems. And if not, someone in San Diego might know something about the missing scientist—something not in the case file due to the classification and compartmentation preventing the team from asking. Then Marcus said, "Get Hank up to speed, and by the time you two get to the NISRA office, there will be a NIR waiting for you with more info."

"You got it, boss. And if all goes well, we might still make our evening flight."

"Don't count on that, Jake. I have a feeling there's something out there that will help the case. And one other thing … the CO of the research center here is new. She came here a couple of months ago after being the XO of that office in San Diego for the past two years. I don't feel anything off about her. Well, my gut says that's not completely true, but I don't have a clue about what's bugging me. She might link to Rembrandt. Keep that in mind as you ask around the place."

"Understand. I always trust your gut."

"And Jake, I know you want to come home, but since you are already out there, it might save some time in the long run. If another day or two is needed, or if you need Neil's help, so be it."

"I hear and I obey. If there is nothing else, I gotta run and get it done."

"Nope. Keep in touch."

The dial tone indicated Jake hung up to get busy with his new assignment. Marcus turned to his typewriter, and using his recently acquired yeoman skills, quickly created a NIR, the slang for an official Naval Investigation Request. That document would cover Jake and Hank in their endeavors and provide the background they needed to ask the right questions. He carried it to the chief yeoman in charge of the AUTOVON communications, who promised it would be on the way shortly to both NISRA Pendleton and NISRA San Diego. Depending on what the guys found, they might need the resources of the San Diego office.

Back in his office, Marcus typed a personal message for Rita to give to SSA Doubleday when she called him at Pendleton. Doubleday usually got into his office between 0730 and 0800 Pacific Time, so Marcus asked Rita to keep calling until she reached him. He then walked to the conference room; Rita would track him down if she needed backup.

He picked up the list of worldwide research center cases the computer techies had left on Carl's desk, as promised. It was a thick one, and his immediate thought was *more dusty files to read*. Oh, well, glamour is slow coming in the intelligence world. As luck would have it, the admiral saw him as he rounded the corner towards the conference rooms.

"Colt, what's the status?" the admiral asked sharply.

"Good morning, Admiral, we are just now getting into the personnel files. Nothing was found in the twenty-nine cases we worked at our research center over the last three years. Last night, we hit upon the idea that other centers might also be working on Rembrandt and there might be some connections there. I have here the list that will require a lot more file analysis."

"Last night? Burning midnight oil already?"

"No, sir. We left at a decent hour. I took the team home for dinner last night. It was done for a bit of bonding as well as an early 'thank you' for their upcoming work. Naturally, after a good meal and with more than enough wine, the conversation turned to the frustrations of this case.

Veronica brought up the question of other centers sharing the project. With that door opened, I called the computer guys, and we have destroyed a tree getting this printout of cases."

The admiral smiled and chuckled. "Veronica, eh? 'Out of the mouths of babes,' right? And she really is a babe. Just don't let her or my wife hear that I said that."

Marcus nodded as the admiral turned toward his office. When the admiral was out of hearing, Marcus could not stop a chuckle from erupting. The admiral may be old, but he ain't dead, he thought. He entered the larger conference room to find Doc and Chris discussing one of the personnel records. They stopped talking when they saw him.

"What did you find?" Marcus asked.

Doc shrugged. "Not much, boss. We're hitting the local center personnel files hard, but so far, nothing very strange jumps out."

"And the look on your faces, and the fact you stopped talking when I entered tells me you're up to something. Spill it before I take away your coffee mess privileges," Marcus threatened jokingly.

Doc shrugged and looked at Chris before saying, "Okay, we have nothing concrete. But, and that is a very big 'but,' the attack on Radarman Second Class Larry Masters looks weird."

"Why?"

"Marcus, he doesn't have any gambling or drug issues. No financial problems came forward. No estranged girlfriend or wife. No personnel problems, yet he was beat hard for no apparent reason and ..."

Chris excitedly jumped in. "And he was assigned to work with Dr. Frederick Monroe on Rembrandt."

Doc shot him a slightly dirty look, shrugged, then nodded. Chris's look showed he knew he had overstepped; he mouthed a "sorry" in Doc's direction.

"Doc, you know how I feel about coincidences, right? I want you two to work that angle. Anything else?"

Doc snickered. "And there are some inconsistencies with his statement."

"And I also hate inconsistencies. What is your next step, gentlemen?"

Doc looked at Chris and motioned for him to answer. "We go back to the hospital and question Masters again, right?"

Marcus nodded and headed back to face the growing mountain of papers on his desk.

28

RITA HAD LEFT FOR LUNCH and the Cold Fog group did the same. Marcus stayed behind to catch up on the pile of papers that never seemed to stop appearing on his desk. In anticipation of working through lunch, he'd confiscated the last crab cake from his fridge, so had at least packed a decent sandwich. He grabbed the crab cake sandwich and a soda and secluded himself in his office.

Carl had arrived early for his new "late shift" and, having finished his update session with Rita, was working on the stack of papers covering his desk. One sheet was a note from Marcus. The knocks on the boss's door casing pulled his attention from the papers. Carl had a quizzical look on his face. "You wanted to see me, Mr. Colt?"

Marcus pointed to one of the chairs in front of the desk and Carl took it. "Sorry to keep you on the late shift for a few more days. But the California team needs to do another project out there."

"Yes, sir, I saw the NIR you generated for San Diego. No problem for me to be here for them."

"Good. This missing doctor case still has us grasping at straws, and one of those straws is the attack that Martin stopped Saturday. Seems the victim was working on the doctor's project and there are some inconsistencies with his statement. Doc and Chris are at the hospital interviewing the victim again in hopes of getting the true facts. It's a thin link, but it's some place to start."

Carl nodded. "And you want them to interview Martin again, right?"

"Not 'them,' just Doc. I'm hoping that Martin going through it again with a new agent will help his memory drudge up something else to help us find the attacker. And not having Chris here should eliminate any leftover feelings from Saturday. I'd like you to be with Doc as he goes through the events with Martin. That okay with you?"

"Me? Of course, I'll help, but why?"

His response surprised Carl. "You know Martin's mannerisms and will be able to pick up on any hesitations that might mean he is holding something back. Don't get me wrong, I know he is the good guy here, but he might be cautious about mentioning something."

"Uh, huh. Your gut's feeling something wrong? Something Martin did?"

"No. No. No. Nothing's wrong, Carl! I just think there's a fact or two he's skipping over for whatever reason. I think he probably saw or heard something he doesn't think is important. In cases like this, everything is important, and Martin might not understand that."

Carl nodded. "I get it, sir. I'll call Martin and have him come here right after he gets off work. That will be a little after 1700—will that be soon enough?"

"That'll be great, Carl. I'll update Doc when he returns from the hospital."

As the door clicked shut from Carl's departure, Marcus tried returning to the stack of paperwork. But the mundane work could not hold his attention. Like a kid at Christmas, he wanted to run down the hall and dig into the "presents," or as they were known that day, personnel files related to Cold Fog.

The decision was an easy one to make: do boring paperwork for the next fifteen minutes as he finished the sandwich, then run down the hall and dig into the Cold Fog files. Being the boss allowed him to make these wild decisions, knowing full well that boring paperwork would not go away by itself. He would pay for that later.

29

THE STANDARD HOSPITAL SOUNDS AND smells hit Doc Stevens and reminded him of his recent past as he and Chris entered the building. Nostalgia is a good thing at times: it reminded him of where he came from and made him appreciate where he was now.

He immediately noticed that this hospital was not as busy as the one in Norfolk where he and Marcus had spent a lot of time earlier that year. Chris led them to the floor where RD2 Larry Masters was recuperating from his attack.

At the front desk, Doc showed his ID to the nurse. "Good afternoon, Lieutenant. What's the condition of RD2 Masters?"

The nurse glanced at the ID and pulled the proper chart. She flipped through a few pages. "Sir, he's doing well. Some pain, but nothing major. No complications."

Extending his hand toward the chart, Doc said, "May I see that, please?"

The nurse hesitated. "Not sure you will understand all that is here, sir. I can answer any questions you have."

Doc chuckled. "Lieutenant, before they forced sophistication on me and made me wear shoes, a coat, and a tie as a NIS special agent, I was a hospital corpsman first class assigned to a SEAL team. I think I can handle it, ma'am."

"Certainly, sir. Here's the chart," she replied with a big smile.

Doc scanned each page and handed it back. "Thanks, Lieutenant. We'll be talking with him for the next little while and would appreciate not being disturbed."

She nodded and winked as she took the chart. "You got it, sir."

Since the door to Larry Masters' room was open, he knocked on the casing and walked in to find Larry Masters sitting up in bed watching TV. The multiple bruises on his face had started turning several colors. Masters pressed the off button on the remote and turned to the agents as Doc closed the door.

Through a clenched jaw, Masters said, "Hello, sirs. What do you want?" His broken jaw hampered his speech, but it was understandable.

"Masters, I'm NIS Special Agent Stevens. You remember meeting Agent McCormick the night of your attack?" Doc displayed his credentials as Chris walked to the opposite side of the bed.

"Yes, sir." Masters' eyes darted nervously between the agents as he nodded.

"Good to see your bruises getting a nice shade of blue and purple. Soon they'll change to yellow as your body heals. How does the jaw feel?"

"Hurts like hell, sir."

"Understandable after that beating." Doc smiled. "Masters, the good news is you'll be out of here soon. But the bad news is the guy that did this to you is still running around free. I just got assigned to help on your case, and need you to go over all that happened again. I've read the reports, but hearing it first hand is always better."

Masters nodded and shared the events of the evening. He started from the time he left the enlisted men's club right before the attack. His story matched what he had said on Saturday night. Although his jaw was clenched most of the time, Doc was able to get the gist.

Doc stopped him several times with additional questions. Chris maintained his quiet stance and requisite blank face while he focused on Masters; perhaps Masters might show a reaction to Doc's questions indicating he's hiding something. At least that's what Doc thought might happen when he'd told Chris to stand quietly and watch his face for tells as they drove to the hospital.

"Okay, Masters," Doc said, "I need you to tell me who you talked to at the club. And what you talked about."

Masters' face developed a concerned look. He glanced at Chris, then looked toward, but not directly at Doc. "Nobody special, sir. Just a couple of the guys from the office, you know, the same guys from the office. We get together every week when we can."

Doc smiled and moved to look directly into Masters' eyes. "Do these 'same guys' have real names?"

Masters nodded and provided names for six people who he said had been with him at the club. They just talked about normal "guy" stuff, he said. Things like which of the girls in the club might want to dance, and of course the latest ball game scores.

Doc continued to write notes, nodding and smiling as Masters gave him more information about the discussions. When Masters said there was nothing else, Doc asked, "And now tell me about your afternoon, say from lunch time until you hit the club. What do you do at the research center?" Doc's tone was that of the friendly older brother.

Again, Masters turned his head to get out of Doc's line of sight. He seemed to become more nervous as the interrogation progressed. After a few moments, he finally said, "Sir, there was nothing special happening that afternoon. As for work, I do the normal boring stuff, sir."

Doc started chuckling and shaking his head. Masters did a double take on Doc and then looked down at his hands. The silence made Masters more nervous.

Speaking with a touch of sorrow in his voice, Doc said. "Larry, the problem you have—well, at least one of the problems—is that you are a terrible liar. Really terrible, Larry. And lying to a NIS agent is one of the things you've done that can lead to seeing you in the brig when you get out of this hospital. Unless your attacker comes back to finish the job while you're resting here. In short, you're in a lot of trouble, and I'm the only one who can help you right now."

Masters sat there, anguish and dread visibly flooding over him, as Doc waited. Nothing was said for several moments.

Finally, Doc quietly broke the silence. "We know you worked on Rembrandt with Doctor Monroe—not boring stuff. We know you were alone in the club. And we know a stranger approached you. Unlike your normal associates, this was a guy unknown to the club staff. So tell us about this guy who confronted you in the club and followed you outside."

It was sad to watch a man implode. Masters seemed to shrink into himself as the realization of his situation hit home. Tears ran down his cheeks. He knew he had been caught. Chris and Doc got started digging out the truth.

30

MARCUS COLT ENJOYED HIS QUIET office, courtesy of the lunch hour. With people out of the office or eating in the break room, interruptions and background noises were at a minimum, making it easy to focus on the job. After handling a good portion of routine paperwork during that break, rather than head to the conference room, he picked up his copy of the Rembrandt location info provided by Captain Collier. He leaned back to read.

Locations for the work on Rembrandt were scattered across the globe. Most of the labs were on Navy bases, which made access more controlled. But three were on college campuses. College and security often do not go together. The relaxed atmosphere of college campuses, where sharing ideas and openly discussing problems is standard, made them easy targets for information theft.

It showed a total of twelve sites working on Rembrandt. With his team in California checking in with the San Diego research center that day, and with his local crew visiting the D.C. lab again the next, that left ten others to consider. Seven of those were military locations that Marcus had visited over the last few years, including Virginia Beach, Virginia; Mayport and Pensacola, Florida; Newport, Rhode Island; and New London, Connecticut. The other two were across the Atlantic, in Scotland and

Italy. The three institutes of higher learning were in Berkeley, California; Cambridge, Massachusetts; and Houston, Texas. Not for the first time, Marcus thought he was facing a problem that would be difficult to solve.

No matter how many labs were in the mix, the key to the success of the Rembrandt project was the knowledge possessed by Doctor Frederick Monroe. Marcus needed to find out who in the project knew specific details about what Monroe was doing—and if anyone else involved with the project had been the subject of strange encounters. Granted, no one else had disappeared, but they might have been threatened. Or perhaps approached to share information. More questions to be asked.

As Marcus leaned back in his chair, allowing his eyes to scan the overhead in hopes of finding answers written there, another "thing to do" popped into his mind. He needed to contact the local police, the FBI, and the CIA to find out if they had any more information on the missing doctor.

The chief of police was extremely courteous when Marcus called, and promised to send a copy of the file over the next day. It's always nice to have some cooperation between agencies. Of course, that cooperation might have something to do with the chief being a personal friend.

Marcus had met the chief late the previous year at one of the many D.C. social functions, and they had struck up a friendship based on their mutual admiration for the Colt 1911 semi-automatic pistol. That conversation resulted in frequent competition at the police pistol range. Their friendly wagers meant the chief frequently bought the beer after the matches, as a good loser should.

For sure, the FBI had done an investigation on the doctor's possible abduction, so there would be something to read there. Perhaps the CIA also looked into it. Not on U.S. soil, of course, since law prohibits that, but who knows what the fine folks in Central Intelligence were actually doing.

Two small problems existed with accessing those files: his friend in the Bureau had left the D.C. area for an overseas posting months ago, and Marcus had never cultivated any contacts with the Agency. Never needed to talk to the Agency in the past, but he did have a contact who could open both doors for him.

Marcus checked the D.C. phone book and dialed the selected number. After only two rings, a pleasant and almost too sexy female voice said, "You have reached the office of Congressman A. Jackson Allen. This is Jessica. How may I direct your call?"

"Good afternoon. Lieutenant Commander Colt calling for Jason Wright."

"I'm sorry, sir, Mr. Wright is in a meeting. May I have your number and I'll have him call you later?"

Marcus frowned and took a breath; not the time to get angry. After a moment, he said, "Miss Jessica, just slip him a note right now that I'm holding for him. He'll want to talk with me ASAP."

"Sir, that is highly irregular."

"That might be true, but trust me, he will be more upset if you delay our conversation."

The line was quiet for a moment, and finally a sigh came through as the lady made her decision. "Hold one moment, sir. I'll try. But I hope you'll hire me when I get fired."

In less than two minutes, a familiar male voice answered, "What's up, Marcus? Good news?"

"Thanks for taking the call, Jason. Hated to bother you in a meeting, but I need your contact help and I need it soon."

"Okay, how can I help?"

Marcus laid out the status of the investigation and his need to get a look at the existing FBI and potential CIA files. Jason agreed that without established contacts in the agencies, the delays and frustrations would waste too much time.

"What say I pick you up from your office at three p.m. and we visit both my friends at that time?" asked Jason.

Marcus smiled, knowing he'd made the right decision. "Let's just do the CIA today. The boys at the Bureau can wait until tomorrow. I'll be outside my office at 1500. Thanks."

Leaning back again to consult the 'oracles in the overhead,' Marcus thought about his team in California. It was way too early to expect their reports on the San Diego Research Lab, and by the time they might be ready to report, he would be leaving to visit the first of the other two alphabet agencies.

He made another decision, and started typing a memo for Carl to read to LT Doty when he called in later. Their California retreat would last at least another day.

31

MARCUS HAD PLACES TO GO and people to see, yet he was able to brief Doc about the upcoming interview of Martin before dashing out to rendezvous with Jason. In return, Doc gave him a quick overview about the chat with Larry Masters as he walked Marcus to the elevator; finally there was a piece of data to put on the board.

The minute hand on his Timex was a couple of notches shy of twelve as Marcus left the building. No vehicles were along the curb, but he wasn't concerned. Traffic around D.C. was always iffy, and Jason was not technically late for the three o'clock pickup.

Checking out the passing cars, Marcus found his attention pulled toward a bright red Plymouth Valiant convertible heading his way with the top down. The 1964 Signet model was decked out with aftermarket "mag" wheels and pinstripes accenting the bodylines. She was a true beauty. It was only when the car stopped beside him that he noticed Jason was driving.

Jason smiled as he said, "Hi neighbor. I guess that silly smile means you like my old car, right?"

"You bet—she's sweet. But I'm a bit shocked you don't have a chauffeured limo, Jason."

"Only on Mondays," Jason joked. "Get in. Time to see what Langley has to offer us lowly civil servants."

As Jason dodged the traffic, Marcus shared the progress of the investigation. Granted, there were not many positives to relay, but Jason seemed happy that something was being done.

In return, Jason shared info about the person they'd be meeting soon. When he'd set up the meeting, he related a bit about the problem they now faced. He also admitted he was glad Marcus had called and pushed to get him on the phone.

"Marcus, you have no idea how boring it is to sit in so many of these meetings. Heading out of town with the top down is great therapy."

Marcus replied with a knowing nod. At their level of management, too many meetings were a shared nightmare.

Jason added, "By the way, I informed my staff that any calls from you get my immediate attention, so you won't be delayed in the future."

"Thanks. Guess I don't need to hire that girl Jessica who interrupted your meeting," Marcus said with a laugh. Jason just smiled and focused on the traffic.

The head guard at the CIA parking lot was expecting them, and after verifying their identification, directed them to the proper parking area. Entering the hallowed halls of the CIA will make anyone with a modicum of emotion stop and reflect. Etched in the lobby wall was a simple Bible verse: John 8:32 *And ye shall know the truth and the truth shall make you free.*

Marcus nudged Jason and pointed to the Bible verse. "Sure hope that is accurate for our upcoming meeting."

Jason grinned and shrugged. "Fingers crossed?"

Marcus nodded and held up a hand with two fingers intertwined.

Checking in with the receptionist, Marcus was required to surrender his weapon. Jason was surprised to see that not only did his neighbor carry a weapon, he carried it with a round in the chamber.

As they were led to the conference room, Jason quietly asked, "Do you always carry a weapon?"

Marcus smiled and gave a small shrug. "Only when I am awake."

Jason's reply was cut off as they rounded a corner and nearly ran into a man standing by an open door. The smiling gentleman nodded. "Good to see you again, Jason. Come in and let's see how the Director of Operations can be of service to both Congress and the U.S. Navy." Extending his hand to Marcus, he continued, "Commander, I'm Leslie Forrester. Officially, I am the Assistant to the Deputy Director of Operations. Often called the ADDO, but I prefer Les."

Chuckling, Marcus shook his hand. "Les, I'm a lowly lieutenant commander named Colt who is the Director of Internal Affairs for the Naval Investigative Service. My friends call me Marcus and, before the day is over, I hope you fall into that category."

Les nodded and pointed to the conference table. He took the seat at the head and Jason grabbed the one on his right. Marcus decided to shake things up by doing the unexpected: he sat across from Jason, but left an empty chair between him and Les.

Les did a small double take and asked, "Has my deodorant lost its punch?"

"No, sir. Just that this position allows me to easily watch both of your faces at the same time. One of you might say something that surprises the other."

Now it was Les's turn to laugh. "Marcus, you and I'll get along swimmingly! Jason told me to be careful around you. Let's talk about Doctor Frederick Monroe."

Jason started. "Les, we need to find this missing doctor. He is vital for a new submarine detection system. It is a case of national security. Sadly, he vanished from his office in the Washington Navy Yard back in June. No trace."

"Okay, first off, the CIA does not operate on U.S. soil. Add to that the fact that four plus months have passed. So why ask me and why ask now?"

Jason pointed to Marcus to handle that question.

"The 'why now' is easy—on Monday, the CNO ordered me to find the guy, Les. As to the 'why you,' I have read all the NIS case files about him, and frankly, with almost nothing to go on in those, I am grasping at any straw I see floating around," said Marcus. "And you're my next straw."

Les nodded, smiled, and gave a *come on* hand signal.

"I am hoping you can dig into your files and see if there has been any overseas chatter about the good doctor, any new sub detection devices, terms like *satellite radar*, or the name *Rembrandt*. That would be a good place to start."

"Damn. Can you narrow that down to a country or two of interest?"

With a slight chuckle, Marcus said, "Sure, Les. Include all of our enemies and at least half of our friends. Think that'll help?"

Les grimaced as he shook his head. "You have no idea the amount of manpower and computer time needed to do that. Sorry, that's not something I am willing to authorize on just a hunch from a guy who is on day two of his investigation. Give me something more concrete and concise—then I might, key word being might, be willing to help. Until then, sorry."

Jason said, "Come on, Les. At least ask around a bit."

"Sorry, Jason. This meeting is over."

Marcus pulled out one of his cards as he stood, sliding it across the table toward Les. He continued his smile as he said, "Well, call me when you change your mind. I appreciate you seeing us, Les."

As they walked out of the building toward the car, Jason looked at Marcus. "You seemed to take that refusal rather well. Is that what you expected?"

"No, I really had hoped for a more positive meeting. But I understand Les's position. It is a big data search requested by a lowly Navy officer. However, the request that Les will get tomorrow, or maybe the day after, will have a bit more punch."

Jason stopped walking and put his hand on Marcus's arm. "What the hell are you planning to do?"

Wearing a left-leaning lopsided smile he learned from Kelly, Marcus replied, "Me? Absolutely nothing. Now when *you* get to your office tomorrow, or later today, and share a cup of coffee with Representative A. Jackson Allen, the chairman of a super intelligence committee, you will tell him about the concrete wall we just ran into. And when you have his full attention about said blockage, you remind him of the importance he assigned on finding the good doctor. Then you will suggest he contact the President and ask him to voice the request to the CIA folks personally by placing a call to ADDO Leslie Forrester or his boss's boss, the director."

Jason's mouth dropped. He shook his head as he said, "Damn, Gallagher warned me that you were dangerous. Are you serious?"

"Completely. I suspect, as the intelligence committee chair, that Allen might get the info by himself, but coming from the executive branch would probably get more traction. Perhaps the VP could make the call if Allen is afraid of the President. All this is assuming finding the doctor is as important as you say."

"I'm starting not to like you so much, neighbor."

32

THE DRIVE BACK FROM CIA headquarters was a quiet one. As they entered the Navy Yard, Marcus suggested they visit the FBI the next afternoon. Marcus would meet him at the Department of Justice at 1400 hrs. Jason gave a small smile and agreed when he dropped Marcus back at the NIS building. But he had not been the friendly, talkative person he was on the trip to the CIA.

Time waits for no one, and as he reached the door, he saw Martin and Carl getting off the elevator. Doc's interview was already over. Both father and son were smiling—a good sign. He waited by the door as they approached, and asked, "Everything okay, gents?"

"You bet, Mr. Colt. I'm just escorting Martin out. Agent Stevens got all the info he needed, sir," said Carl.

Martin nodded and extended his hand. "Nice to see you again, sir."

"Right back at ya, Martin. Thanks for coming in on such short notice," Marcus said as he released the handshake and held the door open for Martin. "We really appreciate your help."

"See ya tonight, Dad. I'll hold some dinner for ya." Martin waved goodbye.

Walking to the elevator with Carl, Marcus quietly asked, "So, how did it really go with Doc?"

Carl snickered. "I can see why you like Doc so much. He is really good. Martin was right on point with his recall of the events—his statement matched the one from Saturday. But he did remember a couple of other things, and Doc will fill you in about that. I appreciate being able to sit in with him."

Marcus nodded. "I'm glad you were here also. Your presence probably helped Martin relax."

"He really is a good kid, Mr. Colt, and I suspect this incident, along with guidance from his girlfriend, will keep him on the right path."

"That would be great. Let me know if there is anything I can do." The opening elevator door interrupted Marcus as the load of people leaving for the day exited. As he and Carl entered the now-empty car, he continued, pressing the floor button. "Seriously, don't hesitate, Carl."

"Thanks," Carl said softly.

As they got off, Marcus started to head to the conference rooms, but stopped and asked Carl, "Have we heard from the 'California Dreamin' team yet?"

"Nothing yet."

"When they do call in, tell them as soon as they finish in San Diego to head to NAS Alameda. Work with them and set up the travel and lodging arrangements. And call NISRA Alameda with a synopsis of why our team is coming their way. I'll finish typing up some additional notes shortly, but the NIR we sent to San Diego will probably be enough info."

Carl laughed. "So I get to tell them the bad news. At least they can't kill the messenger via long distance. You know Jake is anxious to get back home."

"Must be something about newlyweds not wanting to be far from the spouse. I wouldn't know anything about that."

"Of course you wouldn't," said Carl with a knowing grin and a soft chuckle.

"If Jake complains too much, tell him that NISRA Saigon has an opening. That should calm him down a bit."

"Boss, you are mean."

"Just training you to replace me, Carl. Oh, yea, please send an information request to NISRAs Mayport, Pensacola, Newport, New London, Oceana, Naples and Holy Lock—use the same format from the San Diego NIR. Their research centers worked on the project, and they need to sniff around about the missing doctor and any outside talk about Rembrandt."

"Can do, Mr. Colt. And if there is nothing else work related, you are expected at the Gallagher residence for dinner. Kelly said to be 'no later than 1900 hours' so you best get moving. Seems her mom did the driving on their shopping trip and sort of kidnapped Kelly."

Marcus laughed. "Somehow I don't think the victim put up too much of a fight. Message received loud and clear. Thanks."

Carl turned toward his office as Marcus entered the conference room. Chris and Doc were the only ones left. But based on the notes attached to the boards, and the disarrayed stack of personnel files, it had been a very productive day. They stood hunched over a document and were busy mumbling, sort of a soft, underwhelming argument, when they noticed Marcus had entered.

Doc smiled as he straightened. "Evening Marcus. How was your afternoon?"

"You go first, Doc. What ya got? I have a command performance at the CNO's residence in fifty minutes, and I really want to say something positive."

Chris shook his head as Doc did his best bow from the waist to Marcus. "Oh, yes, my master, we have news!"

"Doc, I'm too tired and stressed for that right now. Skip the I Dream of Jeannie routine and stick to a Joe Friday from Dragnet: give me just the facts, please."

The smirk came off Doc's face and his tone changed into a serious business type any FBI agent would kill for. He wasn't offended because he understood Marcus's tone. And he fortunately had the ability to jump between serious and comedy, and back, in a second or two. "Marcus, the interview with Martin Freeman added a couple of things to his previously filed statement. He mentioned that the attacker was a bulky white guy. He saw his hands as he hit the victim. And he heard his voice. Martin couldn't make out any words, but he said the voice was like that of the character Boris, from that moose and squirrel cartoon show. That probably makes it Russian."

"Anything else?"

"Martin thinks the attacker might have a mustache. A dark one. But he's not one hundred percent sure. Not much, but something."

Chris jumped in. "And that description matches that given by the bartender at the EM club and the injured petty officer."

Doc nodded and said, "Masters said the attacker was looking for a file. But Masters did not understand what file, and the attacker just kept saying 'the file' as if there was only one in the building. Not much there either."

Marcus sighed. "Gents, every little piece helps. That is more than we had. As for my afternoon, the CIA slammed the door in my face, but I think I have a work-around. Time will tell, probably tomorrow. You guys get out of here and get some rest. See ya in the morning. I'm heading out too."

After locking the conference room doors, Marcus realized he needed to run back to his office. Carl, busy at his desk preparing the transmissions Marcus requested, looked up. "Forget something, boss?"

Marcus chuckled as he nodded. "Too easy to do—get the 'Cuda keys is the first thing. Second thing—you need to take notes as I tell you about my day at the CIA. And no, I didn't intend to rhyme." It took less than five minutes to relate the events of the day. He asked Carl to type them up, put one copy in the Cold Fog file, and leave one on Rita's desk. Marcus went into his office to pick up his keys and finished typing the notes Carl would pass to Jake.

Locking his office door as he left, Marcus found himself humming a familiar movie theme song. *From Russia with Love* was suddenly on his mind.

33

WHAT TO TELL THE ADMIRAL was on his mind as he drove past the Westwood Country Club with its carefully manicured grounds. His father-in-law, a club member, wanted Marcus to improve his golf game, since that was how senior military officers relaxed and frequently discussed off-the-record stuff. Marcus often commented that his golf scores would look good on the bowling lanes.

He felt more at ease on the tennis court than the putting green. He had taken both golf and tennis courses as his physical education credits at Georgia Tech but had excelled at tennis. He was even asked to join the Navy tennis team after meeting, and beating, one of the team captains one afternoon. But after his time in 'Nam, he wished he had taken bodybuilding and track and field. He could have used those skills over there. Oh well, *hindsight is perfect*, he thought.

The Gallagher Estate—that's how Marcus thought of the nearly two-acre wooded site—was located in an exclusive neighborhood. In a couple of years, it would be the retirement home for the Gallaghers, when the admiral would trade his CNO desk for a golf cart.

A dark blue sedan with a government tag was parked on one side of the driveway: the admiral hadn't been home long, since his aide had not departed for the evening. The junior aide-de-camp, a pleasant lieutenant named Ken, was also the admiral's driver. The CNO felt the standard practice of having an enlisted person as a driver was a waste of a man, since all of his aides were capable of driving any vehicle.

Exiting the 'Cuda, Marcus saw Ken leaving the house. Stopping, Ken popped to attention and saluted as Marcus walked toward him. Marcus returned the salute and extended his hand. "How ya doin', Ken?"

"Very well, sir, and based on the aromas drifting from the kitchen, you will be having a wonderful dinner."

"Sure you can't stay? I might need backup as I brief the admiral on my day," asked Marcus, only half joking. Ken was a relatively new friend in Marcus's world. They'd met at the wedding in September, but cultivated a friendship based on their respect for the admiral and a few shared hours on the tennis courts.

"Sorry, Marcus, I'd like to, but as I told the boss when he asked me to stay, I have a class tonight. Still working on the master's degree." Ken grimaced slightly.

"Good for you, Ken. It will help get those stars on your shoulder boards. But we need time on the court soon. We're both putting on a few extra pounds."

They shared a laugh and a few more comments, then Marcus walked to the door. As he reached for the knob, the door opened and Kelly stood there with a grin. "Glad you came to rescue me, sailor. I was getting worried you might not."

"Hey, agent 006.5 can't resist helping a beautiful princess in distress," Marcus replied as he pulled her into his arms.

"Marcus, do you want a drink? I have the bourbon open," yelled the admiral from the den.

With his arm around Kelly, Marcus strolled into the den to face the admiral. Gallagher had already ditched his jacket and tie and had rolled up his sleeves. He had just poured an inch of Maker's Mark into a glass. He turned and looked quizzically at Marcus. "And your answer is?"

"Not tonight, Admiral. I need a clear head when we talk, sir."

The admiral deeply sighed, slowly shook his head, turned back to the bar, and poured an inch into a second glass. "Consider this an order, then." He handed it to Marcus, who nodded, clinked glasses with the admiral, and took a small sip.

"Son, I love you, but you need to change a couple of things. First off, you were invited to a family dinner and not a briefing. Ditch the coat and tie, stop being a Navy officer for a few hours, and relax as my favorite son-in-law."

"I'm your only son-in-law, Admiral," laughed Marcus.

"True, but you're still my favorite," the admiral said with a chuckle. "Second, I would really enjoy having you call me Dad, Bill, Pop, old coot, or whatever when we are in a family environment. Save the rank and *sirs* for the appropriate time. Please! I really don't want to make that an order."

Marcus knew this moment was coming. Kelly had warned him, and he had tried to be more relaxed around her father since the wedding. But the years of ROTC and active duty had drilled protocol into him, and it was difficult to change. He still couldn't call Kelly's uncle, the admiral's brother-in-law, Humphrey. The most relaxed he got with Captain Humphrey Miller was calling him 'Skipper,' since Marcus had been assigned to his command while in Norfolk.

Marcus nodded and said, "No, sir." Kelly hit him on the upper arm when she heard that, thinking he was refusing. Marcus ignored that and continued, "An order is not needed. I will work on it, but don't get upset when I falter … Bill."

The admiral smiled. "Much better. Thank you. Now dinner is still at least a half hour away. Is there something we really need to discuss?"

In short order, Marcus updated him on the search for the missing doctor. He ended with the slamming CIA door and possible Eastern European involvement.

The admiral was quiet for a moment as he digested all that he'd heard. After draining his glass and pouring a refill, he asked, "Do I need to make a phone call? I know a few people at the CIA."

Marcus shook his head. "No, Bill. I think that problem will be solved in the morning." He explained how he dumped the problem back on the congressman who wanted the doctor found.

That got a belly laugh from the admiral. "Well done. Did you take any political science classes back in Georgia? You are learning to play the D.C. game perfectly."

"At least it will show how important this case is to Congressman Allen. We are spending a lot of our resources on this, and if they are not willing to contribute, that would concern me."

"Me, too," agreed the admiral. "Again Marcus, well played."

Kelly had a worried look. "Does Eastern European mean Russian?"

"Yea, babe, possibly, well maybe. The witness said he sounded like the evil Russian named Boris in the moose cartoon show. He could be from any of several other regions in Eastern Europe."

Elaine leaned around the open door, breaking the tension in the room by saying, "Dinner is ready."

Kelly looked hard at Marcus. "If there is a Boris, there might be a Natasha. Watch your back, hon."

34

"ARE THERE ANY MORE BOXES and bags to bring in? Was there anything left in the stores?" asked Marcus as he finished his third trip from the car to the bedroom. "This is too much like work."

"Oh, quit whining. I think that was the last of them," Kelly said with a laugh. "Besides, you'll agree it was worth it as you enjoy the view when I start wearing these new outfits next week. My new wardrobe gives me a professional yet sexy office manager type look."

"I'm going to miss those ODU sweatshirts and jeans."

"That outfit I'll be saving for our relaxing weekends."

Marcus made a suggestive look, bouncing his eyebrows up and down. "You know my favorite relaxing outfit, Princess. It's the one you didn't need to buy."

Kelly returned the look as she softly said, "Sailor, you might get a special reward shortly for making Dad so happy. Hearing you call him 'Bill' was the best gift you could give him."

"After over four years in ROTC and three-plus years of active duty, my conditioning is pretty solid. And he has been my father-in-law for just under two months. I'll probably end up calling him 'admiral' and 'sir' more than he likes, but at least you both know I'm working hard to do it right. Do you have enough energy for a few minutes of sofa time?"

"You betcha! I'll be down shortly. That should give you time to pour two glasses of wine. I think we have Chablis in the kitchen."

Marcus opened a bottle of Chablis and poured two servings. A quick look in the fridge and cabinet generated a small plate of cheese and crackers: just the snack to finish off the evening. He put a Matt Monro record on the stereo and dimmed the lights.

Kelly padded into the room wearing her relaxing-time pajamas and snuggled beside him. She pulled her feet under her and reached for her glass as Monro started singing one of his biggest hits, the movie theme *"From Russia with Love."*

"Did you plan that song to make me worry more?" asked Kelly softly before she took a sip of wine. Her smile turned up to the right: Marcus knew it well as a not-really-happy indicator.

Marcus gently stroked his fingertips down the side of Kelly's face, pausing as his index finger ever so slightly pushed the upturned corner of her lips down. "No evil intent, Princess—just a nice selection of love songs. Don't look for signs where there are none. Just enjoy a few moments doing our favorite thing."

"Sorry. I'm just worried about you ... especially with this case, Marcus," Kelly whispered. "And now you're getting involved with the FBI and the CIA, and hobnobbing with congressional staffers."

Marcus couldn't hold back a laugh. "I'm sorry, but who says 'hobnobbing' anymore? Have you been watching too many old movies?"

"Dammit, Marcus, I'm serious," Kelly said harshly in a tone that meant frustration more than anger. But unless you knew her well, it was hard to tell.

She pulled back from Marcus, and her face hardened as her jaw clenched. "Don't make fun of me. This case is different from when you went after the vipers. Sure, I was worried then and rightfully so, based on the huge scar on your arm, but deep down I knew you would walk between the raindrops and win. But this one feels ... hell, I don't know, just different, okay? More scary." A tear escaped Kelly's eye and left a trail of sadness down her cheek.

Marcus pulled her close and kissed away the teardrop. He gently ran his hand down the back of her head and massaged her neck. "I'm sorry. I know you're worried, and I'm not making fun of you. Just you say things that completely catch me off guard and drive home just how unique you are. I *am* being careful, and the team is always watching my back just as I watch theirs. Hell, I even have Doc with me, and you know he's a protective mother hen when he's around me."

After a tight hug and a couple of kisses, Kelly softly said, "Stay safe. Shoot straight. I need you, sailor."

"Always for you, Princess," Marcus whispered.

35

THE GLASSES WERE EMPTY AND Matt had finished singing his album. Kelly and Marcus turned off the lights and headed to bed. The day of shopping and the emotions of the evening got the best of Kelly, and she drifted off into a deep sleep. Marcus, snuggling close, listened to her breathing change as it fell into a slow, soft rhythm.

He knew Kelly was right. *She usually is,* he thought. This case was one that could easily lead into a bad place. But Marcus knew he was right too: his team was strong and watched out for each other. Besides, he had been in bad places before. Too many times. As he relaxed and allowed sleep to calm his mind, he drifted from the current problem to relive one from the year past.

◆

The room was dark and hot. Only a small amount of light seeped in around the wooden door: the only means of escape. Soon—well, maybe, since it was hard to tell time in this hole—one of the guards would open that door to throw in another bucket of food, as they did every evening. Well, at least for the two evenings they had been guests in this negative-star location.

It was also hard to call that slop in the bucket edible, but it would satisfy the emptiness for a while. There was no protein in the bucket, only overcooked rice with some unknown green plant pieces stirred into the thin broth. The horrible odor of the room masked any aroma from the bucket. That was probably a good thing.

"This time is going to be it, sir. Follow my lead and be ready to move," Marcus whispered to the older of the two men. They were all sitting on the floor, leaning back against the dirt wall. Marcus knew they had to get out now. The old man was suffering from some intestinal bug and his energy was fading fast. The other man, somewhat younger and in better physical shape, nodded his understanding. The plan was set.

A voice outside the door meant it was time. As the sound of the latch being pulled back broke the silence of the room, Marcus moved to the left of the door. The old man stayed where he was, and the other guy stood against the back wall. Scant light came through the door opening as the guard took one step into the room. He bent over to place the bucket on the floor as he had done before. His captives were too weak to resist, he thought.

But as he prepared to back out, the old man on the floor moaned and fell over to the side. The guard stopped and stared. Marcus used the planned distraction and moved fast, wrapping one arm around the guard's neck and pulling his head around with the other. He pulled hard. With a soft crack, the guard stopped fighting. Marcus pulled the body to the side as the other man helped the old man up. He removed the pistol, extra magazine, and knife the dead guard had on his belt.

A quick look outside fortified his speculation: the guard had been alone. They had only a few minutes to make their escape. He looked back and saw that Nelson was struggling to get the older man standing. Marcus moved to help, and together they got him suspended between them. With his free hand, he grabbed the food bucket.

"Come on, Mr. Secretary, we really need to move out, and quietly," Marcus whispered to the old man.

"Call me 'Harry' or I'm stayin' here, dammit," he mumbled. His grip on Marcus was getting stronger.

Why does he have to do that now, thought Marcus? *For crying out loud, the old man is a member of the President's cabinet, and in addition, his age makes him a man that Mom always said deserved respect.* Calling him *sir* or *Mr. Secretary* was proper, even in these conditions. But now he had to be difficult. *Guess that is one of the things that makes him a good Secretary of State,* Marcus added to the conversation in his mind. And he had been demanding the use of his first name for at least a day. *Okay, we will play your game, Mr. Secretary.*

"Move your ass, Harry," Marcus whispered loudly into Harry's ear. "Now!"

Harry smiled and allowed them to pull him to the door. After another quick check, they stepped out. "Good," Harry said, "now we can escape the Russians."

With the three out the door, Marcus closed it as quietly as he could and placed the bar latch into its slot. Hopefully anyone passing by would think all was well with the prisoners. A look around didn't find anyone watching.

The three moved away from the camp and into the tree line. Speed was essential for survival, but speed at night, in a thick jungle, with a man ready to collapse, was not easy.

When they were brought to the camp—whenever that was, maybe a few days ago—Marcus hadn't noticed any trip wires, so he hoped it was safe to move without wasting time looking. If they did trigger a trap, maybe it would kill them faster than the jungle would. Marcus was fighting depression over the mistakes he had made thus far.

But the good news was, every minute of travel took them farther away from their captives and closer to home. Marcus was still in the lead as he heard a noise: not of the night creatures or the enemy pursuing them. The noise was a buzzing, similar to that of an insect, but much louder and somewhat mechanical.

What the hell is that, he thought. Then a hand was on his shoulder, pushing him. But Harry and Nelson were a few yards behind him.

◆

"Marcus, turn off that horrible alarm and get moving. I'll get the coffee going and meet you in the shower," Kelly said as she kissed his ear and left the bed.

Marcus turned off the alarm clock and rolled onto his back, sighing deeply. His dream had taken him back to the previous year and to the other side of the world. "As if I don't have enough problems right now," he muttered to himself.

Then his memory kicked in and he said aloud, "Did the Secretary of State actually say 'Russians' back then or is that just a warning from my mind?"

36

THE AROMA OF COFFEE PULLED Marcus to the coffee mess even before he checked in with the Cold Fog group or Rita. It occurred to him that the coffee mess should be farther away from the elevator to avoid these distractions. There was always something new to remember to do in case he ever got promoted to admiral.

The slight clink of the spoon on the inside of the filled mug was somewhat hypnotic. As Marcus stirred, his thoughts went back to last night. Kelly was concerned this case was one that could easily lead into a dark place. She was right, but Marcus knew he was also right: his team watched everyone's back. For the present, their big concerns were allergies from all the dust on the old files and potential paper cuts. Not much to worry about yet.

Rita walked in. Her smile was strained as she softly said, "*Tienes un problema, jefe.*"

"Good morning, Rita. And why do I have a problem this lovely day?"

She rolled her eyes. "He arrived about five minutes ago. Would not tell me his name. Just said he was looking for you. I'm getting a coffee service ready. My guess ... he's that Leslie fellow who gave you a hard time yesterday."

"Does he have 'CIA' stamped on his forehead?"

"No, sir, but he might as well have. He acts like he's slumming, if you know what I mean. Like being in NIS is beneath him. But I could be wrong." Rita said the last line with a lilt in her voice and a slight shrug.

"You rarely are. Let's go beard this lion. Should be easy, after all, he's in my den this time. And unlike yesterday at his office, I *am* armed," Marcus said with an evil grin as his hand touched the location of his shoulder holster.

Rita shook her head and whispered, "Be nice, boss."

Marcus carried the tray with the mugs and trappings, and Rita handled the coffee carafe. As they entered the IA office spaces, the Assistant to the Deputy Director of Operations for the entire CIA was staring at his watch and letting out a deep sigh. Fingers were drumming on the armrest.

Upon seeing Colt, he quickly stood and said, "Marcus, we need to talk."

Marcus smiled and nodded. "Morning, Les. Nice we're still on a first name basis. In case you have not been formally introduced, the lady with the carafe of life-saving elixir is Mrs. Rita Howland. Rita, this is ADDO Leslie Forrester from the Central Intelligence Agency."

They shook hands and Rita led them into Marcus's office. She turned to leave, but Marcus stopped her.

"Rita, please get your pad and coffee cup. Join us for this chat."

Forrester stiffened. "We need to talk in private, Marcus. No offense, Mrs. Howland."

Marcus held up his hand in a *stop* position. "Les, the way things work in my office is that I have two senior staff members who are up to speed on everything happening. Rita is one of them. If you insist that Rita retire to her desk, then all that means is I will type up our conversation after you leave and give it to her to read, remember, and file. And who knows, I might overlook something important. If she's here while we talk, then I feel comfortable that she will get everything correct in her write-up, which I will double check before it is filed. Have a seat." Marcus pointed to the conference table.

Les nodded. "Your office—your rules, Marcus. Fine with me."

"Thank you. Should I be concerned that you're being so nice? Sorry, ignore that sarcasm. And what is your mission this morning, Les?"

Les chuckled. "I'm trying to get the Director of Central Intelligence off the President's shit—sorry, Mrs. Howland—eh, bad guy list."

Rita smiled and waved a dismissal with her hand. "No problem. I've heard the word before. Call me 'Rita,' Les. I can tell the boss likes you, and that's good enough for me."

Les nodded and continued, "Thank you. So, Marcus, your call to the President resulted in him calling the director last night, who in turn, much later I should add, called me. He told me he waited for two-plus hours before calling to calm down, but I didn't hear any calm in his voice. You play rough."

Marcus chuckled and cleared his throat. "I play fair when treated fairly. After asking nicely for information, you, sir, slammed the door. But know this fact. I did not call the President."

Les squirmed. "Well, who the hell did?"

"I did plant that seed with Jason as we left your office since he initiated this search for the doctor. I felt that if it really was important to him, he'd take whatever action was needed to get the information I want. I believe in using whatever tools that I have to accomplish a task. Jason is a tool and now you're here." On the last part of his statement, Marcus shrugged and held both hands out in an *and there you have it* gesture.

Rita chuckled and shook her head.

"Whatever you did, it worked. The director ordered me to help," Les said through a small smile. "So, what do you need from Central Intelligence?"

Marcus again laid out the parameters of the case to Les, who frantically took notes. Basically, it was a rerun of the visit the day before. However, this time Marcus was able to add the overseas locations that worked on Rembrandt. He finished with, "How about we head to the conference room and meet the rest of the team? They might've uncovered something this morning that would help your search. Have you got the time?"

Les nodded. "I'm at your service until the doctor, or at least his decomposing body, has been found. Lead on."

Chatter from the conference rooms was far from subdued. The entire team was standing around one end of the conference table, with several of them pointing to various papers lying there.

"Good morning, Mr. Colt. You got here at a good time," Doc said as everyone quieted down to view the new arrival. Since Les was an unknown entity for the team, they were more formal than usual.

"Lady and gentlemen, our guest this morning is the Assistant to the Deputy Director of Operations, Leslie Forrester, from the Central

Intelligence Agency. Consider him part of Task Force Cold Fog, call him 'Les,' make him feel welcome, and give him full access."

Introductions were done all around and they got down to business. Marcus asked that the team provide any key words that the Agency could look for in their data files. As the words started flowing and Les took notes, Doug passed a sheet of paper to Marcus, who slipped out and went back to his office.

Reading while walking, Marcus saw that the team had added names to the list of people to interrogate. More work, but it might just turn over the right rock that led to the doctor.

Rita looked up from the pile of papers when Marcus walked in. "Has he gone?" she whispered as she glanced behind him.

"No, I threw him into the pool of sharks in the conference room. I'll rescue him in a few minutes, but until then, he can swim on his own. Anything I need to know?"

"There is an update from the California team on your desk. Nothing earthshaking there—at least, not yet today," Rita said, smiling at her joke. The February earthquake in the San Fernando Valley was still a subject of conversation. Its thrust actions had killed sixty-five people and injured a couple of thousand. Damage was over the five hundred million mark. Everyone was waiting for the next California 'quake since doomsday fans said that was the lead up to "the big one."

Rita continued, "There are a few NIRs you will want to look over. In addition, there are a couple of NISRAs that might need us to do our magic."

"Thank you, ma'am. On top of things as always."

Back in his office, there was a smidgen of coffee in the carafe on the conference table. Marcus added it to the dregs in his cup and flopped down in the chair behind his desk. Sipping the lukewarm coffee, he leafed through the Navy Yard phone directory until he found the number he needed.

The ringing lasted almost one cycle. The voice on the line responded, "Office of Naval Intelligence. Senior Chief Kirkland speaking. How may I help you, sir?"

"Morning, Senior Chief. Lieutenant Commander Colt, NIS, calling for the admiral."

"Yes, sir. One moment, sir."

"Admiral Beckett," said the new voice on the line. "What can the ONI do for NIS today, Colt?" The admiral's Alabama accent was coming through strong. As the head of the ONI, Clarence Beckett was a vice admiral wearing three stars on his shoulder boards. He was a legend in the Navy intelligence community for his ability to look at a problem and quickly see many of the underlying causes. His laid-back attitude hid a bulldog temperament.

Marcus chuckled. "Admiral, a promotion and a week off would be nice, sir, but I'll settle for some information."

"Hell, Marcus, you just had two weeks off for that honeymoon. And with a quick topic change, how is Kelly?"

"She's fine, Admiral. Thanks for asking. She starts work at Walter Reed next week, so one of her big dreams has come true."

"Wonderful! Pass my best regards on to her."

"Yes, sir. Will do. While she's happy, I'm going nuts with a missing persons case," Marcus said. He detailed what he hoped ONI could sniff around and share.

The admiral agreed there might be some helpful information in their files, and transferred the call to the officer who'd do the actual work. Marcus gave him the details, and he promised to call back as soon as he could check into it properly. Probably it would take at least a day. They concluded the call just as a knock came from the door.

ADDO Leslie Forrester walked over to Marcus's desk and plopped down on one of the chairs in front of the desk. Doc Stevens followed and did the same.

"Why do you two look so tired? The day and all its fun is just starting."

Les just shook his head. "Not tired, I'm just a bit overwhelmed. The key words we need to use for the search are the problem. Too many of them are rather generic. Fortunately, there are a few that are more specific. I'll get back to my office and start the ball rolling. But it sure won't be rolling fast. Assuming you don't have anything else for me?"

"Now you know how I felt yesterday when I came to see you, Les. The needle in the haystack is really hard to find when you don't know where the hell the haystacks are located. And what did you do to make Doc look so down?"

Les shook his head and shrugged. Doc perked up at the mention of his name. "Marcus, I know this is just the start of day three in this search, but it looks impossible. We keep adding places to look and people to interrogate, and have little to show for it. On top of all that, Radarman Larry Masters seems to be holding something back."

Marcus smiled. "And the only hard day was yesterday, Doc. Shake off the negatives or turn in your Trident. What's your plan for today?"

"Most of us are heading over to the research center for a tour of the doctor's old office and to interview key personnel. We'll include questions about Masters also. Want to come with us?"

"No, thanks, I'll pass for now. Paperwork is piling up here. But keep an eye on the CO if she shows up. I think she has more to tell us."

Forrester looked at Doc in disbelief.

"Got something to add, Les?"

Still looking at Doc, Les asked, "You were a SEAL?"

"Hell, yes. Still am, well, technically. Why?"

Marcus failed to hold back a laugh. "Les, Doc was on the team until earlier this year when an opportunity arose for him to work with us. Consider him in a transition phase. That means he'll still tear off your arms if you make him mad, but will do it wearing a coat and tie."

Forrester just smiled. "This place is just one surprise after another. If there is nothing else, Marcus, I'm escaping to my office."

37

THE DRIVE OVER TO FBI headquarters gave Marcus a few moments without having to read another report. Or write one. Since the talk with Les earlier in the day, he had spent the rest of the morning, as well as time through lunch, clearing the piles of paperwork off his desk.

While many thought his job was constant excitement—investigating, chasing, and capturing the bad guys—the reality was that ninety-eight percent was paperwork. The Navy, like all military organizations, moved on a sea of paper.

At least the drive over had allowed him time to clear his mind of the paperwork clutter and think about the case. Doc was right. Day three and still nothing that would help find the doctor.

Jason Wright was standing by the main entrance to the Department of Justice building when Marcus arrived a few minutes after 1400 hrs. He was a bit friendlier than he'd been the previous day, after the CIA visit. "Hi, neighbor. Ready for more fun?"

"Guess I'm off your bad guy list for at least the next few hours. Life is better this way."

"Marcus, I apologize for yesterday's negativity and attitude. After the congressman and I talked about it, he helped me realize I was just jealous of your insight and ability to come up with a quick—and very workable—solution. Besides, being friends with my neighbor, who is also a SEAL, one hell of an intelligence officer, and carries a weapon, is a smart move. Again, sorry."

Marcus smiled and extended his hand. "You've never moved out of my friend column, Jason. At least now you know when I'm handed an assignment, I do what needs to be done to achieve success. Want to go rattle some cages, eh?"

A little over an hour later, Jason and Marcus left the building, each carrying a box of files. They ranged from a full copy of the missing doctor case to files referring to Rembrandt, submarines, or anything else bearing on the case.

Obviously, Jason had placed a few additional calls to his FBI contacts earlier that morning. His warning about the influence of the White House on the reluctant CIA seemed to convince the FBI to have all the data ready before Marcus asked.

As they walked toward the parking garage, Jason said, "I know these boxes will take your crew more than a few minutes to handle. Is there anything else you need from me right now?"

"Nothing about the missing doctor, Jason, but Kelly and I would like you and the family to come over Sunday afternoon late for cookout. Assuming the weather cooperates, I'll fire up the grill. If it rains, plan on eating some of my inside cooking. What say about 1600 hours?"

Jason chuckled. "Damn. Occasionally, but not very often, I do wish I had joined the military instead of getting all those draft deferments that kept me in college through my doctorate. 1600? That is four o'clock for us common civilians?"

"Ya broke the code, amigo! Well done! Yes, four o'clock in the afternoon is the right answer. And no, before you ask, you do not need to bring anything except an appetite. And maybe, if my cooking doesn't kill ya and you like what's prepared, you'll bring the congressman and his family the next time. My father-in-law keeps telling me I need to cultivate such contacts," Marcus said with a laugh.

"See ya then, Marcus." Jason gave a thumbs up and walked toward his car.

With the file boxes secured in the small trunk of the 'Cuda, Marcus hit the ignition switch and enjoyed the sound of the engine. He sat in the driver's seat thinking for a moment before putting the transmission in gear. *Did I miss something in there? The assistant director of the FBI was extremely cooperative. Why does that bother me? Paranoia or premonition?*

Marcus pulled out into the D.C. traffic. As he watched for red lights, jaywalkers, and the ubiquitous crazy drivers, he realized there was too much running around in his mind to be memorable or even helpful. It was a collection of random thoughts. Actually it was more of a clutter than a collection. More information overload. With nothing firm to focus on, he decided to let his mind wind down and just enjoy the drive back to the Navy Yard.

As he carried the two boxes into the conference room, he saw that the "fort" was being held down by only two people. Both were deeply involved with their tasks.

Christopher McCormick was wallowing in a sea of paper; his eyes darted from side to side as he compared information in two different folders. His frown and furrowed brow clearly said he wasn't seeing what he'd hoped. And Veronica Mays, at her end of the large table, was madly typing shorthand notes into something the team could understand. Thumping the boxes on the table got their attention.

"Welcome back, Marcus. Input from our friends at the Bureau?" asked Chris.

Veronica grimaced as she softly said, "Oh, joy. More files to log in and copy."

"Yes, Chris, this is from the FBI, and we have more coming, soon I hope, from ONI and the CIA. Log them in, Veronica, but hold off on the copy work until we go through them. We'll only copy those that might be meaningful," Marcus said. "Everyone else at the research center?"

Veronica gave a thumbs up and went back to typing.

Chris nodded. "Yes, sir. I decided to stay here and continue with the cross-reference of personnel. Some of these folks jumped around between centers, and I wanted to document when and where they worked on Rembrandt."

"With emphasis on the people who were working directly with Doctor Monroe?"

"Yes, sir, and I'm sending those names to the appropriate NISRAs, requesting high priority background checks. Doubt we'll see anyone with a recent large cash inflow, but it's just one of the t's that needed to be crossed."

Marcus smiled at Chris's efficiency. "Excellent. Since you two have things under control here, I'll be in my office seeing what evil things are growing there. Carry on."

With a fresh cup of coffee in his hand, Marcus entered his office area to check with Carl on the status of the California team. Although Carl was on the phone, he held up several sheets of paper as Marcus walked by his desk. A quick glance showed them to be ROIs from the California team. Time to sit and do some heavy reading and analysis.

The good thing about sending Jake and Hank to check on the California connections was that they were very good at their jobs. The reports of investigation from San Diego were long and complete. Nothing seemed out of place out there.

The first report outlined the San Diego research center's work on Rembrandt. Their input was restricted to the launch vehicle and satellite containment device that mounted on top. Nothing involving the missing doctor was done there, and none of the staff had contact with him. The SAs were scheduled to head to NAS Alameda in the morning and would meet with members of NISRA Alameda as soon as possible.

The second report was their in-depth analysis of Captain Jennifer Collier while she was at the San Diego Research Center. As the XO of the unit when she was still a commander, her performance was considered excellent. No negative comments from any of the staff were reported.

And her part of Rembrandt was limited to supervising the work to get the satellite into orbit. No contact with the missing doctor there either. But she'd lied about her knowledge of Rembrandt. *What else did she lie about*, Marcus wondered.

Only negative item was her divorce in the fall of 1970, but military life takes its toll on many marriages, so probably nothing to see there. Perhaps that was why she was rubbing her left hand during their first meet. Missing her ring, perhaps?

Marcus leaned back in his chair and allowed the oracles in the overhead to guide his contemplation on the ROIs. No joy in southern California, but perhaps the team would have better luck with their visit to Berkeley. The ceiling tiles didn't offer more insight, so he checked out with Carl and drove over to the research center. Always good to check in with the team and maybe get a second go at the CO.

38

THE TEAM WAS SCATTERED AROUND the center. Some members of the team had been assigned to interview specific people. Some were looking over the doctor's old office and boxes of stored belongings. The rest were trying to find ways someone could have snuck into the center to abduct the doctor.

With the help of a guard, Marcus found Doc Stevens and John Driscol in an empty office. "Did I interrupt an argument, gents, or did someone steal your puppy?" asked Marcus as he walked in. "Neither of you look very happy."

Doc shrugged. "Neither one, boss, just the frustration from another bunch of dead ends. So far, no one has provided anything of interest."

"And we have not discovered any way to get into this building without someone noticing it," groused John.

"Well, you know the drill. Get all the interviews written up and see what can be pulled from them to add to the board. Someone somewhere knows something—we just have to find that person."

Doc started to say something, but stopped and nodded toward the door. Marcus turned and saw Captain Jennifer Collier standing there. "Good afternoon, Captain. Something we can do for you?"

Collier had a smile Marcus's dad had once described as the "cat that ate the canary" as she looked at the three agents. "Just checking to make sure the agents snooping around my command are getting the support they need from my staff. Is that happening?"

Marcus pointed to Doc, who nodded and replied, "Yes, ma'am, we are. Thank you. After we go over the interviews in the morning, we probably will be back in the afternoon for some follow ups, but it will not be as intrusive as today. Again, we appreciate your understanding with all this."

Collier nodded once and turned to Marcus. "Can I see you in my office, Colt?"

"Yes, ma'am."

Neither Marcus nor the captain spoke as they made the trek to the captain's office. Marcus figured she was going to complain about the disruption of the interviews. At least he hoped that was all she wanted.

Collier held up her hand with palm facing her yeoman as they walked into the office. "No calls." The yeoman nodded.

"Have a seat," said Collier as she pushed her door closed. Marcus selected a chair in front of her desk. Surprising him, Collier sat in the chair next to his and not behind her desk.

"Marcus, my friends call me Jen, and I really hope you will. Okay?"

"Certainly, Jen. I assume you need to discuss something."

Jen chuckled. "Nothing gets past the NIS, does it?"

"We started mind reading courses last year. Seems to be working," replied Marcus with a shrug and his best smile.

"Glad you feel comfortable enough with me to joke around, Marcus— some junior officers are intimidated by my rank and sex. Glad you're not. But seriously, I know what you're doing here is important. What I would like, if possible, is to be kept informed on how the investigation progresses. Would that be possible?"

Marcus caught himself before looking up toward the oracles in the overhead, as he was prone to do when needing a quick answer to an unexpected question. Fortunately, there was an easy stock answer in the NIS Manual of Operation.

"Jen, I will keep you informed on things involving the operation of your command." Marcus paused to let that part sink in. "But the rest of the investigation falls into the 'need to know' category. And right now, I cannot see that you have that need."

Jen Collier sighed; deep sadness replaced her smile.

"Jen, my wife is the therapist in the family, but I've learned enough from her, and from doing this job for years, to know you have something you need to share. I saw it in your eyes the other day, when we met, that you're hiding something. Know this, whatever it is—we will uncover it during our investigation. And getting it out now puts you in front of it. That can mitigate any damage."

She stared straight ahead, tapping her fingers on the arm of the chair as her mental processes fought to make the right decision. Hard as it was, Marcus knew to quietly wait. Nothing he could say would help. Jen had to decide on her own.

"Okay. I know you'll find out eventually. I should've told you on Wednesday, but I was too embarrassed."

"If you mean your divorce, that's nothing to be embarrassed about, Jen. It happens to a lot of people in the service."

She slowly shook her head. The sadness increased as she said, "That's just part of it, Marcus. I knew Doctor Monroe because I worked on Rembrandt while in 'Diego."

"Okay, so why did you lie to me?"

"Because I was embarrassed to admit to you I had an affair with him in the spring of '70. It cost me my marriage and I was afraid it would kill my career," she answered, her voice on the edge of breaking."

Marcus sighed deeply and stood. "Captain Collier, I need you to come with me to the NIS office and answer some questions."

"I thought that might happen," she quietly replied.

Approaching the door out of the research center, Marcus signaled for Doc Stevens and John Driscol to follow them. He motioned for Collier to wait as he stepped aside to talk with the agents.

"John, I need you to head back to the office right now. We, and by 'we' I actually mean you and Veronica, need to interrogate the captain. Use the interrogation room and treat her with due respect, but as a possible suspect. She just admitted to knowing Monroe in both the work environment and in the pure biblical sense. She lied to us earlier. Doc, stay here and continue doing what you're doing."

"Veronica?" asked John with surprise on his face and in his voice.

"Trust me on this, John. I'll explain later."

Both men nodded and went in different directions. Marcus walked back to Collier and said, "Want to ride with me or do you prefer to drive your own car?"

"I prefer to drive, but I thought I was under arrest."

"No. At least, not yet. I trust you to come directly to my office in your car. Meet you there."

Marcus resisted the urge to watch to see if Captain Collier actually went to her car. His gut told him she'd be at the NIS office shortly, so there was no need.

39

MARCUS ESCORTED CAPTAIN COLLIER TO the interrogation room. He asked her to have a seat and said an agent would be in shortly. She nodded as he left and closed the door.

Marcus called John aside and related all that had been said while he and Collier were in her office. "Agent Driscol, I'm not sure why, but it seems Collier believes she can play me. Imagine that! Must be my youthful look, eh?" Marcus said with a laugh. "John, I want you to go in there as the hard ass special agent and get whatever you can from her."

"You got it, Marcus. But what's with Veronica?"

Marcus shrugged. "Gut feeling again, John. Collier might be the type to cry that you made sexual advances. Veronica's presence running the tape recorder will eliminate that possibility. And perhaps a female on the interrogation side will help keep Collier calm. Again, nothing but a gut reaction for this decision."

"Well, your gut is usually right, so I'm happy to go with it."

"Thanks. And before y'all go in, tell Veronica to ask questions if she hears something that doesn't sit right with her. She seems to have some skills when it comes to seeing and tying up loose ends."

John nodded. "Any specific methods you want us to follow? Or special info you want?"

"Methods? Use your normal interrogation style, but avoid using the thumb screws. Well, as for info ... for sure we need to know the locations of her and her ex since the time the doctor vanished. And where the ex is right now. Did he hold a grudge against the doctor because of the affair? Or did Collier get rejected by the doctor and did she seek revenge?" Marcus smiled. "You know, the standard questions we ask the usual suspects."

John nodded. "Going to watch?"

"Probably be the most boring show of the night, but yea, I'll be on the other side of the glass. And I promise not to second-guess or interrupt you, John. My last suggestion is to let her sit and simmer for at least twenty minutes before you start—that will give me time to check in with Carl."

Driscol went to find Veronica. Marcus headed back to his office. He had just entered when Carl looked up from his typing and waved Marcus over.

"You need to see this, boss. Latest update from Jake." Carl held up a sheet of paper.

Marcus held off reading until he was behind his desk. He needed a moment to change gears from face-to-face interrogation to report reading.

The ROI was well written and concise: the standard for Lieutenant Doty. Their digging had uncovered rumors that Collier was having an affair with an older man. No one knew the older guy's name. But most people believed the affair was the root cause of her divorce.

Jake wrote that they hadn't been able to find her ex-husband, Stephen Collier, but had asked the local police to put out a "locate but do not detain order" for him. And he had tasked the San Diego NISRA with doing a quick background information report on him. Jake felt they had uncovered all they could at this time and would fly to Alameda in the morning.

At least we have confirmation on the divorce and a possible on the affair, thought Marcus as he reread the ROI. He added it to the growing stack of paper on his desk and left his office. Time to watch the Collier interrogation.

40

MARCUS WAS ALREADY ON HIS second mug of coffee. It had been an extremely short night of sleep. He'd stayed late last night observing Driscol as he went after Captain Collier. That took a couple of hours. Then Marcus had come in earlier than usual in hopes of having some quiet time to think about the somewhat expected—and a few unexpected—results it had generated.

Collier said she was still in love with Monroe even after he broke off the affair. She provided dates and locations of her contacts with Doctor Monroe as best as she could remember. No, she didn't know where he was or how he vanished. Yes, she wanted to see him again. No, she did not know where her ex-husband was now; they had not talked since the day the divorce was final. Only good news with the divorce was they didn't have children. No little lives to damage. They were both in San Diego when Monroe vanished; they'd had a meeting with the judge that afternoon and a court date the next morning. Standard questions were asked and answered. It was a pretty routine interview.

But the most interesting, and definitely not expected revelation, was that the letter from Monroe breaking up with her was mailed the morning of the day he vanished. Coincidence? *Not very likely*, thought Marcus. But was the timing important?

Collier promised to return that morning with the letter—she had saved it as a reminder of her foolishness, she said—and to answer any more questions Driscol had developed over night. Marcus felt she'd held on to the letter due to her love for Monroe. Whatever the reason, at least they would have a look at the last known communication from the missing doctor. Maybe, just maybe, the letter would contain one of those elusive straws.

As Marcus went over all the information in his mind, he kept going back to one wild theory he had generated. Granted, he said to himself, the theory was just that, with nothing much to back it up. But Marcus was starting to believe that the doctor had left of his own accord. Perhaps the letter Collier was bringing in would help justify that theory. Probably not, but it was past time to start throwing theories against the wall to see what stuck.

But his theory had one really big hole: the *why* of the doctor leaving of his own accord. Yea, it was a big hole. He seemed happy. His financial situation was good. He had a woman that loved him. Everyone said he loved his job at the research center. Day four of "find the missing doctor" was starting off as hopeless as the other three.

The lack of progress had been the deciding factor for coming in early. He wanted to think about the case in quiet, then spend the rest of the day digging into the dusty files from the FBI and CIA. With dusty files in mind, he'd opted to wear civilian clothes that day. Naturally, he kept a complete uniform in his office closet in case of a decorum emergency, but there was no need to get his dress blues dusty.

Marcus decided the next step was to refill his coffee mug. Caffeine is brain food in the Navy. As he left the coffee mess with his steaming mug, the elevator door opened. A rather attractive young lady wearing the Navy uniform of an ensign stepped out and looked around, a slightly confused look on her face.

"You look lost, Ensign. Anything I can do to help?"

"Good morning, sir. I am looking for Lieutenant Commander Colt. Do you know where I can find his office?"

"Just so happens I do. Follow me." Marcus smiled as he pointed down the hall. He led her down the hall to the IA area and ushered her toward his office door. "Go right on in and have a seat."

From the open door she could see the office was empty, so she turned to Marcus. "Do you think that will be okay, sir?"

"Sure. Sit in one of the chairs in front of the desk." Marcus walked in and took a seat behind the desk.

The ensign stood there for a moment, then a combination of anger and embarrassment enveloped her face. "Sir, I don't appreciate being made to look like a fool."

Marcus chuckled. "Ensign James, no foolish appearances were intended, I simply answered your one question. Remember the one about me knowing the location of this office? That was all you asked. Since I knew the location of my office, you are now here. Have a seat."

Ensign Wendy James got her anger under control, but the blush on her cheeks refused to fade. She took a seat in front of the desk. "Thank you, sir."

"Lesson one in the IA division—we usually never start by asking just one question if it is extremely specific: generalizations work much better until you know as much as you can about the person being interrogated. Until that moment, it is much better to ask multiple questions. And lesson two, you will notice I didn't provide more information than what you requested. At NIS and especially the IA division, we gather information and almost never give it out freely. Now what can I do for you this morning?"

"I know I am not due to report in until Monday, Lieutenant Commander Colt, but I wanted to meet you and maybe just get a quick look around. I'm looking forward to working here. And I appreciate the additional training just now even if it was embarrassing."

Marcus chuckled gently. "Well, you will fit in well here, James. We have a tendency to come in early and stay late, if the situation demands. Otherwise, we can goof off with the best of them. And we're all in training every day. As for me, I come in early most days."

"That's why I'm here this early. Agent Stevens mentioned in his class that you often came in early. I have to admit, sir, you are not what I expected."

Marcus slowly nodded. "Yea, I get that a lot. What exactly did he tell the class about me?"

"Sir, based on what we were told, I expected someone much older with lots of scar tissue. Maybe you would have a lightning bolt-shaped scar from a dueling saber on your cheek. No disrespect intended, sir," Ensign James said with a small laugh.

"None taken, James. Another quick lesson. Agent Donald 'Doc' Stevens tends to run off at the mouth. And embellishment is one of his personality traits. You have been warned. Now, let me show you to your office. Hopefully it will meet your requirements and approval."

Wendy was impressed that her new office was ready for her arrival. Everything, including her nameplate on the door and the desk, seemed perfect. After a quick look around and a nod of approval, they left her office. And she immediately got the attention of Mrs. Rita Howland, who was stashing her purse into her lower right desk drawer.

Rita looked at James and then back at Marcus as she said, "Good morning, chief." She switched to Spanish as she glanced over at James. "*¿Algun problemas para compartir, jefe?*" Rita punctuated the question with a single raised eyebrow.

Ensign James smiled and looked at Marcus. "Am I one of your problems, chief?"

"Not yet, James, but the day is young. Wendy James, this is Margarita Howland. She's one of the civilians who keeps this office running. Rita, this is our new ensign who is so excited to work here she came in at a very early hour, several days ahead of schedule, just to meet us," Marcus said. "And yes, she is well versed in Spanish, so watch what you say."

After a few moments of welcoming chatter between the two ladies, Marcus gave her a tour of the NISHQ office spaces, ending with the conference room. Three stacks of sealed boxes labeled "Property of the Central Intelligence Agency" were beside the open door. The lights were on and showed that Doc was also doing the early routine.

"Good morning, Mr. Colt. And hello again, Ensign James. Good to see you."

"Doc, Agent James was just telling me about some wild tales you're spreading in your classroom about some members of IA. I suggest some things are not appropriate for you to share. Got it, Doc?"

"Oh, hell, sir. You know that your adventures make for good training tools," Doc said with his standard grin. "Book learning alone could get them killed out there."

Marcus shook his head and rolled his eyes, knowing that further discussion wouldn't help. Doc was right about using experiences as part of the training. It was critical. But it was also embarrassing for Marcus when he was the subject.

Wendy James broke the silence as she looked at all the files and note cards on the boards, asking, "What is going on in here? Or am I allowed to ask?"

Doc jumped in. "This is the home of Task Force Cold Fog that has been established by the CNO to find a missing research doctor. He has been missing since June, and we are digging through a ton of files, closer to two tons based on the CIA stuff I saw in the hallway, hoping to find a clue or two. Want to join us this weekend?"

Marcus said, "Doc, she is not officially here until Monday. She just stopped by for a quick look around."

Wendy held up her hands in the *stop* gesture. "If it would help, I will be glad to work tomorrow. Sorry, but my Sunday is already relegated to helping a friend and her husband paint their kitchen."

Marcus pursed his lips and took a deep breath. "James, if you want to help, I sure won't turn it down. We need all the fresh eyes we can get. Start at 0800, right Doc?"

"Yes, sir."

Wendy looked at Marcus and asked, "Would it be alright if I hang around a bit this morning, meet some of the team, and soak up some of the knowledge about this case? I'll try to not get in the way."

"Ensign, if you wish to violate the long-standing military rule of never volunteering, who am I to stop you. Take care of her, Doc." With that, Marcus walked back to his office to face a cold mug of coffee.

41

MARCUS NEEDED ANOTHER CUP OF coffee: one that was hot. With his personal mug on his desk, he grabbed a disposable cup and filled it from the "special blend" urn. The aroma of spices in the brew always helped get the brain working.

"Hello again, Lieutenant Commander, Doc asked me to make a coffee run. Thanks for letting me hang around today. It should be interesting," said Wendy in a serious yet pleasant voice as she entered the mess. "Like you, I have a tendency to survive on coffee." Her smile brightened the room and improved his negative attitude about the missing doctor.

Ensign Wendy James, USN, was, at the ripe old age of twenty-three—her birthday was just the month previous—the youngest officer in IA. She was 5'7" and her weight probably barely topped the minimum requirement of 112 pounds. Her uniform couldn't hide that she was well built; Marcus had overheard a guy in the cafeteria commenting that she was built like the proverbial brick outhouse.

Her medium-length reddish brown hair was drawn into a small bun at the base of her skull, and her green eyes, when not partially hidden by the glasses she wore for reading, would pull you in and keep you staring into them. Her face was not one that would excite a fashion photographer, but she sure grabbed and held the attention of most of the males who saw her. Her smile was intoxicating.

More importantly for the work done here, Wendy had a degree in accounting with a minor in business management from Washington and Lee University. She should be great at discovering and following money trails and grasping the nuances of most business operations. Born and raised in Richmond, VA, she had a delightfully soft Virginian accent that disarmed most people. And when she had them disarmed, Marcus suspected she went for the jugular with vengeance. She would fit in well here.

In addition, her father's job had taken him on extended stays, usually two or so years at a time, to several places around the globe, like Rome, Madrid, and Tokyo. Wendy had picked up Spanish, Italian, and a bit of Japanese while going to school in these cities.

"Ensign, I appreciate your excitement and willingness to get involved early. We'll try to make it up to you. As the old saying goes, no good deed goes unpunished." That got a laugh from Wendy.

Marcus returned to his office on that positive note. Rita was hard at it, going through the radio and AUTOVON traffic for the morning. There were three stacks of each on her desk, which concerned Marcus. He knew the big stack was "info only." The second might need the attention of IA. And the small yet growing stack needed immediate IA attention. *Never a good thing*, thought Marcus.

From the corner of her eye, Rita saw Marcus approaching and held up the small stack of radio messages. "Still working on the AUTOVON traffic, boss—I'll bring it into you. Start here. And yes, I think Ensign James will fit in well here."

"Thank you, Rita … for everything," Marcus said as he swooped by like a high-speed train and grabbed the radio traffic from her hand. At his desk, he dropped the radio traffic in the center and reached for his coffee mug. Well, he thought, *it has a bit of warmth left so it's still drinkable*. He added the few sips left in the disposable cup to his mug.

The first message was from NISRA New Orleans: an agent had been involved with a drug buy. That was a normal thing. However, his presence at the local police department drug bust scene was awkward, at the very least, as he tried to explain that he too was investigating. The SSA of NISRA New Orleans didn't have a record of that agent working any ongoing drug cases. So he was buying to use? Or resell? Well, maybe. Marcus nodded silently and attached a note to it. Yes, it was obvious that IA would take further action.

The next two messages involved actions that really didn't need the attention of IA. Almost, but not quite. He jotted some notes for Rita or Carl to send back to the originator, under his signature. He leaned back, pleased that at least one stack of traffic was done.

He returned his focus to the first message. New Orleans was a three-hour drive from Naval Air Station Pensacola, the location of another research center working on Rembrandt. Perhaps this was another opportunity to kill the two well-deserving birds with one flight down south. The lack of IA agents was obvious, so the only one available for the trip was the guy reading the message.

Marcus picked up the phone and notified Rita he needed to get to New Orleans right now. He placed a quick call to Kelly, who promised to get his bags ready and drive him to the airport. And he called Vic and informed him about the new IA case so the admiral was in the loop. He drained his mug and left his office.

"Rita, call NISRA New Orleans and let them know when I'll be arriving. I put some notes on the message. Anything in the AUTOVON traffic I need to see?"

"No, boss. The problems in the AUTOVON traffic are things we can handle while you're gone. I'll call New Orleans. Your ticket will be at the Delta counter at National for a 10:45 departure, so you better get moving."

Marcus ducked into the conference room on the way out. Doc and Wendy were deep in discussion about the cards attached to the boards. A couple of other agents had arrived and were going over the interviews from the day before.

"Doc, I'm leaving right now for NISRA New Orleans—we have a problem down there. If it works out, I'll visit the research center in Pensacola tomorrow. I should be back home Sunday morning, assuming all goes well."

"No problem, sir. We'll stay on top of things. Most of the day will be spent going over the interviews we did yesterday."

Marcus nodded and frowned as he remembered something important. "Doc, Captain Collier will be back this morning and will be bringing a 'Dear Joan' letter she got from the doctor. John is handling the follow-up interrogation, but I want you to observe. Get with John for the schedule."

"You got it, boss. Have a safe trip."

After Marcus left, Wendy looked at Doc and said, "Things certainly happen quickly around here."

"Ensign, it's just another day in paradise. And so far, today is one of the calm ones."

42

SOMETIMES THINGS WORK THE WAY they should in the travel industry. The Delta flight from New Orleans touched down with a chirp from the wheels and a roar from the engines as the thrust reversers kicked in, several minutes before its posted arrival time. The taxiing to the terminal used up those few minutes, and the flight officially arrived at the gate right on time at noon. It took more than a few minutes for the passengers to deplane due to the mass of carry-on luggage crammed into the overhead compartments.

Marcus was in the first group of people off the plane. His carry-on consisted of a simple small shopping bag and his briefcase. Looking around, he failed to see Kelly. *Probably held up in traffic,* he thought, since even Sunday morning traffic in D.C. can be a mess. He turned toward baggage claim.

"Hello sailor, welcome home," Kelly whispered into Marcus's ear from behind as she stepped from the column hiding her. She wrapped him in a bear hug. Marcus inhaled her fragrance, happy to be back where he belonged. He turned and took her in his arms for a proper welcome home hug and kiss.

"Glad my ride home is here," Marcus said after pulling back from the kiss.

Kelly put on a fake frown face. "Is that all I am to you? A chauffer? Guess the honeymoon is really over."

"I think you have a few other wonderful uses, babe, but not here. Let's get home and try them out."

Chuckling, Kelly said, "No time for that, Romeo. Remember we have company coming in a few hours for dinner. Let's go home."

As Kelly grabbed his arm, she noticed the shopping bag. "Well, what did you bring me from the 'Big Easy'?"

Now it was Marcus's turn to laugh. "Most of what's in the bag is to keep two admirals happy—Chance and your dad. I got them each a couple of bottles of Peychaud's Bitters. You know how they love a Sazerac or two after a hard day making my life miserable."

"Hope you picked up a couple of bottles for us, sailor. Besides, keeping the CNO happy is easy—just keep me happy." Kelly grinned as she pinched his butt. "I am his favorite daughter, ya know."

"And only daughter." They both said and laughed at what had become a standing joke with the admiral. "And yes, ma'am, we have a couple of bottles as well as two containers of filé powder. I was so busy down there I had to pick these up at the airport gift store on the way to the plane."

Kelly looked lost in thought for a moment, then lowered her voice. "Busy? No new scar tissue, right?"

Marcus shook his head.

Kelly smiled and whispered, "Tonight, after one Sazerac I will do a full body inspection to make sure you're being truthful."

"Works for me, wife!"

After picking up his bag from the moving line, Marcus was surprised when Kelly handed him the Mustang keys and told him to drive home. Usually Kelly was reluctant to relinquish that driver's seat. But he assumed she had an ulterior motive.

With her smile kicked up to the left, she said, "We have a few more coming to dinner tonight, babe. And that resulted in a few changes— well, more than a few."

Marcus shrugged. "Okay, who else will be there?" He now knew she'd asked him to drive so he'd stay calm. He never got angry while driving.

"Ann came up for a long weekend, so she and Doc are staying with us."

Nodding, Marcus said, "Good. I've wanted Doc to meet Jason. But how did Ann get off this weekend?"

Kelly laughed. "Remember the time she yelled at your surgeon?"

Despite her small size, Ann was feisty and extremely loyal to her friends. Back in the spring, when Marcus was recovering from the stab wound, Ann was there when the surgeon, Lieutenant Jack Ambrose, did the one-week follow-up exam. During the session, the doctor tried to be positive about the recovery and mentioned how a pair of overaggressive SPs had shot a poor fellow in the shoulder the previous week. That man, unlike Marcus, would never have much use of his arm again. He did not know that Marcus and Doc were the shooters and the victim was a murderer who had been holding a gun to the head of Ann's best friend.

Marcus was going to let the comment fly by, but Ann would not. In defense of the two shooters, Ann got a little hostile and loud, which a junior enlisted person should never do with an officer.

He smiled at the memory. "That was one incident hard to forget." Then he got concerned. "Did Ambrose take some sort of retaliation against Ann? Is she okay?"

"She's fine. Better than fine, in fact. Seems Doctor Ambrose was so impressed with her boldness, he had her assigned to his surgical staff when a recent opening occurred. He figured she would be the one who wouldn't hold back if she thought he or anyone else was doing something wrong. He's at a conference all this next week and gave her a long weekend off. She and Doc spent yesterday house hunting. They are so cute discussing locations!"

Marcus waited for the other shoe to drop. He knew those two wouldn't cause a bunch of changes. He didn't have to wait long.

"And I talked with Dad last night. When I mentioned our dinner with Jason, Mary, and their boys, Dad said he had been hoping to talk more with Jason, so I invited them to join us."

"Okay, Kelly, I can tell you're still holding back. Spill it, girl."

The left hook smile got bigger. "Uncle Humphrey and Aunt Dorothy are visiting and were disappointed they weren't able to see you yesterday, so they'll be here this afternoon. And David is coming also."

"Okay, a lucky thirteen for dinner on Halloween, and the rest of the story is?"

"Pay close attention. Mom and I put our heads together and decided the following. Dad is picking up some smoked mackerel and clam chowder. Aunt Dorothy is putting together some bruschetta. I have a three-bean salad and German potato salad done. Mary called yesterday, before all this happened, and asked if she could please bring some stuffed eggs. She's been trying out different ingredients and wants your opinion on several versions. Based on Jason's comment, Mary was afraid you might shoot her since their orders from you were to bring just an appetite."

Marcus had to laugh at that one.

Kelly continued, "Ann is currently cooking the pork roast from the original plan and we will serve it warm with a nice horseradish sauce, which you will make shortly after getting home. David said he'll bring both beer and wine. I think we have it covered." Kelly explained it as if giving a briefing to the CNO.

All Marcus could do was slowly shake his head. The admiral's daughter had taken charge of the entertaining and it was damn the hors d'oeuvres and full speed ahead!

43

BEING IT WAS A SHORT trip out of town, Marcus hadn't taken many clothes, and carried in his single bag with ease. Doc was sitting at the kitchen table reading real estate ads in the paper, and he looked up and waved. Ann was sliding the pork roast into the oven. She smiled when she saw Marcus.

"Hello, adorable," Marcus said as he dropped his bag and picked up Ann in a hug. "Dump Doc and come back to my harem." Doc had started the harem thing earlier in the year when he saw several women hovering around Marcus; he jokingly asked if they were members of Marcus's harem.

Ann laughed. "Tempting offer, good looking, but Kelly might not approve." She kissed Marcus on the cheek and wiggled out of his arms, then reached over and set the oven timer. Ann had become a second sister to Marcus just as Doc had become Kelly's older brother.

Kelly came over and hugged Ann. "Ignore him. I think he is suffering mentally from crossing time zones."

"Hey, it was only one zone, Kelly." Marcus inhaled sharply and asked Ann, "Which spices went on the roast?"

Ann's smile was huge as she said, "Last half of that Simon and Garfunkel song, Marcus, just like you taught me. Parsley for the potatoes, sage for the turkey, leaving rosemary and thyme for the pork roast."

"Ya done good, corpsman."

Marcus turned to Doc. "How did it go with all the CIA files?"

Doc rolled his eyes and shook his head. After a deep sigh, he said, "You will not believe the crap they sent us. Sure, the files mention submarines, detection, and radar, but nothing coherent. It will take a translator to figure it out. We need someone who speaks fluent 'CIA' and we need him fast. I put a copy of one file on your desk upstairs so you can see for yourself."

"I'll see what I can do." Marcus carried his bag and briefcase up to the bedroom, leaving Kelly to keep the kitchen under control.

Marcus wondered if the CIA was stonewalling them with a clutter of data, like the information overload he'd been reading about. Or perhaps they'd provided what they thought would be helpful, not realizing their documentation methods were somewhat cryptic to the uninformed. *A call to Les might bring some help,* Marcus thought as he flipped through the file, but not as fast as they needed.

As he started downstairs, it hit him: there was a translator nearby. At the bottom of the stairs, Marcus opened the front door as he said, "I'll be back shortly."

As he approached his neighbor's door, Marcus wondered if he was grasping at straws. Then he smirked: everything about this case had been a straw grasp. *Situation normal,* he thought as he rang the doorbell, skipping the rest of words for the Army's favorite acronym of SNAFU.

"Well, hello Marcus. How are you?" asked a slender woman, perhaps in her late forties, with a slight British accent. Her face was neither ugly nor beautiful; it fell somewhere in between, but it wasn't one that would stay in your memory if you bumped into her on the street.

"Mrs. Smythe, I'm hoping you can help me."

"Happy to help, Marcus, but only if you stop calling me *Mrs.* and use *Victoria,* as I told you last week," she said with a patronizing smile. "Come in and let's discuss it."

When Marcus and Kelly had made their social calls the previous Sunday afternoon, they found out that Victoria had been widowed at a young age. Rather than remarry, she had thrown herself into her work at the CIA. She had retired a few years ago after twenty-five years with the

Agency, and was splitting her retirement time between writing, painting, and volunteering at the Arlington no-kill animal shelter.

After a short discussion, she agreed to help, and accepted the invitation to dinner. At the Colt residence, they entered the kitchen to find Kelly, Ann, and Doc enjoying a beer and a snack tray of cheese, olives, and crackers while discussing the seating arrangements for dinner.

"Oh, no, looks like Marcus found another potential harem member," Doc said with a slight leering grin.

Marcus, wondering if Doc had reached his beer limit already, quickly took control of the conversation. "I couldn't let that thirteen number stand—especially on Halloween—so our neighbor, the charming and delightful Victoria, saved us from evil spirits and brought the number up to a safe fourteen. Add one more chair to your plan, please."

The laughter settled down and introductions were done. Doc apologized and explained the "harem" remark, which caused Victoria to break up again. She agreed to accept temporary harem status, awaiting Kelly's final approval. The laughter restarted and Victoria realized she truly enjoyed the camaraderie of her new friends. Perhaps, she thought, her life had been too tranquil the last couple of years. She graciously accepted a beer and found the snack tray had been moved to within her reach. She felt she had been accepted.

"Doc, you asked for a CIA translator earlier. Sorry I took so long finding one."

Doc could not hide his surprise and pointed toward Victoria with a questioning lopsided grin and a raised eyebrow.

Victoria smiled and raised her hand. "Yes, Doc. I spent a few years at the CIA and might be able to help you."

Before the conversation could continue, the doorbell rang. Kelly jumped up to welcome the new arrivals. Doc started to ask Victoria a question, but Marcus held up his hand in a *stop* signal. They heard Kelly welcoming her mom and dad, and others. Elaine, Bill, Dorothy, Humphrey, and David Bartow carried food and drinks into the kitchen.

Again, a round of introductions filled the room with noise, as strangers became acquaintances on the way toward friendships. Once things settled down, Marcus noticed David was slow releasing Victoria's hand when they were introduced. Or perhaps it was Victoria. Either way, it was interesting, based upon the smiles they exchanged.

Kelly had introduced her relatives only by their first names, but Victoria said, "Admiral Gallagher, it is a true pleasure to finally meet you." She then turned to Hump and said, "And Captain Miller, your reputation in the intelligence field precedes you well indeed."

Marcus chuckled at the surprised expressions he saw. "Nice to have a neighbor, a CIA veteran, joining us, right?"

"You do know how to keep people off balance, Marcus. It is a pleasure to meet you, Victoria," said Bill Gallagher, "and why do I think you're here for more than dinner?"

"Probably because you are very perceptive, Bill." A twinkle hit Victoria's eyes.

"I suspect we'll have an interesting conversation during dinner," replied Bill.

"Quite."

After food and drink were unloaded, everyone settled down to some friendly talk. Hump Miller updated the Colts about their friends in Norfolk; eventually the conversation turned to the two Norfolk agents currently in D.C. Captain Miller said Sam Maker, the supervising agent of NISRA Norfolk, was anxious for their return.

Before Marcus could address that comment, the doorbell again rang. More introductions were carried out as Jason, Mary, and sons—Jason Jr. or "J.J.," and Clark—arrived.

Marcus relieved Mary of the tray she carried and immediately tried one each of the wasabi flavored and Cajun shrimp stuffed eggs. Mary received a thumbs up on each, and her smile beamed her appreciation. The noise level in the house increased and remained high until everyone prepared to sit down to dinner.

While the food was being pulled together, Marcus and his father-in-law were able to get Jason alone in the living room for a moment. Bill said, "Jason, I hope we can have a few minutes to chat later."

"Yes, sir, Admiral, I look forward to it. When I saw you, I suspected that was part of Marcus's plan."

Marcus snickered. "Nope. I'm innocent again. My plan was to serve you dinner, mostly as thanks for your help with those not-so-friendly agencies. Plans changed while I was in New Orleans for the last two days, and over the six months I've known Kelly, I've learned to roll with the changes."

Bill added one last thought as they returned to the kitchen. "Gentlemen, just remember, no plan survives first contact with the enemy ... or in this case, contact with wives and in-laws. Let's eat." He received the expected chuckles.

The food was excellent, as was the company. During dinner, the conversation turned to Halloween. After all, the sun was heading down and children would soon be knocking on the door in search of treats.

Jason tapped his knife on his near-empty glass to get everyone's attention over the noise. "Marcus, I suspect with the admiral here, we might need to spend a few minutes talking about our project. So I have a suggestion. J.J. and Clark told me they're too old for the trick-or-treating thing, so how about they take a position on the porches here and at Victoria's to handle the candy distribution. Mary can cover our place. Will that work for you?"

Marcus said, "As long as everyone agrees, especially these two young men who were volunteered by their father—fine with me." Heads nodded all around.

After dinner, Victoria and Kelly helped set the boys up on the porches. Mary went home to handle her candy bowls. Ann, Elaine, and Dorothy offered to keep Mary and the boys company after clearing the table. Victoria came back inside, and in a short time, the dinner table was ready for conference duty.

Marcus took the head seat at the table and started the discussion, "Okay, Doc and Kelly will be taking notes, so we'll have documentation on this informal chat. To get started, I invited Victoria to join us, since as an ex-CIA employee she might be able to help translate the files we received Friday from the CIA. Doc says, and I agree after looking at this one sample, that the notation is somewhat cryptic. Now the issue is, and this is directed to Jason, how much info can we share with her?"

Jason's face had a sour look. "Victoria, what was your security level when you last worked?"

Her slight smile almost looked condescending. "Our security clearances do not match those of the military, but it is safe to say that I had access to everything within the CIA control."

Marcus felt there was something not being said, so he pushed a bit. "Okay. And who would we contact to verify that?"

This time, her smile was that of a kindergarten teacher would give a student who asked the right question. "Well, I suppose you could call my replacement. I spent over a year training him, and he knows me well."

"And who would that be, Victoria?" Marcus felt like he was pulling teeth.

"Leslie Forrester. And I suspect you have his number. Right?"

Marcus, hopefully hiding his surprise, got up and left the room.

Jason's look was total surprise as he asked, "You were ADDO before Les?"

"Oh, yes, quite."

A few minutes later, Marcus came back into the dining room grinning. "Well, Les confirmed your security level, Victoria. And he ended our short call with a strange comment. He said, 'we could always ask her school friend, Lizzy.' Then he laughed. Care to elaborate on that?"

Victoria laughed at that. "Oh, that bastard Les. I think it is a bit late for a call to the UK. HM does not like to be awakened and the palace staff would not issue the wake up for her unless World War III has started."

44

THE SILENCE WAS RATHER LOUD. All eyes were open wide and a few mouths were actually hanging loose a bit. Considering the combined experience of the people in the room, it was hard to imagine them shocked. But such was the case. The news was totally unexpected.

Victoria's soft smile was disarming. She sipped of her wine, giving everyone a chance to digest the information she had just revealed.

Naturally, Admiral Gallagher was the first to recover. "Your school friend, Lizzy, is now the Queen of England? 'HM' is Her Majesty?"

"Very true, Bill. Allow me to back up a bit." With that, she laid out her history.

Victoria Spencer was raised in the shadow of the throne. Her cousin several times removed, and best friend through childhood, was Princess Elizabeth Alexandra Mary Windsor, whose father, King George VI, then sat on the throne of England. Vicky and Lizzy went to school together, played together, and did all the things best friends do together, at least within the confines and control of the palace security officers.

When the war came and they reached a suitable age, it was her Uncle Winston who suggested she join Lizzy in the Auxiliary Territorial Service (ATS), the women's branch of the British Army. He was not really an uncle to either Victoria or Lizzy but was another distant cousin who they called "uncle" due to the age difference. They both trained as mechanics and truck drivers in early 1944, but Victoria had a problem in that she couldn't grasp the nuances of driving huge trucks. As a result, she wasn't happy in the ATS.

Again Uncle Winston came to the rescue. As British Prime Minister, Winston Churchill was able to pull strings, and shortly Victoria was working in the London headquarters of the Office of Strategic Services (OSS). The OSS was initially an intelligence gathering operation for President Roosevelt, based on a combination of the Brit's Secret Intelligence Service (MI6) and their Special Operations Executive (SOE).

Later, OSS men went through training to parachute behind enemy lines to help locals disrupt the enemy. Before crossing the channel, they trained on how to silently cut the throats of sentries, plant bombs, wreck trains, and generally become a thorn in the side of the bad guys. These three-man units went to Europe under operation Jedburgh, a name later attached to all who had served behind the lines.

Victoria did not go behind the lines, but her work in the London office made sure those who did had what they needed. When the war was over, Victoria became the wife of one of the Jedburgh survivors, a British Army officer named Colin Smythe, and they both joined the CIA when it was formed in 1947 from the remains of the OSS.

Their marriage and careers in the CIA provided them both with a great amount of pleasure and pride. They moved to America in 1948 and became naturalized citizens. Sadly, Colin died of a massive heart attack in early 1962. On a typical work day, he'd stood up from his desk at the CIA, walked toward his door, and simply fell over dead before he got there. Many of his coworkers believed he was another victim of the disaster known as the Bay of Pigs Invasion; he was involved in the planning and felt personally responsible for the failure. Victoria was devastated, but continued her career with the Agency and retired early, after twenty-five years of combined OSS/CIA service, in 1969.

"And now you know more about me than just about anyone else in America." She took another sip of tea.

Kelly spoke first. "Victoria, you gave up life near the royals for a career at the CIA?"

"My dear, my marriage, and secondly my career, provided me so much more excitement than being near Lizzy could have ever done. You will see that is true with your life with Marcus. That is a fact," Victoria said.

Kelly chuckled. "You are so right. The Norfolk case provided some exciting moments."

Before they went too far down memory lane, Marcus pulled the group back to the main concern. "Okay, so we are in agreement that Victoria should be a member in good standing of Task Force Cold Fog?" Marcus turned to his neighbor. "Jason, this is your circus. Can she be one of the monkeys?"

Jason nodded and succinctly laid out the reason behind the task force and the current status. Victoria's expression changed from comradery to concern as she listened. When he finished, she sat back, quiet and withdrawn.

After an awkward couple of moments, she deeply sighed and faintly said, "I know Freddie, but didn't know he had disappeared."

Marcus failed to hide his surprise as he glanced over toward Doc.

Doc shrugged. "You knew the doctor? When did you last see or hear from him?"

"We dated a couple of times in the late spring of 1970, a few months after I retired. We met at one of those horrible D.C. Christmas parties. I was intrigued by his intelligence, but we really didn't have that much in common. There was a rather disappointing date in early June during which he said he was sorry, but he had someone else in his life. I think that was the last I heard from him."

"Okay, Victoria," Marcus said, "for the moment you are now a witness and we need to ask some questions. Did he ever talk about any projects at the Navy research center?"

"No. We mostly talked about the Navy and old movies. He really enjoyed Bogart in *The Caine Mutiny*, which was a nice combination of both."

Doc jumped in. "Did he know your history with the CIA?"

Victoria slowly shook her head. "Doc, I rarely talk about that, and especially not to strangers. Had I not known that Marcus was with NIS, I would have not told him, either."

"How was his attitude?" Marcus asked.

"Now that I think about it, he seemed somewhat depressed due to his forced retirement from the Navy. Nothing that would raise warning flags about suicide, but enough to know he was not happy."

"Do you think his attitude was sufficiently negative to cause him to retaliate against the Navy?" Marcus asked. "Like maybe cripple his project by vanishing?"

"Sorry, I didn't spend enough time around him. Perhaps, but that seems to be a rather harsh thing to do."

The conversation and questioning continued until Marcus finally said, "I think we have exhausted this line of questioning, and I believe that Victoria has provided all the info that she has about the good doctor. Far as I'm concerned, we need to move on to the use of Victoria as a 'CIA translator.' And I'm in favor, but Jason, this is your show. What ya think?"

Jason grimaced as he shrugged. "Anyone have any negative thoughts?"

A quick glance around the table showed that all heads were moving side to side: no one had a problem with Victoria. She softly smiled. Jason nodded toward Marcus, indicating that all was well as far as he was concerned. Time to get down to business.

"Welcome to Cold Fog, Victoria."

45

HE HAD WANTED TO SNUGGLE more with Kelly, but Marcus knew there was too much to do at the office. His mind going in circles over the case had interrupted most of the night's sleep. He needed to look at some files at the office. So after a grand total of three hours sleep, he left the comfort of the warm bed, quietly dressed, and drove to the Navy Yard.

The petty officer assigned coffee duty for the week plugged in the two urns when he saw Marcus. "Sorry, sir, I didn't know you were arriving this early. These should be ready in a few minutes."

"Good morning, Stan. I think I can refrain from becoming an evil ogre due to caffeine shortage for a few more minutes. You and the computer room team doing okay? Any big issues over the weekend?" Marcus dropped a buck in the coffee fund can to cover his next four cups.

Petty Officer Stan Jackson smiled. "It was a calm weekend, sir. No major problems with the hardware, and I didn't see the chief jumping up and down as he scanned the incoming traffic, so I don't think any new wars started." Stan appreciated the sincere comments and questions. It was nice when a senior officer showed concern for the crew and even took the time to learn their first names. *Lieutenant Commander Colt is one of the really good guys,* he thought, not for the first time.

"Good to know. We appreciate the job you all do. And the coffee is great!" Marcus grinned as he poured his first mug of the special blend. The clocks showed 0500 hrs as he walked down the hall.

The quiet in the conference room helped him sort through the info as he reread the cards posted on the boards. Nothing jumped out and no new links were formed in his mind. Perhaps getting the cryptic CIA data in the mix would help. Victoria would arrive at 0800 to start the translation.

A copy of the "dear Joan" letter from the missing doctor to Captain Jen Collier was in the middle of the table. Doc had attached a note that the FBI verified the signature to be the doctor's. As he read it a second time, Marcus felt there was something wrong about it, but not knowing the doctor personally, it was hard to grasp what. He attached a note to the letter asking Victoria to give her thoughts. *Just another question to add to the growing list*, he thought.

Marcus added his Pensacola lab visit report to the small stack at the head of the table. The other two reports were from Doty and Bates on their visits to the labs at San Diego and Berkeley. Aside from Captain Collier's previous assignment in San Diego, nothing linked the missing doctor to either location except the project name. *Another dead end— okay, technically two dead ends. Yippie.*

Marcus had spent most of Saturday in Florida talking with the research center staff there, and discovered their input to Rembrandt was restricted to testing the computer code that allowed communication with the satellites. There was nothing at that lab that directly involved Doctor Monroe. The commanding officer of the research center remembered being introduced to the doctor at a Washington meeting when the project was in its infancy, but all he remembered about the guy was a quiet demeanor and somewhat negative attitude.

With conference room tasks done, Marcus made another stop in the coffee mess before strolling to his office. Since the official day was still two hours away, Marcus turned on his stereo and let the sounds of the Beach Boys flow around his head. With "Fun, Fun, Fun" playing quietly behind him, he started typing a status report to pass to the admiral. He chuckled, knowing the admiral would enjoy the revelation about the Queen's best friend now working for him.

The eight-track tape had just started over—that was much nicer than flipping an LP over—and was playing "Be True to Your School" when a knock interrupted his typing. Marcus looked up to see Ensign Wendy James smiling at the door.

"Sir, may I approach?" she asked.

"Good morning, James. Have a seat. Isn't 0630 a bit early to start your first official day?" Marcus reached around and shut off the music.

She chuckled. "Not when my boss comes in at 0500 and, based on the sound of his typing, not to just listen to the golden oldies station."

"Ouch! Thanks for making me feel ancient, Wendy. Anyway, how did Saturday go?"

Her lips pursed as she prepared to answer. "I'm not sure I was able to help much, but it gave me a great respect for the work we need to do this week, sir. Honestly, I felt like a junior high kid attending a graduate college course."

Marcus chuckled at the mental image. "Have you heard about the Navy's new Fighter Weapons School at NAS Miramar?" Wendy shook her head. "That's where our best fighter pilots are trained to be even better. They say that the 'best of the best' show up there for training—training that will hone their already excellent skills and make them better, so they can become tagged as a TOPGUN. We believe, as humbly as possible I should add, that being in the Internal Affairs division makes you a TOPGUN of NIS. Here the best of the best get better. The people you worked with on Saturday are the best. And with time and effort, especially watching and learning from some of those there, you will be also. You were selected for this slot because you're already good, and this work will make you better."

Wendy rolled her eyes. "No pressure, right, sir? Now I feel totally inadequate … and doomed."

Marcus snorted. "Bull. Tell me, Ensign, how well did you speak Italian on the day your dad moved you to Rome? Or an even better comparison—on the day you walked into a calculus class, you had a lot of basic math skills, but none in the way the calculus instructor would be teaching. And you excelled in both places. Just pay attention and use the skills you already have as a foundation and build upon them."

"I take your point, sir. Thank you. I'll do my best."

"We expect nothing less. Now, if you have nothing else to discuss, I suggest you retire to your office and read through the intro data Rita left on your desk. By the time you get through that, I will have finished my update for the admiral, and he'll be here, so I can take you around for the introductions."

Wendy smiled. "Thank you, sir. Guess I'll be in my office."

Marcus checked the clock and saw he still had half an hour to finish his update for the admiral and uncover anything else that needed his attention.

46

AFTER DROPPING A COPY OF the update on Carl's desk and the original on Senior Chief Yeoman Victor O'Keef's desk, knowing the admiral would see it first thing, Marcus made his third trip to the coffee mess. He entered to find LT Jacob 'Jake' Doty, USN, and 1stLt Henry 'Hank' Bates, USMC, getting their first cups for the day. They had returned from their multi-assignment trip in California late on Saturday afternoon.

"Mornin' gents. Hope y'all enjoyed sunny California," Marcus said with a grin. "How was the beach?"

Hank just grinned, and Jake started to render the middle finger salute, but reconsidered and sarcastically said, "It was really fun, boss. Ain't nothing more fun than cramming three investigations in different parts of a big state into four days." He took a sip of coffee. "And pray tell, sir, what new fun do you have reserved for us today?"

Marcus shrugged. "All of us, and a couple of imported agents from downstairs and Norfolk, are up to our ears in the missing doctor case. Really glad to have you two back home. Maybe you can look at what we've gen'ed up and see something we're missing."

Hank Bates shook his head as he said, "Sir, they have really compartmentalized that project. Based on what we were told at those two sites,

176

people working in the same office didn't share info. No one out West knew much about the doctor once you get past the name recognition."

"I understand. I read both of your reports this morning. We can touch on them at the meeting later," Marcus said as he left with a full mug. "Again, good to have you home."

Passing Carl's desk, Marcus noticed the radio traffic destined for IA had been left by one of the yeomen. A quick sort showed that the larger stack of messages was simply informational copies. Those directed to IA for action got his attention. And this short stack showed the day would be interesting.

Reading while walking, Marcus saw the first message was an hour old and from the NISO in Naples, Italy. An agent had been accused of rape and would be placed under arrest by the local police as soon as he regained consciousness. This one was unusual and needed immediate attention. The SSA believed the locals were setting the agent up with a false charge. Stuff like that became front-page, anti-American news.

Marcus stepped back and left a note on Carl's desk. When he arrived in the next few minutes, Carl would get the ball rolling finding transportation for the Italian trip, and two members of the IA team would be leaving town. Marcus decided he would call the State Department shortly to give them a heads up about the potential problem.

The rest of the short stack was follow-up traffic about ongoing cases. Nothing to cause any immediate concerns, but they would generate a bit more paperwork getting the files up to date. Rita would handle most of that. Marcus was again glad that he came in early so he could face the Italian problem.

A quick couple of moments on the typewriter generated another brief for Vice Admiral John Chance. But before he went to the boss's office, Marcus placed a call to his contact at the State Department. The secretary there told him it was too early and to call back later. Just as well, since Marcus needed to brief the admiral.

He dropped the carbon copy of the brief on Carl's desk. He would see it when he arrived and jump on the phone with Andrews Air Force Base in hopes of lining up a flight to Italy. Later he'd file it properly.

Vic O'Keef, keeper of the admiral's gate, was placing his cover on the coat rack when Marcus entered his office. "Good morning, Mr. Colt. What brings you in early?"

"Senior Chief, it's just one of those mornings I hate. Here's another brief for the admiral as soon as he arrives." Marcus passed him the single sheet of paper.

"Just have more coffee, sir, it will get better." He grinned while taking the brief. After a quick read, his smile vanished. "Damn, this is not good, sir."

With a chuckle and a touch of friendly sarcasm, Marcus replied, "Even on an early Monday morning, you are the sharp one, Vic. Let me know when the boss arrives. Thanks."

"You got it, Mr. Colt."

Marcus noted the staff had yet to arrive, but it was still a reasonable twenty minutes before the official start time. No need to panic yet. He went to his office and reread the radio message from Naples, but that didn't offer any more information.

He leaned back in his chair and studied the overhead for a moment. Slowly a plan of action came together. In standard Colt fashion, it was probably a bit radical. Picking up the message, he left his office.

Carl had arrived and was on the phone when Marcus passed. He gave Marcus an *okay* sign as he kept his head down making notes and mumbling "uh, huh" multiple times. Reservation seeking was under way.

He glanced over and saw through Ensign James's open office door that she was busy reading the information manual. He knocked.

Wendy looked up. "Sir?"

"Are you about ready to get to work, Ensign?"

"Since this is the second pass through this manual, I'm ready for something a bit more exciting, sir."

Marcus took a seat in front of Wendy's desk just as Carl walked in and announced, "Mr. Colt, we have two seats on a TWA flight leaving Dulles at 1400. Connection in Heathrow will get to Naples around 0900 their time tomorrow. I just need the names to go with the reservations. Nothing out of Andrews would have got there until late Wednesday night. This is the best we can do."

"Excellent work, Carl. Names for Naples will be James, Wendy and Colt, Marcus." Marcus grinned at Wendy's surprised look. "How's your Italian?"

"Me la farò," she said.

Carl had a questioning look, so Marcus translated, "She will get by, she said."

Nodding, Carl headed back to his desk to complete the air travel plans. Around here, nothing surprised him. Wendy had a puzzled look that Marcus hoped to relieve as he passed her the radio message from NISO Naples.

She read it and looked up. "Do we have any more info on this, sir?"

"Not yet, but as soon as you call the SSA over there—they should be back from lunch about now—I hope we have more information. Let them know we will be there in the morning. Remind them to line up the witnesses, dig into the background of the victim, etc. We'll have a status meeting at 0815 in my office—spread the word. That's all."

"Aye, aye, sir."

As he walked back to his office and stood behind his desk, his mind went to the standard question: *what have I forgotten to do so far*?

Before he could form the answer, his phone rang and the internal line to the admiral's office lit up. "Colt speaking, sir."

"The boss has arrived, Mr. Colt."

"Thanks, Vic!" Time to get approval on all the plans he had already set in motion.

47

ON THE WAY TO SEE the admiral, Marcus realized he needed yet another cup of coffee. The coffee police would be after him for having four cups before the staff meeting, but it had already been a rough morning. He grabbed it and, without delay, visited the admiral.

Vic nodded when he entered. "Go right in, Mr. Colt. The admiral is looking forward to your chat, sir."

He knocked on the open door casing and came to attention. "Morning, Admiral. I hope you have a couple of minutes to spare me, sir."

"Colt, just like last week, you certainly do have a knack for messing up a good Monday morning. Any other disasters? And for crying out loud, at ease and sit down," the admiral bellowed, pointing to a chair in front of his desk while waving the brief Marcus had provided.

"Thank you, sir. There are no other issues to add to that disaster list— at least none so far."

The admiral twisted his mouth a bit and took a deep breath. "Okay. Where are we on Naples?"

"Waiting to hear more information, Admiral. I have Ensign James calling the NISO now to see where they are and what new info they have. Carl has laid on two reservations for a flight this afternoon to Naples for us to handle the investigation. Considering the potential international PR damage, I will be going to take the lead on this case."

The admiral nodded in agreement. "Who else is going?"

"Ensign James, sir."

"And your logic for that choice? Hell, this is her first day."

"Multiple reasons, sir. First off, since we are dealing with a potential rape, having a woman conduct the victim interview might be a good thing. There are no female agents in Naples. James speaks Italian, much better than I, so that puts us in a positive position with the locals. And finally, this is an excellent opportunity for me to evaluate her actions in the field. This one might provide a good test of her abilities, and I will be there to evaluate."

The admiral nodded. "Again, I cannot argue with your logic. Just be careful over there, and remember you will have a rookie watching your back. Try not to cause a public relations nightmare or get wounded. And you know I do not want to call the CNO and tell him you're in the hospital again!"

Marcus couldn't stop a chuckle from erupting. "Thank you, sir. We will be on our best behavior with our Italian brothers ... and sisters. Now if there is nothing else, I have a lot to get done."

"Carry on, Colt. Keep in touch."

He got a thumbs up from Vic as he exited his office for the IA area. One of the many clocks on the wall indicated it was 0805, so the day had officially started.

Wendy was sitting in his office with her notepad on her lap. She started to rise when Marcus entered, and he quickly responded, "As you were. What ya got?"

"Sir, this is very interesting and extremely weird. The agent who supposedly raped the local girl is still in a coma. Male friends of the girl almost beat him to death. Now the weird part is, neither the girl nor the friends who did the beating can now be located. They gave their initial statements to the local police, and when our agents wanted to talk with them, not one could find them. It's like they didn't exist. So we have no witnesses either for or against."

"And that's why the SSA thinks it's a setup?"

"Yes, sir. But the big question is why. I asked the SSA, a guy named Anthony Carter, why he thought his agent, William Coleman, was attacked. No idea, he said, so I asked him to give me the case numbers

Coleman was working as well as those recently closed. I asked Rita to pull copies for us and to get a copy of Coleman's personnel file."

"Okay, guess that's all we can do right now. After the status meeting, run to your BOQ and pack. Plan on uniforms and civilian agent-type clothing for five days. Hopefully we can wrap it up by then, or sooner— worst case we go shopping. Wear casual civilian clothing for travel since we'll be in the air for a long time. I'll swing by the BOQ and pick you up no later than 1100."

"That's okay, sir. I can catch a cab."

"I will pick you up. Just say 'thank you' and go round up the team."

After Wendy left, Marcus called Kelly and gave her the news. She would have his packing done by the time he got home around 1030 hrs and would drive them to the airport. No need to leave the 'Cuda in long-term parking.

He had just hung up from that call when an outside line rang. "Naval Investigative Service Internal Affairs. Lieutenant Commander Colt speaking. How may I be of assistance, sir?"

A recognizable voice said, "Hello, Marcus. I see you called for my assistant earlier. Anything I can do to help?"

Being on a first name basis with the Secretary of State was still a bit uncomfortable for him. He kept telling Marcus to call him "Harry," but there was still reluctance.

"Good morning, Mr. Secretary, it was not my intent to bother you, sir. What I need is to pass on some information to your people," Marcus replied. Then he filled him in on the problem in Naples, and the plans to address it.

"Thank you, Marcus, for the heads up. One of my people will meet you upon arrival. And by then, they will have cleared the way for you with the local police. Let me know if you need any further assistance. And damn it, if you don't start calling me 'Harry' I will purge you from the Christmas card list!"

"Sir, yes sir, Harry, I will work on that. I promise," he laughed. "I have a similar problem with my father-in-law."

"Trust me, Marcus, you don't want to get on either of our bad sides," Harry responded with a laugh.

Harry sent his love to Kelly, Marcus sent his to Margo, and that concluded the call. Conversations with Harry were enjoyable, even though they often invoked memories of the previous year.

As he hung up, Marcus saw his team lined up at the door, ready for the Monday status meeting. He waved them in and joined them at the conference table. The three officers included Jake Doty, Hank Bates, and Wendy James. Carl was joined by Rita this time, at Marcus's request.

Senior Chief Vic O'Keef was there again to help keep the admiral in the loop. At the last minute, Doc Stevens came in and took the last chair.

"Welcome to Monday morning. Hope y'all had a great weekend, people, because this week is starting off rather nasty, and I suspect it will only get worse. It usually does." Marcus said his standard opening line and received the expected chuckles.

"Before we get lost in the challenges of the day, please officially welcome Ensign Wendy James to our unit. Granted she is new to the Navy and to NIS, but she brings some talents we need here, and an impressive accounting knowledge. Go easy on her for the first hour or so," Marcus concluded with a chuckle.

He then gave them a rundown on the hot issue from Naples. It didn't take long to share all the info they had thus far. And while there wasn't much to go on yet, you go with what ya got. He announced he would be heading up the Naples investigation and leaving before the day was over.

Marcus then pointed to Wendy. "Naples is a potential political nightmare. On a rape case, experience has shown that female victims will respond better to females doing the questioning. Therefore, Wendy will be heading to Naples with me. We'll leave Jake in charge to hopefully keep the home fires burning bright. Rita, since you're already doing some file digging about Naples, you'll be our point of contact here." Rita nodded in agreement.

Marcus pointed toward Carl and Rita. "You two need to coordinate your new schedules. Hate to ask again, but starting Wednesday morning, Rita, we need you here from 0300 until 1100 hours in case we need help in the morning hours of Naples. Will that be a problem?" She shook her head indicating it was not.

Marcus continued. "Then Carl, you will need to hang around here until 1800. Sorry for the long mixed up days again, but considering the importance of these cases, we need you here to back us up. I'll make it up to you. Say, Vic, would you be willing to loan us a yeoman who can be here at night through the early morning as a bridge between Rita and Carl?"

Vic nodded. "Not a problem. YN1 George Russell had so much fun last week that I suspect he'll volunteer again. I'll get with him, Carl, and Rita later today to work out the schedule."

"Thank you, Vic! And other thoughts, people?"

Bates, shaking his head, interjected, "Boss, I have more case experience than Wendy and, therefore, will be a better asset for you in Naples."

"What is your level of spoken Italian, Hank?" Marcus asked.

"I know some Spanish, so I can probably pick up enough Italian to get by."

Ensign James looked at Marcus and asked, "*Quanto velocemente può imparare?*" Then she nodded over at Bates.

Bates looked at her, then Marcus. "What did she say?"

"Hank, in addition to being a female who might help with the rape victim interview, Wendy knows Italian, both spoken and written, and more so than me. Her question in fluent Italian was 'how fast can he learn?' and I hope she was talking about Italian language skills." That got a few chuckles.

"And while this newly wedded gentleman would much rather stay in the vicinity, or at least the same time zone, of his bride, the admiral agreed that my presence, as the IA division leader, might impress the local Italian police and open a few more doors than the standard investigator," Marcus said. Wendy looked a little uncomfortable.

Bates shook his head in resignation. "Well, that stinks, Marcus, but I hope you both have a safe and successful trip." His smile showed approval.

"Thank you, Hank, for seeing and agreeing with the wisdom of your division leader's decisions. You may kiss my ring later." And with that, everyone broke up in laughter: laughter that was needed to dispel the tension that had been generated.

Doc waved his hand as he said, "Can I throw something out, Marcus?"

Marcus nodded. "Dang hard to stop you, Doc. What ya got?"

Doc provided a concise report on the progress, or rather lack thereof, of the Cold Fog task force, ending with comments about the newest member, the Queen's high school buddy. Then he asked, "Can we have Doty and Bates brief the Cold Fog group before they do anything else? We have the written report, but you know the verbal one is always better."

"Sure, Doc. Soon as this meeting is over. And make sure everyone knows Victoria is one of us."

Doc smiled. "Thanks, and can do."

"Okay, before we lose total control—which I so hope Vic will leave out of his update to the admiral—let's wrap this meeting up since I need more coffee." Marcus paused and realized there was another task to be done. When Carl held up a sheet of paper, he motioned him to hold a minute.

Marcus took a deep breath before looking at Wendy. "But first, there is one more piece of housekeeping I need to cover. Wendy, I apologize for not bringing this up earlier. Anyway, know that in our closed-door meetings like this, we frequently forget the formalities of military as we discuss issues. This is the place to air differences, toss out ideas, disagree with plans, and work together to get our jobs done. I suppose we all had a tiring weekend since we haven't had too many loud arguments this morning or interruptions. And as you have just seen and heard, people chosen for assignments are the ones with attributes, whatever they may be, that will hopefully help close the case in short order. Is it fair when you consider seniority, et cetera—probably not. But for us, getting the right answers and closing the cases properly has priority over personal feelings. Around here, the best qualified person gets the job. Any questions?"

"No, sir … eh, no, boss. I appreciate knowing that and will try to argue more in the future," she responded with a smile. That generated a round of applause.

"You're learning, newbie," Hank said.

"Okay, we need to wrap this up and get moving. Carl, is there something we need to discuss from the AUTOVON traffic?"

Carl frowned, solemnly nodded, and quietly said, "The last NIR in the stack was from one of your friends in Norfolk. And they asked specifically for you."

48

WELL, THAT CAME OUT OF nowhere. Marcus asked Carl to pass it to him, and he gave it a quick read. Everyone sat quietly as he read it again slowly. Based on their facial expressions, Marcus knew his face conveyed concern and sadness.

He had made a lot of good friends while working undercover in Norfolk, Virginia earlier that year. One of the young agents with great potential was Bill Collins from NISRA Oceana. *Was* being the key word. Captain Humphrey Miller, CO of NISO Norfolk, had requested IA to investigate the murder of SA Collins by party or parties unknown around midnight. Damn, this loss hurt. He needed to call the skipper for more details.

Marcus slid the NIR down to Hank and said with more emotion than he could control, "Read that aloud, please."

Hank did, and now the rest of the team knew there was a dead agent. He had been shot while investigating a possible breaking and entering at an office on Oceana Naval Air Station. Only a few details were in the NIR, but he shared them. When he finished, he looked at Marcus and quietly asked, "How soon do you want me down there, boss?"

Marcus looked down to gather his thoughts and get his voice under control. He finally answered, "Hank, let me call Captain Miller first. I want you in on that call also, but first I need a few moments alone. Give me five minutes, Hank, okay? That's all for now, folks. Thanks."

As they quietly walked out, Marcus was surprised by the grief that was taking over. Collins was a good agent. Sure, they had only worked together on the viper case, but still it hurt. Probably he was just tired and emotions were taking control.

Five minutes went by fast and the knock on the door was from Hank Bates. Marcus motioned him in. He closed the door, sat in the chair in front of the desk and quietly waited. Marcus picked up the phone, dialed a number that was burned into his memory, and hit the speakerphone button.

"Naval Investigative Service Office Norfolk. Yeoman Second Class Frost speaking. How may I be of assistance, sir?" blasted a familiar voice into the room.

Sorrowfully, he said, "Sid, Marcus Colt. How ya doing, buddy?"

"Better now that you have called, Mark. The skipper has been climbing the walls because of SA Collins. Damn shame what happened. Let me connect you. Take care, sir."

"Thanks, Sid. You too."

In less time that it takes to blink, Captain Miller came on the line. "Marcus, good to hear from you, although the circumstances are bad. I have Sam with me. When can we expect to see you? And can you send John Driscol and Douglas Knox back ASAP?"

"Sorry for the delay in calling, Captain. It has been a rough morning here as well. Bill's death is tearing me up, sir—he was a fine agent and a good friend."

"We're all in shock about it, Marcus."

"Captain, I'm sorry, but I cannot come to Norfolk. But I will have John and Doug on the way to you later today."

"Damn, we really need your help. What has a higher priority than a dead agent?"

"Sir, I am leaving for Naples in a couple of hours. We have there what could grow into an international incident, so I've got to put the fires out. We have an agent accused of raping a local girl, and her friends nearly beat him to death. He is in a coma, and the girl and witnesses have now vanished. Looks like a setup to cover up something, and I have to discover what—as well as keep the local press from having an anti-American field day."

The captain mumbled something vulgar and said, "Well, I can understand that getting your personal touch. Do you have a backup to send down?"

"On the other side of the speakerphone is one of my people, 1stLt Hank Bates, USMC. He is ready to drive down shortly to handle the investigation. What other information has been found since the NIR was written?"

"Hey, Marcus, Sam here. Ruby is now cutting the tape on an update and we will have Dexter or Rhonda send it to you within the next thirty minutes. It's just too much to cover over the phone. By the way, we miss you around here, buddy."

"Thanks, Sam. Kelly, Doc, and I miss you too, but really miss you always buying lunch. Speaking of lunch, Mr. Bates should be there around lunchtime, so take him to your seafood place for a face-to-face update. He is a good investigator, and Doc made sure he is trained on the index card method, so take good care of him."

The captain said, "We certainly will, Marcus. Lieutenant, come directly to the NISO office and ask for me when you get here. Give my love to Kelly, Marcus. All for now." The dial tone filled the room.

Marcus smiled at Hank. "Glad I didn't have anything else to add."

Hank chuckled. "He is direct and to the point." Then he got serious and asked, "What can you tell me about Bill Collins?"

For the next twenty minutes, Marcus gave Hank an overview on SA Collins, NAS Oceana, and the key players at NISO Norfolk and NISRA Norfolk. He wrapped up the overview by telling him about the yeomen in the AUTOVON room, both Rhonda and Dexter, and finished it off with a description of one person who always made him smile: Ruby, the lady in charge of the NISRA secretaries.

Mrs. Ruby Judge was a hoot. She reminded him of the actress Elsa Lanchester when she was playing the somewhat strange aunt in *Bell, Book and Candle* with Jimmy Stewart. Short, a bit overweight, early fifties, married, glasses perched on the end of her nose, and a big smile that looked like the grin of a tiger. Marcus finished the overview with one final comment: "But she is the one to ask when you need something, so get on her good side quick."

A knock on the door was followed by a clerk from the computer room opening it and sticking his head in. "Sorry to interrupt, sir, but I have a high priority ROI from Norfolk for you."

"Thanks, Jon. Bring it on and give it to Mr. Bates. It's his problem now."

49

MARCUS PARKED THE 'CUDA IN front of his townhouse rather than in the garage. He didn't plan on being there long. He wasn't looking forward to being away from Kelly, and really wasn't looking forward to telling her the news. Bill had become a fixture around their house in Norfolk over the summer, and Kelly thought of him as another one of the adopted brothers.

"What's going on, honey, you look really down," asked Kelly when she opened the front door.

"Your Uncle Humphrey sends his love. I talked with him just a bit ago to get more information on the murder of Special Agent Bill Collins. I'm so sorry, Kelly."

Kelly's eyes filled with tears and she hugged him tight, sobbing. After a couple of minutes, she got control and pulled back. "What the hell happened?"

As succinctly as possible, Marcus gave her the known details and the plans for the investigation as they walked up to the bedroom to get his luggage and change clothes.

"I'll find out about the arrangements, and if you're not back from Italy in time, I'll go to the funeral alone," she said.

"You'll not be alone. Doc knows about Bill, and he offered to go with you if I'm stuck in Naples. It's going to be a rough week for us all."

Kelly had expertly packed all that would be needed, and even laid out his standard semi-dress casual wear for the trip: jeans, yellow button-down oxford cloth shirt, and dark blue sports jacket. Marcus changed and they headed out. Kelly offered to drive the 'Cuda, so Marcus settled down in the passenger bucket seat.

"My partner on this trip is our newest IA agent, Ensign Wendy James. I selected her because she is fluent in Italian, and if we can find the rape victim ... as a woman, she might have better luck with that interview. Since you haven't met her yet, I offered to pick her up."

"What's she like?" Kelly asked.

"Intelligent and beautiful are the first two attributes that stand out. She picks up on things quickly, it seems, and holds an accounting degree from Washington and Lee. She is new to NIS and new to the Navy, so this will give me a chance to give her an initial evaluation. I want your thoughts about her, since your gut is getting to be as sharp as mine."

"Beautiful, eh?" Kelly chuckled and punched his arm. "And now you are taking her to Italy, also. Just make sure you don't consider this trip another honeymoon, sailor."

"I will be on my best behavior, dearest, since my body and soul belong to you."

50

WENDY WAS STANDING OUTSIDE THE BOQ, waving, when the 'Cuda pulled up. Marcus had told her to watch out for a yellow Barracuda. Her choice of casual travel attire was similar to his, consisting of jeans, a light blue oxford cloth blouse, and a dark blue jacket. *It's true that great minds think alike*, Marcus thought.

Spotting Wendy, Kelly looked over at Marcus. "Your vocabulary needs work, babe. I really should have bought you that dictionary back in Norfolk. I think you need to add an adverb or two to that 'beautiful' description—maybe 'outstandingly' or 'extremely' would work, or better yet, use both together. Wow, she's a knockout."

"Jealous?" he asked with a grin.

"No, and don't give me a reason to be."

"You have my heart, Kelly."

"And all the rest of you, too," she said, her smile kicked up in a left hook.

Marcus got out and loaded Wendy's bags into the back of the car. He then climbed into the back seat, giving Wendy the front so she could get to know Kelly. Introductions over, they headed to Dulles International Airport, located about an hour away and east of Reston, Virginia.

By the time they arrived at the short-term parking, Kelly and Wendy were chatting like they had been friends for decades. Kelly was all smiles, showing Marcus that her take on Wendy was a positive one. She winked at him in the rearview mirror.

With the baggage checked, they picked up their tickets and boarding passes. Carl had gotten them seats in first class, since coach was sold out. *We all have to sacrifice at times*, Marcus thought, *and traveling first class is my contribution to the cause.*

Kelly had a meeting with the head psychologist at Walter Reed in a couple of hours, so she couldn't stay until the plane departed. She quickly hugged Wendy and made her promise to watch Marcus's back. Kelly and Marcus walked over to a quiet area to say goodbye in as much privacy as a busy airport would allow.

"I like her, Marcus. Initial gut analysis is that she's honest and she doesn't realize how beautiful she is. You're right, she is very intelligent. I didn't feel any hidden agendas. She can join the harem if she wants." Kelly giggled and winked. "But you can only kiss her in the line of duty, sailor."

"You do know you're crazy, don't ya?" Marcus laughed while shaking his head.

"Crazy about you, Marcus." Kelly pulled him closer and leaned her head against his chest. "Hate to say it, babe, but I have to go and leave you two alone."

"I know. Hope your first day goes well tomorrow. Wish I could be here to see you off and pack your lunch bag. I'll call when I can, but remember there's a six-hour time difference. Love you so much."

After a hug and a couple of kisses, she softly said, "Stay safe. Shoot straight. I need you, sailor."

"Always for you, Princess," he whispered. Her eyes were glistening as she touched his cheek and walked toward the exit. *Ugh, this trip stinks already.*

Marcus hated to see her go, but really enjoyed watching her walk away. He chuckled to himself, remembering an early rock and roll song called *"Poetry in Motion."* Yea, *that's my Kelly.*

The princess had left the building, so it was time to get back in agent mode. Glancing back over to where they had left Wendy, he saw her smile and give a small nod. "What?" He sat down beside her.

"Seeing love is wonderful, and seeing the special love that you two have is even more so. I pray that someday I get to have that. She is a very special lady, Mr. Colt."

"Thanks. I know how lucky I am. Just be patient and the right guy will come along for you, Wendy."

"I'll try, sir."

Since they had time before the flight, and the waiting area was empty enough for some privacy, Marcus decided it was time to share the rules. Well, not official NIS rules, but rules he'd established for working cases.

"Wendy, when we are not in uniform, we usually work on a first name basis. Avoid the 'sir' and other military pleasantries. You'll need to follow my lead, as there might be times when we need to be more formal. If you hear me call you 'Miss James,' then call me 'Mr. Colt,' otherwise stick with first names. When in uniform, we maintain standard military protocol when around others. Alone, we can be less formal. I know it might sound confusing, but after a short time, it becomes second nature."

"I think I can keep up, Marcus," she answered with a smile.

They talked about how other cases had progressed and how the agents handled various situations. Without much to go on for this case, they knew they'd be at a disadvantage to start. Marcus then mentioned that a representative from the State Department would be meeting them at the Naples airport.

"How did that happen?"

"I called the Secretary's assistant this morning to give them a heads up about the potentially damaging situation. The Secretary himself returned my call and offered to have one of his guys assigned to help us. So hopefully, some doors will be easier to open over there."

Wendy had a confused look. "How well do you know the Secretary of State? I don't think he usually goes around making personal calls to naval investigators."

"That was the result of an operation I handled last year in Vietnam. It is still classified higher than the usual NIS levels, so I can't talk about it. Let's just say the secretary and I became personal friends, and he helps watch our backs."

"Wow, now that is interesting. Seems there's a lot more than meets the eye with you, Marcus. I think hanging around you is going to result in some very exciting times."

They talked about NIS methods and procedures until their boarding was called. They were in the nose of a 747–100, row five. Wendy wanted the window seat and Marcus obliged. He had gotten to where flying was boring—the sooner he fell asleep, the better. Especially since he just did the trip to Italy a few weeks ago. *Probably on this same Boeing 747,* he thought. He wondered if this was what Yogi called "déjà vu all over again."

They spent the first few hours reviewing the case files Rita had pulled. Perhaps there was something in them that triggered the situation with William Coleman. They went through them twice without finding anything. At least that info was planted in their brains, just in case.

As they finished the last file and stuffed them back into the briefcase, it was dinnertime. The steak was actually above average, and as Marcus started eating, it hit him that they had skipped lunch. Probably it wouldn't be the last time that week. With dinner over, a round of drinks was served, the cabin lights were lowered, and the in-flight film started. It was one released the previous year—a well-done movie about the Japanese attack on Pearl Harbor: *Tora! Tora! Tora!* Hopefully, the disaster that hit the Navy in 1941 would not repeat for them in Naples. He drifted off to sleep before the first plane with meatballs on its wings took off to sink the USS *Arizona*.

51

NISO NORFOLK WAS LOCATED ON the second floor of the 5th Naval District Headquarters building, on the main drag of the base. 1stLt Hank Bates pulled into the closest visitor-parking slot he could find a few minutes before 1200 hrs. A slight cool rain, heavier than a mist but lighter than drizzle, was falling in Norfolk that afternoon.

But he was ready. The standard Marine saying is to "improvise, adapt, overcome," and while that's a good rule to live by, Hank liked to plan ahead, so had packed an umbrella after calling the base weather office for an update.

The petty officer at the entry to NISO Norfolk had been told to expect a NISHQ agent, and after inspecting Hank's identification, directed him to Captain Miller's office. Hank had just rounded the corridor corner leading to that office when he almost bumped into the captain.

"Excuse me, sir. Captain Miller?" Hank had stepped back to keep from slamming into the naval officer.

"Welcome, Lieutenant Bates. You are just in time to join us for lunch. Good news—I've convinced Sam to both drive us and pick up the tab. And yes, I am Miller. This is SSA Sam Maker." Captain Miller extended his hand, as did Sam.

The drive to the restaurant was filled with the normal pleasantries and the captain's questions about Hank's background and training. The skipper did a great job of interrogating the people working for and around him.

Hank's physical attributes were obvious. He was a Caucasian male in his mid-twenties. He stood about 5'10" and was in good physical shape. *He is probably a body builder,* the skipper thought. A blond flattop haircut and square jaw screamed "Marine Corps" even without the visual of his perfectly creased uniform. After a few specific questions, Captain Miller and Sam Maker knew Hank was single, from Michigan, had graduated from Penn State with a law degree, and had been with NIS for two years.

Between bites of stuffed flounder, Hank asked, "Sir, is there any more information about the shooting, aside from the ROI that was sent earlier?"

Sam shook his head. "Hank, sorry, no. As soon as we finish here, we're heading to Oceana to see the scene. The agents have been on site since the shooting, and all the documentation is there for your analysis."

"Thank you, sir," Hank said, and he looked at Captain Miller. "Sir, Mr. Colt asked that we have LtCol Tiller run a full BI on SA Collins to set a base line. Mr. Colt greatly admired Collins and has no reason to think anything is off. He just wants to make sure everything is done by the book."

The captain grimaced, and with a harsher tone, said, "It will be so ordered. And I agree with Colt, Bill Collins was a fine man and an outstanding agent with a promising career."

Sam saw a confrontation starting and tried to defuse the situation. "Captain, we are just following standard protocols. Hank is doing his job asking to make sure that was done."

The captain nodded, and after a moment or two finally said, "Agreed. Sorry to be short, gentlemen."

"It has been a rough day for everyone, Captain," said Hank, trying in his way to calm the rough waters. "How about we finish lunch and head to Oceana?"

Sam smiled as he looked at Captain Miller. "Marcus taught this one well, Skipper. Let's follow him and see what he finds."

Hank ended up interrogating Sam and the skipper on the way to Oceana. He now understood why Marcus held both men in high regard, and felt proud that Marcus had given him this assignment. Then he prayed he would lead an investigation that would make Marcus proud of his work.

Arriving at Naval Air Station Oceana, a thirty-year-old air base located in Virginia Beach, Virginia, Hank was anxious to learn about the place that was the home of the Navy's most advanced aircraft. The base had a twenty-four-hour flight schedule, with several hundred flights each day. It was the home of all East coast-based F-4 Phantom squadrons.

Driving several blocks from the hangars and flight line, they came to a nondescript building. It was several stories high and featured a truck-bed-high loading dock on the left side. Several large air conditioning units ran down the right side. Hank could not view the back, but he figured he would soon enough. He spotted several official cars parked near the loading dock; strings of yellow "POLICE LINE DO NOT CROSS" barricade tape ran from the dock toward the back of the building.

Sam stopped his car near the front door, and as they exited the vehicle, Hank looked up at the sign over the door. In bold letters it proclaimed, Naval Research Laboratory Oceana.

"Oh, crap," Hank muttered under his breath.

52

HIS INTERNAL SENSORS NOTICED A change and told his brain to wake him up. The engine sound was different, and they were no longer level. As Marcus came to consciousness, he realized they were descending, hopefully toward Heathrow and the next step in this adventure. It was never safe to assume. A quick check of his watch showed it to be just after midnight D.C. time, or a little after 0500 in the UK.

He started to move, then noticed a weight on his left arm, which had been resting on the console between the seats. Wendy was sleeping, using his arm as a pillow. He reached over and gently touched the tip of her nose; it was enough to bring her out of slumber. She opened her eyes, realized where she was, and quickly sat up straight.

"Sorry, Marcus." Her cheeks showed a bit of red.

"Not a problem, Wendy. I'm always happy to help a lady in distress and look, no drool on the sleeve. All is good," he whispered. "We are less than an hour out and it feels like we started the descent. It's time for us to come alive and get ready for the next leg of this journey."

As they walked by the almost middle-aged flight attendant on the way out just under an hour later, she thanked them for flying TWA and commented, "You two make such a cute couple. Enjoy your stay in the UK."

While Wendy blushed, Marcus smiled and thanked the attendant. When farther away, Wendy turned to him. "Well, that was embarrassing. Hope Kelly doesn't hear about it. Why didn't you correct her, sir?"

"Just following some of the rules I try to live by, Wendy. First off, it would have embarrassed her to be corrected when she was just being nice. Now she might have a better day, thinking she helped make us feel good. And there was no harm done aside from your red cheeks. Next point, always graciously accept the honest compliments you receive, for one day they might stop coming. And only object to a compliment if it is a bold-faced lie. Look over there." Marcus pointed to their reflection in the huge glass window. "See, we are a cute couple, at least to the outside world." They continued their walk to the center of the concourse to find the departure board for their next flight.

"Just as long as Kelly doesn't find out about that," she said.

"Actually, I plan to tell her when I call. She'll get a chuckle out of it since she really likes you. And as part of your training, here are a few more facts to keep in mind. If this were an undercover mission, being a 'cute couple' could work to our advantage. It might make it easier to blend with crowds, or at a restaurant. A couple walking arm in arm looks less dangerous than two ugly guys in suits trying to look inconspicuous."

"Yea, I can see how that would work."

"On top of that, an embrace or a kiss is a good way to hide your face from the bad guys. Or if we needed to stay in close contact and watch both directions in this area, standing facing away from each other would be noticed. However, if we were over to the side, embracing like Kelly and I did earlier, then we could watch both directions, and most people would look away from us to give us privacy."

"I have so much to learn. And none of this was covered in the agent training course. Why not?"

Before he could answer, Marcus noticed a gentleman holding a sign that read "M. Colt" in bold letters. His coat and tie, as well as the small bulge on his left hip, told him he was local police, Scotland Yard, or NIS. Marcus hoped for NIS as he walked toward him.

"Hi there. I'm Melvin Colter, are you looking for me?" Marcus asked.

The man with the sign looked him up and down and, with a thick Irish accent, replied, "Sorry, you don't look like a Melvin, bud. But you certainly do look a lot like Marcus Colt, whose photo was in the NIS newsletter a couple of months ago expounding about your great work in Norfolk, sir. Happy to meet you, Mr. Colt." He lowered the sign and extended his hand. "Admiral Chance said if I didn't catch you before you got on the Naples flight, I might never get another day off. I do hope that was a jest on his part, so here I am, very happy to see you. SA Colin Daley, NISRA London, at your service, sir."

"That sounds like the admiral. But for the record, his bite is far worse than his bark, so it's good you are here. This is Ensign Wendy James, Colin."

"Truly my pleasure, Ensign James. Now if you will follow me please. My friends from Scotland Yard offered the use of their office here, for us to have a short private talk. We have something that wouldn't be right to talk about here in the middle of the thoroughfare. This way." And he headed off toward the row of doors across from the bar.

Marcus looked at Wendy, they both shrugged, and walked fast to catch up with Colin. The office had a sign indicating it was a Scotland Yard office, but that was not necessary as police departments have a certain look and smell.

"Tea, anyone?" Colin asked, then continued without waiting for an answer. "You have about two hours before your Naples flight leaves, so plenty of time for a cup or even a snack if you need one."

Wendy shook her head, and Marcus responded, "Thanks, but business first. What did the admiral need?" They all sat around a table to the side of the room.

Colin reached inside his jacket pocket and pulled out an envelope. He handed it to Marcus. "He insisted you get this ASAP. Not good news, I'm afraid."

The envelope contained two sheets of paper in standard ROI format. The first was an update on the Naples case: SA William Coleman died without regaining consciousness. There was still no word on the possible rape victim or the men who beat up Coleman. The admiral had added a note to the bottom—"Stay in civilian attire. The consul general will have special identification for you and will explain. Use it and not your military IDs. Stay safe. Chance." He passed the ROI to Wendy and said, "Well, this trip just got more interesting."

The second sheet of paper was a ROI on the death of Agent Collins: There were a couple of possible leads based on fingerprint evidence collected. Analysis of the slug didn't show any connections to other shootings thus far. Data had been passed to the FBI. It was probably a .38 Special, so there was no casing left at the scene. The building burglarized was the research lab, which held a half-dozen different departments, all focusing on experimental equipment. Nothing else to report at this time. It also went to Wendy. She had finished the first and passed it back to Marcus.

"Thanks, Colin. If there is nothing else, I hope you know which gate we need to use for the Naples leg. My brain still needs a few hours of sleep."

"Nothing else, Mr. Colt. Please accept my condolences on the loss of the two agents. I understand that Agent Collins was a personal friend. That makes it so much harder. All of us in the NISRA hope you get the evil bastards that did that. And yes, I can lead you to your gate, or you both are welcome to enjoy the silence and solitude of this office. I will be happy to roust you out in time to catch your flight."

"I have a better idea, Colin—actually two ideas. Call me Marcus. And join us at the bar across the way for a quick pint to help clean the cob webs out of our travel-destroyed brains." Wendy nodded her agreement.

"Excellent plan, Marcus. I'll just think of it as being late last night and not early this morning."

53

A BEER AND A HANDFUL of salted snacks in the Heathrow bar helped get the mental juices flowing, and they had a great chat with Colin. He gave them a quick rundown on some interesting cases open in NISRA London. After expressing their thanks and goodbyes to Colin, Wendy and Marcus got on the Alitalia Douglas DC-8 for the two-hour trip to Naples.

Italy's airline provided excellent service, and they enjoyed a great breakfast as they crossed the English Channel and France, toward the Mediterranean. The peak of Mount Vesuvius appeared faster than expected, and for the second time in six weeks, Marcus was back in Italy. He reset his watch to local time: almost 0900.

They had just exited the gate area and started looking for the signs to baggage claim when Marcus noticed a serious-seeming young woman standing to the side, intently looking around. She made a beeline for them, a slight smile forming on her face. Marcus hoped she was the contact from state.

Dressed in an expensive, sleek, dark blue suit, with a white blouse and bright red scarf hanging loose around her neck, she gave off an air of power. Her jet-black hair was pulled back in a ponytail, and dark framed glasses seemed to overpower her face. The darkness of the hair and glasses made her face look a bit pale, as did her red lipstick. Her face was average in appearance, and her makeup was light. Marcus thought her nose was a bit large for her face. She was probably a couple of pounds overweight; most folks would call her big boned. This lady could easily fall into the not-very-memorable category were it not for her attire and the attitude she projected. There was power there. And a magnetism.

She also wore a wedding ring and a decent-sized diamond on the left hand, and a nice-sized ruby ring on the right. A small gold chain circling her neck held a small diamond and matched her earrings.

As she neared, her smile got brighter, and she pulled a small black folder from her pocket. She flashed her ID like a professional law enforcement officer would. It was a U.S. State Department ID. Her photo had the serious look Marcus saw earlier.

"Mr. Colt, Miss James, my name is Susan Woodward, from the Public Affairs Section of the U.S. Consulate General Naples. The Secretary called the consul general yesterday, and he sent me to take good care of you. I do hope you had a good flight."

"Thank you, Mrs. Woodward. We appreciate you meeting us. I assume you have a car to get us to whatever hotel holds our reservation. When we left D.C., that trivial stuff was still in the works. They did contact you about that, I hope."

Marcus noticed Wendy looking Mrs. Woodward over, and while her expression was almost a blank slate, he thought he saw a touch of concern.

"Yes, to all, but first we need to step over to that office"—she pointed across the way to several doors on the far wall—"and conclude a bit of business. This way, please." She laid her hand on Marcus's arm and steered him in the right direction before taking the lead.

"Certainly." Marcus motioned Wendy to follow her, and he joined the small parade last.

The door did not have a sign indicating the primary use of the office, but like the room in Heathrow, this place had the look and feel of law enforcement. A man in a dark business suit, presenting a stone face, stood when they entered.

Marcus looked around. "Is this the local Arma dei Carabinieri office?"

Mrs. Woodward chuckled and replied, "No, sir, this is the office of the Polizia di Stato. Since they handle most tourist issues, visas and such, they were happy to allow us its use for a quick meeting to straighten out your status. This is my assistant, Gregory Walker. Please have a seat."

Marcus sat across from Gregory with his hands interlocked on the table, and Wendy faced Mrs. Woodward holding her purse in her lap. "And our status is … what?" he asked.

Her smile expanded as she relaxed a bit. Gregory, still projecting his stone face, pulled a couple of black folders from his briefcase.

Mrs. Woodward continued, "Your admiral and the Secretary put their heads together after you left D.C. We are pleased they figured out the best way for you to do your job here in Naples. We tried, but we failed to convince the Italians that it was safe for you to carry weapons, which I know you have on your persons right now. The admiral insisted that you be allowed to do so. After all, you are investigating what is now the murder of one of your agents."

Marcus nodded his head. "I must agree with the admiral on this issue."

"As does the Secretary. Under his direct order, while you are in Italy, you are now assigned to our office as investigative agents. As members of the diplomatic corps, you now have diplomatic immunity. You may carry your weapons," she explained as she again laid her hand on Marcus's arm.

"So that clears up the admiral's note about wearing civilian clothing and not using our military IDs."

Greg checked each folder, then slid one to Wendy and handed one to Marcus. He checked that his name was spelled correctly and all other data was right. Looking at Mrs. Woodward, he had to ask, "So are we now required to call you 'boss?' And since you have dished out the sugar, what is the vinegar you will now dump on us?"

"Mr. Colt, I …"

"Please call me Marcus."

"Wonderful. Our friends call us Sue and Greg, and I hope you both will fit into that category," she said, and even Greg broke his mold and smiled. "Marcus, I do not have any vinegar, but there are a couple of requirements that I believe you will find acceptable."

For the first time since Sue approached them, Wendy spoke up, asking the question that was on both their minds. "Sue, when was the last time you saw your boss at Langley?" Now Marcus knew what was behind her look a bit ago.

Sue's smile dropped a few percentage points, then she nodded. "I can see the Secretary was correct when he said you two were very good at your jobs. Okay, Greg and I have not been in our Langley offices for a few months now, really almost a year, but we keep in contact."

"I—well *we*—appreciate openness between friends," Wendy replied with her soft Virginian voice, and displayed one of those shark-like smiles.

Marcus nodded in agreement, and pointed toward Sue. "I think the way you displayed your ID was a giveaway that you had a law enforcement background. Where did you work before the Agency? And you were going to tell us some requirements, right?"

"Yes, sir, uh, Marcus. I was with the FBI for a year before I was recruited by the Agency. Greg joined the Agency right out of college. Now as for the requirements, they are not too terrible."

"Do we need to take notes?" inquired Wendy.

"Oh, no. The biggest one is that one of us, Greg or I—more than likely it will be me—will be with you whenever you leave the Consulate General grounds. With one of us driving, you'll be able to get around much faster and we will make sure you don't have any issues with the locals. Just think of us as a driver and a social buffer combined."

"That will work," Marcus said. "And the other requirements?"

"Again, nothing really nasty. The Secretary decided that you staying on the grounds had several advantages. We have a visitor's residence that will provide proper security and allow quick access to high-end communication equipment. Our goals are to keep you safe and help you wrap up the case. Any further questions, or can we take a short drive and get you settled into your rooms?"

"Lead on, Sue, the day is young and the game is afoot."

Sue chuckled. "Do I need to call you Sherlock?"

"No, not yet. We haven't yet solved this case, right, Doctor Wendy?"

Wendy shook her head, exhaled a long sigh, and muttered, "It's going to be a long few days, I feel."

54

GREG PICKED UP THE LUGGAGE while Sue escorted them through Customs. Having a set of diplomatic credentials reduced the hassle and delays. Actually, *reduced* was the wrong word: they were totally eliminated. Marcus decided he could get used to having this black folder.

The small limo, a black Mercedes with diplomatic plates, was parked next to one of the many *no parking* signs right outside the door. The driver, a local hired full time by the State Department, was partitioned off from the seating area. Greg and Sue took the rear-facing seats while Wendy and Marcus rested in the larger forward-facing seats.

Sue was quiet for the first few moments of the drive, then it was like a switch was thrown that made her explode. "Marcus, I have been so looking forward to meeting you," she almost gushed as she laid her hand on his knee. "What you did for the Secretary last year in Vietnam was so amazing."

He felt his anger start to boil and wished Doc was here to help keep him calm. Marcus glanced over at Wendy; she barely moved her head side to side. She had seen his demeanor changing and was pulling a "Doc," trying to keep him under control. Marcus took a deep breath. "That mission is still classified and you should not even know about, much less be talking about it."

Sue smiled, not what he expected. "I was told all about it late last year. And I do mean all the details. I guess the guy who spilled the beans knew I wasn't a foreign agent. And before you blow up, Marcus, you need to know I was with my immediate family sitting around the Thanksgiving table when Dad, also known as Mr. Secretary to many, and Harry to you, told his immediate family all about it. It was a limited and very secure audience. You were invited, but you begged off saying work got in the way. I'm looking forward to meeting Doc one of these days too. You guys are amazing, and our family is in your debt. Thank you, Marcus."

Well, that shut him up. Sue was the daughter that Harry had bragged about so much when the team finally got him back from the bad guys and out of danger.

"Okay, Sue, since you're Harry's daughter, I can see where you might have the need to know. You're welcome and it was my honor, by the way. Has Greg been briefed too?"

Greg opened his mouth for the first time. "No, Marcus, I don't have all the details. I just know the end result, and like Sue, there are many of us in the State Department, as well as in the dark corners of Langley, who are grateful to you and the SEAL teams. And no, we do not sit around chatting about it."

Greg had a rather thick Boston accent. Standing just over six feet tall, he was taller and heavier than Marcus, and his suit failed to hide a muscular physique. Greg looked like he could handle himself. That might come in handy.

Sue chuckled. "I have to admit, Marcus, you are not what I expected."

"I get that a lot, it seems."

"Based on Dad's comments and description, I was sort of expecting you to get off the plane wearing a tux, and introduce yourself as 'Colt, Marcus Colt' while looking around for a shaken martini."

Marcus chuckled a bit. "Well, since your dad is a senior diplomat, he is prone to embellishments."

Wendy was having trouble keeping her facial expressions under control. Marcus knew he'd be hit with more than a few questions when they were alone.

"Enough about classified history. Is there any progress on the situation that brought us across the big pond in such a hurry?" Marcus asked.

Sue shook her head. "Nothing new. After we drop your luggage off and you have a minute or two to freshen up, the consul general wants a moment of your time. After that, we'll head directly to the hospital.

I assumed you want to see the body of Agent Coleman and review the medical records. Then we will go over to the NISO office, introduce you to the staff there, and give you a chance to review their case files. After that, it will probably be lunch time and, if it goes well, maybe SSA Tony Carter will pick up the lunch tab. Does that work for you?"

"Boss, you have a great plan laid out. Let's make it happen," Marcus agreed.

55

IT WAS EASY TO SEE where some of the extensive State Department budget was spent. The rooms in the visitor's residence were more lavish than any of the hotels where Marcus had laid his head, including those in D.C., New York, or even the Fairmont in San Francisco. *Guess they're frequently used for visiting royalty,* he thought. Not complaining: just noting his surroundings and again accepting the fact that sacrifices needed to be made for NIS.

They were given a two-bedroom suite with a common sitting room. The large windows in the sitting room overlooked the Gulf of Naples, visible from the two sofas that faced a coffee table. A carafe of coffee was on the small dining table on the other side of the room. Sue had reserved this space since she thought Wendy and Marcus would need a place to work on the case in private.

It was only a little after 1000 hrs local time, but their bodies were still working on 0400 Eastern Standard time, and the strong Italian coffee was not totally compensating for that. Though tired and out of sync, they still had a job to do, and rest could come later. A quick brushing of the teeth and a combing of the hair was their version of freshening up, and they were ready to move on to the next meet.

Before they left the suite, Marcus asked, "I suppose you had a chat with SA Doc Stevens about some of my facial expressions, right?"

Wendy gave a sheepish smile and nodded. "At lunch on Saturday, he said that if I was ever *stuck* as your partner—his word, sir, not mine—I was to watch your face and give you small signals. Like I did in the limo. Sorry, but he made me promise."

Marcus just shook his head and finally said, "No harm done. Fact is, thanks for your help. Guess we need to go do another meet and greet."

The meeting with the consul general was short and to the point. He was glad they were there, he asked if they needed anything, and he told them not to cause an international incident. *Fair and detailed enough,* Marcus thought. He immediately liked the guy, since he presented a no-bull welcome speech. The consul general concluded by hoping they would find time to join him for dinner while in Italy. That might happen, Marcus told him. After thanking him for his hospitality and extensive support, they departed his elegant office.

Sue was outside his door and guided them out of the building. A cream-colored four-door sedan—Marcus wasn't sure of the make and model, but it was an Italian-built vehicle—was waiting. Smaller than the limo and not as fancy, it would be their chariot through the streets of this Italian town, in search of the bad guys. Sue would drive and be the tour guide that day. First stop was the hospital: one place Marcus really hated visiting.

The U.S. Naval Hospital Naples was north of the airport, about a dozen miles from the consulate. Sue took them down some narrow and congested streets rather than the faster multi-lane highways. About ten minutes into the journey, she pulled over to the side of the street and expressed the reason for the scenic route.

Pointing to a small alley off to the right, she said, "Thought you might like to see the place where Agent Coleman was found. A pair of local police officers noticed several men and a woman standing over a man on the ground. It was surprising they did not run off. They cooperated with the officers after the ambulance carried the unconscious agent to the hospital."

"I assume the NISO has copies of the police reports and photos."

"Yes, they do, Marcus. And your people took their own photos yesterday morning as soon as they were contacted."

"Not much to see here," added Wendy.

"Sue, we will need to do a walk through of this place later. Time to get the hospital visit behind us. I suspect they will want to ship the body home later today."

They drove on in silence. Marcus focused his mind and started a list of potential reasons for the beating, with rape at the top of the list, of course. It was frustrating that there wasn't much information available right then. Before the sun set, perhaps there would be something they could start linking together.

The hospital was a nice-looking building, and reports Marcus had read said it was one of the best-staffed in Europe. Since their car had diplomatic plates, Sue parked right outside the main door under a *no parking* sign. A tall, silver haired, doctor-looking man, complete with the expected lab coat and stethoscope, and a stout, middle-aged nurse holding a large brown envelope, walked up to the car as they got out.

The man extended his hand. "Lieutenant Commander Colt, I am Captain Sean Smithson, commanding officer of this hospital, and this is Commander Karen Caston, chief nurse. Greg Walker from the consulate called to tell us you were coming, and why. And while the circumstances are not pleasant, welcome to our hospital."

"Pleased to meet you both, sir, ma'am. This is Miss Wendy James, one of my agents, and Mrs. Susan Woodward from the consulate. I appreciate you meeting us and would greatly appreciate you not using our military ranks. I promise we will try to get out of your way as fast as possible. First, we need to see the body of our agent."

"Of course. Let's step inside and I'll show you to the morgue."

As with most hospitals Marcus had visited, the morgue was in the basement. They took the elevator down, and the captain led them directly to the morgue office, where they met another captain. This one was the chief forensic pathologist and was in charge of the morgue. His name tag read "Spearman," and he reminded Marcus of his high school physics teacher. Spearman was a large man and had short blond hair sticking out in several directions, from wearing headgear. A slight German accent emitted from a ruddy face.

Captain Smithson did the introductions, and Captain Franz Spearman led them into autopsy and over to a bank of small square doors on a refrigeration unit. He opened the second from the top in the first row, which placed it about waist level for Marcus. He pulled out a tray containing the covered body of the agent, just far enough to expose the head and shoulders. He gently pulled back the cover to expose his face. Even after clean up, it was a mess. A closed-casket funeral was coming, unless the undertaker was damn good with makeup.

"As you can see, Mr. Colt, he was severely beaten. He also received multiple blows to his torso."

"Pull him farther out, sir, and remove the sheet, please." The captain did, revealing that the bruising on the chest and abdomen was extensive. There was more purple and blue coloring than there was flesh tone. His thighs showed evidence of bruising too. His hands indicated that he had fought back to some degree, but with the police report listing five men as the attackers, he didn't have much of a chance. "I assume he sustained similar bruising on his back, also?"

"Yes. Almost the same amount as his chest. My autopsy showed he died from a heart attack. I suspect the trauma of the beating was just too much for him. At the age of forty-eight, he had over thirty years of smoking damage to his body. Add to that a bit of a weight issue and stress from his job—it's surprising he survived the beating for as long as he did. I'm sorry for your loss."

"Any evidence of sexual activity within the last twenty-four hours of the attack?"

"Not a bit. Due to the nature of his assault, he was thoroughly examined upon arrival. For a man who supposedly had just raped a girl, it is surprising there was no semen, no vaginal fluids, no pubic hairs that were not his, and no evidence of minor abrasions on his penis from an unwanted forced entry. No tooth marks either. Furthermore, his body doesn't have any of the usual fingernail scratches or bite marks a victim frequently leaves on the attacker. In my opinion, this man did not rape anyone."

Marcus turned to ask Wendy if she had any questions, and saw that she was standing by the door with Sue. Wendy looked a little pale. Instead, he directed his attention to Sue. "Mrs. Woodward, please contact the Italian medical examiner's office and ask their head doctor to come over here today to confer with Dr. Spearman. I want the Italians to be convinced that the rape did not occur."

"Yes, sir, I'll make the call," Sue replied and left the room.

Marcus turned back to face Spearman, paused a moment as he again looked at the body between them, and finally said, "Thank you, doctor. I will need a copy of your report, all the photos you took, lab reports, etc."

Nurse Caston spoke up. "Mr. Colt, I have all that for you here. I also included a complete copy of his medical records from both the ER and the ward, and his last physical. It's everything we have." She extended the large brown envelope.

"Excellent, Commander, thank you." Marcus stashed the envelope in his briefcase and turned back to Doctor Spearman. "Have all the arrangements been made for sending him home?"

"Yes, sir, they have. He will be heading home later tonight. He was divorced, and his next-of-kin is a son who lives in Portland, Maine."

Marcus nodded and took one last look at SA William Coleman. He'd never met him while he was alive, but he was one of the NIS team. "Rest easy, William," he said under his breath.

Wendy was more than happy to get out of the morgue and the hospital. She admitted it was her first visit to a morgue and first time viewing a body so heavily damaged. Sure, she'd looked at photos in the agent training, but the real thing hits you hard.

"Sorry I let you down back there, Marcus. At least I didn't toss my cookies," she whispered meekly.

"Wish I could tell you it gets easier, but it doesn't," he answered. "No problem."

Sue, having met them at the door, spoke up as they entered the elevator. "He's right, Wendy. It is never easy, but it's part of the job. When I was with the Bureau, I emptied my stomach on the first three bodies I viewed. It still gets to me at times. You did better than me."

56

THEY RODE IN SILENCE FOR the quick trip to NISO Naples. Quick trip was an understatement. The building that housed the Agency was nearly walking distance to the hospital. The offices were on the second floor of the Naval Support building: a simple structure covered in white stucco with a dull-red tile roof. A small sign announcing NISO Naples was attached to the wall next to the door. And for some reason unknown to Marcus, the staff were all civilian and pulled joint duty, handling both NISO and NISRA tasks.

The outer office of NISO Naples was rather small, with two desks, both occupied by ladies; the older one smiled when the three entered, the younger one did not. A man stood by one of the doors on the opposite wall. It was hard to tell if he was entering or leaving the office behind the door.

"I can only assume two of you are Colt and James, but I'm not sure which of you ladies is James," offered the man standing by the door. "I'm Tony Carter, and I am damn glad you're here." He walked toward them with his hand extended.

"Easy to tell them apart, Tony. Wendy James is the one who dresses like me as we both are underpaid NIS agents. The clotheshorse is Susan

Woodward from the consulate. She has an expense account and is our minder, slash tour guide, slash driver. I'm Marcus, by the way."

Sue laughed and punched his arm. Wendy walked toward Tony and took his hand as she said, "Ignore him, Tony, it was a long flight and he is short of sleep. Pleased to meet you, I'm Wendy James."

"Again, we are glad you're here, and with the rough couple of days we've had, a touch of humor is welcome." Tony pointed to the lady on the left and introduced her first. "Mrs. Millie Goshwell runs this office, and Miss Sandra Markham helps her keep us in line. They know why you're here, so if you need anything, they are the ones to ask. Let's head on back and meet the rest of the team."

They shook hands and exchanged pleasantries with the two ladies. Miss Markham showed signs of recent crying and didn't smile. Once Tony punched in the door code, they followed him into the back. It was like entering one of those cartoon tents that is three feet wide on the outside and the size of an auditorium on the inside. Here was a tiny front office with a small-looking back wall; yet behind it, the "back" was a huge room containing six desks, a conference table, and a couple of glass-walled offices on one side. Several men looked up as they entered.

Marcus nodded to the men as Tony started the introductions. John Wright, Adam Richmann, and Ben Baker came over as Tony gave a quick overview of their areas of expertise. Marcus introduced Wendy and Sue, then explained they had just left the hospital.

"Marcus, William Coleman's desk is over there." Tony pointed to an empty desk next to the window. "I suppose you want to start there. Nothing has been touched since his death. We wanted you to have first run at it. I doubt you'll find much there since William was a filing nut and hated clutter. John will show you the file room. You and Wendy can have this office behind me for your work area. I placed all of our photos, reports, and the information we got from the police on the desk. Oh, yea, door code is 5042. So, what else can we do?"

"Thanks, Tony. Critical concerns—where is the coffeepot and the restrooms? And not necessarily in that order." That got the expected chuckles.

Wendy shook her head. "Ignore him, please. Like I told Tony outside, it was a long flight and Marcus is really short of sleep." That got even more chuckles.

Marcus then got serious. "Gents, we really hate to be here under these circumstances. The loss of an agent is difficult for everyone. Know this—we are not here to place blame or point fingers. We will help you find William's killers, and we will determine if that rape accusation has any validity."

They all nodded their understanding, and he continued. "First off, we need to read everything you have on the case and on Coleman himself. And know that all information will be a one-way street. We will ask questions and expect honest and complete answers, but we will not give you any updates on our progress or discoveries until we nearly finish the investigation. That might sound cruel since William was a coworker and friend, and we're all on the same team, but it is the only way to prevent our findings from influencing your answers. Nothing personal—just procedure. Any questions?"

No one had any problems with the rules, so Marcus sent Wendy and Sue into their new office to start looking at the photos and write-up the NIS agents had prepared. Since Sue was FBI and now CIA, and was under orders to stay with them, Marcus decided he might as well use her for something other than as a driver. An extra set of eyes is always a good thing.

Marcus also asked them to carefully compare the NIS photos with those shared by the local police, looking for any minor differences. Grasping at straws described the first part of this investigation, since the victim/suspects in the form of the girl and her friends had vanished, the suspect/victim in the form of the accused agent was dead, and there were no witnesses.

Marcus went to William's desk. Tony was right: it was a clean desk, almost too clean. The desk calendar was still set for last Friday, the last day William was in the office, according to Tony. He flipped back for a couple of weeks, and aside from a dental appointment the previous week, it was clear—except for a somewhat cryptic entry for that past Friday. It looked to have been written in a hurry, scribbled basically, in pencil: "dock 20." Honestly, Marcus was not really sure if that word was "dock," since William's writing was even worse than his. He went backward and forward several months and did not see any other entries like it, or any related to docks.

"Gentlemen, I already have a question," Marcus announced. He showed them the calendar entry and asked if anyone had input about its meaning. No one did. The rest of the desk was also extremely clean. Basic office supplies and a paperback novel were the only items in the drawers. The novel was one of Fleming's *Bond* books and had a bookmark on page seventy-three. Nothing else was stuck between the pages. After pulling the typewriter ribbon, Marcus slipped it into a bag. He carried the ribbon and calendar into his new office and showed it to the ladies. Now they had another couple of straws to add to the pile.

57

THE FIRST AND SECOND PASS over the police report, their photos, the NIS reports, and NIS photos failed to show anything that would be considered a eureka moment. The ladies gave a quick brief on what the multiple folders on the desk held, and Marcus skimmed their contents. It was true; nothing exciting. However, it did lock into their minds the parameters of the case and the evidence collected so far.

Tony stuck his head into their office. "Hate to be a bother, but anyone here have time for lunch?"

"I'm not sure if it's lunch or breakfast time. The body clock is a wreck right now. But some sort of food would be a great thing, since I'm hungry," offered Wendy. Sue and Marcus agreed. They locked the files in his briefcase.

On the way out, they again passed through the outer office. Millie had already left for lunch, and Sandra was holding down the office. Marcus noticed Sandra still had a sad look and her makeup wasn't perfect. *Perhaps from wiping tears*, he thought.

Walking to Tony's car gave Marcus an opportunity to ask about Sandra. He touched Tony on the shoulder and motioned for him to step back. "Tony, I noticed that Sandra is pretty upset. Was she involved with William?"

"Not that I knew, but yea, she seems to be more upset than the rest of us."

"Perhaps we should get her aside after lunch and ask some important questions. Perhaps there's a connection there that needs a deeper look."

"Can do, Marcus, I'll talk with her. But even if they were romantically involved, what does that mean for our case?"

"She might have info about William's recent actions and contacts. Perhaps it would be best for Wendy to do the talk. One of those girl-to-girl things."

Wendy heard her name mentioned and slowed to let them catch up. Marcus gave her a quick update on their thoughts, and she agreed it was worth an effort. But first, lunch was high on the list of things to do, for all of them.

The locals commandeered the front seat to discuss potential eateries. Wendy and Marcus rode in the backseat of Tony's Fiat 124, a bright green four-door sedan that had about as much room as the backseat of Kelly's Mustang—not much room in either front or back seats. At least the small tan seats were soft and comfortable. The drive gave Marcus a few moments of quiet time. His body clock was telling him the sun was just coming up over D.C. and he should be sleeping, not going to lunch.

Tony's restaurant selection won out in his discussion with Sue, and it was just about two kilometers away from the office. It was a hole-in-the-wall place, but the aromas wafting out offset any concerns Marcus held. They all ordered the same item that Tony recommended: bowls of *pasta e patate*. Marcus admitted that having potato with pasta sounded weird, a double starch entree, but it tasted great. And Tony said it was one of the signature dishes of Naples.

Since they'd beat the lunch crowd, the seats around them were empty. The quiet corner of the restaurant provided sufficient seclusion for talking privately about the case. As they ate, they spent almost an hour tossing weird theories on the table, all of which were quickly shot to pieces.

The one positive about lunch was that all the dishes went back to the kitchen with little trace of what they had just contained. They finished off the excellent meal with a small limoncello, helping with digestion. The old "when in Rome" maxim holds true in Naples, and everyone enjoyed the chill of the citrus drink. It was a great lunch place, and Marcus decided that if they hung around Naples for more than a couple of days, they would return.

As the three of them entered the agents' area of the office, Wendy stopped at Sandra's desk. Marcus decided to let her run with the interview. Tony, Sue, and Marcus returned to his new temporary office to plan the rest of the day.

"Sue, who do you know in the local government that has any control over the local docks, wharf, boat slips, etc.? We need to know which of them use the number twenty. Who uses them, who owns them, et cetera," Marcus asked.

Sue nodded. "Just so happens I know a guy. Okay to use your office, Tony?" Sue stood and slowly walked to the door as she watched Tony for a response.

"Sure. Button on the right is an outside line," said Tony with a wave of his hand.

This case needed a break. So far, they had a dead agent and not much else to help find answers. Time to go back to basics. Marcus stood to close the office door.

"Tony, I have to ask. Are there any of these agents, William included, that you have any doubts about?" Marcus asked, and before Tony could reply, he continued, "Look, we need to consider any and all possibilities. And even a concern about something as simple as taking too many late lunches might lead somewhere."

"No, sir, nothing comes to mind. But I promise I'll think on it and let you know. That's something I just have not considered," he said rather stiffly.

Marcus chuckled and lowered his voice, "And now you know why people hate Internal Affairs. We have to consider all these things, Tony, and ask the questions everyone else avoids. No offense intended, really."

Tony smiled. "Glad I don't have your job, Marcus."

Marcus then shared with Tony some of the points to look for in an agent that might have problems outside the office: problems that may affect performance. As the supervising special agent, it was Tony's responsibility to make sure his team stayed on the right side at all times.

When Marcus had finished, Tony asked, "So, what else do you need?"

Marcus shrugged. "Not much to see here, so we need to see his vehicle and his living quarters. But frankly, the time zone change is wreaking havoc on my mind, so I want to put off the living quarters search until tomorrow morning. Maybe then I'll have fresh eyes and brain."

Tony nodded. "The Shore Patrol has his car secured in their garage. It was found at the crime scene and towed here. It's about a five minute drive to get there. How about we go take a look at that, and then you guys call it a day?"

"That's probably a good idea, Tony. I just feel like there is something else I should look at today, but the brain fog is hiding it."

"Do you need to see the closed case files that William had been working?"

Marcus shook his head and said, "No, we pulled copies of all those and read them on the trip across the pond. Nothing there that would raise a red flag."

"Well, we'll never know about his last case. He didn't get it written up before the attack. And no notes were found on his body or at his apartment."

A look of concern flashed over Marcus's face. "And what case was that?"

Tony looked bewildered. "The latest one that came from your office. The NIR we got last Thursday morning requesting Naval Research Laboratory interviews. William worked on that Thursday afternoon and all day Friday. Seemed to me it was a lot of time spent on a few interviews, but I was out of the office when he came by Friday afternoon. I didn't get to talk with him about it."

"Oh, crap," Marcus mumbled between clenched teeth, feeling hit in the gut. Had his simple inquiry caused the death of an agent? He'd been there in Naples about seven hours and never once thought to ask about the NIR he'd sent the previous week. Marcus knew this was sloppy work on his part. He should have asked. His mind rapidly went in different directions, thinking of all the possibilities.

Tony looked at Marcus with concern. "You okay, sir? Sir?"

Marcus stared blankly at him for just a moment, then finally said, "Uh, yea, Tony. I'm fine. Just some thoughts rolling around in my weary head that needed more attention."

Wendy walked in and said, "Well, that was interesting."

Marcus held up his hand in the *stop* position toward Wendy and turned to Tony. "Would you excuse us for a moment? I need to run something by Wendy."

Tony nodded. "No problem, sir. I'll be in my office if you need me." He left and closed the door. Marcus sat behind the desk and pointed Wendy to a chair in front of it. He sat quietly for a moment.

Looking confused, Wendy asked, "What's that all about? I thought he was one of the good guys."

Marcus replied, "He probably is, but until we finish here, we ask questions, but don't share what we uncover. Remember? Anyway, what ya got?"

She grimaced. "Sorry, Marcus. It won't happen again."

"I know. You're still learning, Wendy. Besides, you're safe, since we don't keelhaul anyone until after their second screw-up. What did Sandra tell you?"

"Interesting stuff. Seems she and William had been dating for the last six months. He was thinking about asking for a transfer back to the States—Maine, if possible—to be near his son, and promised to take her with him. He was talking marriage. But he didn't want Tony to know just yet." Wendy paused.

Marcus nodded and gave a *come on* motion with his hand.

"Well, I'm not sure if it relates to the case, but she said that usually she slept at his apartment. But last Thursday night, he insisted they stay at her place. She tried to put him off since she hadn't cleaned lately, but he really insisted. She just thought it was strange. You know, a bit out of character for William, who was always laid back about their arrangements and not very pushy."

"When did she last see him?"

"Sunday, about noon. He showered that morning, dressed in his sports jacket like he was going to work, and kissed her goodbye. Didn't say where he was going or when he would be back. Does that have any value?"

Marcus leaned back in his chair and again consulted the oracles of the overhead for about thirty seconds. He leaned forward and focused his eyes on Wendy. "By itself, it's just another disconnected straw. But now, add this to the mix. I just found out that Coleman was working on the NIR I sent last Wednesday asking for interviews of the research lab staff about the missing doctor. Coleman started the interviews on Thursday afternoon."

Wendy perked up. "And abruptly Thursday night he doesn't want to go to his apartment. Then he stayed at her place on Friday and Saturday nights. Coincidence?"

"In our line of work, coincidences rarely exist, Wendy. I think it's time to head to our ultra-fancy rooms, get some food, maybe a beer or something stronger, and ponder what we've learned in a more relaxed environment. And I want to look over the packet of info the doctor gave me about Coleman. Of course, the unspoken fact is that we both need rest. Let's find Sue."

"Agreed, Marcus. And just how much of this do we share with Sue?"

Marcus smiled. "You're learning. Right this minute, none of it. This might fall under the jurisdiction of Cold Fog, which she hasn't been read into. I decided she's part of the murder investigation, but we need to make sure we keep some info separate for now. Cold Fog is technically the property of the senator's office, and his chief of staff, Jason Wright, has the final say on who, outside of NIS, gets into the group. I need to make a phone call or two."

As they stepped into the hall, Sue came out of Tony's office. She had a sad look on her face. "Marcus, the guy I need to contact is out of the office today but will be back in the morning. I tried a few other contacts, but no one could help. Not sure what else I can do this afternoon."

"Perfect timing, Sue. We're tired and ready to go back to our rooms. We'll pick this up in the morning, okay?"

Marcus told Tony they'd look at the car and apartment first thing in the morning. After bidding goodbyes to Tony and his team, the three left the NISRA office.

"Sue, do you know where the research laboratory is located?" Marcus asked as he climbed into the car.

"No, but I have a map here somewhere that shows all the buildings. Check the glove compartment."

Marcus found the map and showed Sue the location of the lab. It was just a few miles away. "Drive by that place, please. It was where Coleman was working his last case, and I want to take a look."

The lab was a nondescript building similar to the one he had visited in Pensacola: not too many windows, no fancy trim, and a simple sign by the door. They parked and walked around the structure. There was nothing exciting to see, but Marcus felt it needed to be done for some unexplainable reason.

"What goes on here, Marcus?" asked Sue.

"Like the sign says, research. The Navy is constantly trying to find new and improved ways of doing just about everything, and these labs lead the charge. Okay, I've seen enough for today. Let's go."

As they left the base, Marcus turned to Sue. "I guess there are hundreds of docks around the town, right?"

Sue chuckled. "I think you could say that. We have our military docks, and in addition, there are docks for the Italian military, commercial fishing, cargo ships, cruise ships, tourist boats, and privately owned ones. Let's drive by at least part of the waterfront."

She was right. There were more than a few docks along the waterfront. And after an hour in the car, Marcus said he'd seen enough, so they drove to the consulate. Fatigue took over during the drive, and the talk was limited to Sue pointing out other places of interest.

58

AFTER SUE ESCORTED THEM TO their suite and showed them the list of numbers to call for room service, an outside line, etc., she promised to be ready to drive them at 0745 in the morning. She also gave them her personal phone number before leaving.

Marcus laid his briefcase on the coffee table and flopped down on the sofa to the right of the table, while Wendy collapsed on the left sofa. Both let out huge sighs. It might have only been seven p.m. local time, but Marcus had racked up less than ten hours of sleep in the last fifty-five while passing through seven different time zones. And with half of that sleep poor quality from sitting on an airplane, fatigue was catching up.

Wendy was the first to speak after a few minutes of quiet. "Do we really need to look at any files tonight? I think I just hit a brick wall."

"Yea, I know the feeling, but we have a case to work. Fact is, we have two when you include the research lab. Just lay there while I make a couple of important phone calls. But pay attention." Marcus reached for the phone. It took a couple of tries to correctly dial the numbers he needed to get an outside, overseas line, but he finally got a dial tone. Thirteen digits dialed from memory and two rings later, he heard the familiar voice of Carl going through the standard greeting.

"Buon pomeriggio, Carl."

"Damn, Mr. Colt, one would suspect you are calling from Italy. What's happening, sir?"

"Nothing gets past you, Carl. Write down this phone number," Marcus read his number off to Carl, then gave him the main consulate number and explained their housing situation.

"Dang, sir, you're hanging with the big dogs. We'll need to get you a bigger hat soon," Carl said with a chuckle.

"I'll try to stay humble, buddy. You stay sharp, and please switch this call over to the conference room. That is, assuming the mice are still working while the boss cat's out of town."

"Can do, sir, and yes, they are hard at it, digging through all that CIA data. Hold one, sir."

"Special Agent Stevens speaking. How may I help you, sir?' Doc asked.

"Marcus here, Doc. Is Victoria handy to chat?"

"You bet, boss. And she is really great at explaining all this CIA crap … excuse me, *stuff*. Hold one, she's in the other room."

Victoria's voice came on the line in less than thirty seconds. "Hello, Marcus. Everything going well?"

"Doing fine, Victoria. Do you know a CIA agent assigned to the Naples Consulate named Susan Woodward?"

"Certainly, Marcus. She is the daughter of the Secretary of State—Harry is so proud of her. She's ex-FBI and has a good future with the Agency. Good person all around. Why?"

"She has been assigned as our driver, but I think it's more of a keeper position." Victoria chuckled as Marcus continued, "I might want to bring her into Cold Fog, but needed some references first."

"I understand. Call Jason and tell him I vouch for her. Okay?"

"He's my next call, Victoria. By the way, enjoying the work?"

"Oh, my, yes. Thank you for bringing me into this. You have a great team here, by the way."

"Agreed. And thanks. Please pass the phone back to Doc. Keep having fun, Victoria, and again, thanks."

"My pleasure, sir. Stay safe."

There was a moment of background chatter and then Doc came back on the line. "What's up, Marcus?"

Marcus paused for a second to gather his thoughts. "Doc, take notes. The death of the agent here might—key word is a strong *might*—be the result of him pursuing the NIR we sent asking for interviews of the research lab staff. Make sure everyone associated with Cold Fog is watching his or her back. Talk with the admiral ASAP and ask him to get some agents or plain-clothes SPs as bodyguards on Victoria and Veronica. All agents are to be on higher alert. And have the SPs put a twenty-four-hour watch on that guy Masters—I assume he's still in the hospital. Get with Carl and have him send ROIs to all the NISRAs associated with the research labs and issue the warning to them. Use the same distribution list as he did with the original NIRs."

Marcus paused to take a breath and gather more thoughts. "Wait. Back up, Doc. Send the warning to all except the NISO Naples office. I'll handle that when the time is right. Something here is not kosher, but I'm not sure what. Need to hold the cards close for a while."

"Damn, sir. This just got really nasty. What else?"

"Doc, brief Doty and ask him to look deeper into the assault on Masters. See if the Shore Patrol or local police have discovered anything about it. I've got a nagging feeling about that assault. Anyway, that's all for now. Watch your back."

"Can do, Marcus. One more thing, you probably haven't heard that Bill Collins was killed while investigating a break-in at the Research Laboratory Oceana, of all places—it wasn't just another building. Coincidences usually don't exist, right?"

"No, they don't, Doc. We now may have lost two agents to Cold Fog. My higher alert call is coming a day late. Thanks for that info. Oh, yea, give Kelly a quick call later tonight and let her know I'm still alive, but extremely tired. I plan to be in deep sleep by the time she gets off work. I'll call her tomorrow … probably."

"Happy to do it, Marcus. You stay safe. Doc out."

Wendy had a look of surprise when Marcus looked up from the phone. She softly said, "You certainly do have a lot going on inside that head of yours."

Marcus smiled at Wendy. "Yea, my mind is a terrible place to visit. I'm always trying to stay one step ahead of the bad guys, and too often it doesn't work. Bill Collins was killed at the Oceana Research Lab, so my warning was too late for him. Anyway, one call down, and who knows how many more to go."

After telling Wendy the rest of the update from Doc, Marcus reached in his briefcase and pulled out a small phone directory. He found his target after flipping through several pages, and again dialed a bunch of numbers and waited through three rings.

A female voice said, "You have reached the office of Congressman A. Jackson Allen. This is Jessica. How may I direct your call?"

"Hi, Jessica. Jason Wright, please. Marcus Colt calling."

"One moment, Commander."

A couple of moments later, Jason came on the line. "Hey, Marcus, what's up?"

"Jason, I want to bring another CIA employee into Cold Fog. Victoria just vouched for her, and by the way, she is the Sec State's daughter, Susan Woodward. We have some interesting leads popping up and I believe she'll be an asset. Okay by you?"

"Do what ya got to do to find the doc, Marcus. I know her and she is okay. But last I heard, she's in Italy."

"Well, that's good, 'cause so am I."

"Damn, you do get around. Anything else? Hate to rush, but I'm in another damn meeting."

"Nope, neighbor, we're good. Thanks, and take care."

After hanging up the phone, Marcus leaned back and closed his eyes. "I wonder if anyone has tracked the energy used to make a phone call. I'm feeling more tired after those two quick ones."

"There's probably a medical journal article about it, Marcus, but I'm too tired to care. What's next, dinner? And can we order room service?"

"Oh, yea, this is a five-star accommodation, and a quick call will bring on the food. There's a menu over on the sideboard if you care to read it and make a decision for us. Surprise me. I have another call to make first."

Marcus picked up the phone and dialed another number from memory.

"Naval Investigative Service Office Norfolk. Yeoman Second Class Frost speaking. How may I be of assistance, sir?" It was comforting to hear another familiar voice.

"Sid, this is Marcus Colt again. Is the captain available?"

"Always for you. Hold one. Take care, sir."

"Thanks, Sid. You too."

In less time than it takes to blink, Captain Miller came on the line. "Marcus, how's Naples?"

"Skipper, I haven't slowed down enough to see it, sir. Someone said there's a volcano nearby—not sure since I haven't had time to look." He paused while the captain chuckled. "Sir, I just heard from Doc that Bill died at the research lab building. Not good, and it bolsters the reason for my call—we might have a problem."

"Okay, what?"

"We need to get the agents, especially Hank Bates, immediately on higher alert. I just passed the info to Doc that the death of the agent here might—key word is a very strong might—be the result of him pursuing the NIR we sent, asking them to talk with the research lab staff. He started the interrogations, started acting strange, guess you could say somewhat paranoid, and then was killed. I'll hopefully have more to go on tomorrow, but I have a sickening feeling that they both may be victims of this missing doctor investigation. And I didn't see it coming. We have to make sure everyone associated with Cold Fog is watching his or her back."

"Bates is here with the NISRA agents in their office today. We assigned Driscol and Knox to work with him, since they're up to speed on the research center case. I also asked Sam to stick with him for the duration. So he has several good men watching his back. But I'll talk with them as soon as we hang up. Is there anything else I can do for you?"

"Just one more thing, Captain, please call the other agent at NISRA Oceana, sorry, but I can't recall his name, to reinforce the importance of the warning ROI Doc will be sending out shortly."

"Consider it done, Marcus. Look, you sound tired, so try to get a good night's rest. And before you dwell on it, there was no way you could have foreseen the assaults on the agents, so put that out of your mind immediately. I'll get the warnings out here. You just make sure you stay safe. Kelly would be highly pissed to hear you're back in the hospital. Take care."

The dial tone let Marcus know the captain had decided enough had been said. *He is never one for long goodbyes,* Marcus thought. Again, he leaned back and closed his eyes.

Wendy interrupted his quiet moment. "Sir, okay to use the phone now?"

"Yea, sorry … go ahead. And see if they can send up a bottle of bourbon and a bucket of ice. Now I need to think about what I'm going to say in my next phone call."

With Wendy's soft voice in the background placing the order, Marcus closed his eyes and allowed the tiredness to take control, as his mind went back over all that had been said the last ten hours. There was lots of new information, and just like so many cases, not many links. *More information overload,* he thought, then started running the disjointed pieces past the eyes in his mind.

Marcus heard a noise but could not determine what it was. With some effort, he opened his eyes and saw Wendy rattling a couple of ice cubes in a glass in front of his face. She held a bottle of dark brown liquid in the other hand. "Think you can handle this, boss? You look a little wiped out," she asked with a smile.

Dinner had arrived while Marcus was lost inside his mind. Actually, he had dropped off to sleep, but the thinking process continued in his slumber.

"Double shot, please, barkeep."

Wendy smiled as she shook her head and poured. "That'll be four bits for your double shot, cowboy," she said as she passed the glass to Marcus.

Marcus took a small sip. "Do you know why a shot of whiskey is frequently called a 'shot' instead of some other measurement name, or just a *jigger*?"

"No, but I suspect I'm about to get a lecture." Wendy took a sip of her drink.

"Somewhere in Old English is a reference to a *flagon*, a drinking vessel for alcoholic beverages with a handle, being called something sounding like shot. I find that one rather boring. Another is a German guy named Schott owned a glassworks factory and offered small sturdy drinking glasses in his line. My favorite theory goes back to the Wild West in the 1880s where cowboys often, at least as the story goes, traded a .45 round for a small glass of whiskey since they were about the same price. So take your choice," offered Marcus lightly. "Just another case of information overload, Wendy, at least in my brain."

Wendy just took another sip of her drink. "Guess we need to eat and then crash. Hope you like seafood."

Dinner was as good as the quality of the room. Shrimp, pesto, and pasta are always an excellent combination. And Marcus would have wagered that the shrimp were still swimming in the sea that morning. As they returned the covers to the near-empty dishes and replaced them on the serving cart, Marcus said, "We need to go over a few things. Starting with … do you trust Sue? Should we bring her into Cold Fog? Both Victoria and Jason have approved her. Your thoughts?"

"Wow. No stress, right? Okay, as you said, she has good recommendations. Based on who her dad is, I doubt she's a Russian agent. And since she has a major crush on you, I don't think she would mess us over. She's probably safe."

Marcus had to blink a couple of times. "Excuse me? A crush?"

Wendy laughed at his expression and comment. "You bet, Marcus. Whatever you did for her father put you into 'knight in shining armor' status, and if you two weren't already married, I suspect she'd be ready to jump into your bed. And even with the existing spouses, she still might. I'm surprised you didn't see it. You must be really tired."

"Come on, Wendy. There's nothing there."

Wendy rolled her eyes and held up a hand with a closed fist. Extending the first finger, she said, "Okay, first off, remember all the times she touched you at the airport and in the car. Not something strangers do unless there is an attraction."

She raised the next finger. "While I suspect Mr. Secretary probably asked that we be treated nicely, do you really believe this suite is often given to middle and low-level Navy officers? No way, unless the local CIA station chief demanded it."

Marcus shrugged and lamely said, "Yea, that is a bit strange."

The third finger was lifted. "Again, we are not multi-starred admirals, yet the head CIA agent assigned here is now our driver-slash-tour guide. It would have been more appropriate to have Greg, or someone at a lower level, do all the driving."

With his face showing a bit of a grimace, Marcus had to admit to himself that Wendy's logic made sense. "And what is number four?"

Wendy chuckled. "Well, that's more of a feeling I have based upon the twinkle in her eyes, the slight flush, and the increased smile when she looks at you. More of an intuition than anything real."

"Okay, Wendy, let's say you're right. Assuming it really is infatuation because I saved her father's life, then she would be safe to bring onboard with Cold Fog. But we have to think about all possibilities of a situation. What if she is doing what the CIA is notorious for doing—trying to get information any way they can. In this case, she may be willing to use her body. What would the CIA want from us? After all, we have opened the door to the CIA back in D.C."

"I hadn't considered that, Marcus. But while she could fake points one through three, I don't believe she could control the twinkle or flush."

"And to take the conspiracy thought one step further, Wendy, knowing her family and the people who respect her, I doubt Sue would voluntarily be spying for a foreign country, but what if she's being blackmailed to do it? We always have multiple points to ponder when we do this job."

"Now my head really hurts. Thanks for opening that can of worms, boss. Is this the kind of discussion you usually have during the Monday morning meetings?" asked Wendy.

"Yea, and on just about every case we work. Sometimes you end up talking to yourself when you work a case solo. But no matter how much you hash out a problem or situation, it boils down to you having to make a decision on the information you have. Granted, speculation and intuition get involved, but mostly you go with the facts you know unless the gut is screaming otherwise."

Wendy nodded. "Guess a lot of this comes from experience, right?"

"True. But you have just shown you have the inclination to do it based upon your observation of Sue. Now to throw another thought out there. Perhaps she is working for a foreign government and needs something from us. Don't you think she would have a tap on the phone here and bugs in our room? Before you share thoughts, you need to make sure the subject of those thoughts cannot hear you sharing," Marcus said with a grin.

"Ouch! Yes, sir, I can see that now. Sorry."

"No harm done. I trust Sue, but I am not going to share anything about Cold Fog just yet. We'll stick to investigating Coleman's murder, and if we quietly learn something about the missing scientist, that's a bonus. And we need to make sure we keep any new info between us, at least for now. And as you heard me on the phone, we need to watch our backs at all times."

"So you saved the life of the Secretary of State?"

Marcus slowly smiled. "Yes, with massive help from a bunch of SEALs and several months in the jungles of beautiful Vietnam, I did, but sorry, I can't get into the details. I'll write a book in about thirty years and you can go see the movie. Okay?"

"Guess I'll have to wait then. It'll be difficult, but should be worth it."

"Maybe. I think our time before we pass out should be focused on the case. And that case is Cold Fog. While you were ordering our outstanding dinner, I ran some things around inside my head. Think about these things, and then sleep on it. Let your subconscious help, okay? This mess got started for us with the obvious problem of a missing scientist who has been gone for five months. Now there are two dead NIS agents, possibly—but not proven—due to whatever caused the scientist to go missing. Adding to that, we have a needed defense system on hold, an SSA failing to mention a dead agent's current case, CIA theoretically helping us in

D.C., a CIA babysitter here in Naples, and a D.C. sailor who worked with the missing scientist getting beaten up by a guy with a Russian accent."

"That is some interesting stuff you ponder when you're asleep. Good night, Marcus."

59

MARCUS WAS WIDE AWAKE AS he rolled over and looked at the clock beside the bed. The glow of the hands showed it was a little before 0400 hrs. Still time to catch another hour of sleep, but he knew his body clock was in control and that would be a wasted effort. It felt like it was time for bed and, according to Eastern Standard time, it was. Hopefully, the day would allow his body to finally adjust as he watched the sunrise.

The hot shower helped shake out the body aches and clear the fog from his brain. Thinking about the tasks for the day, he knew they had to check out Coleman's car and apartment first thing. Based on the info Wendy got from Sandra, they would need to see her apartment, also. Hope that request would be well received; Wendy would be the one asking her for the address and key, since they had started a friendship of sorts.

And on top of that, they needed to keep an eye on SSA Anthony Carter. Perhaps not mentioning that Coleman was working on the research lab interviews was an oversight on Carter's part. Or perhaps it wasn't. He needed to check on Carter, but there was no way he could ask the local NISRA to do a BI on their boss without it getting back to him. However, there was a way. But first he had to get dressed and get coffee.

The shared sitting room was quiet and dark. No noises were coming from Wendy's room. Marcus called the kitchen and ordered a pot of coffee and some pastries to be delivered. A caffeine and sugar fix would help get the brain cells communicating faster. Then they could order breakfast.

Next he called his office in D.C. YN1 George Russell picked up the phone on the second ring. "Naval Investigative Service, Internal Affairs Division, Yeoman First Class Russell speaking. How may I be of assistance, sir?"

"Good evening, George. Marcus Colt calling and I have a small task for you."

"Hello, Commander. All going well, I hope, sir?"

"Not bad for an old man who has trouble adjusting to different time zones. But I should be better when the coffee arrives. I just woke up."

George chuckled. "Coffee always makes life better, sir. How can I help you tonight? And I do have a message from SA Stevens."

"Start with his message, please."

"Yes, sir. It reads 'Vicky said letter not from the doc. Kelly had a great first day,' and that is all."

"Thanks, George. Leave a detailed note for Rita. I need her to call NISO Norfolk first thing in the morning and talk with Lt Col J. Scott Tiller, USAF. Tell him I need a favor and ask him to contact one of his buddies in the Air Force Office of Special Investigations. I need them to do quick, and extremely quiet, BIs on all the personnel assigned to NISO Naples and the Naples Research Lab, with emphasis primarily on financials. Put a higher priority on SSA Anthony Carter. I don't want any Navy personnel involved with the BIs, okay? Underline that, please. Have her give Tiller my numbers here—I gave them to Carl earlier."

"Can do, sir. Anything else you need?"

"No, George. That will do for now. I greatly appreciate your help with the phone coverage. It really helps knowing you're there for us."

"My pleasure, sir. Good night."

Light knocks on the door announced the arrival of the important brew. Marcus was just stirring his first cup when the door to Wendy's room opened. She came out with her hair down on the shoulders of her white robe. A stifled yawn was quickly replaced with a warm smile as she said, "Coffee, yes!"

Marcus poured her a cup. "Good morning. And how do you take it, ma'am?"

"Two and one—two sugars and one dash of cream. Thanks, boss."

They sipped coffee in silence for a few minutes. Marcus decided a pineapple Danish was the right choice, and as he swallowed the first bite, he asked, "And did your subconscious come up with any answers overnight?"

Wendy shrugged. "Sorry, no. I must have passed out the moment my head touched the pillow. I bet you are already two steps ahead of me."

"Probably not two steps, but one for sure. I got the ball rolling on BIs on the entire staff of NISO Naples and the lab. We'll get the Air Force intelligence folks to handle it for us. Perhaps we'll find someone with unjustified money or large purchases out of their pay range. Just another straw to add to the pile."

"Why everyone, sir? And why the Air Force?"

"Just covering all the bases, Wendy. If Carter is dirty, perhaps he has accomplices. Or he might be clean, and another agent could be bad. Best case is that we find them all spotless. But until we check, we just don't know," Marcus said before taking another bite. After another sip of coffee, he continued, "And by asking the boys in light blue to do the deed on the QT, hopefully, maybe, nothing will filter back to the Navy folks here."

Wendy nodded. "I hope there won't be a test on all this stuff you're teaching me on this trip," she said through a chuckle. "Guess I'll get dressed since we have a full day ahead."

As she stood, Marcus said, "I've got a special request, if you don't mind. Leave your hair down like it is. It gives you an easygoing, friendly look, and I want everyone to think of you as the 'good cop' in case I have to play the part of the heavy. Okay?"

"Can do, Marcus. Anything else?"

Marcus shrugged. "You good for breakfast around 0700? Omelet?"

Wendy nodded. "Western, with a dollop of salsa on the side." She poured another cup of coffee, grabbed a pastry, and vanished into her bedroom.

It was still early; his watch quietly told him it was 0545 hrs, so Marcus nibbled on his Danish and sipped on his second cup while slowly outlining the expected events of the day in his head. Three places needed to be searched in hopes of finding more clues about the murder. If things went well, maybe they could all be done before lunch.

He knew the only clue they had right then, if it really was related to the case, was the calendar note about "dock 20," whatever that was. Sue expected to reach her local contact and at least get a starting point with that.

Then, since Coleman was working the case at the lab, that would be their next stop. But right then, the question was whether to include Sue when they interviewed the staff at the lab. That could easily bring her into Cold Fog territory. He had permission from Jason to do so, but Wendy's comments about Sue's attraction were nagging in the back of his brain. If it was just a simple grateful daddy's girl attraction, that would not be a problem except for Marcus having to watch his step around her. He had to be careful not to lead her on in any way. Maybe events of the day would help make the decision about Cold Fog.

A third cup of coffee was almost gone, as was a second pastry and just over an hour of time, when light knocks again came to the door. Marcus thought *breakfast has arrived.* Expecting the same gentleman from earlier, Marcus was surprised to see Sue pushing the breakfast cart. He stepped aside and motioned her in.

"Good morning. Aren't you a little too high up the food chain around here to be doing room service, Sue?"

Her smile was so bright it would have been perfect for any toothpaste commercial. "Always happy to be of service to my favorite special intelligence officer. Sleep alright in this shabby establishment?"

Marcus immediately thought back to Wendy's comments the night before as he saw the smile and slight blush on Sue's face. *Might be something there.* Out loud he replied, "Sleep was good while it lasted. No bedbugs mind you, but my body clock is still confused and I woke up at 0400. Maybe tonight I can get situated in your time zone."

"Marcus, I hope you don't mind, but when I saw your breakfast order getting ready, I decided to include mine on the cart and join you ... and Wendy, of course, for breakfast. Was that all right?"

"Certainly. Let's get it on the table. Glad there is more coffee—we about drained the first pot."

They had just finished unloading the cart when Wendy came out of her room. Marcus almost did a double take, as she was dressed in dark gray slacks and jacket with a light blue blouse. It was a dead-ringer match for Sue's outfit. And with both wearing their hair down, they looked like members of the same team at quick glance.

Wendy reacted fast. "Looks like we both got the dress code memo, Sue. You look nice." That got everyone smiling.

Breakfast was filled with casual talk about Naples and the Consulate General. Sue seemed to avoid any mention of the reason they were there. Marcus finally asked about her dock contact, and she said he should be in his office around nine. Then the focus returned to eating.

The western omelets, link sausages, and English muffins had been devoured, and the three were finishing up the last of their coffee when Wendy asked, "Sue, is your husband here with you?"

Sue's face darkened as she looked down at her plate. It was only for a second, but it seem longer before she looked up and smiled. "I divorced Charlie just over two years ago, while I was still working at Langley."

Wendy grimaced. "I'm sorry. I didn't mean to touch on a sore topic." She looked at Marcus and cocked her head to the right slightly.

Marcus noted the head position and logged it into his brain as one of Wendy's silent signals. The message from this one might be "See. I told you so," and it would be most appropriate.

"No, it's fine. I'm still angry—no, I suppose I'm more hurt than angry, about it all. He's a college professor who found out he liked the intimate contact with his young female students more than mine."

"He's a fool," Marcus offered.

"Thanks, Marcus, I agree," Sue said. "At least I no longer have to worry about what he's been doing when he comes home late."

"Yet you still wear the ring," Wendy mentioned softly.

Sue chuckled, "Part of my cover. If you hang around Naples long, you will wear one also. Too many locals zero in on the bare finger and get amorous ideas."

"Good to know, Sue. Well, are we ready to face the day and uncover the truth about SA Coleman?"

Sue's smile got bigger as she turned toward Marcus. "There is one piece of good news. I spoke with the local authorities last night and they agree that the rape charge is bogus. And they also agreed to withhold that info from the press for now, while you finish your investigation."

Marcus returned the smile. "Thanks. I'll take any piece of good news. Time to get to work, ladies."

60

THE DRIVE TO THE NISO was filled with Sue's information about the places they were passing, and comments about the many people already out on the streets. A large number of tourists were keeping Kodak in business as they burned film on the many classic sites. Mount Vesuvius was in the background for some of them; thankfully, the volcano had been quiet since the last eruption in 1944. With the sun low and bright in the mostly cloudless blue sky, a bit of fog still hung over the bay, and the temperature hovered a little below fifty degrees. Marcus admitted to himself that it was a perfect Kodachrome 64 kinda day for sightseeing in the cool air.

The NISO office was humming loudly as they entered a few minutes after 0800. Mrs. Goshwell was hammering out a report on the ASR-35 Teletype system in the corner. Yellow paper tape was piling up on the floor at a decent rate. Sandra was typing something on her IBM Selectric at such a high rate of speed it sounded like a machine gun. Wendy had planned to pull Sandra aside to ask about seeing her place, so she lingered by her desk and waited for her to stop typing for a moment. When she looked up, Wendy spoke quietly to her as Marcus and Sue went through the back office door.

Tony Carter and Adam Richmann looked up from their task when Marcus closed the door. They were sitting at the conference table looking over a group of loose papers. The other two agents were not seen.

Marcus started the conversation. "Good morning, gentlemen. Any issues I should know about this morning?"

"Hello, Sue, Marcus. Wendy not with you?" asked Tony.

"She'll be here shortly, Tony. Now is there any traffic I need to see?" Marcus had a bit of harshness in his voice.

Tony looked a little taken aback by Marcus's tone, but he smiled. "No, sir, nothing directed to you, but you are free to join us and look over this morning's traffic."

Marcus went to the conference table. Sue headed to their temporary office to keep out of the way and wait for Wendy. He realized he was being short for no reason, so he smiled and said, "Thanks, Tony. It would be nice to see what all you folks are facing as I continue to get in your way."

Adam said, "Get in the way all you want, just figure out why William is dead, Marcus. I'm getting more coffee—want some?"

"Yea, thanks, Adam." Marcus turned to Tony. "And where are the other guys?"

"SAs Wright and Baker are out looking into a possible robbery at the hospital," Tony replied. "Patients have complained about missing personal items. Not very interesting, but somewhat weird, as the bulk of the missing items were shoes." He chuckled and shook his head. "I told them to start with the psych ward." They nodded and turned their attention back to the stack of messages.

After a few more minutes, the main door opened and Wendy strolled in wearing a face that told Marcus nothing. She already had the agent's nondescript look under control and was wearing it well. She nodded at Marcus and turned to go into their temporary office. Marcus went back to reading the daily traffic.

With nothing of interest in the stack of morning traffic, Marcus finished his coffee and turned to SSA Carter. "Unless you have something more pressing, it looks to be time to check out Coleman's car."

Tony Carter nodded and addressed his fellow agent. "I'll be out with Marcus for a couple of hours. Take care of the small issues in the morning traffic. We should be back before lunch." Adam nodded and picked up the stack.

Marcus excused himself and joined Wendy and Sue in their temporary office. He closed the door and looked at Sue. "Were you able to reach your contact about the dock issue?"

Sue nodded. "Yes, indeed. He promised to have a list of docks with that number for us right after lunch."

"Okay, that will work. It's now time to visit Coleman's car and apartment. Sound *Boots and Saddles* please, Wendy."

Sue had a confused look when Wendy tried to mimic the bugle call through laughter. Chuckling at her own failed attempt, Wendy said, "I'll explain it later, Sue. Welcome to the world of Colt—things do get strange here, I have found out."

Leaving the office, Sue and Tony immediately got into a discussion of which car to take; Sue's had the diplomatic plates and Tony's had the radio communication with the NISO. Since they weren't heading into any areas where there could be issues with the locals, Tony's communication ability provided him the opportunity to drive.

Walking across the parking lot beside Marcus, Wendy touched his arm and slowed her pace, clearly signaling for him to hang back. She softly said, "Sandra agreed to let us see her place. Best time would be before work early in the morning."

"And we will be there. Got her address, I assume?"

Smiling, Wendy responded, "And a map, boss. But I'm not sure what you expect to find there?"

"Neither do I. Only a look at the place will, at least hopefully, fill in a blank or two. With nothing to go on, we have to keep grasping for those straws." Marcus glanced around and saw Tony and Sue standing by the car looking at them. "And we need to walk faster to get to the next potential straw holder."

The drive to the SP garage barely got the engine warm; it was less than a mile from the NISO office building. Coleman's car was inside the garage in the same spot where the SP's had positioned it after towing the car on early Monday morning. It hadn't been touched since Tony and another agent had gone through it on Monday afternoon.

The car was another plain Italian-made sedan. Nothing exciting was visible on the dark blue exterior or in the medium gray interior. It was showroom clean. After a walk-around and a look at the extremely bare interior and trunk, Marcus asked, "And what did you remove from the car, Tony?"

"Nothing, Marcus, nothing at all. William kept his car as neat as his desk. No notes, nothing. Not even a gum wrapper," said Tony. The slightly queasy smile told Marcus that Tony was frustrated with the lack of progress so far.

Marcus nodded. "I know the frustration you're feeling, Tony. We go through it frequently in Internal Affairs. Have the crew here pull the interior panels, flooring, etc. and see if anything is lurking there. Let's head over to his apartment."

On the drive to the apartment, Sue asked what was also on the mind of both Wendy and Marcus. "Was the neatness thing with Coleman a mental issue? I've never seen anyone this compelled to not have anything out of place."

Tony chuckled. "Just his way, I guess. We all have our quirks. Never had any problems with him that would warrant psychological attention, so there's nothing official in his file."

Marcus slowly shook his head and remained silent for the rest of the drive.

61

DOC ALREADY HAD THE COFFEE brewed when Kelly strolled quietly into the kitchen. He was nearly dressed for work; his tie was not pulled tight and his jacket was hanging on the back of the chair. He lifted his mug in a salute and said, "Good morning, Mrs. Colt. Hope you had a good night's rest."

She broke into a huge smile. "Yes, I did, Special Agent Stevens. Thanks for asking." Kelly's smile kicked up to the left. "Ya know, I don't think I'll ever tire of being called Mrs. Colt. I love it! And it looks like you got an early start, Doc. Thanks for getting the coffee ready."

Doc just smiled and nodded as he picked up and drained his second cup. Since Ann had returned to duty in Norfolk on Tuesday, Doc would usually have been back in his quarters on the base. But with Marcus out of town, Kelly asked that he stay. It was a selfish request on her part. She figured if he was there in the evenings, she could pump him for information and get faster updates on what all was happening with Marcus in Naples. And she was right.

Doc didn't mind, as it also gave him more time with Victoria—he'd volunteered to drive her to the NIS offices. They continued their discussion about the case on the daily drives back and forth.

"Princess Kelly, the coffee I can do well, but I don't have the same cooking skills as the boss. You're on your own if you want to eat something decent. Sorry."

"Quit whining, Doc. Your kitchen skills aren't that bad. But I'll feed ya since you're providing me with updates on 'the boss.' Sausage and eggs okay?"

"You bet." Doc paused as he gathered his thoughts. "Uh, Kelly, did you get a call from Marcus last night?"

"No. Why? Were you expecting to hear from him?"

Doc shook his head. "No, ma'am, but just wondering. I know the time difference thing is inconvenient for lots of chats, but I sort of expected for him to be more hands-on with this Cold Fog thing. All I've heard from him was that short phone call yesterday, and he didn't even ask me how things were going here."

Kelly took a sip of her coffee as she let Doc's comment steep in her mind. She realized she was seeing a side of Doc that was totally new to her. And she suspected even Marcus hadn't often seen that side. A bit of self doubt was showing. She smiled softly. "Doc, when you and Marcus were running around 'Nam last year, did you always wait for him to tell you what to do?"

"Hell, no, Kelly. I knew when something had to be done and just did it."

Kelly's smile got bigger and she chuckled softly. "Oh, you mean he trusts you now just like he trusted you then? And he knows you'll do the right thing today without him calling every hour giving you orders or questioning your actions."

Doc looked down at the table. "But this is all so new, Kelly."

"Everything is new the first time. But remember, Doc, you have the rest of the Cold Fog team covering your back. When in doubt, ask them for help just like you did when you were new on the SEAL teams."

"Yes, ma'am, will do. Thanks. You know, I was ..."

The doorbell chime interrupted Doc's comments. Kelly winked at Doc and hurried to the door. Checking the peephole, she saw Victoria standing there, ready to push the button again. She opened the door and welcomed Victoria with a laugh. "My, you're an early bird today. Care for some breakfast?"

"Oh, I hate to be a bother, Kelly. Thanks, but I ate an hour ago. But I do need to talk with Doc, if he is awake."

"He's in the kitchen draining the coffee pot. Is there time to put on some water for tea?"

"None for me, dear, but a cup of that coffee will hit the spot," Victoria said.

Doc stood as they walked into the kitchen. "Morning. Am I late or are you early?"

Kelly pulled another cup from the cabinet and poured the coffee for Victoria, who had already taken a seat beside Doc at the table. As she sat, she placed her hand on top of his and leaned toward him, softly saying, "Doc, I'm sorry. I completely missed it, but fortunately my old subconscious worked overtime and woke me up hours ago. This morning, rather than go to NIS, I need to dash over to Langley and talk with Les."

Looking confused, Doc said, "Okay, not a problem. But what is it that you missed?"

"I'm not sure, Doc. The thing is ..." Victoria paused and her mouth twisted into a confused look. She held her hands in front of her as if grasping for something unseen. "The thing is, there is something in one of the files I read yesterday that triggered a memory about another, yet totally unrelated, case. But I can't remember the details. So I have nothing of value to clutter your mind with right now, Doc. Let me dig around a bit at Langley and get back with you later today. Okay?"

Doc nodded. "I trust your instincts. Call if you need anything while there, and hopefully we'll see you later at the office."

Victoria leaned her head to the right. "I think I'll just ask the nice gentleman watching my house if I can ride with him to Langley. If he follows me, he might not get into the parking lot without my help."

"Either Agents Jasper or Taylor, I'm not sure who is on duty right now, will be happy to give you a lift. It will make their job easier."

62

DOC CHECKED IN WITH RITA. He was surprised, and impressed, that Marcus had Rita call in the Air Force to help with the BIs of the Naples team members. He wouldn't have thought of that, and he looked forward to seeing what they could find. With nothing else exciting from Rita, Doc grabbed another cup of coffee and headed to the conference room.

The large team from the first week had been trimmed down, since Doug Knox and John Driscol were called back to Norfolk to help with the investigation of the dead agent there. Technically, they were still working Cold Fog since the murder had occurred at one of the research labs. And with Marcus and Wendy in Italy, that left Ron Tucker, Chris McCormick, and Ed Dondridge to help Doc keep moving forward on the case. Veronica was there to keep them in line with the documentation, of course, and with her ability to think of not-so-obvious things.

They had worked late the previous day, so Doc told them all to come in an hour later that morning. Doc usually tried to avoid the "do as I say, not as I do" rule, but as the leader needing to keep ahead of the team, he had arrived in the office a little past 0730 hrs.

Veronica waved him over when he entered the conference room. As always, she was the first to arrive, and frequently the last to leave. She had ignored the "hour later" order too. After the customary morning greetings, and snickering at Doc's verbal pseudo-tongue lashing about coming in early, she handed him a sheet of paper and said, "We got this interesting ROI from the Holy Loch NISRA."

Doc thanked her and moved to his customary chair at the other end of the table to study the report. Sipping his coffee, Doc read that the research lab in Scotland had been tasked with gathering drawings and photos of all the submarines in service, belonging to every country, including the U.S. This information was being used to set up data files for each one. These files would be used by the new radar system to identify the specific vessel. Even subs of the same class had minor differences in construction that the system must be able to identify. And similar variations were created after a sub underwent maintenance.

The staff at the lab had minimal contact with the missing doctor, but there was one point in the report that jumped out. One of the lead scientists on the Rembrandt project had met an untimely death while gathering maintenance information from the files of the submarine tender, a type of depot ship, assigned to the Holy Loch base.

The USS Canopus, AS-34, was a large ship with a length of 644 feet; it provided support for the submarines. This support consisted of restocking everything from coffee stirrers to torpedoes, and making repairs for just about anything that didn't require a dry dock. The machine shops on these tenders were an envy of anyone who ever worked with metal.

As with any proper repair facility, especially in the Navy, where paperwork was nearly as important as the barrels of gray paint, the Canopus maintained detailed records of all the work done on the subs under its care. In the record storage room on one of the lower decks, a mysterious fire broke out in November 1970. Several sailors, and the research laboratory scientist, died that day. The cause of the fire was never determined. The data file establishment for Rembrandt was hampered by the death of the research scientist. And it was greatly hampered by the loss of the maintenance records.

Another sip of coffee was needed, but Doc's mug was dry. He looked at his mug, then back at the report, then at the overhead like he'd seen Marcus do from time to time. His gut was telling him this was an important piece of information, but his brain couldn't grasp why. His own "oracles of the overhead" were still in the developmental stage and didn't provide any insight. Remembering Kelly's comment earlier about asking for help, Doc decided to share this with the rest of the team as soon as they arrived, to get their valuable input.

As Doc was getting yet another cup of coffee, Ron, Chris, and Ed strolled into the coffee mess. At least they came in forty-five minutes later than normal: much closer to the hour that Doc had ordered. Doc nodded in their direction and said, "Good morning, gents. Fill your mugs and get ready for another fun day."

Ron slowly shook his head. "Sorry, Doc. I'm not looking forward to another day of reading dry, boring files and beating my head against the wall. Can we at least hope for a break in this damn case?"

Chris and Ed nodded in agreement as they filled their mugs and headed to the conference room. Walking with them, Doc filled them in on the news of the morning, which made things a bit more interesting. The three agents read the ROI. Ed was the first to comment.

"Doc, so now we have three dead—two of them agents—and one injured, and one missing, probably because of this Rembrandt project. At least as far as we know as of right this moment. There might be more victims out there. It's good that we have all agents and members of the various research laboratories on high alert. We need to figure out how this all ties together. And do it quickly."

Doc chuckled. "Usually Marcus tells me I'm the one good at stating the obvious, but Ed, you do it with so much more finesse. Wish we had Victoria's input on this, but it will have to wait. So listen up, 'cause here's the plan, and I really need you to tell me if I'm heading in the wrong direction."

63

AS A MARINE, HANK BATES was used to a strict regimen. That included everything from how he tied his shoes down to the number of times he stirred his coffee. No matter where he was, the regimen stayed the same. Dropping the stirrer into the trashcan after the standard five turns around the mug, Hank turned to leave the coffee mess with his first cup of the day. An attractive female in a Navy enlisted uniform blocked his way.

"Good morning, Petty Officer," he said as a smile spread across his face. An officer was to avoid dating, cohabitation, or sexual relations with enlisted personnel: all three were covered in the UCMJ by the simple term of fraternization. But Hank couldn't find any regulation against smiling at or enjoying the view of the lady that stood in front of him right then. He just had to make sure the smile was a friendly one and not that of a hungry wolf eyeing a cute lamb.

Yeoman Third Class Rhonda Evans was one of the two yeomen assigned to the AUTOVON room at NISO Norfolk. Marcus Colt had met her earlier that year at yeoman training school at NTC Bainbridge, in Maryland, while preparing for the undercover assignment in Norfolk. Later, Marcus ended up working with Rhonda at a Norfolk Navy facility at the center of the murder and drug ring, and Rhonda had helped solve the case. At least the nightmares of having a gun pressed against her skull were finally fading. For her protection and peace of mind, Marcus had her transferred from the Navy facility to NISO Norfolk. She was well liked by the crew there and excelled at her job of teletype traffic control. The AUTOVON room was where messages, such as ROIs, were transmitted to and received from other NIS offices and several other government agencies via ASR-35 Teletype machines. Rhonda was holding one such message.

"Lieutenant, I figured you would want to see this one immediately. It just came in from the FBI," Rhonda said, returning the smile and handing over the message.

After thanking Rhonda, Hank headed down the hall to the NISRA Norfolk office spaces, reading with each step. It contained some interesting information and fortunately, the distribution included Doc Stevens at NISHQ, so he knew Doc would send it on to Marcus.

Supervisory Special Agent Sam Maker had assigned him the same desk that Marcus had used while snooping around months ago. Hank hoped that some of Marcus's luck, magic, juju, mojo, or whatever it was called still lingered there. He needed a lot of it right then.

True to form, SSA Sam Maker was in the office earlier than the rest of his team. His arm impatiently waved "get in here" as 1stLt Bates walked toward his glass-enclosed office space. He knew Sam was frustrated about the lack of progress finding the killer of Bill Collins. Hank felt that frustration in spades.

The term "in spades" is thought to have originated from the card game bridge, where having more spade cards is a good thing; it means either *abundance* or *to a high degree*. In Hank's case, both fit his level of frustration. He chuckled to himself as he thought, *hell, I don't even play bridge.*

It was only a twenty-foot walk from the agent area entry door to Sam's office, but it was enough time for Hank's mind to rehash the case, as there wasn't much to rehash. SA Bill Collins had been shot and killed late Sunday night while investigating a possible breaking and entering at an office on Oceana Naval Air Station. It had been Bill's misfortune that he was nearby when the initial call about an alarm came over his car radio. He beat the SPs to the scene by about a minute and paid dearly for his efficiency.

There were only a couple pieces of evidence. Fingerprints were collected, and the M.E. had recovered the bullet from Bill's heart. Analysis of the slug didn't show any connections to other shootings NIS had investigated. And of the few fingerprints collected, a couple weren't associated with members of the lab staff. The slug and unknown fingerprints had been passed to the FBI for a check against their files.

The slug was interesting. It might have been a .38 Special round, as there was no casing left at the scene. Unlike semi-automatic pistols, revolvers retain the spent casing in the cylinder until the shooter manually removes it. Semi-automatics ejected the casing after firing. Of course, a true professional would police his brass, i.e. pick up the ejected casing so it wouldn't become a piece of evidence. Even at night, with sirens approaching, a professional is still a professional.

And there are many semi-automatic pistols chambered to fire either a 9mm or .380 round, both of which look like the .38 to the naked eye when fired. Hence the need for the lab analysis.

The building being burglarized was the research lab, which held half a dozen different departments, all focusing on experimental equipment. This pointed back to the Cold Fog task force case about the missing scientist and Rembrandt. Some files might be missing, but no one was sure. The lab promised to inventory the files and let NIS know the status.

Hank's face held a smile that bordered on a grimace, but at least things had just changed, if only by a small amount.

"Hello, Sam."

Sam nodded his acknowledgment and waved Hank to one of the chairs in front of his desk. He took a deep breath and said, "Yea, morning, Hank. Do we have anything new this morning?"

"Yes, sir. I just received the report from our friends in the Bureau. The slug was a 9x18mm Makarov and, based on the rifling marks, was shot from a Makarov pistol. It's a nice semi-automatic weapon that holds an eight-round magazine. This Russian side arm has been around since 1948, when it was designed by Nikolay Makarov. It has been the standard Soviet military and police side arm since 1951."

"Any matches to the slug in their files, and what about the fingerprints?"

Hank smirked. "Did Marcus learn that impatience thing from you or you from him? Okay, sorry for my impertinence, Sam, guess I need more coffee. Hang on, I'm getting there. Okay, there are no matches in the FBI database for this slug, so they have sent it to Interpol in hopes they can find one."

"Very well, and the print ..." Sam said through a big grin.

After consulting the ROI again, Hank answered, "They have a match from one partial print to a gent who is now one of the members of the Russian Embassy in Naples, Italy. The guy is named Vladimir Davidovich

Kroneski. He had been with the Washington, D.C. embassy in the past. Since it's a single print match, they give it eighty-percent reliability. They say he is listed as the cultural attaché for that embassy, which is diplomat-speak for the resident KGB agent. But this is the interesting part, Sam—he has been in the States for the last two weeks."

"Where's he now?"

Hank shrugged. "Sorry, no idea. He left for London on Monday morning, and the folks over there have lost him."

Sam shook his head. "Great. A freaking Russian who is a freaking spy with freaking diplomatic immunity is now a freaking ghost. The day has officially just turned to shit."

64

DOC HAD JUST FINISHED EXPLAINING Victoria's absence and was getting ready to issue the plan for the day when Rita walked into the conference room and passed him the ROI from the FBI. Doc read it twice before he turned to the other agents.

He slowly shook his head as he said, "Gents, we have some new info and it stinks." Passing the ROI to the agents for them to read gave Doc time to consider the ramifications of the news. And it allowed him a moment to formalize his now-changed plan for the day. He waited for them to finish with the message before he started. Ed Dondridge was the last to read it, and he grimaced in disgust as he slid the paper back toward Doc.

"Doc, it's looking like one or more of us need to head to Naples to cover Marcus's back. This bastard is probably hiding in the Naples embassy now."

Doc slowly shook his head. "No, Ed, the boss has plenty of help from NISO Naples, and he'll get this new info shortly. Our task is to do some quick follow-up to provide him more information. Ron, I want you to call Les at the CIA. See what they have on this commie. If they have a photo of Kroneski, we need to get a copy here ASAP."

Agent Tucker nodded and moved to the other conference room for some quiet while he made the call.

"Ed," Doc said, "I hate to do this to you, but you need to call our 'friends' at the FBI and find out what they know about Kroneski. See Rita and get the name of the guy Marcus talked with last week—start with him. Hopefully he'll be helpful. If not, we can get nasty."

Doc continued with the assignments, looking at Chris McCormick. "Chris, please type up a quick ROI for Marcus. Include all this info about the Russian, and the info we received from Holy Loch. Tell him what we're checking on this end. Flag it 'Operational Immediate' so they'll get it to him quickly."

Chris said, "You got it, Doc." He picked up the two ROIs and paused before going to his normal desk for some quick typing, looking ready to ask something.

Ed also stood to leave, but beat Chris to the question: "And what else do we need to do, Doc?"

With a quick shrug, Doc said, "Only one other thing comes to mind. I get to call the Secretary of State and see what he has to offer."

After Ed and Chris left, Doc sat there for a moment. He realized that Kelly had been right: when the pressure was on, he did know what to do, and he didn't have time for self-doubting. *Her insight is amazing*, he thought. And with that on his mind, he looked at Veronica. "Do you have the Sec State's number handy?"

Minutes later, Doc was on the line with the Secretary of State. While they moved in totally different social circles, the fact that Doc was one of the men who saved his life the previous year brought them together. It was a bond sealed with blood.

"Good morning, Mr. Secretary. Thanks for taking the time to talk, sir."

"Doc, you are just as bad as Marcus. The name is 'Harry' and you had better get used to saying it, son. Hell, you know Margo and I have just about adopted you. Anyway, so what's up, Doc?" Harry chuckled at his humor. "You know I never tire of saying that!"

Doc shook his head and slightly blushed at the familiarity with a man he held in high esteem. He swallowed and replied, "I'll keep working on the name thing, Harry. Just have patience with this old sea dog. Reason I called is we need some info on a member of the Russian Embassy in Naples really fast. Specifically, we need background, a photo, and his U.S. entries for this year. He might be the one who killed one of our agents in Norfolk earlier this week. Can you point me in the direction of who I need to call to avoid the standard runaround?"

"Damn. Not good on some many fronts. Okay, I'll do you one better, Doc. give me the guy's name and I'll call the right people who will contact you shortly with all we can dig up. Will that work?"

"Hate to put you out, Harry, but yea, that will work fine. Greatly appreciate it, sir." Doc paused to pick up the ROI and continued, "Name of the man is Vladimir Davidovich Kroneski. He was in the States for the last couple of weeks up, until this past Monday morning. No known location right now."

Silence on the line concerned Doc. Harry finally said, "Doc, that is one slimy bastard. I will make sure my people get back to you very soon. Hang tight!" And without further comments from either end, the line was filled with a dial tone.

65

AFTER ALL THE YEARS SHE'D spent in the CIA offices and the many friendships she'd generated, Victoria hadn't been back since she retired. It was part of her makeup that when you leave something, it "stays left" in the past. She enjoyed seeing her former coworkers in other environments, but never felt the need to visit the office.

Knowing her quirk about visiting, Les was more than a little surprised by the call from the front desk to meet her. Since she was his old boss, he was a bit worried that he was being taken to the woodshed. After all, the previous day's phone call from Marcus let him know she was now working with him. And after the way that damn swabbie had pulled strings and gotten the CIA involved in his cold case, she might be here to give him a tongue lashing. *Oh, well, time to play nice*, he thought.

"Good morning, Leslie. You are looking splendid this morning."

Les chuckled. "Victoria, you just brightened my sorry day. Nice to see you back on your old turf. How can I help you?"

Victoria smiled, winked, and extended her hand.

After the smiles and handshakes and a few more words of greeting, Les signed her in and passed her the access badge. It had *Guest* in large letters across the front. He shrugged and smiled. "Sorry, we never got around to getting badges made that said 'Retired Super Spook,' so I hope this will not offend you." Victoria again smiled and said nothing. Les felt even more concerned.

A short, quiet elevator ride and a stroll down the hall brought them to the office that Les now called his, but for eight years had belonged to Victoria. They approached the chairs across the room from the huge desk and faced each other across the coffee table.

"Can I get you some tea or coffee?"

Again Victoria smiled and gave a quick shake of her head.

"Victoria, you have always been one to use the fewest number of words, but this morning you are extremely quiet. What can I do for you, or should I ask what can I do for Marcus Colt?" Les said with what he hoped was a disarming grin.

"Vladimir Davidovich Kroneski," she softly said.

Les dropped his happy face, a look of total concern replacing it. He leaned forward toward Victoria and quietly asked, "And what about that devil?" They spoke as if mentioning his name would actually bring forth that evil one into their presence.

She inhaled deeply and exhaled slowly while the right words formed in her mind. When she spoke, it was with a voice of authority that had been honed over the decades. "Leslie, working on the Cold Fog case has released some information I thought I had completely buried and locked away in the back of my mind. It came to me around four o'clock this morning that he has to be involved with this. You know we almost had him back in 1960. There was that case of potential submarine sabotage that you and I felt so very sure was his doing, remember?"

"Yes, ma'am, I do. It was the work on that case that got you the seat behind that desk," said Les as he pointed to what was now his desk. "And put me in a position where I could follow you. You think he's involved with this mess?"

"Oh, yes, quite sure. Submarines are his specialty, and he could not resist the temptations of Rembrandt. He probably is the controller and has more than a few minions under his command, but he is the one pulling strings as well as doing some of the wetwork. You know he cannot resist the feeling of killing someone."

Les nodded in agreement. "So, Victoria, what do you need from me?"

She shrugged. "Just every piece of information you have on Kroneski. And I need it right now. I want him closely watched 24/7 with NIS in the loop, being updated in real time. Nothing hidden from Marcus and his team, Leslie. They are the 'good guys' too."

Les cocked his head to the side and grinned. "You haven't told them about Kroneski yet, have you? Still playing games, Victoria?"

She shook her head slowly. "You are correct, I have not told them, but it's not part of a game, Les. I didn't want to just throw a name out there until I had more information. No need to give them false leads. And I needed my hunch to steep a bit before I released it. Hence my visit to you to get some confirmation and the information I need for my new teammates."

Before Leslie could respond, his outside line phone rang. Catching it on the second ring, he listened to his secretary as he sat down at the desk. He said, "Please put him through." Les waited for a moment. "Good morning, Agent Tucker. What's up?"

The look of frustration takes several forms, and Les used them all up as he listened to Ron Tucker. When Ron ran out of steam, Les finally got a word in and said with unexpected calm, "Happy to help, Ron. Victoria is here now for a chat, and I will make sure she has copies of all we have on him before she leaves. Anything else I can do for you?"

Again Tucker was on a roll and kept the line hot. Les finally got his chance to interject, "No, Ron, again, we are happy to help. We are all part of the same team. Do I need to come over there in person?" Les listened for another minute, said his goodbyes, and hung up the phone.

"Well, Victoria, it seems your team is keeping up with you. Doc asked Ron to call over here and get what we have on Kroneski. You can deliver it, okay?"

Before Victoria could answer him, his internal line phone rang. After the standard line of identification, Les went into listen mode for at least two minutes. Finally, he said, "Yes, Director. I can handle that, sir." He hung up and grabbed his jacket.

"Well, Victoria, it seems that Marcus has transferred some of his audacity over to Doc." Les chuckled. "Doc called Sec State himself, and he just called the director asking for the same thing you did. Great minds really do run along the same path."

Les pointed toward the office door. "Let me help you carry some data over to our friends at NISHQ. I have been assigned by our director to stay there and work under Marcus Colt until he releases me. Interesting times, eh?"

Victoria smiled and whispered, "Quite."

66

THE DAY WAS STARTING TO warm up as the sun climbed higher and burned off any remaining morning fog. Coleman's apartment was near the water, on the western side of Naples, in an affluent residential area called Posillipo, where steep cliffs and small beaches fight for space with apartments and restaurants. Tony pointed out several good potential lunch spots as they drove down the main highway that paralleled the waterfront.

The apartment building wouldn't fit into the American definition of a complex; it was a simple, multi-story structure, probably built way before the turn of the century. The parking area was extremely small, but clean. Only one other car was there when they arrived.

Realizing the building was extremely old, Marcus half expected to see a plaque that said "Julius Caesar slept here" as he surveyed the exterior. The painted stucco was cracking and falling off in places, revealing the original crude brick walls. It was easy to see that the stucco had received many coats of paint over the decades. Dead vines covered some parts of the lower walls. Sadly, the window casings would need another paint job soon to slow the rotting of the wood. A large wooden door provided access to the interior; it too showed signs of a rough life, including at least two bullet holes.

The climb to the second floor of the apartment building was done single file. Tony took the lead ahead of the ladies, with Marcus bringing up the rear. The stairs were too narrow for two, and if someone was coming down, the meeting parties had to turn sideways and press against the wall to allow clearance. If one person happened to be a bit overweight, physical contact was unavoidable. Marcus wondered how furniture was moved up these tight spaces.

A heavy oak door with two locks was the entrance to Coleman's place. One lock was ancient and needed a huge, black cast iron key, while the second was a modern dead bolt. Tony had the keys—both locks gave out loud clicks with the turn of the keys—and he entered first. The three people in the hall heard him yell, "What the hell?"

Marcus pushed ahead of the ladies with his weapon drawn, and entered to find Tony standing just inside the door looking at a total disaster. Furniture was turned over; most pieces were destroyed. Pillows shredded. Drawers dumped on the floor and tossed into a corner. Nothing was left on the walls.

The floor was covered with hundreds of broken pieces of Coleman's life.

Wendy couldn't hide her shock. "Not as neat as his car, that's for sure. What a mess." She and Sue had pressed into the foyer right behind Marcus.

"Nobody go any further. Tony, when did you last check on this place?" Marcus asked quietly.

"We checked it Monday afternoon. Everything was neat as a pin at that time. Nothing was out of place. Doors and windows were secured when we left."

"Stay here," ordered Marcus before he carefully checked each room. No one was hiding, so Marcus holstered his weapon as he came back to the foyer.

"Well, that brings up a few questions. First off, what were they looking for? More important, who were they? And did they find it?"

Tony just shrugged.

Marcus threw Tony a slight look of disgust. *You're not a lot of help, bucko.* He took a deep breath to calm his frustration and finally said, "I know you use the Shore Patrol for most of your evidence collecting. My question is a simple one—are they better than the local police? And by 'better' I mean more thorough and faster."

Tony nodded. "Hate to admit it, but the locals have greater resources, both in the number of people and the size of their lab. We use them on big cases."

After closing his eyes momentarily to focus his thoughts, Marcus concocted the plan for the next step. He opened his eyes to find the other three staring at him.

"Here's the plan. Sue, use your diplomacy skills and call the local police chief. We need a forensic crew here ASAP to go over this place in hopes of finding a fingerprint, footprint, or whatever. But it needs to remain an NIS-controlled case. Okay?"

Sue smiled. "No problem. Can I check to see if that phone still works?" She pointed to a phone lying on the floor under one of the sofa cushions.

"No. It would be better for you to use a neighbor's phone. Stay right here until Wendy returns." Marcus ushered Tony and Wendy out the door and pointed to the stairs. "I'll catch up," he called after them.

Turning back to Sue, he said, "There are two cases that are intertwining here. Wendy will fill you in shortly. Use your FBI skills and don't take anything for granted. Keep alert. I'll be back."

Sue gave him a rather warm smile and touched his forearm as he turned to leave; that quietly reminded him of Wendy's speculation. Warning lights were triggered in his mind as she softly said, "No problem, Marcus."

Catching up with them at the bottom of the stairs, Marcus said, "Tony, give the apartment keys to Wendy, and go get the car. I need to talk with Wendy a moment."

Tony didn't look happy, but did as he was ordered and walked to the parking lot. Wendy stood there, patiently awaiting orders. Marcus took a moment to look around the area. Nothing seemed out of place or strange, once he got past the fact he was in Italy and everything looked strange. At least no one was seen lurking in the shadows.

Turning back to face Wendy, Marcus said, "Watch your back and keep your weapon handy. While I doubt whoever created that mess will be back, don't take chances. Keep the door locked and stay with Sue at all times. Go with her when she makes that call. As soon as you get back up there, fill her in on Cold Fog. We really need more help right now."

"Can do, Marcus. Anything else?"

"Yea, too much. I'll be sending Sandra here as soon as I get back to the NISO. She'll have one of the agents with her for protection. Have her look around to see if there's anything missing. If the forensic people get here first, have them wait for Sandra's look around."

Wendy snorted. "How can anyone tell if anything is missing in that mess?"

Marcus smiled. "Never said it would be easy. But I suspect after all the time she spent here with Coleman, she might see something that just doesn't look right. Or not see something that should be here. Think of it as another straw to grasp while we keep going in circles, chasing the wild geese. I must be tired, since I can't think of any more metaphors to mix right now."

Wendy laughed, nodded her understanding, and waited.

Marcus let out a sigh. "Oh, and one other thing, I will be sending over a Shore Patrol officer. Have him take charge of the people the local cops send to help. Our case, our evidence, etc. Again, don't let the locals start until Sandra has finished her look around and the SP rep is here. Okay?"

"Got it, boss. When will you be coming back here?"

"Soon, I hope. But first I need to have a long talk with Tony and get the SPs involved. Remember, stay alert and take care," Marcus said as he turned to get into the car Tony had just driven over. He sat there for a moment after closing the car door, and watched Wendy reenter the building.

Tony glared at Marcus and sarcastically asked, "Are you planning on telling me where we are going? Or am I to start reading minds?"

Coldness came over Marcus's face as he faced Tony. "Carter, your attitude is putting you about a minute away from being placed on suspension. Get on your radio and tell the head of the Shore Patrol that we will be there in about thirty minutes and we need to have a serious talk. Then drive us to your office while I decide if suspension is enough."

After a terse radio conversation with the commanding officer of the Shore Patrol unit, Tony signed off and again faced Marcus. "Colt, I don't appreciate being ordered around like a rookie. And I feel you are intentionally keeping me in the dark about something. So, yea, that has kicked up my attitude a bit."

Marcus held his thoughts for a good thirty seconds. "Carter, when it comes to an IA investigation, you *are* a rookie and you should be happy about that. Your record is spotless and you've had no reason to meet anyone from IA before this incident."

Marcus paused to let that sink in. With a stern command voice, he continued, "And less than twenty-four hours ago, I told you emphatically that information was a one-way street. Nothing has changed about that, so enjoy the damn dark."

Tony flinched, knowing Marcus had just cut him off at the knees. Marcus added with a calmer, softer voice, "Carter, James and I need all the info we can get from you about Coleman, as quickly as we can get it, and yet you seem to be holding back. Like why not lead yesterday with the fact his last case was checking on the research laboratory? I don't believe it's because I've hurt your feelings."

A sigh and a slight shake of his head were the only physical signs Tony showed. His voice calm and quiet, he said, "Mr. Colt, I'm sorry. Nothing has been held back on purpose. It didn't seem important in light of William's beating and death. I need to stay involved—he was my agent. Please, sir."

The soft rumble of the engine was the only thing that broke the silence in the car, for at least a minute. "Okay. For now, I'll trust that. Let's go," Marcus said. In the quiet of his mind he realized that he believed Tony's excuse. Considering the death of Coleman, everything else seemed trivial. Especially since Tony hadn't known all the ramifications of the research lab investigation.

Again, he hoped his gut was holding true about the SSA. "Tony, I just decided you can be more helpful knowing more, so here is what is going on with the research lab and how it relates to your dead agent." It took the entire drive back to the NISO to explain just the high spots of the case intersection.

◆

Sandra Markham was surprised when Marcus told her to go with SA Adam Richmann to Coleman's apartment. Her surprise turned to utter shock when Marcus explained why she needed to leave immediately, and what she had to do when she got there. Shock turned to sadness, and the tears started flowing again as she grasped that she had to face destroyed memories she'd shared with William. It reopened the wound just as it started to heal.

While Marcus was talking with Sandra, Tony made sure that Adam understood the new complications of the case. And he emphasized that Adam was to stick with Sandra at all times and to be ready for trouble. With two dead agents, the stakes had gotten higher.

Millie Goshwell said she'd contact the agents in the field and bring them up to speed on the new security developments. Before she could walk to the radio, the bell of the ASR-35 rang. After a short phone chat with the sender, she pressed a sequence of buttons, and the teletype started chattering as it typed out the short message while dumping a pile of punched yellow paper tape on the floor.

She glanced at the header of the message from NISHQ, where the distribution was specified as she removed it from the ASR-35. She turned and handed Marcus the ROI that was addressed to him.

67

As expected, Captain Wesley Boxer was not thrilled to have been left sitting on his hands, waiting to talk with a Washington-based NIS agent. With just under twenty years in the Navy, and over a year of skippering a large Shore Patrol unit, Boxer was a man who carried a large amount of prestige and power. His star was rising, figuratively and literally, since the first star of an admiral was in his near future. He had been told unofficially that it was just waiting on the approval of the Senate and, if the gods in D.C. were happy and acted, he would soon pin on the one star of Rear Admiral (Lower Half).

Anyone looking at his expression would immediately know that almost-admiral Wesley R. Boxer was having trouble maintaining his cool as he waited for his "guest" to arrive. Fingers on his left hand drummed rapidly on the desktop, playing an unrecognizable drum solo; it was not the one from "In-A-Gadda-Da-Vida" since the Iron Butterfly drummer was not that fast. But Buddy Rich's drum work on "Cherokee" when he was with Harry James might be closer. Or perhaps it was something from Gene Krupa. Both of these gents drummed fast, and they were from an earlier time that fit Boxer's age. It would be difficult to decide which of these fine drummers the soon-to-be-admiral was channeling now.

Granted, as the head of the NIS Internal Affairs division, Colt could—just as he did—issue orders to the commanding officer of any Shore Patrol unit and expect those orders to be followed. And through the SP grapevine, Boxer had heard from a buddy in Norfolk that this investigator had a lot of pull with the CNO. With Colt having friends in high places, Boxer decided it would not cost him much to play nice. He passed on his lunch, sipped on some nearly cold coffee, and waited.

Fortunately, the wait was short. The intercom came alive and his yeoman gatekeeper announced regally that two NIS agents were here to speak with him. He ordered that they be allowed to enter. A sharp rap on his door generated his response. "Enter!"

Carter and Colt walked into the office, came to the captain's desk, and assumed an attention position. Well, Carter tried to assume one, and it was close enough for Boxer to be impressed by the gesture. Marcus said, "Sir, Lieutenant Commander Marcus Colt and NIS Supervisory Special Agent Tony Carter request a moment of your time, sir."

With his knowledge of the man, Boxer had to admit to himself that Marcus Colt was following proper procedures and not abusing his position of authority. Or usurping that of his higher-level contacts. Boxer was impressed with what he saw and heard, so he immediately decided he liked this guy.

"At ease, Mr. Colt. You too, SSA Carter. Take a seat and tell me how the Shore Patrol can rescue NIS today," Boxer said with a chuckle.

Marcus smiled and chuckled at the interagency jab. He decided right then that Captain Boxer was one of the good guys and a perfect one to have on his team. "Thank you, sir." He cleared his throat. "Skipper, it would probably save some time and effort if you just called us Tony and Marcus. We have too much to do to stand on formality right this minute."

Boxer nodded and smiled; *easy going and humble,* he thought. His first impression about Colt was spot on: he was one of the good guys. He waved a *come on* motion, and Marcus took the lead. After Marcus's short but detailed explanation, confirmed by Tony's nod, the commanding officer of the Shore Patrol immediately called for his XO and two petty officers to come to his office.

Working with the local police was the XO's specialty, and he had a great relationship with the police and the various groups within the forensic community there. He and Marcus hit it off immediately and connected via mutual friends in the service.

After the XO and his team had been briefed, then departed to control things at the apartment, Wesley Boxer leaned back in his chair and took a deep breath. He twisted his hands together and looked at Marcus. "The thing that just doesn't seem real is that the local commie bastard from the embassy was in the States, probably killing your agent in Virginia, when your agent here was killed. So how many evil commie bastards do we have attached to the Naples Russian Embassy?"

Marcus grimaced and shook his head. "Skipper, you have just asked one of the more interesting questions so far in this investigation. Wish the hell I had a clue."

Boxer nodded. Another deep breath and sigh followed. Tony Carter shrugged as a frown crossed his face. Frustration was mounting with the three men.

"You know," Marcus continued, "there are no rules that would have prevented good ol' Vladimir Davidovich Kroneski from making a quick phone call on Sunday, telling some local guy not associated with the embassy here, to take out our agent who was looking into the lab issues. Do we know of any local thugs that the Russians have in their hip pockets?"

The skipper smirked. "Easier to list the criminals the Russians *don't* have influence over, at this time."

"That bad?"

"Oh, yea, Marcus. The Russkies have contacts, and probably contracts, with every evil group in Italy. Hell, probably all of Europe."

Marcus frowned. "And do you know any friendly agencies who might have a list of said contacts?"

Boxer nodded again, but this time with the grin of an attacking shark. "One of *my* specialties, Marcus, is keeping in good standing with head guys at the Polizia di Stato and Polizia Municipale. Those agencies sort of equate to our state troopers and city police, and both have been very cooperative. We have a decent list, but I can make a couple of calls and add the new ones they've found."

"And when you do, can you ask them if 'dock 20' rings any bells?"

His brow knotted as Boxer answered, "What the hell does that mean? I'm happy to ask, but if I have a context, it might generate a better response."

"No idea, Skipper. It was the only notation on our dead agent's desk calendar for the week he died, so we're grasping at straws looking for any clues and connections," Marcus said with a shrug. "Appreciate you asking them about it anyway."

"Consider it done. Anything else?"

Marcus passed a card to Boxer. "Sir, we can be reached through the NISO, of course, and these numbers are for the consulate where my partner and I are staying. Call anytime and both locations will know how to reach us if we're out."

Right before they left, the skipper agreed that the Shore Patrol would keep the research lab under surveillance, with personnel stationed both inside and outside the lab at all times. Marcus thanked him for his assistance and promised to keep him apprised as things progressed. They left and drove back to Coleman's apartment.

68

THE SERENITY OF THE SMALL apartment complex had been totally destroyed by the arrival of the Shore Patrol, the local police, and the forensic team. Official vehicles crowded the small parking area, and too many flashing lights provided a circus feeling to it all. Tony had to park down the street.

After they walked the block to the apartment area, Tony flashed his NIS credentials as Marcus displayed his diplomatic folder to the local police who were securing the perimeter. Two Shore Patrol petty officers were cloistered near the door with four men. Each man was carrying what looked like mechanics' toolboxes, but Marcus knew their reason for being there: obviously the cases contained forensic tools.

Flashing their IDs at the guards controlling the building door, they were finally able to return to the apartment. Sue and Wendy were in the hall outside Coleman's door talking with the SP XO, Commander Paul Dillon. Sue's face lit up as she saw Marcus approach.

"Miss James, what is the status?" Marcus asked in a formal way. He looked into the apartment and saw Sandra Markham in the middle of the living room. Her hands were covering her mouth as she looked at the destruction of what had been her love nest. SA Richmann stood to the side against the wall, observing.

Wendy flashed a quick half smile. "Glad you're back, Mr. Colt. On her first pass through the place, Sandra did not see anything that might help. She asked to try again. She's a trooper since this is so painful for her."

Marcus nodded his acceptance of Wendy's report, and with a quick turn to the commander, continued, "Unless there is anything else you need from us, Commander, the ladies and I will leave you here. Gather what you can quickly, with emphasis on fingerprint recovery. You can have one of the locals take Sandra's prints when she feels ready to leave. I'll have the NISO send over a copy of Coleman's prints."

"That will work, Mr. Colt. My team will stay to monitor the forensic crew. I suspect we'll be here for at least another three hours, then we'll go with them to their lab. May I have the keys to this place? I'll send them back to the NIS office after I lock up."

After a glance at Marcus's and seeing a curt nod, Wendy passed the keys to Commander Dillon.

"Anything to add, SSA Carter?" Marcus asked.

Tony Carter simply shook his head and turned to start back down the narrow staircase. Sue and Wendy followed, leaving Marcus on the landing with Commander Dillon. He leaned toward the commander and quietly said, "Watch your back, Paul. We already have enough bodies generated by this case. Take nothing for granted."

Dillon chuckled. "Marcus, my survival is always high on my priority list. But thanks for the concern. We got this end covered."

Following a nod and a handshake, Marcus hurried back to catch up with the rest of his team somewhere in the parking lot. He glanced over and saw Wendy addressing the petty officers and local forensic team. Marcus couldn't hear all the words, but her Italian was spoken with authority.

Whatever she was saying had garnered their full attention. Each man was constantly nodding in agreement and responding "*Si signora*" in a respectful tone. When she had finished, she shook each man's hand and came over to where Marcus had joined Sue and Tony.

"What was that all about?" Marcus asked, noting the men were watching her carefully. Their expressions were a mixture of deadpan and serious.

"Just a little pep talk to the men. I explained the importance of finding any evidence. Especially any fingerprints. Of course, I happened to mention that my boss, a very important investigator from America, had selected them based upon their expert reputation. I figured"—she smiled and put more emphasis in her soft southern drawl—"a little sugar goes a long way."

"Perfect." Marcus turned toward the men and yelled, "*In bocca al lupo!*"

They all broke into smiles and yelled back, "*Crepi il lupo!*"

As they left the parking lot, Sue latched on to Marcus's arm. "Impressive that you would know that saying for good luck. You constantly surprise me, Marcus."

He noticed that Wendy did a slight eye roll and barely moved her head to the right side again. *Yep, he thought, that is an "I told you so" head movement.*

Tony asked, "What exactly did you say? My Italian is centered on the basic communication stuff like ordering meals, and stock phrases like 'drop your gun' or 'get me another beer.' What was with the 'wolf' comment?"

Wendy took the lead. "It's a local way of wishing them good luck. Marcus said, 'Into the mouth of the wolf' and they gave the standard reply, 'Die, wolf.' I'm just glad he remembered not to give them his usual thumbs up hand signal."

Marcus chuckled. "Kelly and I were fully attentive during our Italian class last summer. And we really enjoyed the night colloquial sayings and gestures were explained. I fortunately remembered most of the ones to avoid. That class just came in handy."

Marcus gently extracted himself from Sue's grasp, and he led them off the sidewalk onto a small open area between buildings. He looked at Sue and asked, "Did you reach your contact on the dock issue?"

Nodding, she replied, "Yes, I did. He said he would prepare a list of docks using the number twenty, but nothing jumped out at him at first glance. He promised to send it over to the NIS office before he goes home today."

A grimace spread across his face as Marcus sighed and looked down for a moment. When he looked up, determination was all that showed as he stared at his three associates. Glancing around to ensure privacy, Marcus said, "Okay. Now that Sue and Tony have been read into Cold Fog, we have two more sets of eyes to use. The death of Coleman is now part of Cold Fog, and while I know Tony and his people have a personal interest in catching the killer or killers, the primary mission is to solve the disappearance of the doctor. When we do that, finding those responsible for Coleman's death will be much easier. Understand?"

Tony said, "I don't like it, but I understand. The rest of my team will also." Wendy and Sue nodded in agreement.

"Good. Tony, where can we catch a quick bite to eat before we head over to the research lab?"

"Happy to oblige, boss. Just so happens there is a great place about a three-minute walk that way." Tony pointed to a small side street across the Via Angelo Compagnone.

69

THE QUICK LUNCH ENDED UP being a panzerotti for each of them, passed through the small open window of a narrow shop. The small, calzone-shaped fried pastry was filled with mozzarella, freshly chopped San Marzano tomato, spinach, and a small amount of fried lamb. Flavor was outstanding, and it filled the emptiness they were feeling. But it did nothing to eliminate the frustrations of the case.

After a quiet stroll back to Tony's car, Marcus shared a decision he'd reached over lunch. "Tony, let's head back to your office." As they drove back to the base, Marcus explained to Wendy and Sue the ROI he had just received. The new information was disturbing to them both.

"Sue, we're going to drop you off since I need you to spend some time at NISO. While you wait to get the dock list, check with every contact you have to get a list of personnel at the Russian Embassy. We need photos of all the players, if possible. And find out if they are in town or not."

She nodded. "Can do, Marcus. I happen to know another local guy who can help."

"Perfect. Glad you know so many people. Just tell him we need the info, but not the reasons why. Rest of us will be at the research laboratory for a while. Not sure what we'll find there, but we have to take a look and ask around. Hopefully we can discover, and be able to retrace, Coleman's steps when he was there last week. Perhaps that will lead to something. More damn straw grasping," said Marcus with obvious frustration in his voice. "Oh, yea, Sue, see if Sandra saw anything and if so, call us at the lab."

Again, Sue nodded. No further words were needed, so the four rode in silence for the rest of the drive.

With Sue dropped off to handle her assignment, the remaining three ventured on to the lab. Marcus spotted the SP members that Captain Boxer promised would be handling guard duty for a while, and was damn glad to see them on duty.

Checking in with the reception desk, Marcus introduced himself and asked to see the commanding officer. The civilian clerk on duty was one of the local hires, very fluent in English. Mario Morelli was the name on his badge. He called the CO's office, and shortly a yeoman arrived to escort them back.

The name on the door indicated Commander Wilson G. Montgomery was the man they needed to see. The yeoman opened the door and stuck his head inside as he said, "Sir, I have Mr. Colt and party here."

A robust and somewhat gruff voice replied, "Send them in, Brady." The yeoman pushed the door open and stepped aside.

As they walked to his desk and came to attention, Marcus did an announcement similar to the one he'd done with Boxer. Montgomery was not what Marcus expected. His slender build and youthful appearance did not match the gruffness in his voice. Standing behind his desk, he had to look up at Marcus, which put his height at no more than 5'6". Even Kelly could have pinned him in a wrestling match within a few seconds.

"At ease, Mr. Colt. I understand you are here to investigate the death of one of your agents. Correct?" asked the commander as he pointed them towards the chairs to the side of his desk.

"Yes, sir. My partner SA James and NISO Naples SSA Carter are assisting with that investigation, and with the case SA Coleman was working here right before he was murdered. We believe they are linked." Marcus had decided that good ol' Wilson might be one of those who pushed the military etiquette to the limit and beyond, if he could. So he decided to stay formal, unlike his demeanor with Captain Boxer. Perhaps it was a way for Montgomery to compensate for his lack of physical presence. That was a guess best left up to Kelly and other shrinks.

"Very well. What are you asking of this office?" Montgomery had rested his elbows on the edge of his desk and locked his hands, with fingers intertwined in front of his chin.

"Sir, we will need to interview anyone who had contact with SA Coleman last week, and everyone who has any knowledge of the Rembrandt project. Hopefully they will be the same list of personnel, but there might be someone knowledgeable of Rembrandt who was not interviewed. Therefore, every staff member is a person of interest at this point. And while James and Carter get started with the civilians and military, respectively, I will start with you, sir."

"Of course. I suspect the unit responsible for Rembrandt should be the first?"

Marcus nodded.

"Very well. We will start with a quick tour of the facility." Montgomery pressed a lever on the rather old-looking intercom unit, and said, "Brady, get in here."

When Yeoman Brady came in, Montgomery pointed to the agents and said, "While I take them on the nickel tour, set up two conference rooms. Assign Yeoman Nelson to SSA Carter and you work with SA James. Set each of them up with a complete personnel roster. Escort them to whatever part of the lab they feel they need to see. And when they are ready to start the interviews, bring in Lieutenant Commander Fukuhara's staff first. Assist these agents as they ask, until I relieve you."

"Aye, aye, sir." With that, Brady departed, closing the door behind him. For a moment, Marcus had expected Brady to slightly bow, but that didn't happen.

The tour of the building lasted almost an hour, with most time spent with the team that had focused on Rembrandt. They were now on another project, since Rembrandt was on hold, but all had instant recall about Rembrandt. Their part of the project was setting up the computer code necessary to allow rapid analysis of the discovered submarine's physical characteristics. Glancing out one of the few windows that broke the solid walls of the lab, Marcus saw the shadows growing: a sure indication they were running out of time for the day. They needed to pick up speed.

Turning to Montgomery, Marcus quietly said, "Sir, I think we have a good feel for the building layout now. And we appreciate the introductions to the staff. Time for us to get going on the interviews."

"As you wish, Mr. Colt. Let's head back to my office."

Stopping in the outer office, Montgomery looked at Yeoman Brady and issued the needed orders. "Take SA James and SSA Carter to the conference rooms. If he is needed, Mr. Colt will be with me."

When they again entered Montgomery's office, Marcus was a bit surprised to see the starchy CO take one of the chairs to the side of the desk and point Marcus to another. With his face on a borderline anger setting, Montgomery said, "Okay, Colt. Now that we are alone, what is your problem with me?"

Marcus gave out a slight chuckle as he responded, "Commander, I don't know you well enough to have a problem. I admit your voice doesn't match your physical structure and that's a little disconcerting. But as long as you cooperate fully with my investigation, we'll get along very well."

Montgomery could not stop the laugh that erupted. "You have no idea how refreshing it is to talk with an honest and open Navy officer. Too damn many of them are so busy polishing their skipper's brass that they fail to show the respect that comes with honesty. So, what do you need to ask?"

After that outburst from the CO, Marcus felt more comfortable around him and started pulling the information and answers he felt he needed. The good news was the CO was open and forthcoming on all questions. Bad news was he had only spent about five minutes with Coleman. The agent hadn't shared any information past the fact he was asking around about a Washington-based doctor who had been missing for months. Montgomery did mention Coleman seemed a bit nervous when he left, versus the laid-back attitude he had upon arrival.

"How long was he here?" Marcus asked.

The CO shrugged. "Perhaps five hours on Thursday afternoon. But I can check the entry log for specific times if you need them."

Marcus nodded. "Please. I would like those times, Skipper."

As the CO reached for his phone, Wendy and Tony were deep into their rounds of interviews. With the yeomen ushering in the personnel by rank and rate, Tony and Wendy became efficient with their information gathering. Although it seemed an overwhelming task, the fact they were focused on two specifics—the missing doctor and the dead agent—made things go much faster. Of course, they were watching for signs of stress as each member was interviewed.

The interviews were over. Marcus had put the research laboratory command staff on his list, using the CO's conference room as his interview space. And after the CO, he talked with everyone except the unit's

XO. He got the same answers: not much contact, if any, with Coleman, no direct contact with Doctor Monroe, and nothing strange going on in the lab. No one had any clue about "dock 20."

Tony and Wendy had returned to the CO's conference room after completing their interrogations. They reported that nothing worthwhile had been uncovered, and collapsed heavily into chairs around the table. Marcus was wrapping up his notes when the SP XO Paul Dillon was escorted in and sat down.

"Care for an update, Marcus?" Dillon asked. "Boxer said I would find you here."

"Sounds like a good plan, Paul. Have a seat and spill your guts," Colt said with a grin.

"The NISO secretary noticed that two photo albums were missing. She said both contained mostly local scenic shots and that Coleman fancied himself as a bit of a camera bug. Other than that, she was not too helpful. The local forensic team pulled a ton of prints but nothing else. They will be running them overnight, and maybe we'll have something by tomorrow afternoon," Dillon recited.

"Thanks, Paul," Marcus said.

The yeoman knocked on the door and opened it a small amount before announcing, "Sir, I have Lieutenant Commander Matthew Lane out here. He just came back from a meeting with the base commander."

"Send him in, please," replied Marcus.

Entering the room, Lane came to attention and said, "Lieutenant Commander Matthew Lane, reporting as ordered, sir."

Marcus liked what he saw. He stood and extended his hand. "At ease, Matthew, and have a seat. You're among friends, so relax. I'm Marcus, and these folks are Wendy, Tony, and Paul. We are wrapping up our questioning of your staff, but we do have a couple of questions for you before we call it a day."

Lane nodded and sat back, waiting.

Marcus proceeded to ask the same things he had been asking all afternoon. After getting the same responses, he was feeling another dead end.

About that time, a strange look went across Lane's face, giving him a constipated appearance. "Ya know, I think last Thursday was when the cleaning contractor was running a little late and had a new guy on the crew. They usually show up around 1400 hours, but that day they finally got here closer to 1530."

He stopped and pulled a small notebook from his pocket. Flipping through several pages, he smiled and tapped the book when he found the needed entry. "Yep, last Thursday was the day, and they had a new guy on the cleaning crew. He looked and sounded Eastern European—dark hair, stocky, and slight beard—and, sorry, I didn't get his name. But I can call the service."

Softly, Marcus asked, "What's the name of that cleaning service, Matthew? And are they here now?"

Lane shrugged as he said, "No, they only come in a couple days a week: Tuesday, Thursday, and occasionally on Saturday. They have a weird name in English—maybe it sounds better in Italian. Clock Twenty Cleaning."

Marcus felt blindsided with a gut punch. The word on Coleman's calendar was not *dock*. A lowercase *c* was written close to the *l*, making them look like a *d*. They had been chasing an incorrectly named straw.

After a moment of quiet contemplation, Marcus said, "Paul, do not let that company come back on Navy property until I clear them. Contact the base commander's office and make sure they get the word out—that company is off limits effective immediately. Matthew, please get that info to Captain Boxer ASAP."

Lane looked shocked. "What the hell is going on?"

He looked at Wendy and Tony as he said, "We need to get back to the NISO ASAP. That note on Coleman's calendar was not about a *dock*—he wrote *clock*, but I failed to see it."

70

AN EXTREMELY BRIEF EXPLANATION OF the changing situation was given to Lieutenant Commander Lane. Marcus asked that he pass the comments on to the CO. He also asked Lane to check around to see if anyone on the staff had noticed any strange behavior with the cleaning crew. Especially this past Thursday when Coleman was in the office spaces, and doubly so because of the dark-haired Eastern European.

While Marcus would have preferred to brief the CO himself, and he felt the CO would be expecting that, time was critical and he needed to get everyone together at the NISO immediately. The direction of the investigation needed to be changed, and too many people needed to be updated.

He wanted to see what info Sue was able to get about the local Russian Embassy staff. Montgomery would eventually understand, Marcus hoped, and he would probably buy him drinks and dinner later as a peace offering.

With Tony handling the driving, Marcus started thinking out loud and issuing commands. "Soon as we get there, Wendy, start typing up a ROI for NISHQ with the changed and new information we have right now. Leave it open so we can add whatever Sue has been able to dig up from her contacts."

"Yes, sir," she said.

A slight frown crossed his face, but it vanished as Marcus continued, "Tony, call Captain Boxer. Paul has probably updated him on the cleaning company, but ask him to have unmarked surveillance started on their facilities. The big question is simple. What the hell do we tell him to look for at the place?"

"Maybe I should just ask him to start setting things up and then we'll get him photos soon as we can? Unless his contacts have gotten him the photos already." Tony said.

Marcus nodded. "Yea, that'll work. Tell him we hope to have more info soon, but at least he can start by finding the place. And he may need to surveil the Russian Embassy and watch who is coming and going, that is, if our friends at the CIA haven't done that already. Maybe Sue can find that out. We need to find Kroneski and see what sort of mischief he is creating."

When they got to the NISO, Wendy asked Millie Goshwell if she could use the offline ASR-35 Teletype. Millie agreed, so Wendy took the seat and started keying the ROI.

Entering the back office, Tony and Marcus found all the agents and Sue in a huddle around the conference table. Surprisingly, Sue's associate, Greg, was the center of attention as he pulled papers and photos out of his briefcase and laid them on the table.

Sue rushed over and said, "Your people in D.C. lit a fire under someone, Marcus. Greg just got here with a good bit of information on the Russian Embassy staff."

Marcus gave her a slight smile. "Good. Get any info on 'dock 20' yet?"

She looked down and softly said, "Sorry, Marcus. Nothing stands out in the dock list he sent."

"Not to worry—things have changed and that lead is dead." Marcus then raised his voice and announced, "Listen up, people. We have new information that necessitates an immediate change in thought and direction."

The background chatter stopped and everyone look to Marcus.

"Okay, where to start?" Marcus paused and shook his head. "I missed it. The word on Coleman's calendar was not *dock*. A lowercase *c* was written too close to the *l*, making them look like a *d*, and because of that, we have been chasing an incorrect clue. Sorry. The correct word is *clock*, which would still be somewhat incoherent had we not been talking to the right person at the lab. Luck was on our side today."

Several agents mumbled that they had only seen the word "dock" themselves. Coleman's neatness did not carry over to his penmanship.

"Thanks, but we have wasted a full day on that screw-up. Good news is that Clock Twenty meant something to the XO of the lab. He said it's the name of an outside cleaning crew they use. And it just so happened that a new guy was on their crew the same afternoon Coleman was looking around. Coincidence? I don't believe it. So once Greg explains the treasures he just dumped on the table, Tony will call the SP to set up surveillance on their offices."

Wendy had finished the start of the ROI and came into the agents' area. She maneuvered herself to stand between Marcus and Sue.

Everyone turned to face Greg. He cleared his throat and said, "Marcus, Sec State sends his regards. His orders were to get all the information that we, the CIA and the consulate, have locally on the staff at the Russian Embassy to you ASAP. More will be coming from other places, I have been promised."

Sue looked a little shocked. She turned to Marcus and softly said, "Strange I haven't heard from Dad."

Greg answered her unspoken question. "Sue, your father explained that the request came to him directly from SA Stevens and that Stevens considered it vital to get the info to Marcus. Since you were here, and not at the consulate, I took the call and handled the task."

With a smile, Marcus said, "If Doc felt this was serious enough to talk with Sec State personally, then it is serious." Seeing the confused looks, Marcus offered further explanation. "SA Stevens, called 'Doc' by his friends, is very reluctant to ask for favors, and extremely reluctant to jump the command structure and go directly to someone like the Secretary. Tell us what ya got, Greg."

It took Greg a few minutes to put names on each of the Russian photos. He had travel information on each based upon entry and exits from various countries, but nothing about local travel. He also had background info on each one. After each piece was passed around and read, one of the NISO agents made a dozen sets of copies.

Marcus rapped on the conference table to get everyone's attention. "At least now we know who some of the players might be. Burn the face of Vladimir Davidovich Kroneski into your memory. But we need a lot more information before we can do anything. And that will require the good guys watching the bad guys for a while. Tony, take a couple sets of the copies over to Captain Boxer. Work with him to set up surveillance on both the Embassy and the Clock Twenty Cleaners. Try to incorporate your agents with his SPs."

Tony nodded and asked, "What else?"

Looking at SA Adam Richmann, he issued another order. "Adam, please take a set of the data over to the lab. Brief both the CO and XO. They need to show the photos around to all the staff members and see if anyone recognizes a player. If Montgomery has to call staff members back in tonight, so be it."

Richmann simply said, "Can do." He took the set and left.

Marcus turned to Wendy. "Finish that ROI with all that you just heard. Get Millie to send it highest priority to NISHQ and NISO Norfolk. In the ROI, tell Doc to share it with Jason and the CNO. And aside from that, I can't think of anything else we can do except wait."

As the agents dispersed to do their jobs, Sue turned to Marcus. "You two need a good dinner. That lunch was tasty, but not very filling. Wish I could take you out, but I have to go to a cocktail party at the Consulate of the United Kingdom with our consul general. Some sort of NATO thing, and he demands that I attend. If all goes well, we'll be back around midnight. But Greg is available to you for the evening."

"Not a problem. It will give us a chance to get to know Greg better and give you a break from babysitting duty," Marcus replied with a relaxed grin.

71

IT HAD BEEN A ROUGH day with many twists and turns. Wendy felt a couple hours of down time would help clear their minds. She also knew Marcus had been awake for too long; he'd had maybe sixteen hours of sleep in the last ninety-six. As they drove back to the consulate, she asked Sue to recommend a quiet restaurant away from maddening, frustrating, and very noisy Naples.

Arriving at the consulate, Sue told Greg to take them to a little restaurant she liked on the road to Mount Vesuvius. Greg called the trattoria, Pesce Lavico, and made the reservations for 2100 hrs. Their normal relaxed attire—jeans and jacket—would be fine, he said. The specialty of the place was seafood served on hot slabs of lava rock.

This little place was about one-third the way up the slopes of the volcano, tucked alongside the very curvy, and very narrow, two-lane road. That it was a small place would keep the conversational noise down, providing a restful dinner. Greg told them to meet him in the foyer around 1900 so they would have plenty of time for the drive.

While Wendy was still in her room changing into less business-like attire for dinner, Marcus sipped on a small amount of bourbon on the rocks, dialing all the numbers necessary to call home. Well, he called where he thought Kelly would be at 12:40 p.m. EST. And wherever she was, that was home to Marcus. The operator at Walter Reed transferred the call to the psychological department. Since this was just her second day, and some people had not yet met her, it required a few minutes of waiting and transfers to wrong offices to finally get Kelly on the line.

"This is Mrs. Kelly Colt. How may I help you?" the sweet voice on the phone asked.

Marcus couldn't contain his happiness as he blurted, "I think I need more help than a phone call can provide, babe."

"Well, hello sailor. Just got into town on liberty and looking for a good time, eh?" she said with love and laughter in her voice. "Glad to finally hear your voice again, husband—it's been way too long. Still in Italy?"

After a few more minutes of loving banter, and getting details about her new job, Marcus explained the situation he faced. He wrapped up the overview with, "And since Naples looks to be the key to the case, I'm not sure when we will be heading home. I can only hope something breaks in the next twenty-four to forty-eight hours."

"As long as whatever breaks is not your neck, no problem, Marcus." Kelly knew he was doing all he could, so there was no need to whine about the situation. She offered encouraging and loving words while avoiding any negatives, knowing Marcus would rather be home with her.

"Yea, I have enough scar tissue already. I'll be careful, and Wendy is doing a great job watching my back."

Kelly snickered. "Watching is good. Remember that touching is off limits! Seriously, make sure you take excellent care of her too. I like her, Marcus, and I'll even give her a harem application when you get back." Over their combined laughter, Marcus heard some background noise. Kelly lowered her voice and hastily continued, "Honey, I hate it, but I have to go. My next patient just arrived. You know the drill. Stay safe. Shoot straight. I need you, sailor."

"Always for you, Princess."

The dial tone sounded so lonely to Marcus. He held the phone for a moment, enjoying the remaining electrical bits of distant connection before carefully replacing it in its cradle. He looked up to find Wendy standing in her doorway.

"You okay, boss?" she asked gently as she sat on the sofa across the coffee table from Marcus.

"Oh, yea, it just takes some getting used to—having someone I care about in my life who cares for me, as much and probably even more. It's really different from my past experience."

She smiled. "You are one very lucky man, Marcus Colt, in so many ways. I hope you never forget that."

All he could do was nod. A couple of moments of silence ensued, then Marcus broke it with, "What are your thoughts on today's discoveries, Wendy?"

She laughed. "He asks, changing the subject and breaking the slightly uncomfortable silence."

Marcus smiled and shrugged. "Hey. We all have our talents."

Wendy got more serious. "Okay, I hate to say anything that might jinx it, but it looks like if we can get a bit more info, we're close to breaking both cases wide open. On Coleman's death, we need to find a link between the cleaning company and the missing people who beat him. Now knowing that the Russians have contacts with most of the local crime underworld types, it isn't a stretch to think they did it under Russian orders. But we need proof."

"Very true. So how do we get that proof, super sleuth in training?"

"Find the culprits who did the beating or the Russian who hired them?"

"Right. And finding both would be better. On top of that, we need one more piece of info. Working under the assumption that Coleman was killed because he asked questions around the lab, how the hell did the Russians find out about him being there, and find out so quickly?"

It was Wendy's turn to shrug.

Marcus continued, "Of course, there's one obvious answer—someone in the lab is on the Russian payroll. Hopefully, the BIs that Scott Tiller is getting done will soon point out that person. But the way things usually go, probably not."

Wendy exhaled a huge sigh.

Marcus stood and held out his hand. "Come on, super sleuth in training. Time for dinner."

72

TRAFFIC WAS THE USUAL MESS that locals in Naples had come to expect. The workforce was mostly home by the time the three left the consulate, but that didn't reduce the number of crazy drivers on the larger highways. And it definitely didn't reduce the excitement on the narrow side streets of Naples.

Greg had years of experience with wild drivers in Boston and Washington, so he was somewhat ready for Italy. And during the year's service in Naples, he had honed his driving skills to a point where Marcus believed he was just as crazy as the locals. Marcus was glad he selected the back seat, where he could focus on the back of Wendy's head and not the oncoming drivers who seemed hell-bent on crashing into them.

Perhaps it was part of his cover, but like Sue, Greg kept a running narration about the roads, drivers, and sights around them as he weaved in and out of traffic. Wendy thought that going to dinner was the most dangerous part of this case and regretted not ordering room service back at the consulate.

Marcus had to admit that Naples held a special feeling. It was one city during the day and a totally different one at night. The sun exposed the wonderful architecture and the volcano, but it also exposed the shabbiness of parts of the city. The night hid the bad, and some of the good, but it greatly accented the good with lights. A level of excitement followed Naples at night. It was probably the same in all big, old cities, but there was something Marcus could not explain that just felt different. It was a comfortable feeling. Marcus leaned back and returned his focus to Wendy's head.

Finally, after over an hour of horrid traffic, Greg turned left onto a somewhat quieter street and scooted past the sign indicating that the Mount Vesuvius Observation Area was so many kilometers ahead. The restaurant was about two kilometers short of the observation area, but Greg decided to drive all the way up to show it to his guests. Granted it was dark and there wouldn't be much to see, but Marcus believed logic was something CIA employees avoided too frequently.

Were it not for the cloud cover and chance of rain, the night would have been much brighter. There had been a full moon the previous night and, while it was technically on the wane, the illumination was only slightly reduced from that of the night before. But it did them no good, as the dark rain clouds covered the sky and threw a wet blanket over any lunar light.

The road up the volcano was similar to other side roads in Naples, both too damn narrow and very curvy. Tight hairpin turns emerged one after another as the road climbed the side of Vesuvius. The grades were too steep in places, giving the impression they had simply paved over donkey paths. And while the posted speed limit was greatly reduced, Marcus doubted the locals observed those limits. A small wooden guardrail was the only thing stopping a vehicle from driving off the side of the volcano. But since it was dark, the two out-of-towners did not see the shear drop-offs.

Marcus had been looking out the side and back windows, now that the amount of oncoming traffic was greatly reduced. He thought he saw a car behind them, but it had vanished in the dark. *Probably turned off*, he thought. There were no streetlights on this road, but as they passed their restaurant, the lit sign cast a soft glow onto the roadway. Marcus was sure he saw a shadow several car lengths behind them.

They rounded another hairpin turn and slowly climbed farther up the volcano. As yet another hairpin turn approached, Greg slowed even more. Marcus leaned forward over the seat and started to mention the possible tail to Greg when a violent jolt shook the car.

Greg yelled, "What the hell?"

The screeching sound of metal against metal and the squeal of tires as Greg hammered the brake overpowered the yell from Wendy as she saw the guardrail right in front of their car. They hit it with a loud *thunk*, and things got quieter as the car became airborne.

Marcus reached over and somehow pulled Wendy into the back seat. He held her down as the car tilted forward and the front wheels slammed to earth. The back wheels landed even harder, and all three people inside the car took a beating as a different noise started.

The new noise was tree branches slapping against the front and side windows. At their speed, the runaway auto simply mowed down small trees as it plummeted uncontrollably down the steep slope of Vesuvius into greater darkness.

After what seemed to be forever inside the battered auto, the foliage noise abruptly stopped following the ear-splitting sound of metal compressing as the car slammed into a tree too large to overpower. Pain enveloped the three passengers. Blackness filled their eyes as their brains triggered unconsciousness to grant some relief from the pain. The intense noise was replaced with a soft ticking sound as ruptured coolant lines spewed their liquid on hot metal. The downhill ride was over.

Back up the hill, two men stood by the side of the road, looking down at the trail of destruction left by Greg's car. Aside from the damaged guardrail, a small amount of skid marks, and disturbed small trees and brush near the road, nothing else about the attack was visible from where they stood. The car's headlights had gone out as it crashed down the slope and was swallowed up by the darkness.

The unconscious occupants of the car could not hear the heated discussion between the two men. A short stocky man wanted to climb down to make sure the targets were dead. The other gent, taller and holding a weapon, believed no one could survive that drop. He said, "No, we leave immediately. No need to tempt fate with the authorities, Mario."

The presence of the weapon was the deciding factor in the argument. A few moments later, a dark Mercedes with a now-damaged front bumper did a quick three-point turn and sped back down the winding road.

73

HE KNEW THE LITTLE GUYS in black pajamas were close. And when they caught them, he and Doc would be in for—at the very least—some nasty beatings. More than likely death would follow, and by then it would be a blessing. The pain they felt now was nothing compared to what might be coming. Marcus listened carefully and, after hearing just the sounds of the forest and the rain, he tried to move. But Doc latched on to him tight. Marcus was surprised, since Doc had been unconscious for hours.

The slight movement and the grasp of Doc's arms caused pain to explode from every inch of his body. The burn of the bullet wounds in his head and side was replaced by a dull ache everywhere that increased as Doc held tighter. Marcus grimaced as he whispered, "Damn it, Doc, let go of me. We need to move."

A weak female voice said, "I can't move, Marcus. You're lying on top of me. My leg hurts."

Marcus was slowly starting to remember he was not back in Vietnam and felt relief—just another dream. Then that relief was replaced by panic. "Kelly, what's wrong?" he yelled.

"Not Kelly—Wendy. I think we've been in a car wreck. I'm hurt, Marcus," the voice replied.

Memories of the last few minutes flooded into Marcus's mind. They had been followed and forced off the road. Were they still being hunted? And who did the attack? He checked and found his weapon still in place. But those questions would have to wait until the immediate medical situation was under better control.

First challenge was to get out of the car, but Marcus needed to assess their injuries before making any big moves. But the night was so dark it was as if he hadn't opened his eyes. Black was the only thing he saw. Through the mental fog, he remembered seeing a flashlight under the back of the driver's seat.

"Hold on, Wendy. I need to find the flashlight. I think it's on the floor somewhere." He felt around under the front seat until he touched the cold metal flashlight housing.

As Marcus felt for the switch, he realized whoever ran them off the road might be looking for them to finish the job. Moving slowly, he pulled the bottom edge of his jacket up and covered the lens of the light. Wendy moaned with each small movement he made. Turning on the light created a soft blue glow. It was enough to check for damages while not providing a locator beacon for the bad guys. At least, he hoped.

Wendy was on her back, directly under Marcus. Their heads were positioned on the driver's side of the car. Marcus used his empty hand to push his upper body up off Wendy a small amount. There was blood on the seat and her face, but he saw no wounds on her face or neck, and both eyes looked and responded okay. The space in the backseat was limited, and Marcus realized he needed to get the door open to have enough room to lift completely off her. Turning slowly and reaching back, he found the passenger side door handle and pushed it down.

There was a soft metallic click, but the door did not move. He placed one foot on the door and pushed. The metal moaned as the disfigured door opened a small amount. Wendy matched that moan as the jolt on the door sent stabbing pains throughout her body.

"Sorry, Wendy, but we need to get clear of the car. One more jolt should do it, so grit your teeth and hold on."

"Okay, I'm ready," she grunted through the pain.

This time Marcus gave the door a swift kick. A loud creaking noise filled the car as the door moved enough for Marcus to slowly climb out. Wendy let out a partial scream and went quiet.

Marcus almost lost his balance as he stood beside the car. The pain in his head increased and nausea almost got the best of him. At least the cool night air and the gentle rain felt refreshing. He took several deep breaths, which caused more pain, and rubbed his forehead; his hand came away sticky and wet. A medical degree wasn't needed to know he had another head wound. Therefore, it was a good guess the blood on Wendy and the seat was his.

A quick check of his extremities found them all working. There was pain everywhere, more so in his right knee. He listened for sounds of the bad guys approaching and looked around, figuring up the slope was where they would appear. Nothing caught his attention, so he hoped they'd been left for dead.

Looking back in the car, he again turned on the flashlight to check Wendy. Her lower left leg was slightly bent forward from an obvious break. Fortunately it didn't look to be a compound fracture, but she could still be bleeding inside. Leaning into the car, he saw that she had passed out. At least her breathing was normal, and her pulse felt strong. No other wounds were visible. He prayed there were no further internal injuries.

Marcus looked forward over the seat. Thick tree limbs had wiped out the windshield. One, slightly under three inches in diameter, had impaled Greg through the chest. His lifeless eyes seemed to stare at the limb in disbelief. Fighting for control to the end, his hands still clutched the wheel. A second limb was imbedded in the passenger seat, where Wendy had been sitting.

One piece of good news about the crash was the car had taken down several small trees. Marcus released the Fairbairn–Sykes knife from his calf and grabbed several somewhat straight branches about four feet long. The sharp knife removed the small branches, resulting in four mostly smooth splints, needed for Wendy's leg. With his knife, he removed her left pants leg from about eight inches above the knee. He cut this lengthwise into several four-inch wide strips. Then he took off his jacket to get access to his dress shirt, which he removed and also cut into strips about an inch wide.

Wendy being passed out made his task a bit easier on her. Marcus worked to straighten her leg as best he could. For padding, he wrapped the pants leg strips in four spots: around her leg above the knee, just below the knee but above the break, just below the break, and at the ankle. He aligned the splints around her leg and tied them in place with the shirt strips. He made sure the bonds were tight, but not tight enough to cut off circulation.

With her leg immobilized, he carefully reached into the car, slid her across the seat, and gently picked her up. The pain in his head increased with the exertion, and blood ran into his eyes. He gently placed her on the ground near the trunk of the tree and sat down beside her to fix his leaking head. Not being able to see his wound, he guessed its location from the pain and used the sleeves from his shirt as a compress. The last two shirt strips held the compress in place. He wiped the blood from his eyes as best he could with the help of the rain.

A quick search of the car found Wendy's purse wedged under the front seat. Marcus wanted her weapon, of course, but he hoped to find a small bottle of aspirin; they both needed that pain relief right then. Luck was on his side as he found a small flat tin of Bayer in a side pocket of the purse. He swallowed three of them dry to get the pain relief started.

He looked around the car in hopes of finding anything useful. Right then, he needed something to catch the rainwater. The trunk had sprung open and a fast rummage revealed a waterproof tarp and a small blanket. He spread the tarp on the ground a few feet beyond the limb coverage of the tree, and made sure all the water that landed on it ran into the depression he had made on the downhill side. With that task done, he covered Wendy with the blanket. She was still unconscious.

The car trunk held several critical items Marcus needed. In addition to the tarp and blanket, it held a grungy winter jacket, a carton of empty soda bottles Greg was probably returning to the market, a length of lightweight rope, and a floppy canvas fisherman's hat with a brim all the way around. Marcus positioned the hat on his head to help hold the bandages in place and keep the rain out of his eyes. Then he added the winter jacket over his own.

He grabbed two of the empty soda bottles, and after verifying no insects or mold had made a home there, carried them to the tarp in anticipation of the forthcoming water supply. A third bottle he placed under a fender of the car where water was flowing off the crumpled hood in a small stream. Granted, it was not the cleanest, but it beat not having any water.

The glove compartment contained another smaller flashlight, and a critical thing for their survival: a map! Marcus sat in the back seat to keep the map out of the rain and studied the road that now lay above them. He tried to remember how many hairpin turns they had taken before the crash. If his memory was right, and he prayed that it was, they were on the third tight turn past the restaurant, so the car had come crashing down pointing to the town called Torre del Greco.

Considering the distance he walked carrying Doc in 'Nam, the three or so miles to the town should be considered a walk in the park. But Marcus was enough of a realist to know that, like 'Nam, the terrain was sloped, rugged, and now very wet. The darkness added to the danger of dropping Wendy and making her injuries worse.

As he sat looking at the map, all Marcus wanted to do was lie back and close his eyes. The pain from every part of his body and the bleeding head wound tried to take control. Fatigue, from the blood loss and lack of food and sleep, was doing its share to get him to lie down. But he knew Wendy needed medical care.

He checked his watch: it was 2230 hrs, which meant they had been down here for over an hour and a half. No sirens or flashing lights meant no one was nearby to rescue them. And since Sue was dining out for most of the night, no one would miss them for at least another hour or so. And more than likely, no one would notice their absence until morning, when Sue tried to find them for breakfast.

Marcus knew there was only one option. He had to carry Wendy the rest of the way down the freaking volcano and find medical help in the middle of the night. *Oh, well*, he thought. *The only easy day was yesterday.*

He folded the map and stuck it in his jacket pocket as he walked to where Wendy was lying. She was still out, so he started packing for the journey. He drank the water collected off the car and transferred the tarp-collected rainwater to one of the bottles; the tarp had already collected a couple of ounces. The bottle with the precious liquid was placed in the inside pocket of his jacket, where it would stay vertical … unless he tripped and fell. He rolled the tarp like a western bedroll and tied it using the rope from the trunk. The sling he'd created from rope positioned the tarp over his back, and it hung out of the way.

With the large flashlight stuck in his back pocket, Marcus decided the smaller one would work better as he carried Wendy. Her leg injury would make a fireman's carry challenging, so Marcus decided the more difficult cradle-carry would work best. He carefully tucked the blanket around Wendy like a cocoon, placed the flashlight in his right hand, and gently lifted her in his arms.

Again, he silently thanked Doc for forcing him to do additional reps as he rebuilt the damaged muscles in his left arm over the summer. Without that exercise, he would not have been able to carry Wendy. A final nod towards Greg Walker's body was all Marcus could do for him right then. Well, that and give a silent promise to severely punish his killers.

Hopefully, recovery of the body would come soon after he found a doctor for Wendy.

It was still an hour away from midnight when the journey began. Marcus started off with small steps as his body adjusted to the weight in his arms. The aspirin dumped on his empty stomach had kicked in a bit, and the pain had eased off from a level of "please just let me die" to mere extreme discomfort. He could handle that for a while. And with the image of Greg's body in the front of his mind, he allowed the anger for the bastards, which he'd been ignoring, to build. He was determined to make them pay. That anger gave him extra strength, and his steps became more confident as he carried Wendy down the slopes of the volcano to safety.

74

RIDING IN THE BIG LIMO with the consul general himself was always a treat for any of the consulate staff. And while Sue had become used to such amenities growing up, because of her father's career, even she felt a bit special that night due to that treatment.

The affair had gone on for hours and would probably continue for several more. The consul general took his leave due to a growing sinus headache, and for that reason, they were able to depart early and still save face. While it had been fun, it was also tiring.

Not seeing Greg's car in its usual parking space gave her a bit of concern. Perhaps he had dashed out on an errand for Marcus. Sue decided a quick check with her guests was probably a wise decision; besides, she was curious if any new events had happened. And seeing Marcus always gave her a slight tingle.

There was no response to the knock on their door. *They might be sleeping already*, she thought, but that seemed unlikely. Using the phone in the hall, she called the suite. There was no answer to the many rings. With concern growing, she used her master key and entered the suite. Both bedroom doors were open and no one was there.

Her next thought was that perhaps they were running late coming from dinner. Nighttime traffic in Naples can be a bitch. And it was raining, which made it rougher. Finding the phone directory, she called the restaurant. Fortunately the owner answered. They had been friends for some time now, and she knew she could trust him. He reported that the reservation for three was never filled. They had not phoned to cancel nor had they arrived. He was sorry, since he'd looked forward to serving her friends.

Since it was still too early to panic, Sue went to her office. Her private directory contained office and home phone numbers of just about every important contact in southern Italy. Checking with the Polizia di Stato told her there were no reported traffic accidents that involved a diplomatic-licensed car or anyone named Gregory Walker, Wendy James, or Marcus Colt.

The Shore Patrol duty officer told her he hadn't seen nor heard from Mr. Colt since earlier in the day. He would radio the patrols to be on the lookout for Greg's car, but he had no other info to offer at this time.

Sue then considered that maybe something broke in the case, and they'd gone back to the NISO. A call to that office resulted in a recorded message from the TAD. The Telephone Answering Device told her that the office would open at 0800 hrs and if there was an emergency, to call the Shore Patrol office. So that was a dead end.

Consulting her directory again, she found the home number for Tony Carter and placed the call. It only rang twice before a voice came on the line.

"Carter," a sleepy voice answered.

"Tony, this is Sue Woodward. Have you seen Marcus tonight?"

"Uh, not since he left the office with you. What's up?"

"We might have a problem, Tony. My assistant was escorting them to dinner earlier. And that restaurant was the only destination he gave the security personnel when they left. They aren't here at the consulate and the restaurant said they never arrived there. According to the Polizia, there are no reported accidents with their vehicle. And the SP duty officer has not seen them."

Tony yawned. "Hell, maybe Greg took them for a quick pizza and some sightseeing, Sue."

Sue shook her head as she replied, "No way, Tony. They were both dead tired, and sightseeing, especially on a dark rainy night, was definitely not on their list of things to do. Besides, Greg would have called in a change of plans to security. I've got a bad feeling about this."

"Okay, you call the SP duty officer back and ask him to get Captain Boxer into his office pronto. You head over there now. I'll call my agents and we'll all meet you there. Since the SPs have radio-equipped vehicles all around the city, it will make coordination much easier to use their office. Move!"

Sue looked at the phone as if expecting more than the dial tone that filled her ear. She redialed the Shore Patrol office and passed the needed information to the duty officer. He was reluctant to call the captain at that hour until Sue told him all the people who were descending upon his office right then for a meeting. The lieutenant decided that information justified the CO being the best choice to handle such a meeting.

Before she dashed out to the SP office, she alerted the consulate guards about the situation. They would call her if the missing people showed up. As she stood to leave, one more thought hit her. She grabbed the phone and called a special number in Washington, D.C.

"White House. How may I direct your call?"

"Susan Woodward calling the Secretary of State please."

The operator's voice lightened up a notch. "One moment, Sue. We'll get your father on the line quickly."

There were a number of people who had special White House-connected phone lines that were to be answered within sixty seconds of the first ring. The Sec State had one in each of his homes, at his office, and in his car.

And as protocol dictates, he answered promptly and, having been alerted to the caller, with a happy voice. "Hello, darling. Good to hear from you. I'm just heading home now."

"Daddy, I might have a problem. Marcus and his partner may be missing. And so is my assistant, Greg. Does Marcus have a habit of running off on a tangent without letting anyone know what he's doing?"

Seriousness took over the Sec State's voice. "No, he's very good at keeping everyone in the loop or at least finding a way to leave messages, if he can. Give me all the details, honey."

Her FBI training took over, and she gave a succinct update on the situation. She finished by saying, "And based on the needed surveillance, no one expected anything to bubble up for at least another day or two."

"Looks like someone may be a step or two ahead of the good guys. Hope not. Get on over to the SP office and keep me posted. I'll call Doc Stevens and give him an update. Perhaps by then they'll have returned on their own to the consulate after stopping for a movie or limoncello. Love you, Susan."

"Can do, Daddy. Bye."

A short time later, as she walked into the Shore Patrol headquarters and received smiles from the men on duty, she realized that taking the time to change out of her black evening gown would have been wise. *Too late now,* she thought as she approached the duty desk.

"I'm Susan Woodward. Is Captain Boxer here yet?"

The lieutenant said, "Yes, ma'am, he is expecting you in his conference room. The petty officer will escort you back."

"Fine," Sue replied. "There will be at least four NIS agents arriving soon, so make sure they join us upon arrival. And there may be a call from Washington, so be ready to transfer it back to me. Thanks." She gave the lieutenant a smile he would never forget and followed the petty officer.

75

THE RAIN HAD INCREASED FROM just over a drizzle to just short of a deluge. Visibility, even with the flashlight, had been bad, and now it was non-existent. Marcus had to walk slower to avoid trees, rocks, and other obstacles that nature put in his path. He was determined not to drop Wendy, even though his arms were starting to burn from the load. *Just one more step*, he kept thinking. *One more step.*

Wendy was stirring slightly, and soft moans were her means of communicating her pain. She was starting to wake up again. Marcus remembered Doc doing similar the previous year, as he carried him to safety. With his eyes searching the ground for obstacles and his mind pushing to get one more step before he collapsed, Marcus was caught off guard as he nearly walked into the wall of a small wooden building.

Walking around the structure, he used his light to find a door with a simple wood latch. He turned it and stared into a void so dark that black took on a new meaning. Fortunately, the flashlight pierced the darkness and allowed Marcus to see inside a storage shed holding sacks of something. Whatever it was, Marcus immediately decided it would provide a decent, dry resting place for a short time. He lowered Wendy onto a level layer of sacks and allowed his arms a moment of freedom and relief.

Marcus turned off the small flashlight and pulled the larger one from his pocket. Using it, he looked around and was disappointed not to find any source of light. While he had doubted he'd find electricity, not even a lantern or a candle was seen. He propped up the flashlight so it would shine to the ceiling and give soft light to the immediate area. Going back to Wendy, he started to remove the blanket. He wanted to check her leg, since swelling could disrupt the blood flow if the splint was too tight.

"You sure know how to show a girl a good time, Marcus. I see why Kelly snapped you up," Wendy said through gritted teeth. Her hands were clenched at her side.

Marcus smiled. "Damn glad to have you back, partner. It was getting lonely talking to the trees. Here are a couple of aspirin I found in your purse." He held her head up and placed the aspirin in her mouth, then handed her the water bottle.

She choked a bit on the water, but got the meds down. "Where are we? What happened? All I remember is pain, and I still hurt all over."

Marcus checked his watch and saw it was 0130 hrs. He looked at Wendy and said, "The attack happened just before 2100. A dark-colored car pushed us off the road and down the volcano side. No idea how far down the slope we came, but a tree finally stopped the car. Greg is dead. You have a broken leg. We both came to around 2230, then you passed out again. I started carrying you down the volcano just before 2300."

Marcus paused and took a small sip of the shared water. "It's 0130 now, and we are in a storage shed somewhere between the wreck site and hopefully a town called Torre del Greco. Assuming I haven't gotten too far off my proposed path through the woods. With the dark and the rain, we might be in Greece by now for all I know. Note to self, always carry a small compass. But before anything else, I need to check your leg."

The swelling was minimal, but Marcus loosened the binding nearest the break a small amount. Wendy wanted to sit up, but the lieutenant commander insisted she move as little as possible. His next task was to check outside for water and to try to find some geographic locator. He explained this to Wendy and stepped out of the shed.

There were no signs on the shed, and the overcast sky and rain prevented him from seeing far into the distance. Luck was on his side with one thing: he found a water spigot and filled the two soda bottles. He drank half of one and refilled it before carrying them to Wendy.

Back outside, he decided to check out the area around the shed. It backed up to thick woods on the uphill side. On the downhill side,

Marcus found rows and rows of plants. From his years helping his family with the vegetable garden in West Virginia, he recognized tomato plants. He saw a couple of ripe ones and picked one to test. The flavor was excellent, although it could use a few more days on the vine. Since lunch was many hours ago, Marcus didn't complain and picked several more.

But he couldn't tell how large the farm was or where any farmhouse might be located. No lights were cutting through the rain. He could be fifty feet from a house and not see it. And if he decided to head in any direction, it could be a costly mistake. He chose the only logical option for the moment and went back inside.

Wendy was breathing slowly and seemed more relaxed. Perhaps the aspirin had helped cut the pain level. He walked over and knelt down beside her.

"Figure out where we are?" she asked.

He shook his head and handed her a couple of tomatoes. They ate their feast in silence for a moment, then Marcus cleared his throat.

"Here's the deal, Wendy. I can't see a damn thing out there except rows of tomato plants. The land is more level here, unlike what I just covered, so I can't rely on just going 'down hill' to get us where we need to be. In the dark and rain, I could easily walk parallel to the shoreline for hours instead of heading perpendicular to it. Hell, it might be a hundred yards past the last tomato plant! If we were both healthy, I'd just stay here until dawn. But you need medical attention, and I could use some myself. My thought is we rest here a bit until the rain backs off and then try to locate a house, or some other landmark. What ya think? The decision is yours since you have the worst wounds."

Her smile showed the pain she felt. "I don't know how you carried me for the last couple of hours. You have to be exhausted. Your work on the splint would be the envy of any first aid class and I don't see any signs of internal bleeding. Sure it hurts, but I'm for staying here a while. Take a couple of aspirin, get some rest and we'll let the rain go past. Okay?"

Marcus nodded as he touched her hand and said, "I knew you were perfect for this job the minute you walked off the elevator." He stood and covered her with the blanket, then leveled out several other sacks to create a bed for himself beside her. In hopes of sharing body warmth, Marcus pressed against Wendy's side and pulled a small section of the blanket over him. Sleep came immediately.

76

CAPTAIN WESLEY BOXER HAD MADE several calls after he got an update from Sue. Now approaching 0200 hrs, there were representatives from three Italian law enforcement agencies stationed in his office to co-ordinate the search: the Polizia di Stato, the Arma dei Carabinieri, and the Polizia Municipale. In American terms, these three agencies are equal to the state, military, and city police forces. Boxer had friends in high places that he could call for help.

The combined forces of the five agencies, the three Italian agencies, NIS, and the Shore Patrol now numbered over several thousand officers. Considering the vast area of Naples and Mount Vesuvius, it might not be enough.

The facts were painfully simple. Three persons and their consulate car were still missing. As each hour passed, concern mounted, since there were already too many deaths associated with this case. And while the death of a Navy officer can cause international repercussions, the death of a diplomat, no matter how low on the food chain, was much worse for the Italians.

Phones were constantly ringing and the incessant, high volume of talk in the offices made thinking difficult. But it continued as new ideas on where to look were shared between the five agencies.

SSA Tony Carter had his agents checking the surveillance logs of the teams watching the research lab, the Russian Embassy, and the Clock Twenty Cleaners. They needed to know who had come and gone. And they needed to know when the movements had occurred. They were looking for times that would coincide with the consulate car moving from Naples to Mount Vesuvius.

Shore Patrol members across the area were now on a sweep looking for the car. Extra personnel had been called in from a couple of ships in port. Everything short of roadblocks and lockdowns was being done in the search. And the Italian law enforcement teams were checking and double checking every known criminal and every known place a car could be hidden. So far, nothing had turned up.

Sue was sitting in the captain's office. She and the CO had been batting ideas around and finally reached the point of having nothing new to say. So they sat quietly and waited. Sue was sipping what had to be the fourth cup of strong coffee when the phone rang. The captain answered immediately and passed it to Sue.

"Susan Woodward speaking."

"This is the White House. This line is not secured. Go ahead, Mr. Secretary."

"Any updates, Susan?" her father asked.

"No, sir. Still missing. We're using the Shore Patrol office as our command center and have full cooperation from the Italians. Every rock they can find is being looked under at least twice."

"Anything I can do to help, honey?"

"I wish I could think of something, Daddy. Right now, prayer is high on my list."

"Well, I won't keep you. Just remember the full force of the United States stands waiting your call. You sound tired, so try to get some rest. Love you so much."

Sue smiled as the dial tone replaced her father's voice. As she returned the phone to the cradle, the CO gave her a quizzical look. "He is never one for long goodbyes. I usually get the 'love you' immediately followed by the dial tone. Tonight he showed more concern by adding the 'so much.' Just his way, I guess."

"Ma'am, my hearing is pretty good, and I must say I agree with your father. You look like you need some rest. We have an office set up down the hall where the duty officer can grab a nap. You can use it, and I highly suggest you do. I'll wake you if anything pops."

Sue put on a sad smile. "Captain Boxer, your advice is sound and your warm smile is impossible to resist. I'll go close my eyes for a bit. Thanks." As she left the CO's office, Sue glanced around and took in all the activity and people just in the office working the case. She was impressed that so much came together so fast. She just hoped it worked. Losing Marcus on her watch was simply unthinkable.

77

DOC HAD BEEN AT THE Colt house for only an hour when the call from the Sec State came in. The Secretary had called the NISHQ only to be told that Doc had left for the day. After identifying himself, the yeoman handling the phone explained why Doc was at the Colts' house and gave him the number. Their call lasted just a few minutes, but long enough for Doc to understand the severity even more than Sec State did.

He was now fighting emotions that ran between the need to break something in anger and the need to break down in tears. Marcus might be in trouble and he was half a world away, unable to do a damn thing. And his gut churned as he tried to think of an easy way to tell Kelly. She was running very late because of a challenging patient but was due home within the hour or so.

Doc had made what Marcus often called a "management decision," which meant doing what he knew had to be done even though it was difficult. Doc had called Kelly's father, the CNO, right after hearing the news from Sec State. That was not an easy call to make. The CNO said he and Elaine would head to Kelly's house as quickly as possible and be there when she got home. He also said Elaine had a way with Kelly that would help.

Doc had started pulling leftovers out for dinner when the doorbell announced the arrival of Kelly's folks. Not surprising Doc at all, David Bartow followed them inside.

"Any more news, Doc?" Admiral Gallagher asked as he put his arm around Doc's shoulder, offering emotional support.

"Sorry, nothing else yet, sir."

David went to the liquor cabinet and held up a bottle of bourbon. The admiral nodded a *yes* and said, "All around please, David."

As he poured, David tried to relieve the anxiety. "I hope the team in Naples is not running in circles like the headless chicken too soon. We know Marcus can be counted on to do the impossible, and sometimes he works outside of the box a little. Technically, his whereabouts have been unknown for only a few hours."

Doc nodded. "I agree, David, but we may be facing a real nasty bastard—please excuse me, Elaine—a nasty criminal with this Kroneski guy."

Elaine said, "No problem, Doc. Living with Bill all these years, I've heard that word a time or two. I'll get into the kitchen and see what can be done there. It will be hard to get Kelly to eat, but she'll need to get something down."

As she stood to go, the doorbell rang again, so Elaine dashed to answer it. Opening the door, she found Victoria standing there with a sad look on her face.

"Oh, hello, Elaine, I'm glad you're here. I so hope I am not disturbing anything, but I do need to speak with Doc a moment, if he is free," Victoria said as Elaine motioned for her to enter.

Entering the living room, Victoria looked at the men facing her. "I see my news has already arrived. Les called me right after the director spoke with Sec State."

Doc came to Victoria and said, "They just arrived and I was getting ready to come get you. We need all the ideas we can generate. We have bourbon open, want some?"

"Indeed."

David handed her a glass of bourbon. The visually upset five touched glasses as the admiral said, "To the safe return of our people."

After a sip and a moment of silence, Doc looked at Victoria and said, "Last info I got was well over an hour ago. You probably have the freshest news. What did your director say?"

"Sec State spoke with his daughter, Sue, less than thirty minutes ago. The local authorities are working with the NIS and SP personnel on an area-wide search. Nothing has yet to turn up, but in proper Navy tradition, all hands are on deck."

The admiral chuckled at the reference and added, "And we know Kelly will think that's too few."

As if on cue, the back door opened, and Kelly's tired expression turned to happiness as she spotted the group in the dining room. "Hi, Doc, glad to see we're having a party tonight. I could use some … oh, hell, what happened to Marcus?" Concern replaced the smile and a touch of anger entered her voice when she saw their faces.

David was the first to move to her side and put his hands on her shoulders as he softly said, "We don't know, Kelly. Marcus, his partner, and their CIA driver have been missing for a few hours and a search is underway. That is all we know."

Bill Gallagher handed his daughter a glass of bourbon and said, "David's right. We're all probably overreacting, but we wanted to be here with you."

Her fatigue from the patients of the extended day and her climbing worry took control, and she lashed out with venom in her voice. "Finish your sentence. Don't you mean 'just in case he's dead?' You just *had* to send him on yet another dangerous mission, didn't you, Dad."

The pain on her father's face caused her to take him in her arms in a hug. She cried as she whispered, "I'm so sorry, Dad. I know none of this is your fault."

"Yea, it is, honey. You're right, I selected him for the case. But know this, I would do it again because he *is* the very best. And being the best, no matter what crap is thrown his way, he will dance between the raindrops. Hell, he's probably drinking wine and relaxing right now at some hole-in-the-wall restaurant in Naples trying to get the last drops of seafood stew from the bowl."

78

THE SHED SEEMED LIGHTER WHEN Marcus opened his eyes. While still too dark to see specifics, it was as if a soft glow was starting to grow. He still ached all over, and the pain in his head was reaching an unbearable level. His stomach needed food, and a glass of wine would have helped numb the pain.

But not much food and no wine were available. His hat, coat, and jeans were still cold and soggy from the rain. But he knew he had a mission to complete and a partner to get to the doctor. Marcus checked his watch and was surprised to see he had slept for about three hours. It was just after 0500.

Moving slowly and quietly, he sat up to check on Wendy. Using his jacket as a filter to reduce the glare of the light, Marcus saw that she was sleeping. Her breathing was soft and steady. He gently touched her forehead and didn't feel any fever. So far, things were looking good. He took another aspirin and drank one of the bottles of water. Water he hoped was not filled with bacteria.

Opening the door as quietly as possible, Marcus stepped out to find that the rain had finally stopped. The cool morning air was still damp from the last of the showers, and the clouds were clearing. The bright moon was heading down toward the horizon, but the cloud cover still blocked most of the light. The soft glow from the small amount of moonlight was like a spotlight to a man who had spent hours in near total darkness.

Checking all directions showed the tomato fields extended over a small rise toward what Marcus believed to be a westward direction. Looking to what he considered the north and south, the fields ended at forest several hundred yards from his location. The forest looked as thick as the one behind him running up the volcano. A few lights gave off a faint glow visible miles away in the west-northwest direction. That was probably Naples.

He looked back up the volcano. Dark, dense forest was all he saw. No flashing lights spoiled the darkness. He smiled slightly as he thought, *at least I have added 'walked down the side of a volcano' to my list of accomplishments.*

After the scouting, Marcus took a minute to relieve his bladder pressure and then splashed some water on his face from the spigot. He didn't dare remove the hat for fear of more bleeding, deciding to leave well enough alone for now. Then he harvested a couple more tomatoes for breakfast.

Leaving the door open, Marcus could see Wendy starting to stir, so he went over and knelt beside her sack bed, softly calling her name. She opened her eyes and a look of fear crossed her face.

Marcus took her hand and quietly said, "Wendy, it's okay. We're still on Vesuvius and still hurting, but the rain has stopped. We can get moving when you're ready. I'm going to check your leg, so keep holding still, okay?"

She tried to smile as she said, "Whatever you say, Marcus. I'm hurting too much to argue or move, anyway."

Marcus saw the swelling was about the same as earlier, but some discoloration was building around the break area. Her eyes were still dilating properly and equally. No fever or nausea, so they had some positives to celebrate.

"Well, Ensign James, my engineering degree says you have a stable leg brace. Perhaps my best work, considering the available materials. And my first aid training leads me to believe we both will survive this ordeal. I don't see signs of a concussion and you don't have a fever, so let's hold on to those positives."

Wendy tried to smile, but it was weak. "And what about you, boss? I see blood residue on your cute hat, the ugly coat, and the sides of your face. You okay?"

"Not too bad for an old guy. I have a head wound, but don't know the extent. Head hurts like hell, but at least I got the bleeding stopped. Like you, every part of my body hurts from bouncing around the backseat of that car."

Wendy's face clouded over with sadness. "Greg's dead, right?"

"Yea, a tree limb came through the windshield and into his chest. He went quick."

They both were quiet for a couple of minutes, remembering the man they had met only two days ago.

"I know our primary concern is getting off this volcano alive, but I suspect your brain has been working overtime figuring out who did this to us," she said. "Care to share?"

"Someone in the research lab is on the payroll for whoever is behind all this. Speculation—probably the Russians. That person saw us asking a bunch of questions, probably heard Coleman's name mentioned, and jumped on the phone sharing that info with their contact. That contact put a tail on us. I suspect we've been followed since we left the lab, and they saw an opportunity to act when we came up that narrow road."

"Makes sense."

Marcus nodded. "And I'll wager the same damn thing happened when Coleman was in the lab on Thursday. I guess he went into hiding at Sandra's place after seeing or hearing something we have yet been able to find. They either lost him when he went to Sandra's or had to wait until he left on Sunday before they could take him out. We'll probably never know for sure how he ended up in that alley. A logical guess would be he spotted the tail and tried to shake it. During that attempted evasion, he got trapped."

"And I guess the BIs you ordered from your Air Force buddy might show someone with more money than is normal, right?"

"Hope so." Marcus handed Wendy the last two aspirin and a bottle of water. With her now awake, the trek was going to be more painful for her.

He gave her instructions in short sentences. "Take these right now. Here are a couple of tomatoes for breakfast. Get those down to cushion the aspirin. Then brace yourself for the pain of another journey. We need to find a local doctor."

Marcus helped Wendy into a sitting position and placed a couple of sacks of whatever it was behind her back for support. She grimaced as she moved, but succeeded in making it happen. After she ate the tomatoes and passed the empty water bottle to Marcus to refill, an unusual look came across her face.

"What's wrong, Wendy?" Marcus asked with concern in his voice.

She gave out a small giggle. "Sir, this is one of those times when the ladies' room is not very handy but desperately needed. Got any suggestions?"

A few minutes later, he got to use his engineering degree again to rig up a place of convenience and modesty. The broken leg and improvised splint system hampered the efforts, but in due time, Wendy's bladder felt much better. Marcus had sacrificed his handkerchief to the cause. A roll of TP was not something he usually carried out to dinner.

Back in the shed after the improvised restroom break, Wendy had a puzzled look as Marcus packed up their small stash of belongings. He decided not to leave the tarp, even though both water bottles were filled and the skies were clearing. She finally asked, "How did you carry me down here, Marcus?"

With a chuckle, Marcus said, "Did you ever watch old horror movies? I used the cradle-carry, just like the Mummy and the Creature from the Black Lagoon as they carried off the unconscious beautiful lady. Seemed fitting."

Wendy chuckled. "Would piggyback work better now that I'm awake?"

"Perhaps. We'll start with the cradle-carry, and change if we need to. My arms can handle a bit more, I think," he said. "If you put your arms around my neck, that will transfer part of the load off my arms. But either way, you are going to hurt. Sorry."

"Well, boss, let's get out of here and go find the bad guys."

79

FRUSTRATION WAS PRESSING AGAINST EVERYONE. It was suffocating, and there was nothing they could do about it. Only a sighting of the missing trio would grant some relief. The car still had not been found, and the three people had simply vanished.

None of the surveillance had provided any positive information. The Russians were snug in their embassy, and no one was active around the lab or cleaning company.

The local law enforcement officers had taken charge of checking the areas known to be frequented by criminals. They checked and double-checked the sites. Nothing was found, and their many CIs offered no help.

All the calls coming into the office had told the same frustrating story: no sign of either missing agents or car. Now that daylight was approaching, some of the rural areas void of the ambient light provided by buildings, signs and streetlights were being rechecked. Finally, a radio report from an SP unit gave them something positive.

Captain Boxer tapped on the door to the room where Sue was resting. The noise brought Sue back to consciousness and to the feeling of dread she had faced since midnight. She knew she should have been with

Marcus instead of Greg. He was her responsibility. Well, Wendy also: both of them were her responsibility, she admonished herself.

She had finally admitted to herself, a few hours ago, that she had feelings for Marcus that ran deeper than just an appreciation for saving her father. And because of that, she kept pushing Wendy's presence aside. Acting like a jealous schoolgirl was not something expected of a CIA agent. Now she had to find a way to overcome those feelings. Time to act more professional.

She opened the door and found the captain walking away. She caught up to him and asked, "Any news, Captain Boxer? Sorry I was slow answering the door."

"Some, and it's not looking good. The early light and lack of rain allowed an SP detail to spot some short skid marks off the Strada Provinciale 114. That's the narrow road that runs up the side of Vesuvius. They just radioed in that a guardrail is down at the end of the skid marks on one of the upper hairpin curves. Nothing is visible from the road due to the dense undergrowth and steep slope, but we have dispatched a rescue team with climbing gear. Thought you might want to change into something more appropriate and head up there with me. I'm sick of sitting on my ass waiting."

"Of course, thank you. But you go on. I'll run back to the consulate to update the consul general and change. That will take me about twenty minutes, and then I'll head that way to join you there."

The captain nodded. He turned to go back to his office, but stopped. "And how about your father? Shouldn't he get an update also?"

"Not yet," she said, shaking her head, "because he is one who prefers facts, not speculation. The only fact we have right now is that they are still missing. Which was the same status as it was a few hours ago."

On the drive back to the consulate, Sue started thinking like an FBI agent and not a lovestruck teenager. She had the same data that Wendy and Marcus possessed; she just needed to use it. Perhaps she could pull a clue from that data.

The consul general appreciated the update and offered whatever support Sue needed. He told her he planned to call the Sec State and give him an update while Sue changed into clothing more appropriate for traipsing through the forest. She preferred he didn't, and told him so, but finally agreed it wouldn't hurt. She warned him to make sure he didn't give out any false hope.

As she fought the early morning traffic through Naples, Sue allowed her mind to go back over the facts. Now, in addition to Coleman, two more NIS agents were … no, she flatly refused to think of them as dead. At least, not until their bodies were found. But for sure, whatever had happened to Wendy and Marcus occurred after visiting the lab. The lab was the key. But how did it fit? And where the hell was Greg?

She continued the analysis while weaving in and out of the growing morning traffic. Naples was a tough drive at any time, but the morning work rush was horrific, with everyone in a constant state of hurry. Her eyes and part of her mind focused on the traffic and the rest of her mind on the case. According to the reports, none of the Russians had left the embassy, but that wouldn't stop them from calling in hired help. And there were too many criminal groups in Naples to surveil.

That pointed back to one or two people who worked at the lab. The cleaners were suspect, but they hadn't been there the day before. Someone had reported the agents' presence and caused them to vanish. She prayed they were not gone like the doctor whose disappearance started this mess.

80

BY THE TIME MARCUS GOT their few possessions together and arranged on his body for the trek, the sun had finally exploded up from the horizon. But they couldn't see it, as they were still in the shadow of Vesuvius. After the difficult night in extreme darkness, the light seemed brighter than normal. The brighter glow coming in through the open shed door perked up their spirits. It provoked a touch of a positive feeling as the warm glow pushed against the stress.

As he was bending over to pick up Wendy, Marcus had a thought. He paused for a moment, stood up straight, and said, "We can't just walk into any hospital, Wendy. Whoever ran us off the road probably has enough manpower to be watching the hospitals and clinics to see if we are brought in alive. Then they could try again to kill us. We need to get to the Navy base."

"Okay, how do we do that? It's too far to walk."

"True. We need to find a phone and call the SP office. Captain Boxer can arrange secure transport for us. Okay, let's take leave of this fine establishment." With the plan as set as it could be, Marcus gently lifted Wendy again. She wrapped her arms around his neck as they walked out into the day.

Keeping Vesuvius at his back, Marcus walked between the rows of tomato plants. Unlike the forest, the ground was clear and the walking, unobstructed by potential trip traps, was easier. At the top of the rise he had spotted earlier, the end was in sight. Below him in the distance, what he hoped was the town of Torre del Greco touched on the Gulf of Naples. Directly in front of him, the tomato fields changed into rows upon rows of grapevines. On either side of the cultivated fields, forested ridges rose, so the decision to keep going straight was easy.

Marcus walked slowly. He saw that each step resulted in a wince or soft slight groan from Wendy. But she just gritted her teeth and didn't complain. "Let me know if you need a break," Marcus said.

"I'm fine. Keep going and carry me to a soft bed," she said, then chuckled. "Guess I might want to rephrase that in case Kelly has long-distance hearing."

Marcus just smiled and shook his head.

Wendy continued, "I should be really happy right now. My dream of a handsome hero carrying me to safety has come true. Just my luck that the hero is married to a wonderful person."

"Like I said before, your time is coming. Just be patient and never settle for second best," Marcus replied softly.

Leaving the rows of tomato plants created a small problem. The tomato rows ran in the direction they were heading. The grape rows ran perpendicular to the tomato rows, and the pair could not cut between them due to the horizontal supports and interwoven vines. Marcus decided to go right and find an opening that would allow them to continue heading westward.

In about a hundred yards, they came to the end of the row. At the end of the field, the woods were only a few feet away. Marcus turned and continued his slow pace west. After what seemed to them hours, they reached the end of the grapevines. Ahead was a collection of small farm buildings. Marcus slowly walked toward the center of the group.

An older gentleman was lost in concentration as he worked on the engine of a farm tractor that had to be a few years older than he. He jumped when Marcus walked up behind him and said, "Buon giorno, signore."

The old man dropped his wrench as he spun around in shock. No one was expected from the direction of the fields. In Italian he said, "Who the hell are you and what are you doing on my property?" He retrieved his wrench and held it as a weapon.

Wendy responded in fluent Italian, "Sir, we were in a car crash up the slope. Both of us are injured and we need a telephone. May we use yours to call our friends for help?"

The old man's shock turned to disbelief. "No one walks down that volcano." But as he looked at the condition of the two strangers, he realized that yes, they probably had done just that. "Very well, come with me. The telephone is in the house." The house was at least another hundred yards away, and to Marcus it felt like a mile.

As they walked slowly to the house, introductions were offered. Enzo Costa was the fourth generation to own this piece of land. His wife had passed away several years ago, and his three children were off chasing their own dreams. He hoped that one day perhaps a grandchild would show interest in the family business. But for now, he and several hired hands kept the tomatoes flowing to the packinghouse, and the grapes to the winery. It was a good life, he told them.

The house, like Enzo, was old, but like the farm it was kept in great condition. Enzo pointed to a large sofa, and Marcus carefully lowered Wendy onto the soft cushions. Her sigh told him it felt good to her. Marcus was thankful that he hadn't dropped her during the trek. Enzo offered coffee that was eagerly accepted and enjoyed.

Marcus had some difficulty getting the operator to connect to the base. It took several tries, but eventually the Shore Patrol headquarters was reached. The clock on the mantel chimed 0730 as the Shore Patrol duty officer came on the line.

"Naples Shore Patrol. This is Lieutenant Chambers. How may I help you, sir?" he asked in the standard method. He sounded tired and slightly disinterested as he spoke over the background noise.

"Listen very carefully, Lieutenant. This is Lieutenant Commander Marcus Colt from NIS. I need to speak with or get a message to Captain Boxer immediately."

Abruptly the tiredness was gone from his voice and excitement took over. Marcus heard him yell out, "Shut up, everyone. I have Mr. Colt on the line."

Chambers came back on the line. "Sir, damn glad to hear your voice. Where are you? We've had a massive search underway for you since midnight. The CO is at a possible accident scene on Vesuvius. He left here about an hour ago, but I can reach him by radio. What's the message, sir?"

Marcus was relieved to know someone had been looking for them. He told the lieutenant to hold one moment and asked Enzo for his address. He relayed that to the lieutenant and finished by adding, "Immediately send an ambulance and at least a dozen armed men in several vehicles to the address I just gave you. Make sure the CO knows we were attacked on that road up on Vesuvius and our car was shoved over the edge. Greg Walker was killed in the crash and his body is in the car. I have Ensign James here with a broken leg and we need to get her to the base hospital. Got it?"

"Yes, sir. Sit tight and we will be there in no more than twenty minutes. I'll dispatch the team to your location and brief the skipper. Glad you are alive, sir."

Hanging the phone back on the wall mount, Marcus muttered a quick "yea, me, too" before he smiled at Enzo and begged for another cup of coffee. He looked at Wendy to see if she wanted more, and found her asleep. He smiled thinking the relief of being back in civilization must have knocked her out. It was good to feel safe enough to toss out some humor.

Enzo and Marcus took their coffee out to the front porch, where they could see the road. Enzo understood the English word "ambulance," so he was watching for it. Marcus knew they were still vulnerable, and he was watching for anything that looked like trouble. His weapon was still in his shoulder holster, and he planned to be ready if the bastards came again.

But before he could settle down to wait, Marcus knew he had one more call to make. He told Enzo to keep watch and went back inside.

81

ABOUT TWENTY MINUTES BEFORE COLT called the SP office, Sue was getting more frustrated as the seconds flew by. Traffic delays had cost her too much time. And now there was a roadblock where Via San Vito ran into Via Vesuvio, preventing her from turning onto the smaller road leading up the volcano. After heated discussions with two different Italian officers, her diplomatic credentials finally got her past their barricades. She hurried up the road to find the suspicious location. On this small, curvy road, *hurried* takes on a new meaning: it becomes more the speed of a really fast walk, even though you're driving.

Rounding yet another curve, Sue approached the right hairpin turn. Flashing lights were everywhere and multiple police cars blocked the road. She parked close to one and again had to use her credentials to get to where a group was looking over the edge. She spotted the skid marks the SP had reported and finally located Captain Boxer.

"What have we got?" she asked him.

"Not much yet. The team went down about five minutes ago. They report there are vehicle tracks and a lot of torn up foliage. The slope is too steep and wet for fast movement, so we have to be patient."

"Patience is not one of my strong points, Captain. Any way I can get down there with them?" Sue begged.

"No way. This is my crime scene and you *will* follow my rules. We have people doing what they're trained to do, and we will wait right on this spot for their report."

"Yes, sir," she said. There was something else she muttered under her breath, but the skipper wisely chose to ignore it. He understood her frustration because he wanted to go down there too.

Minutes passed. No positive messages came back up the slope. The team was following a trail of carnage, but no car yet. The captain and Sue were discussing her belief that there was a leaker working in the lab when a petty officer approached.

"Excuse me, Captain. I have Lieutenant Chambers on the car radio. He just got a message from Lieutenant Commander Colt, sir."

Captain Boxer and Sue Woodward took off running to his car.

82

IT HAD BEEN A LITTLE over six hours since Kelly had returned home and gotten the news about Marcus. Elaine and Doc had pulled together dinner, but little was eaten. The biggest part of the evening had been spent speculating about what could have happened to Marcus and Wendy. In a case with one man missing for five months and three killed, their situation was difficult to put a positive spin on.

The rest of the time was spent by the admiral telling Kelly and Doc why they could not fly out to Naples in the morning. It had been a difficult argument. But since he was still on active duty, it was easy for the admiral to issue a direct order that he knew HM1 Stevens would obey. Doc didn't like it, but he would obey it. Victoria smoothed his ruffled feathers by reminding him how much he was needed to work the case from this end.

As for his daughter, that was a totally different situation. Both family and friends knew Kelly as a "force of nature" who usually got her way. Only Marcus had been able to calm what he jokingly named Hurricane Kelly, and he was missing. She needed to be with him and kept putting out reasons why she would leave in the morning. The admiral loved his daughter and kept explaining why her reasons were not valid. She was not happy. He was getting more frustrated.

When the phone rang, everyone stopped talking and stared at it for a moment. On the third ring, Doc answered, "Colt residence. SA Stevens speaking." After a moment of listening, Doc enthusiastically said, "Absolutely, operator! You bet we accept the charges!" He pressed the speaker phone button and placed the handset in the cradle.

"Go ahead, Naples," the operator's voice said.

Marcus's voice was slurred, tired, and filled with pain. "Doc, I got an update for you and need to talk with Kelly. Wake her up, please."

"She's right here, Marcus. And so are the CNO, Elaine, David and Victoria. We've been a bit worried about you, buddy," Doc said, his voice slightly breaking.

Kelly ran to the phone with tears flowing down her cheeks and cried, "Are you okay, babe?"

"I think I have a new scar or two for you to yell at me about, but nothing too serious," Marcus said with a soft chuckle. "Wendy has a broken leg, but her spirits are good. We both have more than a few bruises."

Doc looked up and saw the CNO hugging his wife, and David embracing Victoria as relief flooded over them. He reached over and put his arm around Kelly's shoulders. As he did it, he wondered if it was to support her or for her to hold him up. The relief he felt hearing Marcus's voice hit him hard.

It took about five minutes for Marcus to relate the events of the evening. Another few minutes were spent answering specific questions. Doc feverishly took notes and promised to get updated ROIs out first thing. The CNO said he would pass the update to Sec State and Admiral Chance. And he would get the ball rolling to inform Wendy's parents of her injuries, as soon as they had the official doctor's report to confirm nothing else was wrong.

In the background, they heard sirens, and Marcus finally said, "I need to get Wendy and me to the hospital. Our ride just got here. Y'all keep the home fires burning and I'll call again as soon as the docs get through with us. And Kelly, don't come over here. And don't tell me you hadn't been planning on doing just that. I can *hear* your smile kicking up to the left."

Kelly giggled and smiled for the first time that evening. Her tears flowed freely as she replied, "You know me so well, sailor. Please be careful and come home soon. I'll be here waiting. Love you."

"Love y'all also. All of you get some sleep. There's nothing else to worry about for now. It will probably be a few hours before I can call back. Gotta go."

The dial tone filled the silence in the Colt house for a moment until Doc pressed the off button.

David Bartow said what the others were probably feeling. "That man knows how to leave an impression."

83

MARCUS WASN'T AWARE OF IT, but the CNO made another call before he updated Sec State and Chance. Master Chief David Bartow pulled his standard magic and found the home number the CNO needed. With that information, Gallagher placed a call to the home of Captain Sean Smithson, commanding officer of the Naples hospital. He was told Smithson had already left for the hospital.

The call to the hospital took a couple of routing turns, but shortly the CNO heard the captain on the line and said, "Captain Smithson, this is Admiral Gallagher. I hope you have a moment."

"Sir, of course. I have a staff meeting shortly, but it can be delayed. How may I be of assistance, sir?"

Gallagher chuckled. "Captain, you have two NIS officers I care greatly about heading your way in an ambulance. They were in an auto wreck a few hours ago and, at least from what I've been told, their injuries are not life threatening. Ensign James has a broken leg, and probably has other injuries, so she will not be difficult to handle. On the other hand, Lieutenant Commander Marcus Colt says he's okay with a few cuts and bruises. He frequently ignores pain and injuries, and may have a tendency to ignore medical advice."

Surprised by the names, Smithson interjected, "I met them both a couple of days ago. Colt is a good man."

"Yes, he is. But as I was saying, he might tell you he's fine and try to walk out of the hospital. I would greatly appreciate it, as a personal favor, mind you, and not an order, if you would ensure he is fully checked over and not released until you are happy with his condition."

"Admiral, we treat every patient that way, but I will personally verify that Mr. Colt has a complete exam. I'll be happy to give you verbal and written personal reports on both of the agents."

Smiling, the CNO said, "That would be perfect, Sean. I'll be in my office in about four hours, so please call me there. And you need to know their accident was actually an attack by unknown assailants. There will be a few armed guards with Colt and Ensign James 24/7, and their safety is important. Sorry for the added stress and confusion to your hospital, but trust me, it is a requirement."

"Not a problem, Admiral. If there is nothing else, I need to head to the ER and brief the staff."

"Thanks. Gallagher out."

Captain Smithson hung up the phone. *Interesting man*, he thought. That was his first direct contact with any CNO after many years in the Navy. He called the chief nurse and briefed her on the situation. "Get your ducks in a row and meet me in the ER," he concluded.

As he passed through his outer office, he turned to his XO. "Rick, find the chief of security and chief of orthopedics and have them meet me in the ER. We have a couple of VIPs coming in. Join me there after you find those two."

The XO nodded and grabbed his phone.

The senior staff entourage startled the hell out of the usual ER staff. The chief of security had cordoned off two of the ER bays at the end. He set up a couple of his men on the perimeter of the area to keep it secure. The CO, XO, and chief nurse waited just inside the door and watched as, minutes later, three SP jeeps and a staff car sequestered an ambulance as it backed up to the ER door. Members of the ER staff rushed out with two gurneys. SPs formed a ring of armed men around the ambulance.

As they carefully removed Wendy from the ambulance, a man in a dirty coat and floppy hat stood a little off to the side, and with compressed lips and darting eyes, watched carefully. He limped, following Wendy into the ER as the rest of the ER staff outside looked for the second patient. A Navy captain and a good-looking female civilian walked right behind the disheveled man with the limp.

Captain Smithson stepped in front of the rumpled man and said, "Mr. Colt, sorry to see you again under these circumstances. Come with me."

"Just as soon as I make sure Ensign James is taken care of, sir," he replied in a slightly slurred voice that conveyed authority overwhelmed by fatigue and pain.

"She is in the hands of the chief of orthopedic surgery. I think he'll do an okay job without your supervision. And you are in my hands, so get your butt on the gurney over there." Frustration overpowered the normally level-headed attitude of the hospital commanding officer.

Marcus just stared at him as Smithson pointed to the second bay. "I don't have time for an argument, son, so cooperate or we will put you under," Smithson said with a somewhat evil smile. He turned to the two who had followed Colt and pointed to a small office area. "You two can wait over there."

In his usual difficult manner when under stress, Marcus ignored Smithson and limped to the bays. He looked around the curtain and got a smile from Wendy. Two doctor-looking guys were working on her leg. Several nurses fluttered around doing this or that, Marcus wasn't sure what. Satisfied that she was indeed in good hands, he pulled off the dirty coat and his still-soggy sports jacket, dumped them on the floor, removed his shoulder holster, and climbed onto the waiting table. He waved Sue over and passed her his weapon and shoulder holster.

It didn't take Marcus long to describe his injuries and what he had done to stop the bleeding. The nurse started an IV line immediately, replacing his lost blood and supplying some antibiotics to fight off any infections. Removing the hat and cloth strips was painful, since dried blood had stuck to that improvised bandage, but the nurses were as careful as possible.

The trauma surgeon on duty told Marcus that the wound on top of his head was C-shaped, about three inches across. It would take more than a few sutures to secure it properly after it was cleaned. He failed to mention it would be painful, but Marcus wouldn't be feeling it. Captain Smithson had decided that this patient would be more cooperative when he was unconscious, so an injection in the IV line did the trick.

84

IT WAS DARK WHEN MARCUS started to wake up; well, at least it felt dark to him. He mentally chuckled as he realized it was weird to put a feeling on the level of light in a room, especially since his eyes were closed. There was an insidious beeping noise that pulled him totally from his rest and reminded him of an earlier, and very similar, situation back in the spring. *It has to be more of that déjà vu all over again, just as Yogi Berra may have said a few years ago*, he thought. Pain, noise, that strange antiseptic smell, and the inability to coherently focus his thoughts told him he was in a hospital bed and coming out of anesthesia. Someone was holding his hand. Through dried lips he muttered, "Kelly?"

Sue squeezed his hand slightly. "No, Marcus, it's Sue. Kelly is back in the States. You're in Italy and in the hospital. Here, take some ice chips."

He forced his eyes open and saw Sue standing there. The ice helped relieve his dried lips and tongue, which made talking easier. And in the time it took for the ice to melt, he remembered all that had transpired on the volcano.

"How's Wendy? She okay? What time is it?" he asked, fighting the confusion in his mind. He needed to stay focused. Check that, he just needed to focus, which was difficult to do right then.

Wendy let out a laugh. "About time you woke up, boss. You act like you didn't sleep much last night. It's around 1630, Naples time."

Marcus followed the voice and saw Wendy in the other bed in the room. Her leg was in a bright white cast from her foot up past her knee, and it was elevated on a pillow. She looked much better than she did when they got to the hospital. He returned her smile.

Sue continued, "They stitched up your head and you're going to be okay. Eventually. Tony was here for a short while, then headed back to the NISO to keep the investigation going."

Nodding, Marcus asked, "Any updates on who did this to us?"

"Nothing yet," she said.

Before he could ask any other questions, Sue stepped back as two doctors, complete with the standard lab coats, stethoscopes, and take-no-bull looks, came forward, one on each side of his bed. She recognized them from the ER earlier. The nurse with them grabbed his chart from the end of the bed and checked various things on the noisy monitor. He recognized the older doctor as Captain Smithson. "So, when can I get out of here, sir?" Marcus asked.

The captain snickered. "If I had my way, Colt, you'd be here for a couple of weeks. You're damn lucky to be alive. In addition to a rather nasty laceration on top of your skull, you have a small subdural hematoma, a couple of fractured ribs, and a severely bruised right knee. And contusions everywhere except maybe one of your toes. I don't know how you carried Ensign James down the mountain in your condition. Remarkable, to say the least." The nurse handed Smithson the chart.

Marcus tried to shrug, but the pain in his chest stopped that movement. "It's a SEAL thing, sir. Yesterday was the only easy day. And the bottom line is it had to be done."

Smithson slowly shook his head as he said, "In other words, you are as crazy as the rest of them. Perhaps I should put you in the psych ward for a week or two." Both doctors laughed.

Ignoring Smithson's last comment and looking at the other doctor, whose nametag identified him as Lieutenant J. Summers, Marcus asked, "I remember you from the ER, Lieutenant. How many stitches did you put in my head?"

"Mr. Colt, you now have thirty-seven new ones to add to your growing collection. I saw the other scars on your body and must say you look to be a trouble magnet. Now the important question is how do you feel? Give me honest specifics on all areas of your body."

Marcus did a quick inventory of pains from head to toe and relayed them to the doctors. Yes, his head hurt like hell, now his chest hurt when he breathed, and there was some discomfort in his knee. His left forearm ached a bit from the overuse, but it was tolerable. He finished the overview by saying, "A couple of aspirin will take care of the other pains."

Smithson had finished reading the updated chart and turned to Marcus as he ordered, "No aspirin. They could make the hematoma worse, and that thing can kill you. You're on a small amount of IV pain medication. That's all we can do for your injuries. They need time to heal. We will give you a prescription for oral pain relief medicine when you're discharged."

"And when will that be, Captain Smithson?"

"I would prefer you to stay here for at least a few days, but I understand from the CNO that you're needed on a sensitive mission. If you promise to get full bed rest until tomorrow morning and limited duty after that for a month, you can leave in the morning. That is, after we look you over in the morning and do a dressing change. Will that work for you?"

Marcus nodded. "Yes, thank you, sir. And how about my partner over there? When can she get out and how soon can she fly back to the States for R&R?"

"Ensign James may check out with you tomorrow. From all indications, you took the brunt of the damage in the wreck protecting her," Smithson said. "She'll have some of the same body aches as you for a couple of days and will be on crutches for the next few weeks. Travel is not a problem for her."

Summers interjected, "And Mr. Colt, avoid getting your head wound wet for about a week. I recommend a loose-fitting hat to cover the bandages and cut down on the strange stares. My surgical team members never went to barber school and it shows. In addition, you'll need to be back here on Saturday for another dressing change."

With a smile, Smithson said, "By the way, the orthopedic team sends their regards. You did a good job on the ensign's splint. I'll see you in the morning before you leave. Until then, bed rest."

"Can do, sir," Marcus replied. "Oh, how about removing the IV line?"

Smithson nodded toward the nurse. "Take that out, please. He'll be okay." He turned back to face Marcus and said, "I hate to rush off, Colt, but I've two phone calls to make. The CNO is extremely concerned about you and is expecting yet another personal update. He mentioned that Mrs. Colt works for a friend of mine at Walter Reed, so I called her while you were in surgery. I'll talk with her after I call the CNO to give her an accurate update on your condition. She also told me that you frequently gloss over some critical points, and she wanted an honest assessment. I'll pass on your regards and tell her to expect to hear from you no sooner than tomorrow. Now you need to rest."

"Thanks, Captain."

As the medical team left, Marcus closed his eyes for a moment and let out a deep sigh. "Okay, Wendy, you heard about all my aches and pains. Aside from that beautiful cast, how are you doing? I want all the details."

Wendy shrugged. "Fair enough, boss. Partners should know each other's weaknesses. My body aches are nasty, similar to yours, but have eased off some after taking only a very small amount of the oral pain meds. Feels like I just over exercised every muscle. Ignoring the broken leg, there are no other big issues. My hunger was handled at lunch, so I'm really feeling much better. Short answer, I'm gimpy and slow, but good to go."

"That's good news." Marcus sighed with relief.

"But I am not going back to the States until you do. I can work from the NISO office for now. Don't try to change my mind, sir."

"You're lucky I'm hurting too much to argue, Ensign," Marcus said, smiling.

Wendy's voice dropped into her soft southern tone. "And thank you, Marcus, for saving my life. Sue told me about the limb that would have taken me out if you hadn't somehow pulled me into the back seat."

"You would have done the same for me. That's what partners do," Marcus said, trying to hide his embarrassment. "Just wish I could have helped Greg too."

Marcus turned to Sue and frowned. "Have they recovered Greg's body? Sorry he went out that way."

With visible sadness, Sue said, "Yea. They found the car shortly after we got you here. He's in the morgue downstairs. Langley is handling notifications. Greg never mentioned family. As for transport, I don't know when that will happen."

"How far down the slope did our car travel?"

"Just over a quarter mile. They said it was easy to find since they just followed the path of mowed-down underbrush and small trees. And the recovery team couldn't believe you walked the rest of the way down the volcano. It was steep and extremely slippery in that area," Sue added.

Trying to lighten the mood, Marcus pointed at Wendy and asked, "When did hospitals go co-ed? Or is that just an Italian thing? Not complaining, mind you."

Sue laughed. "Actually, it is a Captain Boxer thing. He insisted you two share the room. It makes security easier, and since you shared a fertilizer bed last night, we didn't think this arrangement would be a problem."

"Fertilizer?" Marcus asked with a grimace.

"Yea," Wendy said, "Marcus, you made us a bed on bags of processed chicken poop. Talk about romantic. Now that is going to be a great break room story!"

The laughter hurt his ribs; but even as the pain was nasty, Marcus was glad he was alive to laugh.

"Okay, ladies, that's enough of the fun stuff. Time to get back to work. Where are we on the case?" Marcus asked.

"Tony was here earlier," Wendy replied. "He said no activity has been seen around either the Russian Embassy or the cleaners. He also left a copy of the ROI that he sent to NISHQ."

Sue handed the ROI to Marcus and waited for him to scan it. Then she added, "My Naples historian, a local who was born here nearly eighty years ago, said the cleaners got the name Clock Twenty from one of the American GIs who captured Naples in October 1943."

"What? Did he elaborate on how that came about?"

Sue smiled and continued, "Oh, yea. He had lots of information and I thought I'd never get off the phone. Seems the cleaners' founder and owner, Gabriele Greco, was a young teen hiding in an old curved building called the Convitto Nazionale Vittorio Emanuele when the Americans arrived. Loosely translated, that is the National Boarding School of Vittorio Emanuele II, which still stands at Piazza Dante. He was so happy to see them he later recalled the first words he heard from one of them and used it for his business."

Wendy had a confused look. "And why would a soldier say 'clock twenty' or any variation of that?"

With a knowing nod, Marcus said, "I suspect that building has a clock tower, right Sue?"

"So true. And I'm willing to bet the soldier had been a cop in civilian life and was on a radio giving his position. In the heat of battle, he probably accidently dropped back to the police jargon, the common 10-codes, when he was asked for his location. 10–20 is the code for location. He probably yelled, 'my 20 is the clock tower. Clock 20' or some variation of that, which Ge-Ge picked up."

"Ge-Ge?" asked Wendy.

"Greco's nickname among his friends. Possibly originated with his family or maybe his friends. According to my source, confirmed by the local police, Greco is clean. No police record and nothing hinted at by any of the lowlifes around here."

Marcus frowned and asked, "Have the local police tried to find Ge-Ge today?"

Sue shook her head. "They discovered that Greco has been on holiday in New Jersey since the end of May. Greco, his wife, and daughters have been visiting some relatives that immigrated to the U.S. after the war. His son, Antonio, has been running the cleaners for a few years now with his dad, so he is in charge while papa is gone. And before you ask, Antonio is not as spotless as his papa."

"And can we assume the locals provided more info?" Wendy asked.

Dropping back into her FBI training, Sue checked her notes and recited, "You bet. Antonio Greco, age twenty, single, eldest child of Gabriele and Maria, two siblings–both sisters. Gina, age seventeen and Emma, age fourteen. He has been in and out of trouble for the last three years. Nothing really major. But he is suspected of being in one of the local teenage gangs, Cattivi Ragazzi. That translates to 'bad boys,' and most of their crimes have been related to small-time gambling."

Marcus slowly shook his head, then sighed. "You know I don't believe in coincidences, right? So do y'all think it is one that Doctor Monroe vanished a few weeks after the Greco family, sans Antonio, went to the States?"

"And the connection between the cleaners, the lab, and SA Coleman is definitely one of those coincidences you hate, boss," Wendy added.

Marcus nodded. "And you can probably include the attack on us." He started to make another comment, stopped, and rubbed his forehead. "Sorry, I need to put this discussion on hold and shave. Ah, no, I mean shower. The hot water might help reduce the head and body pains and get the mental processes flowing faster. So maybe I'll shower and shave. And when's dinner?"

"You're rambling, Marcus. Remember you have brain damage. Sure you're okay to stand and walk?" A concerned look spread across Wendy's face.

"Yea, I'm fine," Marcus replied as he slowly maneuvered out of the bed. Carefully, to keep the back of his gown closed, he looked around. "Question is, what do I put on after the shower? I hate hospital gowns."

"Good news on that front, Marcus," Sue said, "while you were in recovery, I dashed back to your room and grabbed some clothing and toiletry items for you and Wendy. If you like what I picked out, it might give you a break from the hospital gown." She pointed toward the wardrobe beside his bed.

Marcus grabbed a pair of jeans and jockey shorts from the wardrobe as he nodded thanks toward Sue.

Sue added, "And you both know your sports coats were toast, so I picked up a couple of new ones for each of you courtesy of the State Department. Since you technically work for me, I felt you two are entitled to use the standard clothing allowance. And to replace her jeans that you skillfully destroyed for the splint, I purchased a couple of skirts for Wendy—after all, her jeans won't work well with that cast."

Marcus grinned as he said, "Keep that up, Sue, and I'll have you transferred to NIS working for me. We need people who think ahead."

Sue beamed at the thought, and gave a quick shrug.

As he slowly walked to the bathroom, carefully trying without much success to keep the open back of his gown closed, Marcus earned a wolf whistle from Sue. Wendy snickered as she said, "Keep your head dry, boss, and by the way, know that your back door isn't closed."

85

As Marcus was allowing the hot water of the shower to work its magic on his aching body and fuzzy brain in the hospital, a couple of blocks away SSA Anthony Carter realized he didn't enjoy the NISRA office being quieter than usual. He was feeling grossly understaffed.

Once Wendy and Marcus had been found and determined to be out of danger a few hours ago, he had hurried back to the office to put some plans into motion. There were just too many things to do, and scanning the empty agent office space, he knew there were too few people to do them.

His first action, after updating Millie and Sandra, was placing calls to NISRAs Rome, Venice, and Rota to get an update on the arrival of his backup team. When calling Admiral Chance earlier to update him on the status of Colt and James, he had begged for more agents. NISO Naples was already short staffed before Coleman's death, both James and Colt were now impaired and, with things heating up, more hands were needed. The admiral agreed and promised to get at least two agents from each of the three closest NISRAs on the way to Naples.

With nothing pressing at the moment, SSA Tony Carter had sent two of his men home to get some rest until midnight. It had been a long morning that had started way too early for them all. And with the SPs providing security at the hospital, the NIS agents had greater freedom to work the case.

Later that night, when the clock read 2400 hrs, one of the now-resting agents would replace the one who was currently supervising SP surveillance of the Russian Embassy and the team at the Clock Twenty Cleaners building for the more difficult overnight period.

So far, both locations had been too quiet. No one was in the cleaners' building, which was considered strange for a business. And no one coming or going from the embassy. But stakeouts frequently have long hours of boredom. Just part of the job.

The second agent coming back on duty at midnight would take over the watch in the office so Tony could get a bit of rest. Naturally, all these schedules would drastically change as soon as the six temporary agents arrived the next day. Until then: "you make do with what you have."

Tony had decided that twenty-four-hour office coverage would be the standard until this case was over. With Washington being six hours later than Naples, important AUTOVON traffic could be delayed otherwise.

The clerical staff of two had been busy all day keeping up with the coming and going ROI traffic generated by the news of the Russian as a lead suspect, the discovery of the possible connection to the cleaners, and the attack on the two IA agents. Captain Boxer had set up security for the two NIS ladies, and armed escorts would be with them around the clock. Millie had just left for home and Sandra had decided to stick around for a couple more hours. Her sadness over losing William was still an issue, and sitting alone in her apartment was difficult. It was easier to just spend time working.

The sun was slowly setting, casting long shadows all across the Bay of Naples. Tony stared out the window of his office as he ran the events of the last few days over in his head. He could not find any flaws with the actions of his team. Well, except he wished Coleman had talked with him about his suspicions last Friday. Perhaps he would still be alive. Or not. Best not to go there.

The lack of activity bothered him. It was like the bad guys knew they were being watched. Well of course they did, he realized. He had to admit the search for Colt and James had turned into a true Chinese fire drill, with law enforcement personnel running in every direction, and in some cases tripping over each other. Only a dead man would have failed to notice. More than likely the activity had spooked the Russian, and he ordered a complete stand-down of all his people.

So, how do we cool things down and still keep an eye on the bastards, Tony thought. He needed to come up with a method of extremely discreet surveillance, and that was not happening.

86

IT WAS DARK IN HER bedroom. But there was enough ambient light coming from the other room to see his beautiful smile. *Dreams do come true*, Sue thought. At least hers finally had. The only thing separating their naked bodies was a thin layer of shared perspiration generated by their initial bedroom foreplay and anticipation of what was coming. His fingers and tongue had searched and found spots that excited her to a level she never thought possible. Heavy breathing had become standard for them both.

To return the pleasure Marcus had freely given, she moved on top, and after a dozen passionate kisses, guided her tongue down his body. Tracing a thin line with the tip as she stopped to kiss each of his battle scars, he groaned, and then …

"Sue, you need to get out of here and get some decent sleep," Marcus said softly as he touched her shoulder. He had finally left the hospital bathroom after a prolonged hot shower and a quick shave to find Sue asleep in the overstuffed recliner. Wendy had also drifted off, allowing the quiet, the dimmed lights, the painkillers, and the relief of being safe to pull her into much needed rest.

Confusion crossed her face as Sue jumped awake and replied, "What? Oh, no. I'm … uh, oh, yea, good plan, Marcus. Guess I drifted off."

337

Marcus looked at her with concern. "Are you okay to drive, Sue?" In addition to looking confused, her face was flushed and her breathing rapid.

"Sure. Just let me splash some water on my face, and I'll be fine." Sue got up from the chair and dashed to the bathroom.

Less than a minute later, Sue exited the bathroom, wiping her face with a towel. Marcus stopped her as he blocked her way and placed his hands on her shoulders. Looking deep into her eyes, he whispered, "Are you sure you're good to drive home, Sue? We've had enough accidents today."

She whimpered, dropped the towel and wrapped her arms around him. She laid her head against his bare chest and softly said, "I'm sorry, Marcus. I should have been with you last night. Perhaps I could have done something different. I was scared that I had lost you. I'm so sorry I let you and Greg down." Sobs escaped from her as she pulled tighter against Marcus. "I'm so sorry. How can I make it up to you? I'll do anything."

The pain from his fractured ribs was intense, but Marcus understood that Sue's needs outweighed his discomfort. "No, Sue, you driving us would've not changed anything. Except maybe I'd be attending your funeral while failing to convince your father that I did all I could to keep you alive. You do not have any responsibility here. The bastards that hit our car are the guilty ones," Marcus whispered.

Sue continued to quietly cry, so Marcus picked her up and carried her to his bed. He laid her down carefully and held up his hands in the stop position as she tried to sit up. He turned off the rest of the room lights and came back to his bed. Sue gave him a quizzical faraway look as Marcus removed her shoes and pulled the sheet and blanket up to her chin. He softly kissed her forehead and stroked her hair as he said, "Rest easy, sweet lady."

Marcus pulled a spare blanket from the wardrobe and settled into the reclining chair to get the rest he knew he needed to face the next day. And to keep Captain Smithson off his butt. While his body rested, his mind was in high gear.

Now that he and Wendy were safe and on the mend, Sue was facing a guilt trip. One of her crew, a man who was also a friend, was dead. And two of the people she was responsible for were in the hospital. That was easy for Marcus to understand, as he still fought the demons created from his mission to save her father. He had lost friends and seen his people wounded. Hopefully for Sue, it would be over after a good night's sleep, but it was hard to say.

Everyone handled it differently. He would be there to help her, if needed, but had to be careful not to become a further physical attraction for Sue to use as a crutch. What he needed, or rather what Sue needed, was Kelly and Doc to do their mind-mending magic. He was not equipped to handle this situation.

Marcus pushed that to the back of his mind and returned to what he knew and did best: case analysis. He started back at the beginning of the assignment and went over all the details one more time. Granted, the details for the last twenty-four hours were a bit jumbled due to the crash, but he kept coming back to the research lab being the key and someone there keeping the bad guys in the loop. Hopefully, the BIs he asked for would point the way to the bad guy.

And as he laid out the index cards in his mind, he saw there were just too many of them pointing toward Vladimir Kroneski. The frustrating part was that as a diplomat, he was not subject to the law. The worst that could legally happen to him was being kicked out of the country. Not much of a punishment for his long list of probable crimes.

Marcus was naturally more concerned about those crimes that directly affected him. In addition to the missing doctor, there were two NIS agents whose deaths were either done directly or at least ordered by this Russian bastard. Vlad was the key. Somehow, someway, Marcus was determined that Vlad pay for his evil deeds.

As he ran the "knowns" about Vlad around his brain, he realized he was dealing with a seasoned and smart adversary. This guy had gotten away from two people in the CIA that Marcus knew were far better at dealing with Russian spies than he was. Marcus silently chuckled as the thought hit him that Vlad had slipped away from Victoria and Leslie about the time Marcus was still in junior high. Marcus softly muttered, "Oh, yea, I'm so out of my league."

After that depressing realization, he started another mental list of the actions taken thus far in the Naples area. Surveillance was in place on the Russian Embassy, the research lab, and the Clock Twenty Cleaners. Information was being gathered about the people in all three locations in hopes something would be out of the norm. Well, at least they knew good ol' Vlad was guilty, since he'd left his fingerprints at the lab where Agent Collins was killed.

The room door opened and a nurse quietly entered. She was surprised to find a woman in the bed assigned to LCDR Colt and started to rouse her awake.

"Hold on, ma'am. I'm over here," Marcus whispered.

She came over to the chair and also whispered, "Sir, you need bed rest. What is going on here?"

"Nurse"—Marcus paused slightly as he looked at her nametag—"Hadley, what I really need is a cup of coffee. As well as a heating pad for my aching neck and an ice pack for my bum knee. Can you fix me up?"

"Sir, you should be in that bed." She pointed over to where Sue was sleeping.

Marcus twisted his mouth in frustration. "Lieutenant, what is your first name?"

She smiled and replied, "Karen, sir."

Marcus returned her smile. "Karen, my friends call me Marcus. And I really, really need that cup of coffee. It has been too many hours without a caffeine fix. As for the bed, that lady needs it more than me right now. And besides, my wife wouldn't appreciate me sharing that bed with Mrs. Woodward. It will all be okay."

Shaking her head, Nurse Hadley said, "Sir ... uh, Marcus, I understand about the bed, but I can't get that coffee. It's not on your chart and the CO will have a fit if I break protocol."

Marcus chuckled. "Karen, the CO is the one who gave me a knockout shot this morning. Coming from the States on Tuesday, I was just about adjusted to Italian time, and now after sleeping all day long, my body clock is back out of sync. So it's entirely his damn fault I'm wide awake. Trust me, I'll tell him I forced you to get the coffee."

"Um, I don't know, Marcus," she said, putting on a slight grimace.

Marcus pulled his wallet out and handed her his special card from the CNO's office. With a somewhat knowing grin, he said, "You know, we really don't want to bother that man about a cup of coffee, do we?"

With a slight chuckle, Karen handed back the card. "Never knew coffee was critical to national security. I'll see what I can do, Marcus."

"Thank you so very much! Two sugars and a dash of cream, please. And forget about seeing that card."

After the door closed, Marcus heard a chuckle. Wendy elevated the back of her bed and softly said, "And what exactly did that card say, boss?"

Walking to her bed, Marcus showed her the card and quietly told her the history behind it. He concluded, "Sorry, I forgot you didn't know about that. I hate to use it, but it does come in handy."

Wendy smiled and whispered, "Guess you hate it when your charm and good looks fail to woo the ladies, right? And now you're going to tell me why Sue is in your bed?"

Marcus shrugged. "She got hit with the emotions of the day. She's not up to driving and needs her sleep—that is the nearest bed. Besides, I'm wide awake and enjoying that comfy chair. Go back to sleep, Wendy."

"Aye aye, sir. You get some rest also."

Settling back into the chair, Marcus appreciated that Wendy was now on his team. She was a good fit and, like Doc, seemed to see inside his head when he needed it most. Now it was time to get back to the case and figure out a way to catch Vlad.

His plans had slammed into a wall with a sign that read "that won't work, fool." He hit that dead end at least twice before the room door next opened. Nurse Karen Hadley quietly pushed in a small cart. She rolled it over to his chair and smiled as she whispered, "Remember, you promised to rest and protect me from the wrath of Smithson, Marcus. Here's your coffee. And I also have the heating pad and ice pack." She positioned the heating pad behind his neck, picked up the ice pack and asked, "Do you need help getting out of those jeans so we can cool that knee?"

Marcus snickered. "No, I'm good. I'll just put the ice pack on top of the jeans. I was drenched to the skin all last night, so a slightly damp knee won't be a bother. Many thanks, Karen, for getting this for me. It will be good to put this knee on ice."

She nodded and mouthed, "You're welcome," then turned and silently left the room.

As the heat saturated his neck, Marcus sipped his coffee. It had been a long day without his usual multiple cups. And while it wasn't his special blend, the flavor sat on his tongue, triggered all the right taste buds, and provided the comfort and stimulus he needed. He decided that after a few more sips, he would put his knee on ice.

He had to restrain himself from yelling out loud: *On Ice!* That was the way. He finished his coffee as he rolled the budding plan around in his mind. *Yea, that just might work*, he thought.

Marcus threw on a robe and limped out the door. One of the two SPs on duty asked, "Sir, is there something you need?"

"Yea, petty officer, I need a phone located in a private place. Got any ideas?"

"Wait here, Lieutenant Commander, and I'll find you one."

It took a couple of minutes, but the SP returned with Nurse Hadley pushing a wheelchair; she did not look happy. "Sir, you promised me you would rest. I know you're a VIP, but I'll be the one getting the wrath of the CO, who expects you to stay in bed. At least get in this chair before he sees you walking around. And then I'll take you to a phone."

Marcus smiled. "Thank you, Nurse Karen, you're an angel." After a quick trip down the hall, she pushed him into an empty office and closed the door.

She pointed toward the phone and said, "Make it quick."

"Yes, ma'am. How do I get an outside line?"

"Dial nine, sir. Should I step outside?"

Marcus shook his head and joked, "No, stay here. I might pass out from the stress of these calls when my boss yells at me during the second one. Anyway, no big secrets will be told." He dialed the first number after checking his notes.

"Naval Investigative Service, Senior Special Agent Carter speaking," Tony Carter answered, failing to hide the weariness in his voice.

"Glad you're working late, Tony. This is Marcus and I think we need to change things up a bit."

Surprised, Tony perked up and blurted, "Marcus! How ya doin'?"

Chuckling, Marcus answered, "Been better and much worse, so not too bad from the adventure. Hate to rush ya, but I need to call D.C. also. It hit me that some in the local law enforcement might feed info to the bad guys. I know they were very helpful finding Wendy and me, but we need to cut them loose. At least for the next phase."

With a bit of hesitancy, Tony said, "Okay, I'll handle that. And do you have the next phase planned out?"

"Well, it's a work in progress. I'll know more after I call D.C., and we can go over it in the morning. Will that work for you?"

"Of course, just let me get on the phone to the locals. Ciao."

"Quick enough, Nurse Karen?" Marcus asked.

Karen Hadley just nodded and softly smiled.

Pausing to gather his thoughts, Marcus took a deep breath and called the second number from memory.

The phone was answered on the second ring. "Naval Investigative Service, Internal Affairs Division, Carl Freeman speaking. How may I be of assistance, sir?"

"Good afternoon, Mr. Freeman. Marcus Colt calling and I hope things are well in our nation's capital. I have a small task for you."

"My, aren't we being formal today, sir. You must have been hit on the head really hard to bring that about," Carl said through a laugh, then his tone changed to one of concern. "We've all been worried sick. Seriously, how ya feeling, boss?"

"Not too bad, Carl. I have a beautiful nurse watching over me right now, and there are more than a few painkillers floating around my blood stream. I'll probably need more once you set up a conference call with the admiral and Doc. I assume they're around and the boss is as gruff as always."

"Yes, sir, he's none too happy about you being injured … again. Give me a minute."

"And you stay on the line also, Carl." While waiting for the setup, Marcus looked at Karen and saw she was looking at him like he was a total nut case.

"Don't worry, Karen. Doc is actually a SEAL corpsman who is transitioning to NIS special agent status. I'm not looking for a second opinion on my health care."

She shook her head. "I was warned you are different from the standard lieutenant commander. And I see the warnings were grossly understated, sir."

Marcus heard some commotion on the line and asked, "Everyone here?"

Admiral Chance cleared his throat and said, "And you are once again in the damn hospital without my permission. Perhaps you need to transition to the medical corps, Colt, since you like it there so much."

"I'm here, Marcus," Doc interjected quickly to defuse the situation.

"Sorry to be so late calling, but I was sedated most of the day. Seems the doctors here really want me to rest."

That got the expected chuckles and Marcus continued, "Good news, Admiral, I'll be out of here tomorrow morning. Ensign James is doing really good and will be working a desk due to her lack of mobility."

The admiral snorted. "She should come home for R&R with her family."

"I tried to push that, Admiral, but she wants to keep on the case. I hate to put the damper on devotion and enthusiasm. And frankly, we need her."

Doc jumped in. "I know you've been sedated for a while, but does this call have anything to do with a case update?"

"You bet. I just had an epiphany about the case. Doc, you and Carl need to document all this. Admiral, if you agree with my plan, I need you to pull a few strings. I think, with all our surveillance, that we're making things too hot for the bad guys and they have gone into hiding. Here's how we can cool things down."

Marcus talked for several minutes, answered the questions they threw at him, and finally concluded the call. He looked at Karen with seriousness. "You didn't hear anything just now, right?"

Karen shook her head at Marcus in disbelief of all she'd heard. "I understand, Marcus—I didn't hear anything. But I won't be happy until I get you back into bed." The awkward silence that followed was as thick as the proverbial London fog. Seeing Marcus's grin, she blushed. "Oh, hell, that didn't come out right."

Marcus laughed. "I would say it sounded really good to me, but then I didn't hear anything either."

87

EVEN WITH THE SHADES DRAWN, the morning sun cast an eerie glow of soft light over the room. It wasn't much, but just enough to bring Marcus out of his dream. Since his dream was of Kelly, he was not pleased to be awake.

He did a quick physical inventory. The heat had reduced the neck pain. The ice pack had melted and was now a lukewarm, slushy container of water, but it had helped ease the knee issues. His head still held a hellish pain, both inside and out, but that was expected. Other body aches had lessened with the long hot shower and the overnight rest. Since he was still breathing, albeit through the discomfort of fractured ribs, Marcus felt ready to face the day.

A check of the room showed that Sue and Wendy were both still asleep. The rolling cart with the coffee tray had been removed while he slept. He guessed Karen wanted to hide the evidence of her indiscretion.

A glance at his watch forced him to realize that the doctors would be showing up in an hour or so. At least he had gotten nearly seven hours of sleep, and just maybe he would now be in sync with Naples time. A short time spent in the bathroom, shaving again and brushing his teeth, helped him overcome the desire to go back to sleep and prepared him for the next step of the day.

After asking one of the SPs guarding the door to find them some coffee, Marcus decided the best way to get the ladies moving was with light. He hit the two light switches and the soft glow in the room changed into a sanitary white light. As if on cue, both ladies started minor body movements. Feeling a bit like a voyeur as he watched them wake, Marcus noted that Wendy was the first to open her eyes. He walked over to her bed and asked, "Do you need help getting up?"

"Morning, boss. Just hand me the crutches and don't get between me and the bathroom. I'm pretty good with these things—I had practice when I broke the other leg in junior high," Wendy said while rubbing her face and running fingers through her hair. "I do need some quality time with the hairbrush and mirror to get shipshape."

"You look fine, Wendy. I'm here if you need me," Marcus said, moving away from her bed.

"Thanks, Marcus, but I doubt I look fine." Wendy groaned as she maneuvered off the bed and to the bathroom.

He walked over to his bed with a plan to get Sue moving, hoping this morning wouldn't be a rerun of last night's physical contact. Things were complicated enough without a lovesick CIA agent running around. Marcus used the controls on the end of the bed and raised the head about twenty degrees. It was enough. Sue opened her eyes and smiled. "Good morning, Mr. Colt. How are you feeling?"

"Well, the headache is a true bitch, but otherwise I'm ready to chase a few bad guys. How 'bout you, Mrs. Woodward?"

Sue glanced around the room, and not seeing Wendy, she slipped out of bed, walked up to him, and softly said, "I am so sorry about last night. I don't know what came over me, Marcus."

Nodding, Marcus replied, "Yesterday was a rough day for you. Bad things happened and you lost a part of your team. I understand that all too well, and emotions took control. But today is a new day and you need to get, and keep, your mind in the game."

Lowering her voice even more, Sue whispered, "I know. But I really do appreciate your self control last night. You know I would have done anything for you."

"I know, and I suspect it would have been wonderful. But Sue, I have too much respect for you, your father, and your family to ever take advantage of a situation like that. And it cannot happen again, so pull yourself together, okay?"

"But I can't stop wondering what if you had made it to Thanksgiving dinner last year, where we … you and I, would be right now. I keep thinking 'what if' scenarios, you know."

Marcus chuckled slightly. "You do know that 'what if' games will drive you nuts, don't ya. Imagine this—we met last Thanksgiving, felt this attraction, got married, and then this past March, as it actually happened and probably would again, I meet Kelly who knocks me totally off my feet. Then you have another husband straying and a second divorce."

"Or I could have made you so damn happy, no one else would ever catch your eye," Sue said with a big grin, then a shadow came over her face and she sighed. "Or last night I could have been the one to make you stray and poor Kelly would be the one getting hurt. I get it, Marcus. Maybe trying to bring dreams to reality has consequences. I know I appreciate you having the control that I did not. Again, I'm so sorry."

"Sue, just remember that some dreams and thoughts are not meant to be acted upon. If you do, you might enjoy it at the time, but you'll regret it. 'Maybe not today. Maybe not tomorrow, but soon, and for the rest of your life.'"

Sue backed up and laughed. "Did you just go all Bogie on me and quote *Casablanca*?"

Marcus gave her one of Kelly's lopsided grins. "Of course. I could never have said anything as smooth as Rick Blaine did. Besides, we'll always have Naples, right?"

Again Sue laughed, and gently placed her hand on the side of Marcus's face. "Now I really understand why my father loves you so much. And I do think 'this is the beginning of a beautiful friendship,' Marcus, but only a friendship. I get it."

"Just think of me as your older brother, sis. Family is important, and I consider your family as part of mine. Okay?"

A tear came to Sue's eye as she softly whispered, "Agreed. Nice to have a brother who is older, and so damn much wiser, than me." She wiped her eye and cleared her throat, then strongly said, "And on the business side of this mess, I'm out of here for now. I'll get back to the consulate, freshen up, change into more appropriate attire, update everyone, and get back here in time to pick you and Wendy up when the docs let you go. Around 0900 work for you?"

"Yep, should be fine. Be careful, sis."

Marcus opened the door and motioned to the senior SP on duty. "Petty Officer Canton, I need you to escort this lady to wherever she wants to go and back here safely. Got it?"

He nodded, but said, "Sir, my orders are to keep you and the ensign secure."

Marcus pulled open his robe and showed Canton that his pistol was resting in his shoulder holster. He winked and pointed to the other SP. "Between Jackson over there, and John Browning's excellent creation here in my armpit, I think we will survive without you for a couple of hours. I'll take the heat from Captain Boxer should he show up."

Canton smiled and said, "Aye aye, sir. Ready to go whenever you are, ma'am."

As Marcus started to close the door, one of the nurses approached with a cart containing a coffee carafe and a couple of domed containers. She called out his name and said, "Sir, the CO suggested you might be friendlier to him if you had coffee and breakfast before his visit. He mumbled something about a fed lion being less of a threat."

She let out a slight giggle as Marcus winked at her, saying, "He is a very wise man. Thank you, and him, so very much. That coffee smells super."

Before closing the door, Marcus prepared a cup of coffee and handed it to the SP, who was obviously not used to being served by an officer. He stammered his appreciation. Marcus gave him a quick nod as he pulled the cart into the room.

As he poured two more cups of coffee and added the appropriate amount of sugar and cream, Marcus heard the sound of crutches behind him. Wendy said, "Yes, thank you, sir, I do need coffee."

"Yep, I can read minds, Wendy. I've got it ready." Pulling the sheet over her as she settled back into bed, Marcus handed her a cup, and with a slight British accent said, "Coffee and breakfast are ready. Allow me to serve, ma'am."

The coffee was a needed fix for both of them. Quiet and caffeine is a good way to start the day, and for NIS staff, the coffee was mandatory. With the first two cups drained and the scrambled eggs, bacon, and toast devoured, they were finishing the third cup when Wendy asked, "How many courses of psychology did you take at Georgia Tech?"

"One, why?"

"Well, I didn't mean to eavesdrop, but I was leaving the bathroom when I heard most of your conversation with Sue. Figured it would be better for me to just stay there and not interrupt the flow. I won't ask what happened last night, but you get extra points in my book for how you handled things this morning."

Marcus shrugged. "Thanks. Maybe some of Kelly's knowledge has rubbed off on me. I just go with what feels right. I know Sue is hurting after the loss of Greg and feeling responsible for our injuries. Guilt has her emotions running in circles. I've been there. And I fully understand what's going on inside her head. At least I had a month in a Saigon hospital without a fantasy lover nearby to start dealing with my issues. And over a year later, I'm still a work in progress."

Her brow knotted up. "So rescuing her dad wasn't a walk in the park?"

He sighed and shook his head. "Far from it." Marcus decided right then that Wendy's security clearance was adequate, and as briefly as possible he gave her the highlights of the events from the previous year. Better that she understands where her partner was coming from at times than to waste valuable time guessing.

"And Doc was wounded also?"

"Oh, yea. We spent a lot of the time saving each other's lives. I think I have one up on him, but I let him think we're equal. He had a few more months of hospital time than I did, so it balances out."

"Wow. Hell, that's all so impressive I'm about to have some fantasies about you myself, Marcus."

Laughing, he said, "Don't you dare!"

The door opened and Captain Smithson said, "Glad to hear everyone is in good spirits. Much better than yesterday. Good morning."

Marcus stood and came to attention as Smithson came over to Wendy's bed. "Morning, sir. Just enjoying the fact we're still alive, Captain. And especially enjoying the coffee you had delivered. Thanks, so much, sir."

The other doctor was missing, but nurse Karen Hadley followed Smithson and grabbed the charts from the end of the beds. She winked at Marcus from behind the doctor's back. Wendy noticed, but didn't say anything.

Smithson chuckled. "Yelling 'attention on deck' or jumping to your feet is not required in my hospital rooms, Mr. Colt. At ease, and get your butt back in your bed."

"Aye aye, sir," Marcus said as he lay back on the bed.

It didn't take the doctor long to check Wendy's status. She was ready to get out of there and return to duty. But it was to be limited duty due to her mobility issue.

Captain Smithson was careful to make sure Marcus was ready to be discharged. He inspected the head wound after Karen removed the bandages. It looked good. He asked about every bruise and scrape before he stepped back and announced, "While I'd rather keep you another day, after applying a new dressing to your head, Nurse Hadley will do all the release paperwork and you both can get out of here."

"Thank you, Captain. We appreciate all y'all have done for us."

The captain nodded his acceptance of the remark. "Marcus, come into the ER anytime tomorrow for another dressing change. Let them know when you are on the way so they can call me. I want to be here when you arrive. I have a standing request from the CNO to keep him in the loop on your recovery. Okay?"

"My pleasure, sir. None of us want to get on his bad list. Of course, I'm already there for getting injured again on one of his assignments."

Smithson laughed. "Somehow I don't expect the CNO's son-in-law to be on his bad list too long. And no, he didn't mention that. But the newest issue of the Navy Times has a nice article about your wedding last September."

Marcus laughed. "Captain, as you can see by all my scar tissue, I don't get soft duty based upon my marital connections. And now that I think about it, he might be trying to get rid of me. Who knows!"

"You have nothing to worry about. I hear the affection in his voice when we talk about you, Marcus. Now, I really have to call that man and give him an update on both of you, even at 0130 hours his time. Try to get more rest today. Stay safe and I'll see you tomorrow." He shook their hands, turned, and left.

Nurse Karen applied a new dressing to his head and departed to handle the paperwork that the Navy loves so. Her departing smile was one that could have led to trouble if Marcus wasn't married.

As the door closed behind the departing nurse, Wendy had a quizzical look. "CNO's son-in-law? Really?"

Marcus grinned, shrugged, and started to reply when the door opened again. Marcus got back out of bed as Petty Officer Jackson stuck his head into the room and said, "Sir, I have two Air Force officers out here asking for you."

Interesting, Marcus thought. He nodded and quipped, "Let them in, Jackson, but stay on this side of the door with your hand on your weapon in case they go berserk."

Jackson chuckled and replied, "Aye, aye, sir."

A natty Air Force captain and a second lieutenant with a briefcase basically marched into the room and came toward Marcus. At attention, the captain asked, "Sir, are you Lieutenant Commander Colt? I need to see some identification."

Marcus tilted his head to the left and looked between the two officers for a moment. He decided to be the quirky patient as he allowed his robe to open to reveal his sidearm, then solemnly asked with the authoritative voice of a senior officer, "That depends. Exactly who are you? What are you doing here? And where is your identification?" He allowed that to hang for a moment before he smiled and said, "I'll show you mine after you show me yours."

Not expecting any of that, the captain had a slightly confused look. "Sir, Captain William Maxwell and Lieutenant Paul Coffee of the Office of Special Investigations. Lieutenant Colonel Tiller asked that we deliver this package to you as soon as possible, sir." Both officers held out their identification cards.

Marcus checked them over and responded in kind, holding his identification out for them. "Thank you, gentlemen. Yes, I'm Colt, and this is Ensign James, also of the NIS. You can speak freely in her presence. What have you got for me?"

Captain Maxwell nodded at the lieutenant, who opened his briefcase and handed a thick package and a clipboard to the captain.

"Sir, we need your signature on this transfer document, please," he said as he handed the package to Marcus.

Marcus signed and passed the clipboard to the lieutenant. He took the package from the captain and said, "Many thanks, gentlemen. Unless there is anything else, Jackson will see you out."

The captain nodded. "Nothing else, sir. Thank you. And we hope your recovery goes well, sir." They turned and left, with Jackson following them out and closing the door.

As Marcus opened the package, Wendy said, "I hope that's the BIs."

"Ah, yes, enough reading material to keep us both busy for a few hours." Marcus held up the five-inch-thick folder. "Fortunately, my good friend Scott included a one-page executive summary. Everyone at the NISRA is clean. And the only person of interest at the research lab is the local-hire clerk at the reception desk, Mario Morelli. Remember him?"

"He didn't cause any alarm bells with me when I met him. He's interesting in what way?"

"Scott's 'CliffsNotes' comments tell us Morelli has recently paid off his house and has a new bank account set up on Capri with just over $20,000 as the initial balance. Another $5,000 was deposited over the weekend. On his salary, that's pretty much impossible without a rich uncle dying and leaving him a fortune. And no sign of that having happened, according to the Air Force investigators."

Passing the package to Wendy, Marcus added, "Give me a few minutes to get my shoes and jacket on, and I'll vacate to room to give you some privacy to dress. I suspect Sue will be returning shortly, if you need any help. Okay?"

Wendy laughed. "I'll call *you* if I need any help, Marcus. That's what partners are for, right?"

88

AN HOUR HAD PASSED BY the time Sue got back to the hospital. By then, Wendy had dressed, without any help from Marcus, and was ready to face the day. The navy-blue skirt and jacket Sue had picked out fit her perfectly. It looked tailor-made, and even with the cast and crutches, it helped project a professional, take-no-prisoners attitude. And that attitude showed she was anxious to catch the people that put her in this cast.

While waiting, Marcus made a couple of calls to find out what was what. SSA Tony Carter had taken the lead on the investigation while he was doing his volcano stroll—as he called it now—and subsequent recuperation. Marcus's first call was to the NISO to see what had popped since his call to Tony last night. He got a complete update on the situation in Naples. Basically, nothing had happened since the crash, but more agents were on the way to help when things finally broke loose.

His second call was to NISHQ, and he was surprised to find Carl Freeman manning the phone desk. Carl provided a concise update on the situation status from the HQ viewpoint. He passed on the fact that the admiral had spent the afternoon and most of the evening on the phone arranging the support Marcus had requested. That was why Carl was still there at 0230 hrs; the admiral had just left and Carl was wrapping up the paperwork. Things were looking good so far except for the lack of sleep, Carl had said.

With the status calls behind him, Marcus gathered up his and Wendy's extra gear into the suitcase that the ever efficient and organized Sue had provided.

He selected the steel gray jacket Sue had purchased; he had to admit it went well with his dark blue jeans and burgundy dress shirt. *That lady has good fashion sense*, he thought.

Checking the mirror in the wardrobe, he also had to agree with the doctor that his head was not pretty. They had shaved a good portion off the top of his head in a haphazard way, and the bandages added to the revolting mess. He needed a hat, and soon, or he'd be the center of much undesired attention.

"Well, as I expected, the jacket looks great, but that head needs some work," Sue said as she came into the room. She handed a bag to Marcus. "Here, try this on for size."

Marcus removed a black cap from the bag and offered his thanks.

Sue smiled. "Officially, it's called the Greek Fisherman's Hat, but I've heard it referred to as a skipper's cap, so it seemed right for you since you're the skipper of this operation. It's made from Merino wool—only the best for my brother."

Marcus gently lowered it onto his head. It covered the bandages and bad haircut perfectly. He had to admit, it did look good and fit well.

Wendy came out of the bathroom. "Nice look, boss. I recall the Bolsheviks loved those caps during their revolution. Appropriate since we're chasing a Russki."

Marcus's grin turned into a fake grimace as he said, "Bolshoe spasibo, tovasisch."

Laughing, Sue said, "Your Russian pronunciation needs work, but 'thanks a lot, comrade' came through good enough to get you by in Moscow."

"I just exhausted fifty percent of my Russian vocabulary on that," replied Marcus. "Guess it's time to get to the NISO and do some work."

Sue shook her head. "Not there. When you guys went on your 'field trip,' we moved the operation's HQ to the Shore Patrol office. They have more space and better radio communication. And now it has the added benefit of no stairs for Wendy to negotiate."

"Speaking of my complication, now I just need to fit into your small car," Wendy said.

"Not a problem. The consul general was extremely upset by the attack and your injuries—he ordered that one of his large limos be available to us for the duration of this operation. It comes complete with bulletproof glass and a Marine driver."

That extra man might come in handy, Marcus thought. Out loud he simply said, "Lead on, Sue."

None of the three talked on the way to the SP HQ. Each was lost in thought. Marcus was worried about both Sue and Wendy: Sue for her attraction to him and Wendy for her injuries. He was afraid Wendy was too much like him and wouldn't admit to being in pain in order to get the job done. He probably should have sent her home. In addition, he was anxious to get this operation successfully behind him before anyone else got hurt or got dead.

The limo stopped, bringing them back to the present. The driver exited the vehicle and opened the rear door faster than Marcus could reach the handle. He helped Wendy and her crutches out, and Sue exited from the other side.

As Wendy and Sue started toward the door, Marcus turned to the young Marine in his dress uniform. "At ease, Marine. What's your name?"

"Gardener, Richard, sir." He was still standing at attention.

"Didn't you hear the 'at ease' order I gave, Corporal? And do your friends call you 'Dick' or 'Rick'?"

Gardener relaxed from attention to a position closer to parade rest rather than the ease stance. He looked uncomfortable. "Sorry, sir. Gunny demands that we maintain a certain attitude when on duty. And my good friends call me Rick, sir."

"I understand and appreciate that attitude, Rick, but while you are assigned to me, there are a couple of different rules that you will follow. And you are assigned to me until I say otherwise. Are you armed?"

"Sir, no sir."

Marcus paused for a moment. "Go back to your quarters and change into civilian attire similar to mine. Get with your gunny and have him issue you a sidearm ... 1911 .45 caliber is best. And carry a couple of extra magazines. Then hustle back here and find me inside. Got it, Rick?"

"Sir, that's highly irregular. I'm not sure the gunny will let me do that, Mr. Colt."

Marcus snickered. "If he is foolish enough to question my orders, have him come see me. But warn him that my current headache makes me grouchier than normal. Carry on."

"Aye aye, sir." Corporal Gardener turned to get back behind the wheel.

The two SPs had followed from the hospital in their jeep and were standing by it, awaiting further orders from Marcus. They popped to attention as he approached.

"At ease, gentlemen. What are your orders for this assignment?"

Gunners Mate First Class Kevin Canton responded, "Sir, we, and four other men, are assigned to guard you two until you release us. We are on rotating eight-hour shifts, and Jackson and I will be relieved at 1600 hours. Captain Boxer made it clear we are at your orders, sir."

Marcus quickly gave the same orders to the SPs as he had his new Marine driver: get into casual dress civvies, keep your weapons handy, and get back as soon as possible. He also instructed them to each drive an unmarked, radio-equipped sedan. He concluded, "Canton, you and your relief will stick with Ms. Woodward, while Jackson and his relief do the same with Miss James. Pass the word to your reliefs and find me as soon as you get back here, okay?"

Canton smiled. "Aye, aye, sir." The two SPs jumped into the jeep and sped off to their barracks.

Marcus limped into the office and was startled by the round of applause he received from all those inside. He gave a slight smile and waved as embarrassment tried to overcome him.

Captain Boxer came to him as he motioned everyone quiet. Shaking his hand, he said, "Mr. Colt, we are all happy that you and Miss James survived your ordeal. And we are greatly impressed by your actions. We have the conference room ready for you."

Looking at the crowd around him, Marcus raised his voice and said, "We appreciate the welcome. And James and I have heard all about the extra time and effort you all put into our rescue. It *is* greatly appreciated. Knowing you have our backs makes this job much easier. Thank you."

Some gave a thumbs up, while others nodded their appreciation of the recognition. Marcus turned to the captain. "Thanks, Skipper. Lead the way. First to the coffee mess, please."

As the needed personnel drifted back to the conference room, Marcus pulled Sue aside as he poured himself and Wendy the next round of coffee. "I need you to call your office. I just sent our Marine and SP guards back to get into civvies and to pick up weapons. If they are going to drive us around, they need to be armed and a little less conspicuous. Get them whatever credentials needed to conform to Italian law, please. Names are Richard Gardener, Kevin Canton, and David Jackson. There are four other SPs, but Canton will have to give you their names when he returns. Okay?"

"Can do, Marcus." Sue left to find a phone.

Marcus was pleased to see that the crowd in the conference room included the agents he knew, several unknown men who looked like NIS personnel, eight officers wearing the gold wings of naval aviators, and four enlisted men sporting senior aviation ratings. A handful of Marines in fatigues stood against the back wall. It took more than a couple of minutes to complete the introductions.

Captain Boxer called the meeting to order, and all quieted down as they took their seats. He started by sharing an important piece of information. "Through the hard work of our State Department, the Italian government will allow us to arrest Italian citizens as we work this case. Sadly, the primary person of interest is a Russian diplomat, so it is hands-off with him."

Glancing over at Colt standing by the door, Boxer pointed to the head chair and said, "Mr. Colt, take the lead. We're here to follow your plan … as soon as you let us know what it is." That got the expected chuckles.

Marcus smiled and stood behind the chair where the captain usually sat. "Captain, I'll do my best. But know this, people—my plans are rarely set in stone. And this one is probably more fluid than my usual. It was, after all, developed while I was partially sedated in the hospital from a head injury. So its fluidity justifies calling it Operation Quicksilver. Pay attention, because I really need y'all to shoot holes in the thing so we can firm it up. Our big problem is that there are too many people noticing we're looking for a couple of evil people, so we need to look like we are backing off. And here is how we can do that."

As he started the briefing, Sue slipped into the room and nodded to Marcus before taking her seat next to Wendy. That nod told him she had accomplished the credentials mission.

Marcus held up a copy of the handout. "Study the faces and information about these suspects. These are the bastards we need to watch and catch. The first one, Vladimir Kroneski, is the worst of the lot, but as the captain mentioned, he has diplomatic immunity so we can't do much about him. However, that immunity does not prevent us from watching him 24/7. Right now, we believe he's holed up in the Russian Embassy, but when he moves, we need to see where he goes and whom he meets. Those other people we can pick up."

Marcus paused to get a sip of coffee while everyone took a minute to look through the handout. Then he continued. "Most of you are aware we need to find the persons responsible for the death of a Naples NIS agent, and for the attack that put Miss James and me in the hospital. And while I only have a gut feeling to go on, I believe a Navy scientist missing from D.C. for the last few months was kidnapped and is being held in this area, probably by the people in this handout. With the excellent assets we have in this room, I know we will succeed."

He paused to let that tidbit sink in. Wendy did a double take, as that last piece of information caught her completely off guard.

Marcus outlined the problems they faced and how his plan might overcome each one. Glancing at the clock, he realized he'd been standing behind the chair and talking non-stop for over forty minutes. No wonder his head ached and knee was throbbing. He wrapped up. "Okay, that's all I've got for now. Let's take a quick coffee break, and then you can tell me how bad this plan is. Thank you."

Marcus hurried out to beat the crowd and limped back with two more cups of coffee, passing one to Wendy. He plopped down in the chair next to her. "Well, did that sound as foolish to you as it did to me when I said it out loud?"

"Boss, I hate to tell ya, but it was concise, professional, and seems to handle each issue we're now facing. But don't let that go to your aching head, okay?"

Captain Boxer walked over and said, "I concur with the ensign. Assuming the fly boys can do their part, it should work, Marcus."

Sue just smiled and shrugged. Not being accustomed to military operations, she was reluctant to offer any comments, but she added, "The State Department and CIA are ready to help—just ask."

A scrunched-up nose accented Wendy's smile as she asked, "And you were going to tell me about the doctor being held around here when?"

"Sorry, Wendy, it just came to me as I was talking. But think about it—it all fits. Vlad is the key. He's located here. He was in Norfolk at the lab there and probably killed Collins when he interrupted his break-in. He was in D.C. and here in Naples. It just makes sense that Coleman was killed and we were attacked because we're getting close. Too many coincidences otherwise, and you know my feelings about those things."

"Okay, boss. I can see where your logic is leading. Makes sense to me."

As the rest of the team returned to the room, Marcus noted there was little chatter and lots of serious faces. He was about to find out if that was good or bad.

SSA Tony Carter remained standing as the rest of the group took their seats. While many heads nodded in agreement, he said, "Mr. Colt, the consensus over coffee was that your plan is as solid as we can get, considering all the variables. So let's wrap this meeting up and get it into play, sir."

Marcus was a bit stunned by that announcement, but as the team leader, he rolled with it and quickly moved on. "Thanks, Tony, and to you all. But please, do not hesitate to offer improvements as it progresses."

Heads nodded around the room and he heard a few positive comments.

"Okay. You all have the radio frequencies we'll use. And on the last page of the handout, you will find the code names we have assigned to the various elements. If the Russians are listening, which I suspect they are, hopefully they will waste valuable time trying to decipher them."

Marcus continued, "This base of operations is now Homestead. Our air assets will be known as Bluetick One through Four. Odd numbers will be surveilling the Russian Embassy, now known as Tree, and even numbers will watch the Clock Twenty Cleaners, hereafter known as Swamp. Back in West Virginia, Bluetick Hounds were the best at tracking and treeing raccoons, so hopefully the P2Vs and our Marines will carry on that fine tradition."

That last comment got laughs, and most of the aviators gave thumbs up signs.

"There are three people we want to follow. Our Marine snipers, with the help of the Bluetick aircrews, will take the lead finding and following these people—they are our missing lab reception clerk, Mario Morelli, who will be called Pest. The cleaners' operator, Antonio Greco, is Ratfink, and the most evil one, Vladimir Davidovich Kroneski, is Viper. That code name for a bad guy worked well for us earlier this year on another case, so maybe the luck will hold. Any questions?"

Captain Boxer asked, "And what is your code name?"

"Use R1 for me, sir. Since I'm going to be running around in circles until this case is closed, calling me Runner seems right. Miss James is R2, and Mrs. Woodward is R3. If there is nothing else, this is *Boots and Saddles* time, people, so mount up and get going."

No further comments were given, and the members of Quicksilver left to do the things they did best. Marcus walked over to sit next to Wendy and Sue. He pressed his left thumb and middle finger into his temples, in hopes of reducing the headache pain that was trying to overcome his head. After a long sigh, he quietly said, "Well, the horses have left the gate, ladies. Now all we can do is watch and wait to see if our horse succeeds in this race."

Wendy's glance at Marcus was filled with concern. He looked worse for wear from the briefing, and she knew from everything Doc had told her that Marcus wouldn't slow down until the case was closed. "You okay, boss?"

Marcus continued stroking his temples as he said, "Just peachy. Trying to adjust to the constant head pain while I wish I had a dark, quiet place to hide. And more important, I'm worried about what the hell I've missed today." Marcus focused on the cup as he sipped more coffee.

To lighten the mood, Wendy quipped, "Well, with a name like Vlad, I suspect he has an evil lair somewhere around here. Maybe some dark castle on a tall hill, like Vlad the Impaler, that he might share with you for some R&R."

Sue laughed. "Not many castle-like structures in this area, and our tallest hill is your favorite volcano. But I like where you're going with this. Maybe we can rent a villa for Marcus so he can have a quiet recovery week when this is over."

With a laugh and a shrug, Marcus said, "I wish."

A knock on the door casing interrupted that thought. Canton and Jackson came in. Their attire was spot on for Marcus's parameters, including the slight bulge on their sides indicating a holstered weapon.

"Welcome back, gentlemen. You both look perfect," Marcus said. "Take a seat and relax for a moment."

As the two SPs were getting seated, Corporal Gardener returned. Marcus gave him the once over and was pleased with what he saw. Rick Gardener was decked out in jeans, a white dress shirt, and light gray jacket. He opened his jacket to show Marcus he was armed.

"Sorry I'm late, sir," Gardener said as he walked toward the group.

"You're right on time, Rick. Have a seat and we'll go over the rules of engagement for this operation."

Gardener handed three sets of credentials to Marcus as introductions were done.

Sue pointed to a chair next to her. "The military look is almost gone. We'll need to pick up a hat to hide the Marine haircut, though."

"Get all three of them ones like mine." Marcus chuckled as he passed the credentials to the men, then he turned serious. "Rick, did you have any issues with your gunny?

"Not after I mentioned your name, sir. He told me he remembered you from 'Nam, and if I pay attention, I'll learn a lot from you. He also added a few things to your list. There's a pair of M16s, an M40, an adequate amount of ammo for both of them and our .45s, a couple of AN/PVS-2 Starlight Scopes, and a can of frag grenades in the trunk. He also added a case of smoke grenades and some flares. Just enough to start a small war, sir," Gardener listed with a small laugh. "He also said to tell you to call for Rattler if you need backup."

Marcus perked up. "Is your gunny named Jasper Railey by any chance?"

"Yes, sir. But no one is allowed to use his first name. And he also said I was now your bodyguard, and if anything happened to you on my watch he would hang me from the flag staff by my … uh, delicate body parts, sir," Gardener said with a sheepish grin and a glance at Wendy and Sue.

"Yep, that's Jasper all right. Tell me, Rick, what is your knowledge of the M40?"

"Sir, the M40 is the Corps' designated sniper rifle. It is a bolt-action rifle based on the Remington Model 700 and has a Redfield 3–9x variable scope mounted. It features a five-round internal magazine for the 7.62x51mm NATO round, which has a muzzle velocity of 2,550 feet per second. Effective range in the hands of an expert is around 2,600 feet. And this weapon has been modified by Gunny Railey, sir—trigger pull has been reduced to just under three pounds, and it has a suppressor installed," Gardener recited from memory.

"And have you shot the M40?"

"Sir, I have shot expert with both the M16 and the M40. I have a MOS 8541, indicating I am a scout sniper."

Marcus broke into his biggest smile of the week. "Outstanding! Ladies, things just got much better with the arrival of Kevin, David, and now Rick and his arsenal. The cherry on top is that we have Jasper as backup. I think it's time to do this brief over a quick lunch."

89

THE NAVAL BASE IN NAPLES is typical of all other U.S. military bases: the basic needs of personnel are very well covered, and the officers' club is no exception. With one phone call, the O-club was able to set up a private dining room for Captain Boxer and his entourage on short notice.

Never wanting to waste a minute, Marcus asked Boxer and SSA Carter to join his team for a working lunch. They needed to get Rick, Kevin, and David up to speed, as well as go over the operation parameters one more time. And to keep everyone on the same page, Marcus mentioned that Canton and Jackson were now on bodyguard duty.

Captain Boxer decided that since he was picking up the tab, everyone would enjoy the Maryland Crab Cake special and it would save time ordering. Hearing no objections, the lunch order was given to the steward. Marcus passed a copy of the handout to each of the three guards and told them to memorize the faces and code names.

As they enjoyed the superb lunch, Marcus looked at the three enlisted men and said, "Those people in that handout might try to kill you. Therefore, it is imperative that you know them on sight. We believe that the one on the first page, code name Viper, is the ringleader—and, in addition to probably putting us in the hospital, he was involved with the death of three people. Two of them were armed NIS agents, so be forewarned. For the duration of this operation, you are assigned to the consulate and are technically working under Sue Woodward, who is with the State Department. Officially, you're to answer to my orders. SSA Carter will now brief you on Operation Quicksilver."

The three bodyguard/drivers were brought up to speed. Marcus firmly believed everyone involved in an operation needed to know the whys and the hows. He sat back, and as they all finished their lunches, he let Tony impress upon the three men the importance of their new roles.

And as he half listened to Tony, his mind also worked on something that was nagging at him. He fast-forwarded the conversations of the day through the intense pain in his aching head and slowed down when he remembered something Sue had joked about earlier. But the pain was blocking the attempt to pull the details to the front of his mind. He clutched onto that thought as he closed his eyes and waited for Tony to wrap up the overview of the operation.

The men asked various questions, and Tony provided answers based on what was known. It was easy to see they were impressed with the seriousness of the situation and would therefore be more diligent in their duty. Marcus heard the voices but had tuned out the actual words. It became a soft drone, easy to ignore.

"Marcus, I asked if there was anything else you wanted to add," Tony said as Wendy gently shook his shoulder.

"Did you drift off?" she asked.

Marcus shook his head. "Actually, no, but I did get lost in thought for a moment or two about something Sue said earlier." He paused as the details he needed finally came to mind, and took a quick sip of his now-cold coffee. "Sue, does the Italian government allow foreigners to own property?"

"Sure. Considering a retirement place already?"

"Not me, but perhaps Viper has already bought a place ..."

Wendy jumped in. "And while we're watching the embassy and the cleaners, he is free to move about from his unknown home."

Captain Boxer frowned. "So all of our surveillance work has been for naught?"

"Not at all, Skipper," Marcus said, "we had to start somewhere. We expected to add more places as time progressed. Now we need to go off on this tangent. Sue, does the local government have some sort of hall of records or courthouse where deeds are filed?"

"Sorry, no. Copies of Italian deeds are kept by the notary public who witnessed the property sale. There are hundreds, probably thousands of them." After a slight pause, she continued, "But we might find something in the IMU records."

"IMU? What's that?" Marcus asked.

"It is the Imposta Municipale Unica—simply translates as single municipal tax, which is due on property twice a year. Think of it as the same as our property tax."

With a slight snicker, Marcus asked, "And why do I suspect you just happen to, quote, *know a guy*, unquote, that can help you search these files?"

"Of course, Marcus, it's part of my job description to know all the right people. Excuse me while I make a fast call," Sue said sweetly.

"Canton will stick with you, Sue, and we'll go on back to the SP HQ. Catch up with us there," Marcus said as Sue stood to leave.

After Sue and Canton left, Tony threw another complication into the mix. "And what about all the rentals that populate the area? There are probably hundreds of them. I'm not sure we can ever discover who is renting them."

Wendy said, "Nothing's perfect. All we can do is work with what we have. And pray that it's enough."

Marcus stood and addressed the group. "Skipper, unless you have anything else to add, time for NIS to do the boring part of an investigation. We have a ton of files to look through, and maybe something will turn up there."

90

THE NAVAL BASE IN NAPLES, officially known as the U.S. Naval Support Activity, is located adjacent to the Naples civilian airport, and it shares the use of the runways. Various hangars and support buildings are located on the edge of the airport. Four P2V Neptune patrol aircraft, normally stationed in Sicily, were positioned outside one of the Navy's hangars.

The Neptunes are beautiful aircraft designed and built by Lockheed. They are powered by two Wright eighteen-cylinder radial piston engines and two Westinghouse J34 turbojet engines, one of each per wing. Armament can include rockets, free-fall bombs, depth charges, and torpedoes, depending upon the demands of the mission. The aircraft are outfitted with air and surface radar, as well as sonobuoys and a magnetic anomaly detector, to aid in the submarine search. The P2V aircraft are in constant use as they patrol, watching for Russian subs as well as ships in distress.

For this mission, the aircraft were basically unarmed. The addition of several Marine snipers to the crew could constitute armament if they had their weapons with them. However, for this mission they just needed their scopes.

Lieutenant Commander Robert D. MacArthur, called Bob by his friends, enjoyed the challenges he faced as the executive officer of VP-73:

the last operating Fleet squadron flying the Neptunes. The following year would see the aircraft he loved transferred to a Naval Air Reserve unit, and he would transition to the new P3-C Orion. He knew it would be a sad day for him, but that it was just one of the challenges progress brings.

Though moderately tall, he stood in the back of a jeep at the front of the closed hangar so he could see and be seen. He faced a group of men he had helped train over the last two years. They were relaxed and carried on low conversations as they waited. MacArthur could count on his aircrew members to do their jobs correctly; they were his well-oiled machines. He was proud of them.

To the right of his men stood thirteen Marines: one lieutenant in charge of twelve enlisted men. They stood by quietly, each man carrying a small black case.

He had to admit, at least to himself, that Operation Quicksilver, as proposed by Lieutenant Commander Colt, fell into the harebrained category if he ever heard one. But last night the skipper had said the order came directly from the CNO's office. Since they were the only ones in the skipper's office, Bob gave a lazy salute and said, "Aye, aye, sir, three bags full, sir." This was his standard sarcastic comment about orders he considered unreasonable or downright ridiculous. But he only said such things in private, and only to his best friend, who happened to be his commanding officer. His CO just smiled and wished him a ton of luck, then dismissed him with a wave of his hand.

Bob leaned down and pressed the jeep's horn once to get everyone's attention. He cleared his throat and said, "Gather round, people. I'm only going to say this once, so get the crap out of your ears and pay attention."

The murmur stopped and all eyes focused on Bob. He held up a handout from the earlier meet in one hand and a set of binoculars in the other.

"As you heard earlier, we are now part of a manhunt in Operation Quicksilver. This should be interesting and, if the powers that be ever declassify this mission, it will provide great entertainment around the scuttlebutt. But for now, it is classified extremely high, so no chatter outside your aircraft." MacArthur briefly paused to let that part sink in.

"The public affairs office has informed the locals, in print and on radio, that we are doing a test of some new low-altitude equipment. Hopefully that will keep the bad guys from being concerned about us circling over Naples at Angels 2.5, or lower if needed. Unless you are flying the aircraft, I expect all air crew eyes to be looking for the subjects in this handout. Learn their faces. All comms will use the code names provided."

MacArthur turned toward the Marine contingent. "Lieutenant Bailer, I wish your men good hunting. Select the three-man crew for each aircraft and get them ready. Just let my people know if you need anything."

"Aye, aye, sir," the Marine responded.

Turning back to face the aircrew group, he asked, "Any questions?"

The lack of questions was a sign that aircraft commanders and senior enlisted personnel, who had attended the morning briefing with MacArthur, had already drilled the mission specifications into the heads of their crews. Only thing needed now was the *go* command.

MacArthur looked around, gave a quick nod, and said, "Make it happen, people." He jumped down from the jeep and walked toward his temporary office. His leadership philosophy was simple: once you give an order, get the hell out of the way of your people and let them do their jobs.

Bluetick One and Bluetick Two were airborne in less than twenty minutes, and started their four-hour surveillance of the target locations known as Tree and Swamp. The XO suspected most of the men felt it was an impossible task, but none said that out loud. They had a mission and would do it to the best of their abilities.

91

TWO CUPS OF STRONG COFFEE helped counter the head injury, pain meds, and lingering anesthesia that was trying to pull Marcus Colt into a near comatose state. He really just wanted to close his eyes and sleep, but there was too much to do. Perhaps later, he promised himself, already knowing that was a lie.

After the phone call, Sue Woodard and Kevin Canton had dashed off to see the man about the property tax records. Marcus wasn't holding his breath, but like so many investigations, it was necessary to look under every rock. Crossing every t and dotting every i was frequently a royal pain in the butt.

The air cover was in place. In addition to the Blueticks' surveillance, additional Navy aircraft were flying over the Naples area to hopefully prevent the bad guys from noticing the watchers. Colt just wanted his plan to work, and he prayed the Blueticks could actually see Viper, Ratfink, and the Pest from their perches in the sky.

They had spent the last hour plus digging through the BIs the Air Force guys had provided. J. Scott Tiller had done an excellent job on his overview; nothing else of importance was found in the files. Another group of i's were dotted or t's crossed. Whatever!

"Since it is getting close to 1500, we need to take a short break from this." Marcus closed the last file folder with yet another yawn. "Walk around … well, not you Wendy, but you guys take twenty, grab a candy bar, soda, smoke, or whatever."

Not needing to be told twice, Rick and David immediately left for a much-needed break. Marcus turned to Wendy. "Honestly, how ya holding up? Much pain from the accident?"

She let out a deep sigh. "Don't sugarcoat it, Marcus. It was an attack and not just an accident. The leg's fine. I hurt some from the bruises, but my anger for the guy that pushed us off the road overpowers that. You are the one with the more complicated injury. You need to stop pushing yourself and take it easy."

"Sounds like you've been talking to Doc," Marcus said with a chuckle. "I'm okay for now, but looking forward to a decent night's sleep in the Eastern Standard time zone after we quickly wrap this case up."

Wendy rapidly tapped her pen on the stack of folders in front of her, mouth twisting into a grimace of disgust. "I don't know how you can keep such a positive attitude right now. We have nothing—unless you consider speculation and assumptions as something valid. It is so frustrating!"

Smiling, Marcus replied, "Like I said on Monday morning, welcome to Internal Affairs. Most cases are not handed to us on a platter. We have to use logic, common sense, and gut instinct to work these types of cases. Taking what little hard evidence we find, we analyze it to see where it fits in the overall scheme, and from there develop a plan. Frustrating at times, but that's why they pay us the big bucks."

Wendy scoffed, but had to smile. "Aye, aye, Skipper. I'll work on improving my 'can do' attitude. Guess all the body aches put a damper on it. So, what do we do now?"

"Now we do the thing I hate most. We wait. And while we wait, you get on that phone and call your folks. They need to hear an update directly from you. I'll check in with Kelly, and then call Doc to see if anything's cooking on his end. Okay?"

"Yes, sir," Wendy softly said. "Thanks, Marcus." She reached for the phone to do exactly what Marcus ordered.

Marcus checked in with Captain Boxer and was told all was quiet from the watchers. Radio checks had been done and no movements had been seen.

With the skipper's blessing, Marcus used the privacy of the XO's office to make his calls. Kelly had just gotten to work and was thrilled to hear from him. After a few moments of newlywed chat in hushed, sexy tones, she wanted a full update on the status of his injuries. After the report, she naturally counseled him to get more rest and not do anything foolish. Marcus could only chuckle at that "foolish" remark knowing that, to many people, everything he did could be considered foolish.

Hearing her voice gave Marcus the boost of energy he needed. He wanted to finish this case and hurry home to her soft warm arms and other fine attributes. As seemed to be standard during calls to her office, Kelly's next patient arrived, forcing an end to the call they both wanted to continue.

His second call was to NISHQ. Since it was 0930 in D.C., he was hoping to find everyone he needed in the office. For once lately, his luck held.

After hearing the standard spiel, Marcus asked, "Hi Rita, how goes your morning?"

"Well, hello Mr. Colt. Feeling better, I hope."

"Yea, nothing that a month off won't cure."

Rita scoffed. "Your luck ain't that good, boss. There are a bunch of folks looking forward to you getting back to your office—me most of all, since I'm the one who hears all the whining. The admiral is grumbling. Lieutenant Doty is bitching. And poor Doc is running around like the headless chicken. Hurry home!"

"Rita, my darling, you just gave me three great reasons to stay here in Italy a bit longer."

She chuckled. "So, who do you want to get yelled at by first? The admiral?"

Marcus sighed and stifled yet another yawn. "No, get me Doty, Doc, and then the admiral. Maybe by then I'll have some positive news to tell him."

"Can do. Hold one while I track Lieutenant Doty down."

92

THE OBVIOUS PLACE TO FIND Lieutenant Doty should have been Marcus's office, since as his backup, he needed to address the growing pile of paperwork. He didn't have time for goofing off, but the big office chair was empty. However, Yeoman Neil had the right idea. He stuck his head into the coffee mess and said, "Lieutenant, Rita is looking for you. Mr. Colt is on the line, sir."

"Thanks, Brad. On the way," Doty said as he tossed the coffee stirrer into the trash can and dashed out the door. He mumbled an obscenity as a small amount of hot coffee splashed onto his hand as he hurried back to his temporary office.

"Lieutenant Doty speaking, sir," he said as he plopped down behind the desk covered with file folders and messages.

"Having fun yet, Jake?" Marcus asked with a chuckle.

"Oh, things are just peachy keen, sir, thank you so much for asking." After rattling off the expected and sarcastic reply, he became serious. "Frankly, Marcus, I would prefer to have your head injury than your desk. But enough of my whining—what's up, sir?"

"Doing the waiting routine here as we hope the surveillance will locate the bad guys. We know several of the probable key players, but they have gone into hiding. Figured I should check in with my favorite replacement. Any nasty issues?"

"No, sir. Nothing I couldn't handle if I had a twenty-eight-hour day. I don't know how you do it, man. Good news is that Naples is the only hot spot right now. Everything else is same ol', same ol' kinda stuff."

"At least that's some good news. Remember Carl and Rita can handle some of the minor issues. Don't be afraid to get their help."

"Will do, sir. Anything else?"

"No, just transfer this call on to Doc so I can pull his chain a bit. Take care, Jake. I really do appreciate your help."

The silence on the line was a welcome break to Marcus. Thankfully, NIS had never opted for the canned and usually disgusting elevator music when on hold. His headache couldn't handle that right then.

"SA Stevens speaking. How may I help you, sir?"

"Guess Jake failed to mention it was me, Doc. What's the status, buddy?"

Doc chuckled. "Yes, sir, he warned me it was you. But I figured you might be on speakerphone since you like it so much, and wasn't sure who's the audience."

Now it was Marcus's turn to laugh.

Doc continued, "Nothing much new on Cold Fog on this end. Today Victoria is back at the CIA with Les, doing more file digging. She keeps thinking there is something she's overlooking. That lady is tenacious— glad I don't have her chasing me. Oh, did Lieutenant Doty tell you about his digging into PO Masters?"

"No, he's so covered up with paperwork he failed to mention that."

"Yea, the piles are getting deeper by the day, so hurry home or you may never find your desk again. Anyway, Masters is out of the hospital, and we have him under arrest."

"What are the charges?"

"Lying to NIS agents is one. Failing to mention contact with a foreign agent is the other. Seems he had been approached before the beating by the guy we've been calling 'Boris' who we now know is your buddy Vlad. We found a witness who saw them together before the attack. Masters said Vlad had been pushing for him to get a Rembrandt file from the lab."

"And because he didn't deliver the file, he received the beating, right?"

"Yes, sir. Doty got him talking after threatening him with spying and treason charges. But the wildest part, which we're not sure we can believe, is that Vlad told Masters that Doctor Monroe is alive. Vlad said the doctor had wanted Masters to get a special file for him."

"Now that's interesting."

"My thoughts exactly, Marcus. The rest of the team is skeptical about the validity of it all. General consensus is that it could be his way of creating a diversion away from himself to mitigate his crime … which might be true. While I hate to admit it, I sort of believe him."

"Yea, Buddy, sometimes the excuses are so far out there that they just might be true. Not sure if Masters is smart enough to come up with that on his own."

Doc laughed. "Or I could be so green that I fall for anything."

"Doubtful, Doc—you're pretty perceptive most times. Maybe I picked up on your thought waves earlier today. I threw that speculation out during a team briefing this morning. It hit me that Vlad could be his kidnapper and forcing Monroe to finish his work for the Russians. I had nothing firm until Masters' comment, and that is as firm as quicksand, but it might justify Vlad being around the labs. Key word is might."

Doc let out a deep sigh. "Well, that's a bit far out there, but it's as solid as anything else we have, with all our other speculations and theories."

"Tell ya what, Doc—go back over Monroe's financials that were run at the time of his disappearance. If I remember right, the investigators were concerned just about recent bank and credit card activity to see if he skipped town on his own. Do a new BI with in-depth analysis of his financials, going back at least five years, looking for anything that might point to something hidden. Get Scott Tiller to help with that. While Scott is doing his magic, get the team together and search his house again, but this time think of the doctor as the bad guy and not the victim when you give it a good going-over. Okay?"

"You got it, boss. Anything else?"

Marcus took a deep breath and exhaled before he said, "Oh, yea, one other speculation to ponder. At lunch we hit on the idea that Vlad might have bought or rented a villa around here, and he's got another hiding spot besides the embassy. I sent Sue to check property tax records—it's a long shot, but nothing else to do around here while we wait."

"Yep, that's some major straw grasping, Marcus." Doc chuckled. "I'll run that by Victoria to see if she thinks Vlad is the villa type. That rat might prefer a dark basement apartment. Only thing I have left to say is take good care of Wendy and get your wounded butt back home."

"Working on both, Doc. Please get the admiral on the line for me. Thanks, buddy."

The few moments of silence on the line provided Marcus a respite from the stress and discomfort of what he had started calling *thinking while under the influence of head pain.* He knew there were people who had constant headaches, many of them up to the migraine level, and he was getting a new respect for their strength in facing them daily. He prayed his pain would subside soon.

"Chance here. What ya got, Colt?"

"Admiral, we are just starting the surveillance measures we discussed last night, so nothing solid there yet. We also have a few new thoughts—mostly wild theories I have to admit—that we are pursuing. But for now, only fact I have is a nasty headache."

With a sharp exhale, the admiral said, "Your father-in-law mentioned that several times before he suggested I order you home and put you on recuperation leave."

"Sir, I'm glad it was just a suggestion. Please ignore it. My gut's telling me I'm close on this. I just need a bit more time. And I appreciate your patience, sir."

"I can only ignore the CNO if, and that is a big damn if, you don't get hurt again. We don't want daddy's little girl to become a widow. Do you understand me, Colt?"

"Aye, aye, sir. I'll do my best to avoid both death and the doctors."

The admiral chuckled. "Glad we're on the same page, Colt. Wrap this up and get back here soon."

The admiral had one other issue to discuss. The conversation went on for several minutes, ending with both parties firmly agreeing. And after a shared laugh over the coming announcement, the admiral said, "Chance out."

Just as he hung up the phone, Doc knocked on the admiral's door. "Enter."

Doc approached the admiral's desk and came to attention. "Sorry to bother you, sir, but I had hoped to talk with Mr. Colt before you concluded the call. I'll head back to my desk and call him, sir."

Chance shook his head and pointed to a chair in front of his desk, then slightly smiled. "Perfect timing. Close the door and sit. Doc, your call can wait a minute or two. Tell me what you have for Colt."

Squirming slightly in what he considered the hot seat, while sitting ramrod straight, Doc said, "Sir, Mr. Colt told me he was thinking that the Russian might have a hideout away from the Russian Embassy besides the cleaners. They're checking on their end. I called and mentioned it to Mrs. Victoria Smythe, who's at the CIA office right now. She's there looking for some missing link that's been bugging her. She quickly called me back. Seems she did some fast digging and, with the help of ADDO Forrester, finally remembered Vlad had a girlfriend who owns a villa south of Naples, near the town of Amalfi. I need to pass her name and location on to Mr. Colt, sir."

The admiral nodded. "Interesting piece of info, but it can wait a moment. First I've got a couple of questions for you, Doc … you've worked with Colt when he was injured. Twice, right?"

"Yes, sir."

"As his closest and most experienced medical professional, how do you think he's holding up right now, considering his injuries?" the admiral asked quietly.

Doc had to smile. "Easy answer, sir. Mr. Colt thrives on stress, and pain amps up his abilities. While I wish I was there to help watch his back, I know he is the best person to handle the situation, even with his injuries."

"And is this judgment any way colored by your friendship?"

"Honest answer—probably more than a little bit. But hell, Admiral, I've watched that man dance through situations where others would be curled up in a ball calling for their mamas. He's not perfect—he's not invincible, but he sure has an uncanny ability to get the job done no matter the obstacles. Carrying Ensign James down a volcano in the dark after both being injured in a car wreck is just the latest example."

"Okay. I'll trust your medical judgment. Now the last question." Chance took a deep breath and glanced at the overhead. After what seemed like an eternity to Doc, the admiral asked, "Are you happy with your assignment here, Doc?"

There were a thousand things Doc expected the admiral to ask, and this was not one. He started to answer, then paused. His face slightly contorted as he posed his own question. "Sir, may I speak freely?"

"Nothing else is ever allowed in this office, Agent Stevens. We don't have time for BS or you blowing smoke up my butt," Chance said with hardness in his voice. He then softened. "Answer my question, Doc."

"Aye, aye, sir." Doc let out a sigh. "Admiral, sorry if my response is a bit scattered and long winded, but it is the only way I can hope to explain myself. It's not a yes or no thing for me. Okay, sir?"

Chance nodded and gave a *come on* hand signal.

"Sir, if you had asked me about becoming an NIS agent around the first of the year, I would have told you my place was on a SEAL team kicking ass and taking names. But Marcus has shown me that the job we do here is just as important in the overall scheme of things. And in this situation with Rembrandt, it is much more complicated and challenging than running around the jungle with the teams. At least mentally, that is. While I know I have so much more to learn, I am extremely happy with my current assignment on Cold Fog. When this case is over, I know I'll go back to teaching, where I feel somewhat out of my element, but I believe this case will make me a better instructor, sir. And I will do my damnedest to be the best instructor NIS has ever seen."

Slightly shaking his head, Chance gently said, "Sorry, Doc, you are not going back to instructor status. While you have done a decent job over the last few months, we both know it is not your strong suit."

"Sir, are you kicking me out of NIS?"

"Oh, you're not getting off that easy, Doc," Chance quipped with a smile. "I just talked it over with Marcus, and he's in full agreement with my plan. You are now permanently assigned to Internal Affairs. I'd be a fool to break up such a good team. You still need to finish your degree—and when time permits, you will go through the standard agent training."

Doc's face showed the highest level of surprise. Emotions made it hard to talk, but he finally stammered, "Thank you, sir. I'm more than a bit flabbergasted by all this."

The admiral chuckled. "I want you to know this was not Colt pushing to get you the assignment, although I fully expected him to do it one day soon. The decision is all my idea, and it was a surprise to him. It came to me after watching you without Marcus around. You have handled yourself well. Granted, I did ask the other people involved with Cold Fog how they felt working for you, and everyone gave you high marks for leadership and ability. Things will stay the same with your Navy enlistment until you get your degree. For now, just continue as you have been doing. You might want to keep this between us and wait for Colt to get back so he can make the formal announcement. He might want to shift his organizational table around a bit now that he has two new people."

"Yes, sir. And thank you, sir, for your confidence in me. I won't let you down, sir."

Chance smiled. "You're welcome. Now get back to work. You have a call to make, I believe."

93

IMPORTANT PHONE CALLS BEHIND HIM, Marcus had wandered back to Captain Boxer's office. They were deep in discussion about the next possible steps when a senior CPO stuck his head in the office and announced, "Cap, we got problems. I need you out here." Both men stood and followed the chief.

"Sir, we just heard from Petty Officer Canton," the chief said as they hurried down the hall to the radio console. "They've been attacked at the tax office and Mrs. Woodward is missing."

"Talk to me, Canton," Marcus almost yelled over the radio as he grabbed the mike from the operator.

"Sir, she was looking over tax record books and I went to the rear of the office to pull the next one for her. When I turned with my arms wrapped around a big record book, some SOB hit me in the face. I didn't have time to register who it was, but I came to quick enough to see Ratfink forcing R3 out the side door. I'm sorry, sir."

"Anyone hurt? Do you need medical attention?"

"No, sir. One clerk was knocked out, but he'll be okay. I did get outside fast enough to see a black sedan speeding around the corner. It was about two minutes ago and I'm in pursuit heading southwest. I might catch up to them unless they ducked into an alley."

Marcus rubbed his forehead and grimaced. "Kevin, we're sending additional cars your way. If you spot the bastard, hang back and follow. Do not try anything alone, okay?"

"Aye, aye, sir."

Marcus turned to Boxer. "Can you get several more unmarked cars heading that way pronto? And we need one to secure the tax office staff."

"Consider it done," Boxer said as he walked toward another radio console.

"And pass the info on to the Blueticks, sir," Marcus added.

Boxer nodded.

Keying the mike he was holding, Marcus asked, "Kevin, how many clerks were on duty at the tax office?"

"Two, sir, that I saw. One was knocked out and I don't know where the second went."

Marcus sighed deeply. Looked like another person could be added to the list of people helping the Russians. He keyed the mike again. "Okay, Kevin, stay on the radio and keep the guys here posted on your location. I'm heading back to confer with Miss James."

"Aye, sir."

Marcus passed the mike back to the operator, who had been just sitting there, watching things happen around him. They looked at each other for a moment and both nodded in an unsaid agreement. They both knew what had to be done.

Rushing back down the hall to the conference room, Marcus checked his watch. It was only 1545 hrs, Naples time, but it felt like midnight.

Entering the conference room, Marcus saw Wendy on the phone as she waved and frantically said, "Hold one, Doc. Here he is."

Grabbing the phone from Wendy, Marcus barked, "What ya got, Doc? Be quick, brother, as we got some bad crap happening here."

"Got it, sir. Victoria found a reference for a villa owned by a past girlfriend of Vlad. Stand by to copy."

"Go ahead, Doc."

"Stefania Morelli. She's the older sister of Mario, who works at the lab. The villa is located south of Naples. No real address—it just contained directions. To get to it you head south past Pompeii on 'the main road.' Turn left onto ..." Doc rattled out instructions to the villa for several minutes. He finished by saying the villa was painted yellow with a red tile roof.

"Well, that doesn't narrow it down much, Doc. Just about every house here is painted in pastels and has a reddish tile roof." Then Marcus frowned as he asked, "When were Vlad and Stefania connected?"

"Sorry, Marcus, no idea. This info dates back to when Victoria was chasing Vlad, so that's about ten years at least. She's still at the CIA office and I failed to ask that question when she called."

"No problem. So while they could have painted the place over the last decade, at least it's more info than we had an hour ago. Glad to have it. Anything else to pass on to me?"

"Only one thing. I just had an interesting chat with Admiral Chance. Thank you for the permanent assignment to IA, Marcus."

Marcus chuckled. "All I did was approve a logical choice by the admiral. You earned it, buddy."

"Thanks, Marcus. Now what's going on over there?"

Marcus took a deep breath and let out a huge sigh. "Doc, Sec State's daughter, Susan, has been kidnapped. We have an SP in pursuit trying to catch up with the suspected car, and more agents zeroing in on him, but it looks like Vlad has reared his head again. Best not to tell Harry until we know something more solid. Okay?"

"Agreed, boss. I'll call Victoria and Les to see if they can help more."

"Thanks, Doc. Colt out."

Wendy's shocked look conveyed her feelings. "What can I do, Marcus?"

He took a deep breath and gathered his thoughts. After a moment, Marcus said, "Call the consul general. Don't tell him about Sue's abduction, but ask if he has any high-level contacts in the Italian government who we can call for info on Stefania Morelli. We need to know if she's still alive, and where we can find her. And I'm not sure we can trust all the local police."

"Can do, but what if he asks why Sue is not doing that?"

Marcus shrugged. "Tell the truth—she left here to check on another lead."

Wendy's nose scrunched up, giving her a confused look. "And why don't we want the consul general to know one of his people has been abducted?"

"He'll feel obligated to call her father. Harry doesn't need the stress of it while we have nothing specific to tell him. His heart is not one hundred percent. As soon as we get some solid info, I'll call him. Okay?"

"Got ya," Wendy said as she pulled the phone closer and lifted the handset.

Colt headed back to the CO's office. He wasn't sure why, but by the time he knocked on the door casing, the reason popped to the front of his mind. Captain Boxer waved him in and pointed to one of the chairs to the side of his desk.

"What ya need, Colt?" The skipper sounded more than a little grouchy. He was not having a good day and it was starting to wear on him.

Thinking he might have done something to irritate the CO, Marcus played it safe. He marched to the front of the desk, snapped to attention, and sharply asked, "Captain, does anyone on your staff know how to find locals without going through the local law enforcement? I need to find a woman."

The captain sighed deeply. "Marcus, sorry I snapped at you—bad case of frustration and worry mixed together. At ease," Boxer said with regret in his voice as he again pointed to the chair. "And for crying out loud, sit, please, before you fall over. Who do you need to find?"

Marcus slightly smiled as he nodded. "No apologies necessary, Captain. I feel the same way. It has been a true bitch of a day."

Having taken the seat, Marcus said, "Anyway, the woman is Stefania Morelli—sister of our Pest, Mario. My CIA friends found a reference to her as a sweetie of our boy Vlad back in the day … probably about ten or so years ago. She had a villa somewhere south of Naples. It might be Vlad's hideout, where he might have Sue stashed. As for the hideout reference, hope I'm allowed to use old cowboy movie terminology. And before you say it, you bet I'm grasping at straws, sir."

Boxer chuckled. He stood and said, "For that, we consult one of the foundation stones of the U.S. Navy. Let's go talk to my master chief of the command."

94

PETTY OFFICER KEVIN CANTON WAS mad as hell. Mrs. Woodward's kidnapper was high on his list for that anger, but he was angrier with himself. He had let Lieutenant Commander Colt and Mrs. Woodward down by not paying full attention. He should have kept one eye on the lady. He slammed his left hand onto the steering wheel in frustration as a vulgarity escaped from his mouth.

He still hadn't caught up with the sedan that was carrying Mrs. Woodward. Granted it had a head start, but with all the speed limits he was now breaking, he should have seen the car by now. *Maybe they turned off onto a side street*, he thought. Kevin faced the fact that there were too many options for the bad guys.

The car radio crackled: "KC. Homestead. What's your status? Over."

Kevin keyed the mike. "Homestead. Still in pursuit. Have not seen the target, but think I'm in a good position to catch up. Over."

"KC. Bluetick Two has moved toward your location. Can you provide any more info about the subject vehicle? Over."

"Homestead, like I said before, a black sedan. That's all I got. Sorry. Over."

"KC, we understand. Keep us apprised. Be careful. Over."

"Homestead, roger. Out."

Kevin returned his full focus to the road ahead and the side roads branching off from it. Nothing. Looked like he'd lost them, and that fired his anger. And that anger caused his leg to push the accelerator even more. Again he slammed his hand against the steering wheel as he muttered another profanity.

If nothing else, Kevin Canton was a logical person. He analyzed every situation and usually let logic, not emotion, control his actions. He realized that emotion was controlling his actions right that moment, so he backed off the gas and slowed to a legal speed. His emotions were on edge because he was blindsided and because his assignee had been kidnapped.

Furthermore—he hated to admit it—but he was drawn to Susan Woodward. Not a good thing considering their positions in life. He was a sailor and she was a married bigwig in the State Department. It was one of those princess and the pauper things. Wouldn't work, but still he felt something when she smiled at him. Enough of this crap, he told himself.

Logic told him the sun was closer to setting than he liked, the car carrying Mrs. Woodward was not in sight, and the probability of finding them was not good. No matter the odds, Petty Officer Canton would not stop. At a slightly slower rate of speed, he was able to glance down each side road and alley for a more complete look. Still nothing.

At times like this it seemed the gods of ancient Rome worked against you. Kevin's attention was focused on a small dark alley to the left for a few seconds too long. When he looked back at the road ahead, he was just a few feet from a black box truck in his path. And closing fast. While his focus was on the alley, the truck had backed out from a parking lot, blocking the entire road.

There wasn't enough time for his foot to completely move from the accelerator to the brake. It was still moving between the two pedals when the front of his sedan slammed, at 55 kph, into the side of the box truck at the rear axle. In what seemed like slow motion, Kevin saw the front of his sedan crumple against the truck as the hood folded up like an accordion. The collision caused the truck to shudder slightly, but the effect on the sedan was much worse.

Kevin lucked out: his body damage was much less than that of the sedan. He had stiffened up when he saw the truck and held his flexed arms tight to the steering wheel. He bounced back and forth a small amount, but sustained no major damage. His mind told him the next day or two would allow a few aches and pains to come forth, but for now, all was well. Not so with his car, as steam exploded from the damaged front end and the engine shuddered to a stop.

Shaking his head, Kevin added a few vocal comments to his mental discussion as he mumbled, "Damn it. How much worse can this day get? Crap!"

As he stepped out of his now-dead car to make sure the truck driver was all right, he noticed a light blue Volkswagen van pull out of a side street and slow as it passed him. He wasn't able to see who was driving, but logged the vehicle into his mind just in case.

At least he had a couple of moments to check the car radio. It was still working, so he called his status change in to Homestead.

95

THE FOG WAS SLOWLY DISSIPATING from her vision as Sue came back to the first level of consciousness. The room was dark except for a small amount of light sneaking in under the door. Her hands and feet were securely bound. Her mouth was dry, but at least it wasn't stuffed with a gag. The mental disorientation was intense.

After that quick tally of her condition, her next thought was ... *and aside from that assassination thing, how was the play, Mrs. Lincoln.* With a chuckle, she realized that Marcus's sarcastic humor was rubbing off on her. At least she was on a soft piece of furniture; it felt like a double bed, not a mattress tossed into the corner, on the floor. And unlike Abe Lincoln, she was not dead.

Her FBI training kicked in as the fog finally lifted; time to go back over the known parameters of the situation. She had been at the tax office. While digging through the first two of the requested tax record books, she had noticed one of the clerks on the phone continuing to glance her way. *Well*, she thought, *he is kind of cute*, and she had smiled at him. And he had smiled back.

Now Sue realized he was probably calling whoever had put the black cloth bag over her head, not really flirting. And this guy who grabbed her also injected a knockout shot into her left buttock as he pushed her into a car. The injection point was still sore.

She couldn't remember if she had mentioned Vlad's name or not. Since Kevin was helping her look through the dusty books, more than likely she had said the name out loud at least once. And the clerk had probably heard her. Stupid move on her part, she realized.

The next thing Sue did was to consider how to get out of wherever the heck she was right then. Maybe she was in the basement of the Russian Embassy. Listening carefully, Sue did not hear any sounds. No voices, no footsteps, no music nor traffic noise could be heard from her prison cell. At least she still had her clothes on, that was a big positive. But the cold steel of the handcuffs on her wrists painfully let her know she was not going to chew her way out of those. Too bad she no longer carried the standard handcuff key, as she had while in the FBI.

Sitting up, she ran her cuffed hands down to the bindings on her ankles. The cloth strips she could easily cut, if she had a knife—something she needed to start carrying in the future. "Well, yea that's a really good idea, albeit a tad late," she softly said out loud. "Note to self—carry a damn knife." Sue realized her only option was to untie her legs.

She started to reposition, hoping to reach the knots securing the bindings to the bed frame. Sue found out that you couldn't easily move when your legs are bound, your hands are joined tightly in front of you, and you're sitting on a soft mattress. *Nope, this is not an easy task*, she thought.

It took several minutes, but by wiggling her butt and contracting her leg muscles to scoot her along, she was able to move closer to the place where she hoped the end of the leg bindings were tied. If she was lucky, the ends of the cloth binders would be tied to the footboard of the bed. Any farther away and she would be out of luck. She stopped moving as a faint noise came from beyond the door.

There was a rattle as a key on a key ring was selected to unlock the door. A moment passed before the sound of a knob turning and a spring-loaded bolt being pulled back from its casing echoed through the still room. The door quietly swung inward.

Light poured into the room around the dark shadow of the person standing in the doorway. What felt to Sue like a long time was, in reality, no more than fifteen seconds as her captor stood quietly watching the captive. Finally, a hand reached off to the side of the door and, with a slight click, an overhead light came to life.

"Good evening, Mrs. Woodward. I hope the method of bringing you here has not been too stressful." The thick Eastern European accent filled the silence of the room. The comment from Marcus about Vlad sounding like the cartoon character Boris from the flying squirrel cartoon show was accurate. Hopefully there wasn't a Natasha hiding around here.

Sue did a quick inventory as she studied her jailer from head to toe. Dark hair in need of a trim covered his head, with just a touch of gray. A dark mustache and trimmed goatee hid portions of his face; both had gray hairs softening the dark color. His pockmarked face was not impressive, with pale blue eyes that sat too close together and a nose that must have been broken in the past. That nose now twisted to the right somewhat, indicating it hadn't received the services of a decent surgeon at the time. His body had the bulky look of a bodybuilder, with broad shoulders tapering down to a slightly thinner waist. The sleeves of his suit coat did not cover the roughness and bulk of his hands, with fingers like sausages.

Sue knew from his BI that this man was accustomed to getting his way and, when he didn't, wasn't afraid to use violence. She ran several scenarios in her mind on how to handle this guy, then chose the forceful direct route. "Kidnapping is always stressful, Vladimir Davidovich Kroneski, and diplomatic immunity will not protect you from the repercussions." Sue paused to gather her thoughts, and with arrogance she didn't know she had, continued, "Vlad, you're such a pompous ass. Cut the crap and tell me what you want before my team arrives."

Kroneski snorted and slowly shook his head. A sneer replaced his smile. "Ha. No one knows where you are. No one will come to rescue you. And unless you tell me what I want to know, no one will ever know what happened to your body. And believe me, Susan—*your* diplomatic immunity will not protect you here."

Knowing that bullies thrive on their victims' fear, Sue laughed. "You are so screwed, Vlad. Just believe your lies and remember that pride goes before the fall. Your only option …"

Moving faster than expected, Kroneski reached Sue, pushed her back down on the bed and yelled, "Shut up, bitch! You have no idea who you are talking to. But you will soon talk more and tell me all that I want to know."

Sue decided that silence was the best response at the moment, but she could not prevent a smile from developing. That smile irritated Vlad even more, so he took out his frustration with a backhand slap to Sue's face.

The slap was painful, but Sue was expecting it. She kept as much of a smile as pain would allow while licking the blood away from her busted lip. With a slight lisp, Sue said, "And what the hell do you want to know, you sadistic bastard?"

Vlad looked down at her and said, "Everything." He pulled a syringe from his shirt pocket and quickly injected Sue with the contents.

96

MARCUS HAD LOST TRACK OF the number of times he had hit the coffee mess in the last couple of hours. *Yea, it was a lot,* he thought, but he had to remember he was fetching coffee for Wendy James as well. At least, he believed that was a good excuse for the overdose of caffeine.

Taking care of an injured partner gave him pause, and he made a mental note to thank Doc again for all he had done for him earlier that year. Now that he was the caregiver, he better understood the amount of work and stress involved. Hoping he was doing almost as good a job as Doc, Marcus properly doctored the two steaming mugs with sugar and cream, and headed back to the conference room to ensure Wendy was properly caffeinated.

With the empty food containers pushed to the end of the table, Wendy was back on the phone with a contact at the consulate. She shook her head negatively when Marcus gave her an inquisitive look. Doc had called back just a bit ago after checking with the CIA; no other info was available about the villa, but they would send out feelers. Two more negatives, and Sue was still missing.

Following his own sage advice about grabbing on to any positives no matter how small, Marcus was glad Kevin was safe and back there at Homestead. The captain had called the local police chief as soon as he heard about the accident, smoothing over any potential rough spots. Kevin was upset with his failure, no matter how much Marcus tried to rationalize the situation.

More bad news was that the police chief was not able to give any clues on finding Morelli's sister. At least he'd promised to make a few calls to local friends and see if they had any clues.

The three enlisted men refused to leave after their watch was over. Marcus appreciated their dedication, and assigned Rick Gardener, Kevin Canton, and David Jackson the task of studying the local maps. Their mission was a challenge: use the decade-old vague instructions from the CIA to locate Morelli's villa.

It was not an easy task in an area where some roads are ancient animal paths filled with only slightly newer, two-thousand-year-old Roman paving stones. But technically these men were local boys, each having been in Naples for at least a year, so they were more experienced than either Wendy or Marcus.

And the two new SPs who should have been relieving Canton and Jackson jumped into the map studying task with great enthusiasm when they arrived at 1600. At least they were rested and had fresh eyes.

Marcus took a minute to think about what he might have missed in the last few frustrating hours. Nothing came to mind as he rehashed the events. His pain and fatigue were gnawing on him, and he suspected Wendy was suffering in the same way. Both tried to conceal their issues, but one person could see through it all.

"Mr. Colt," the CPO said as he entered the conference room.

"What's up, Chief?"

"Sir, you and Miss James are needed in the skipper's office."

Standing and helping Wendy get her crutches in place, Marcus nodded. "On the way."

As they maneuvered down the hall, Wendy chuckled and whispered, "Why does this seem like we are being summoned to the principal's office?"

Marcus shrugged. "Yea, it does. At least we know you weren't running in the hall, right? As for me, I seem to stay in trouble."

Captain Boxer met them at his office door. He pointed farther down the hall and said, "Follow me."

Opening a door, the captain led them inside. The room was set up with a cot, sofa, and a small kitchenette area. He studied their faces for a moment, then said, "Thanks for joining me. I just had a nice talk with your doctor. Considering you both were released from the hospital with some fairly nasty injuries just this morning, and it has been a true bitch of a day, he agreed with me ordering you both to get horizontal and rest for at least an hour or so. He'd prefer not to bother the CNO about this."

Marcus shook his head. "Too much to do, Skipper. We need to find Sue. And as it looks …"

Holding up his right hand like a police officer indicating *stop*, Captain Boxer interrupted the complaint. "You have put everything into play. All that can be done is being done, and having you two fall over from pain and exhaustion will not make it go any better. So stop your complaints, take your pain pills, close your eyes, and don't come out for at least an hour and a half. Better yet, make it two hours. I'll let you know if anything happens."

"Aye, aye, sir," both Marcus and Wendy said over each other.

The captain left and closed the door. Marcus shrugged, then pointed to the cot. "You get that comfy spot since your cast will not let you scrunch up on the sofa."

Wendy softly laughed, "And again, you know how to show a girl a good time, Marcus. At least no fertilizer in here."

Back in the conference room, the five enlisted men were pouring over several maps. As they traced roads and plotted distances, each man muttered various oaths and frequently condemned the efforts of the CIA to document the location. Every trail became a dead end.

Corporal Rick Gardener saw the problem first. "Guys, check the map dates. We are using current maps to plot directions that Mr. Colt said were at least a decade old. Who's to say that some of these roads didn't change over time?"

Kevin looked up from his map. "Could be. I'll check with the chief to see if they have any older ones around." He left in search of the unit's master chief petty officer.

After hearing Kevin's request, the chief said, "Sure, Canton. We get new maps every year. And we properly archive the old ones in the evidence storage room. Hold on and I'll go dig out maps from around 1960. Okay?"

"That'll be perfect, Chief. Thanks!" Kevin replied.

As he carried several tubes of maps the chief had found, Canton stopped by the CO's office to find Mr. Colt. The skipper saw him at the door and asked, "What ya need, Canton?"

"Sir, I have something to pass on to Mr. Colt. Do you know where I can find him?"

Captain Boxer chuckled. "Of course, as your captain, I know all." After another laugh at his own joke, he continued, "He and Miss James are getting some needed rest. He can't be bothered. So, pass on your info to me."

After a quick explanation from Kevin, the skipper joined the men in the conference room as they compared the old maps with the new. They were surprised to find that many roads had changed their designations. Some had gone from old local street names to route numbers, while others seemed to have been completely removed from newer maps. Perhaps growth from urban sprawl had caused new structures to be built over old road locations, with new roads built nearby. And sometimes not built. It was a mess.

The muttered comments started to overpower the room, so the skipper cleared his throat and said, "Okay, people, here's what we're going to do. Each of you will study a different year map—1958 through 1962. Glad the Chief was thinking ahead and gave us multiple years. I'll read out the instructions, and each of you will try to find them on your map. Okay?"

Multiple *yes, sirs* filled the room. The noise of large sheets of paper being unfurled and flattened was quickly followed by total silence as they waited for the skipper to recite the directions.

It took almost an hour of careful study, but the map from 1959 almost matched—at least, closer than any other map—the directions provided by the CIA. It took another chunk of time to correlate the roads on the current map with those on the one from 1959. And finally, they felt comfortable that they could find the villa—that is, assuming it still existed.

A few paces down the hall, Marcus slowly came back to consciousness from the imposed, yet much needed and appreciated sleep. A small part of him was glad Captain Boxer had ordered it, while the bigger part was frustrated by what he considered a delay in finding Sue. The dark room offered an opportunity to get mentally lost in the blackness for a couple of minutes and not think about all the challenges he now faced.

A soft sound caught his attention. He focused his hearing and realized it was Wendy's slow, steady breathing. She was still out. With no need to disturb her, he decided to lie still. If something were happening with the case, they would've been notified. Besides, Wendy had been through a lot in her first official week at NIS's Internal Affairs. She needed the rest too.

Wrapped in the comfort and silence of the darkness, Marcus considered all the reasons Sue had been kidnapped. Every one came back to the same place: Vlad wanted to know what the NIS team was doing, what they had discovered, and if they were closing in on him.

Marcus focused on the obvious problem: Vlad. He knew the Russian was the reason he was in Italy. He was the reason at least two NIS agents were dead. And the bastard was the reason Sue was now missing. And there was a great probability that Vlad was holding Doctor Monroe captive. The Russians wanted to have the doc's knowledge, and Vlad was the weapon to get it.

Add to all that the fact that the Russians owned many of the local criminals and their friends, and it was obvious the bad guys had a serious advantage. Marcus felt his frustration rise as he sought a way to get ahead of them.

97

CAPTAIN BOXER DID WHAT HE did best: he made a difficult decision. Knowing what to do and having the courage to do it were just two reasons he was on the admiral's advancement list. He needed to know if the villa was still there and, if it was, who was in it. Since four of the enlisted men were part of his command, he sent the two who would know Mrs. Woodward by sight on his surveillance mission. He emphasized this was a fact-finding mission and they must not be discovered. "Take no action on your own," the captain ordered.

Shortly thereafter, David Jackson sat in the backseat of a sedan while Seaman Sully Eden drove. Kevin Canton grabbed the shotgun position in the car and played navigator as he focused on the map. The CIA data made much more sense after finding the old roads from over a decade ago. Good progress was being made since the evening rush hour traffic, which usually lasts for several hours, had passed; the roads were somewhat empty.

The Marines had come to their aid, and Corporal Gardener had moved some of his equipment over to the SP's car. Kevin and David were armed and ready for whatever they found. Kevin had heard the skipper's orders about it just being a research mission, but Kevin knew if he had the chance to rescue Sue that he would. *Orders be damned this time.*

Forty minutes later, Kevin quietly said, "According to our map, Eden, we are about a half mile from the villa's location. Time to find a place to stash the car and for two of us to go on foot while you man the radio."

"Can do, Canton. Looks like a couple rows of those 'pencil trees' ahead. I can put this beast there, okay?"

Kevin sighed and brusquely replied, "For crying out loud, Eden, those are Italian Cypress, not freaking 'pencil trees.' Come on, kid, learn the area."

Snickering and using the nickname for a gunner's mate, Eden sarcastically answered, "Aye, aye, Guns. I'll get right on that flora and fauna study crap in my spare time." He slowed the car and pulled in behind a row of cypress trees. It wasn't perfect concealment, but it was less noticeable than parking on the side of the road.

A quick check of the area showed it to be quiet and deserted. No traffic was ahead or behind them. No human-controlled lights were visible, but the partly cloudy sky provided some starlight and moonlight. And the silence was so intense it was almost loud.

Quietly opening the trunk, the two Shore Patrol petty officers grabbed flashlights, binoculars, and a very unusual item from the trunk of the sedan. Namely, they each grabbed an AN/PVS-2 Starlight Scope.

Jackson whispered, "Glad we have a gyrene on the team. Nice toys."

Nodding his head, Canton replied, "Glad you're showing some respect to our Marine, Jackson. Not only is he letting us use his toys, he was the one who realized the age difference in the maps that got us here. He's sharp."

Jackson agreed and headed off toward the villa. Canton told Eden to keep alert and that they would be back soon, finishing with, "Hit the horn with an SOS if you need us, but only if it's a real emergency. Okay?"

Sully nodded his understanding. Canton left in a jog in the direction of Jackson. Catching up with his partner, they moved off the road as they walked toward the potential location of the villa. The walk went faster than they expected. They had reached their destination.

"Well, Dave, that's interesting," Canton whispered as he lowered the binoculars. "It's even painted the same color as it was back then. Do you see any sentries?"

"None visible so far, Kev. At least they left the outside lights on for us," Jackson replied with a quiet snicker.

The villa was pretty much a standard single-family structure, which was a usual sight around the Naples area. The relatively small rectangular structure consisted of two stories. In most houses like this, the second floor held only the bedrooms, and perhaps a bath or two if it had been modernized. Of course, the locals called the second floor the first floor since it is the first one above the ground floor: just another confusing difference between the Old World and the new, and another opportunity for Americans to look stupid.

The exterior was a local standard too. The rounded tops of the doors and windows were capped with architectural details: large, white, arched decorative headers stood out from the mostly smooth, stuccoed yellow walls. Black wrought iron metalwork was visible on the doors. Vines turning brown in the fall weather covered a small amount of the walls, providing an older look to the villa. Faded red tiles covered the roof.

A smaller, separate building, constructed and painted the same as the house—probably a garage or storage shed—stood to the left of the main structure; both buildings faced north. A stone driveway ran from the road and circled in front of the main building. The back of the main building provided a view of landscape rising up the ridge.

There were no fences or hedges around the property. The corner of a small wall, perhaps three feet high, was visible around the back of the villa. Security lights were installed under each corner of the roof, with lamps pointed in multiple directions. Their bright coverage overlapped and made clandestine access to the villa challenging—actually impossible, they realized.

Checking out the driveway made Canton frown as he saw a light blue van parked behind two black sedans. The guy in the van was here, and was probably the one who got the truck to block the road. He would bet the van driver was Pest.

"Okay, Dave, it looks like Viper, Ratfink, and maybe Pest might be here, so be careful. I want you to work your way around the right. I'll go left and we'll meet about halfway up on the ridge around back. Just keep away far enough so you're not spotted," Canton whispered.

"Can do, Kevin. And like you told me before, I'll focus on what I can see in the windows. Looks like the night scopes will be worthless."

"Yea. Be careful."

With the road on Kevin's side of the house, he had to travel farther out to keep hidden. But it was an easy walk on the far side of the Italian Cypress trees that bordered the road. He noticed no activity around the front of the villa, and no lights were on in any of the windows.

Circling around the left side, Kevin started the climb up the hill. Good news was it provided a great view of the back of the house. The bad news was the amount of cover was reduced, since the Italian Cypress trees were not growing on the slope and brush was not high. At least there were depressions, almost trenches, probably created by water runoff over the years, which allowed him to move without crawling on his belly. And the security lights didn't reach his position, so the darkness offered some cover.

Quietly moving into position beside Dave, Kevin whispered, "See anything on your side?"

"Just the old man sitting on the back patio. He's not moving, so he might be asleep," Dave responded *sotto voce*. "All the windows on the side were dark."

As the two SPs contemplated their next moves, another man stepped onto the patio from what was probably the kitchen door. He had turned to face the old man in the chair, so neither of the watchers saw his face. The distance didn't carry his voice, but the animation of his arms indicated he was not happy.

Kevin quietly said, "Stay here. I'm going to move closer. Keep your head down."

Dave nodded and lowered himself behind an exposed rock, bracing his binoculars to get a good view.

For a gunner's mate who was used to firing loud weapons and making lots of noise, Kevin Canton knew the way to move through brush quietly. Unknown to Dave, Kevin had grown up in rural western Pennsylvania, where deer and turkey hunting were normal activities that required stealth. In a short time, Kevin was within thirty feet of the wall. And he stopped before he ran out of any form of concealment, since the brush-covered slopes turned into fairly well-maintained lawn. Kevin settled down to hear what he could.

The new arrival to the patio said in a deep, heavily accented voice, "Doctor, you should know that the American diplomat"—he said *diplomat* like it put a bad taste in his mouth—"just told me that your Naval Investigative Service has Washington agents here, which I knew, and they suspect you are here also. That I didn't know. She also confirmed that Mario and I failed—we did not kill them like we thought. They have their aircraft searching for us. And now they have a lead to this villa. Your thoughts?"

The old man leaned forward and started rubbing his temples with the thumb and middle finger of his left hand. His right hand was waving like he was directing an orchestra. Kevin saw that a grimace covered the old man's face as he said in American English, "Vladimir Davidovich, they will stop you. With you killing that agent a few days ago, and then trying to kill the two new ones, they are even more determined to find you. You're a fool. As for our location, they're just guessing. No one knows about this place. Besides, it is so remote, we would hear them coming."

Vlad shook his head and laughingly replied, "No, Doctor, again you are so wrong. Woodward said they knew of my connection to this place, but they just didn't know where it is … yet. So we still have some time, but probably not much, so we need to be ready to move quickly. Mario will help you. I need to make a call and get things in order to leave this place."

Kevin had heard enough, so he quietly backed out of his position. Finding Dave in the same spot, he leaned in and whispered, "I've got to get on the radio. Move over to the side of the house so you can watch both the front and back. Okay?"

Dave nodded. "You got it." Both men started a slow trek from the back of the house.

Canton had an inspiration and gave Dave one last order before he headed off to the car to access the radio. "Give me ten minutes to get back to the car so I can contact the Bluetick, then you start flashing dot-dot-dot-dash straight up from the other side of the road every thirty seconds for five minutes. And make sure they can't see it from the villa. And hopefully, Bluetick Two will see it."

"Can do, but what does that code mean?"

"That's Morse code for V, like in Viper."

98

WAITING IS THE HARDEST THING for any member of the military. "Hurry up and wait" is an old expression, common in all branches of the military. So is the fact that military life is hours of endless boredom punctuated by a few minutes of pure terror. That boredom was taking over the Shore Patrol headquarters. The phones were silent, and the last status reports, via radio from those watching on the ground and in the air, were basically the same old "nothing new to report."

The noise from the radio was like thunder following the first lightning strike of a sudden summer storm. The radioman nearly fell out of his chair as he jerked to full alertness. Kevin Canton's voice sounded hurried as he said, "Homestead. KC. Over."

"KC, we read you. Over."

"Homestead, we found the place as expected. I believe R3 and Viper's there and possibly the other two who wear black hats. Also, I think the person missing from D.C. is there. Bluetick Two and DJ have eyes on it. Over."

"KC, hold while I get the skipper."

Before the radio operator could stand, Captain Boxer was towering over him, asking, "What ya got, son?"

"Sir, its Petty Officer Canton. He found the villa and believes Mrs. Woodward, Viper and other persons of interest, as well as the missing scientist, are there."

The captain developed a grin that bordered on evil. "Tell him to hold one while I roust Colt."

The sharp rap on the door brought Marcus out of his quiet contemplation. Moving fast, he opened the door and saw Captain Boxer. "Yes, sir?"

"Come on. We got a lead." Boxer filled him in as they hurried down the hall.

It didn't take long for Canton to go over all they had found at the villa. He described the target and where his assets were located. And the knowledge Viper had about the aircraft, proving R3 was there.

"KC. R1 here. Well done. What's the time to your location? Over."

"Fifty-five minutes about. I can send SE back to the main road, and he can lead you in faster. The main road is the one our Marine called 'Baker,' since it was the second road you will travel from the Homestead. Our target is on the south side of 'Foxtrot,' so you have a few turns to make. Some are fairly well hidden. A guide will help, sir. Over."

Colt gave the skipper an inquisitive look. "SE?"

Boxer replied, "Seaman Sully Eden. I sent him as their driver."

"KC. Understand. Make it so. R1 will meet SE at the end of Baker in about thirty. Head back and join with DJ. Copy? Over."

"Homestead. Read you loud and clear. Executing. Out."

Marcus looked up from the radio to see Wendy James leaning on her crutches and staring with a furrowed brow of concern. Captain Boxer was nodding in agreement to what he figured Marcus was thinking, and said, "I'll get the other Blueticks over the area. What else do you need from me, Colt?"

The moment of silence was actually only a few seconds, but for Marcus it felt longer. Marcus knew his headache was not helping his thought process, but he formulated a plan anyway. Well, it was a rough plan. *Hell*, he thought, *it is barely the start of a plan.* Yet he firmly believed that when you know where the bad guy is, doing something was much better than doing nothing, so he forged ahead.

"Skipper, how many cars do we now have watching Swamp and Tree?"

Boxer said, "Three each. Two vehicles with my people and one with Tony's."

Marcus nodded. "Perfect. Get word to both locations for Tony's guys to meet me at the Sully rendezvous in about thirty minutes. Update your men with the current status."

The captain turned to the radio operator and gave him the order to make it happen. He then asked, "And what else do you need?"

Chuckling, Marcus replied, "A barrel full of luck would be nice. But I'll just go with what I got—my 1911 pistol, my favorite Marine, and the other two SPs you assigned to us."

The captain pulled Marcus aside and quietly asked, "Based on the comments from the chief doc of the hospital, you should still be in one of his beds. This is your show, Colt, but are you sure you're up to it with these few people?"

Marcus let that question sit for a few seconds. "Sir, I got this. As for backup, that gives me a total of ten good guys going up against three bad guys. I think we're safe on numbers. Frankly, my concern is that too many vehicles and people will spook the bastards and make our chances slimmer. We need to sneak up on their hideout."

"Okay, cowboy, this is your rodeo. Ready to saddle up and cut 'em off at the pass?"

With a mild snicker, Marcus said, "Right after I put out a potential forest fire with my partner, sir. Know this, Captain, I do appreciate all your help, counsel, and concern."

It was time for the captain to smile. "Hell, don't let my concern go to your head, son. I just don't want to be the one calling the CNO to let him know his favorite son-in-law is dead. Be careful out there."

Marcus laughed and gave a quick nod. "I like you, too, Skipper. Thanks."

After receiving a quick chuck on the arm from the skipper, Marcus turned to Wendy. He motioned for her to head back down the hall to the conference room. He also indicated for his Marine and his two SPs to follow; none of them looked happy.

Closing the door, Marcus turned to his team. "Looks like we need an injection of positive attitude here. What's on your minds? In proper military form, lowest rank first. What say you, Boatswains Mate Third Class Mallory?"

When asking opinions, the procedure was to start with the lowest rank or rate. That way they wouldn't be intimidated by, or feel it was safer to copy, a senior person.

John Mallory started to stand, and Marcus waved him back down. He cleared his throat, a nervous reaction rather than an actual physical need, and said, "Sir, it would be nice to have more backup, sir."

Turning to face the only Marine in the room, Marcus pointed. "So, Rick. Do we have enough manpower—no offense Miss James, guess I should have said shooters—to handle this assignment?"

Gardener paused for a moment. "Sir, we got this. However, I think we should call Gunny Railey and have him head toward our rendezvous."

Marcus's smile twisted up to the left. He nodded. "Agreed. Call Rattler as soon as this little chit-chat is over."

Marcus pointed toward the other SP, Machinist Mate Second Class Tim Helms, for his opinion.

"Sir, if the number of bad guys is accurate, we're probably okay. But I agree with Mallory and Gardener—a bit more backup would be nice."

"Thanks, Tim. Okay, Ensign James, talk to me about your negative expression."

"Lieutenant Commander Colt, we all know you've only been out of the hospital less than a day. You were almost killed in the accident, and then you pushed yourself too much on that Thursday morning jaunt down the volcano. I'm not sure you are up to this, sir."

"Thank you, Ensign. Your honest and heartfelt concern is duly noted, and very much appreciated. But I think there's enough of me left to see this through. And I am a bit more mobile that you are right now. With the pride of the Marines here watching my back, and SP warriors spread out around me, all should be well. Right?"

Wendy just stared at Marcus with a sad look of acceptance. There was nothing left to say. Her superior officer had made his decision, and she had to live with it. She hoped Marcus would live too.

"Sound *Boots and Saddles*—time to move, people," Marcus said as he headed to the door.

All Wendy could do was shake her head and shrug. She pointed to the three enlisted men and motioned them to follow Marcus. As the last one passed through the door, Wendy whispered, "Stay safe." She then bowed her head for a moment of prayer.

99

THE ROOM WAS NOT TOTALLY dark. While there were no distinct shadows in the artificial twilight, there was enough light to allow Sue Woodward to see she was alone ... alone, and in terrible pain. She assumed her headache was sufficiently nasty to qualify as a migraine. It even hurt to blink. Her legs were numb and cramping. Her wrists were on fire.

Ignoring the pain, Sue focused on listening. Only her nervous breathing filled the room. There were footsteps and doors closing somewhere. Faint voices filtered under the door, but they were too low for her to grasp the words.

She remembered the injection given by someone dark, but nothing beyond that. And not much from before. At least she knew her name and was still dressed, so unless she was in the hands of a really considerate rapist, nothing along those lines had happened. Hands and feet were bound. It was time to get out of the bondage before something did happen.

Steel cuffs on her wrists were not something she could do much about. They were so tight they cut into her flesh. She raised her head and remembered that her ankles were tied to the old iron bed frame with cloth strips.

She could not get out of the cuffs; however, she might be able to reach down to the ankle bindings and work on the knots. *Knots* being plural since there were so damn many of them.

As she fiddled with the knots, memories started returning. At first, they were mere flashes of things she didn't recognize, then they solidified, gaining form and structure. People, places, and events flooded her memory as the drug wore off and normal brain functions returned. As did recent memories.

She stopped fidgeting with the knots and said, "Marcus! Oh, Marcus!"

The mental door had opened and Sue knew why she was there. She also knew she needed to get away from Vladimir as soon as she could. And she had to warn Marcus.

Down the hall, Vlad was verbally pushing the old man. "Get moving. We have to get out of here now."

The old man sighed and waved a dismissing hand at his keeper. "I will not leave without my research. Hell, that is why you keep me, right?"

Vlad sneered. "Little good it has done Mother Russia. After all this time, all the money we gave you, nothing is working. The project is a failure. People are tired of your excuses, old man."

"It's your fault. I keep asking for files, and you just give me nothing. How can I make it work without the data I need?"

Vlad rolled his eyes. "Enough, Doctor. The bulk of your research will safely remain at our warehouse. At least, for now. Pack what little you have here and Mario will make sure it gets handled properly. Just do it quickly." He spun on his heel and marched down the hall to the stairs, looking for another man.

Finding Antonio Greco was an easy task. He was in his usual place: sprawled in one of the sitting room chairs, pouring more red wine into his glass. He looked up when Vladimir walked toward him. "What ya need, *Capo*?" Antonio asked innocently.

Holding his temper in check, Vlad just stared at Greco for more than a moment. "Get your sorry ass up to the first floor and help the old man pack. We need to be gone from here soon."

Vlad turned and left the room. He knew Mario was busy gathering the doctor's research. He had several boxes to load into his van and stash at the warehouse. Antonio would get the doctor ready to move. That left Vlad with only one small task.

He unlocked and opened the door to the room that was the temporary prison of Susan Woodward. A quick flip of a switch bathed the room in light. Susan was sitting at the end of the bed, trying to get relief from her bondage.

"Going somewhere?" Vlad allowed a smirk to replace his scowl. For a moment, as he watched Susan jerk her head around to look at him, Vlad considered that this woman would be a good lover. There was a fire in her eyes as she stared at him. Granted it was a fire of pure hate, but such emotion would greatly enhance the lovemaking. But it was only a moment's thought, as he had places to go.

Sue ignored him and continued to pull on the tight knots. She had already broken several fingernails, and the effort had caused the cuffs to dig deeper into her wrists. Blood from the deepening gashes flowed down her hands.

As Sue remained silent, Vlad continued, "Guess my hospitality was not as welcome as a kiss from Marcus Colt would be, eh? Oh, yes, among all the important business things you freely chatted about, you went on and on about your feelings for Colt. He's a fool for not bedding you. Anyway, that's not my problem. I came to say goodbye."

She returned her focus to the knots, ignoring Vlad and his comments. Her peripheral vision saw him just watching her, arms crossed over his chest. Logic told her he was going to kill her. His comment reinforced her belief; the noises she heard were the sounds the villa being deserted. And it was clean-up time.

Vlad walked closer to the bed, but remained several feet away. His voice softened and a smile crossed his face. "Susan, I am sorry for the treatment you have received, but I didn't have time for long friendly conversations. I'm leaving now, but you will be staying. I figure Colt will find this place by tomorrow and release you then. I hope we meet again under more social circumstances. Goodbye."

He turned and walked toward the door.

Sue could not hold back any more. Blazing anger saturated her voice as she slowly fired out each word. "We won't meet again. You killed my friend when you ran them off the volcano road. Your actions injured Marcus and his partner. He knows you killed his friend in Virginia and the agent here. And you did this to me. He *is* going to kill you, so this *is* our last time together. Enjoy your eternity in hell."

Vlad took on the look of a sad, broken man. He shrugged and raised his hands in front of him in a gesture of accepting the inevitable. He turned off the light as he walked out the door.

100

THE INTERSECTION OF ROADS KNOWN to Operation Quicksilver members as Baker and Charlie didn't offer much in the way of a rallying point. It was a small, T-shaped intersection, with Baker as the horizontal part of the T. The Baker roadway had a sharp drop-off opposite road Charlie, and the small shoulders on both sides offered little available space. The shoulders were not wide enough to hold a single car.

Seaman Sully Eden knew that at least four more vehicles were now descending on that point. That would create a very visible traffic jam; not good for a clandestine operation. He turned West on Baker and found what he needed.

Keying the radio mike, Sully said, "Homestead. SE. Over."

"SE. We read you. Over."

"Homestead. Pass to all hands. Moving the rally point from the intersection of Baker and Charlie to a position half a klick further West on Baker. Parking on South side. In position. Over."

"SE. Acknowledge west Baker, south side location. Will do. Over."

"Homestead. Out."

The new location was a good choice. It was the parking lot of an old tomato cannery. From the looks of it, the cannery had shut down now that the season was nearly over. Or maybe it had gone out of business.

Either way, the lot was big, dark, and vacant: it was perfect. Sully leaned back from shutting off the engine when he saw a vehicle turn into the lot. His radio crackled.

"SE. R1. Flash once when you see us. Out."

The next two vehicles arriving were Tony's men, SA Adam Richmann and SA Ben Baker. Each was accompanied by a borrowed agent from another NISRA.

Gunnery Sergeant Jasper Railey was the last to arrive, but he came ready for action. Three other Marines were with him: two corporals and a staff sergeant. All were decked out in utilities, the Marine's fighting uniform, with Ka-Bar knives and holstered 1911 automatics on their belts. Each man carried an M16.

Within a five-minute period, all four of the incoming vehicles had arrived.

Railey approached R1 with his hand extended. "Congrats on the new stripe, Mr. Colt. Sorry I missed the wetting-down. And thanks for the invite—consulate duty is boring. Hope you don't mind that I brought a couple of friends to the party."

The handshake turned into a brief hug between comrades who had fought together.

"Damn good to see you, Jasper," Colt said. He looked at the other Marines and continued, "and you men also. Your help is greatly appreciated."

As the quick introductions wrapped up, the car radios crackled to life. Sully was first to respond. Marcus leaned into the driver's side window and listened. Bluetick Four had observed a blue van leaving the villa and heading toward the Baker/Charlie intersection. Only one person was observed entering the van.

With that new information changing things, Marcus looked over at SA Baker. "Ben, you and your new partner need to hustle back to the intersection. Follow the van and see where it leads. Take two of Jasper's Marines with you. Don't be seen and call Bluetick Three for tracking assistance."

Ben nodded. "You got it, boss."

Jasper pointed to the staff sergeant and said, "Keep them safe, Mike."

With a sharp nod, Mike Stump selected one of the corporals and followed the agents back to their car. They vanished into the night, heading to the intersection.

Marcus turned to the men gathered. "Okay. Hopefully that means we only have two bad guys to overpower. With eleven of us, we might have a good chance of success."

That remark earned the expected chuckles, but all that vanished when Marcus continued, "Don't get too comfortable. The one called Viper is a very dangerous SOB and shot a NIS agent to death Sunday night. And we suspect under Viper's orders, Ratfink had a NIS agent beat to death a few days ago. Keep that in mind as we proceed. Here's the plan …"

101

THE PLAN WAS SIMPLE. IT had to be, since the pain in Marcus's head discouraged complexity. And the plan harkened back to the earliest foundations of warfare: overpower the enemy with greater resources. In his case, Marcus believed there were only two bad guys in the villa. And he had ten armed men backing him up.

Marcus decided not to focus on the complications that would result if Vladimir was killed in the assault. It was never a good thing for diplomats, even evil Russian KGB ones, to die at the hands of a cold war enemy. As for Antonio Greco, that would not be an issue. He was facing kidnapping charges for his work that day, and Marcus was ready to wager that he was the force behind William Coleman's beating and death.

With the bulk of the forces waiting a few hundred yards back on road Foxtrot, Rattler and Marcus approached the villa for their first look. Kevin Canton had positioned himself where he could watch the side of the villa as well as the approach from the road. He spotted the men, who were well hidden, and moved to intercept.

"Nice night for a stroll, eh, Mr. Colt?" Canton whispered as he slid in beside them from the dark.

"Hey, Kevin. Anything new to report?"

Shaking his head, Canton briefed the two new arrivals. No further signs of Susan or the doctor. He thought it strange that when the doctor and Viper were talking, it sounded like the doctor was in charge, or they were at least equals. One man, Pest, had loaded some boxes into a VW microbus and tore out of there a short time ago. He left alone.

Marcus shared a quick overview of the plan and told Canton to share it with Jackson, leave Jackson to watch, and join the crew up the road as soon as possible.

Rattler and Marcus had only been back with the crew for a moment when Canton jogged up to them.

Catching his breath, he said, "Jackson's in position on the west side, sir. All still quiet."

Marcus nodded and raised his voice slightly. "Okay, people. Here are the highlights one last time. Rick, you are in overwatch on the front. Find a position that will provide the best angle of fire. Remember the signals I gave you. When we break, you will have ten minutes to get into position."

Corporal Gardener nodded his understanding.

Marcus continued, "Rattler, send your shooter up the hill in back to do the same."

Rattler nodded and pointed toward Corporal Martinez, who nodded his understanding.

Marcus pointed at the Naples agent and the remaining Shore Patrol members. "Adam, Mallory, and Helms will be with me at the front door. We will drive up and park in front of the first black sedan."

A quick count showed there were still several people he had not mentioned. "Eden, you will drive your car to the villa after me and park it behind the second sedan. Hopefully that will pin them in. And remain in the car manning the radio. You might want to stay down best ya can."

"Aye, aye, sir," Eden sharply replied.

"Rattler, I want you and Canton to breach the back door one minute after you hear my banging on the front door. Or immediately, if you hear gunshots. You are to find and secure R3."

Rattler's deadpan expression was more than scary as he said, "Will do, Mr. Colt. Assuming we hear the knocks on the door."

"That won't be a problem—trust me." Colt looked at the last man. "Agent, uh, sorry, I can't remember your name."

"Sam Falla, NISRA Rota, sir."

"Thanks. Sam, you get into position on the east side of the villa. Jackson is already in position on the west. Everyone hang tight until we exit our vehicles. Any questions?"

As Marcus expected, Rattler had a question. "Sir, you failed to mention what you are going to do after you bang on the door."

Marcus shrugged. "Not totally sure. I hope to distract Viper long enough for you to rescue R3. If I'm lucky, he won't be shooting, and maybe the three of us can secure him and Ratfink. That will give me a chance to possibly find the missing doctor—assuming the old man Kevin described is really him. Guess I'll start off with a stern 'let my people go' or something like that."

Rattler let out a huge sigh, followed by a chuckle. "Not sure the 'Moses routine' will work with a godless commie bastard, Marcus. Bottom line, we'll have more of last year's shenanigans that earned your team the name of Colt's Crazies. Right?"

"Afraid so, Jasper."

With no more questions forthcoming, Marcus pointed to the men who would approach the villa on foot. "Clock is ticking, gents. You have ten minutes before we crash the party. Good luck."

102

HE HAD BACKED THE CONSULATE'S limo into the circular driveway and positioned it snug against the front of the first black sedan. Marcus saw that Eden had successfully placed his vehicle against the back of the second black sedan. With the vehicles boxed in, they advanced to the door.

As instructed, his three companions had positioned themselves off of Marcus, about four feet to each side and a couple of feet back. Marcus slammed the butt of his large metal flashlight against the door several times. The sound in the still night was like a series of rifle shots. After a short moment, he heard the interior latch being thrown. The door opened inward, revealing a shadowed figure in the dark foyer.

The figure said, "Good evening, Navy Lieutenant Commander Marcus James Colt. You are earlier than expected." The figure paused and harrumphed. "Actually, until just a few hours ago, I hadn't expected *you* at all. I had hoped I'd killed you on Vesuvius, but alas, no plan is perfect."

Marcus smiled at the man as he flicked on the flashlight and pointed it towards the voice. "Plans change, KGB Colonel Vladimir Davidovich Kroneski. Mrs. Woodward and Doctor Monroe will be coming with me. Best for you to not be difficult. As they say in the old movies, we have you surrounded."

Vlad squinted as he snorted, "How rude. Making demands as soon as I open the door. What? No hello. No time for a drink of vodka or chit-chat amongst civilized warriors? Please, Marcus, at least come inside for a limoncello."

Marcus shook his head. "I'll pass on that, Vlad. Better for you to step out into the fresh air."

"And if I don't?"

The left side of his smile kicked up, and Marcus held his left hand up with one finger extended.

The only sound was a smack of jacketed lead traveling at over two thousand feet per second and drilling a hole in the wood door. It land-ed close to Vlad's hand, and he jerked back when he realized what had happened.

Marcus held his smile and kept his hand in the air. "The second finger tells him to put one of those 7.62 NATO slugs into your knee. So please step outside, Vladimir, before that second finger rises."

"Well, Marcus, since you insist on continuing this harassment." Vlad left the door open and stepped out to face Marcus. "If you will kindly move your vehicle, I and my wonderful diplomatic immunity will drive back to my office at the Embassy of Mother Russia and start typing my complaint to your Secretary of the State."

"Not going to happen." Marcus's voice became harder and more au-thoritative. "Sit your ass down right now before Petty Officer Helms here throws you down. You can whine and file an official complaint about me later."

Anger was the only emotion on Vladimir's face as he started to follow the order. He lowered himself to the porch deck and crossed his legs.

"Shoot him in the knees if he tries to leave, Helms. Adam, with me, please," Marcus said as he stepped around Vlad and walked into the darker hall.

The noise of the gun had barely registered with Marcus as the muz-zle flash impaired his vision. Through it, he briefly saw the outline of a man standing at the end of the hallway. Marcus threw himself flat mere seconds before another four shots destroyed the silence of the night. He hadn't had time to reach for his own weapon.

Adam Richmann had his weapon pulled before Vlad opened the door. As one of the many NIS agents who had never fired his weapon except on the pistol range, he often wondered how he would react in a crisis situa-tion. He heard the report of the shot and watched as Marcus fell forward in what seemed like slow motion. Without a second thought, he raised his weapon and fired two shots at center body mass of the man in the dark hallway. At the same time, two more shots came from a different direction, slamming the shooter's body against the wall. The now-dead target lingered against the wall for a moment before sliding to the floor, leaving a blood streak on the wall.

Thinking that Vlad might use the confusion to bolt, Helms pushed the barrel of his M16 against the back of Vlad's neck and yelled, "Stay!" Vlad froze.

Lights clicked on in the back of the hallway. Rattler reached down to the body and removed the weapon from the dead hand. He walked to where Marcus lay just inside the door and asked, "You okay, Mr. Colt? Ratfink's dead."

Marcus whispered a profanity as he realized his right arm was not responding to his commands. He rolled over and looked into the face of Rattler. "Jasper, why the hell aren't you with Canton? Hell, since you're here, help me sit up. I think my arm caught that bastard's bullet."

"Canton's heading upstairs with Corporal Martinez. I told him I'd catch up. I saw Ratfink when we came in and followed him. Sorry I was a bit slow shooting the bastard."

Extra noise filled the hallway; the other agent and SPs had rallied to the sound of the gunfire. Adam pushed them back outside and issued a few orders. "Sam, take Jackson, search the house, and find the doctor and Mrs. Woodward. Mallory, go with Helms and take Vlad over by the garage. Keep him there."

Rattler had helped Marcus remove his jacket. Marcus noted his new jacket now featured two small round holes and stain from the resulting blood leakage. "Damn, another fine jacket destroyed," he whispered.

Blood was quickly soaking the upper arm of his shirt. A quick couple of slashes with a Ka-Bar removed the shirtsleeve, giving Jasper access to the wound. The bullet had passed through the outside edge of his arm. Rattler said, "No big deal, Mr. Colt. Looks like it nicked the bicep and barely touched the tricep. Couple of stitches will make you good as new. Hold still while I wrap it up."

Jasper Railey was always prepared for just about anything. One pouch on his utility belt contained a small first aid kit. A thick gauze pad covered in an antiseptic powder was held in place over the wound by several wraps of rolled gauze.

Marcus grunted when the gunny tied the gauze tight. With the adrenaline of the shooting working its way out of his body, Marcus was starting to feel the throbbing pain of the wound. The sarcasm in his mind told the gunshot pain to get in line behind that of his head. Yep, it was true: the only easy day was yesterday.

103

A FEW MINUTES EARLIER, RATTLER had been positioned at the back door and heard the distant door knocks. *Yep*, he thought, *Colt was right*: it was impossible to miss that sound on the front door. It seemed to echo in the night and reverberate off the hill behind him. Pumping his fist up and down, he signaled for Martinez to join them. With a fast nod to Canton, Rattler tried the door; strangely, it was unlocked, and it silently opened into a nearly dark room.

Retreating footsteps were audible enough to get Rattler's attention, and he held off turning on his flashlight. He tapped Canton on the arm and pointed. Someone had just left the room.

With hand signals, Rattler sent Canton and Martinez upstairs to look for R3, and indicated he was going to follow the departing figure. Canton didn't look pleased with that decision, but followed orders. They had just reached the first floor when the first shot rang out.

The noise of the gunfire startled Sue. She was not sure if it was a rescue attempt or Vlad getting rid of witnesses. Maybe he lied about leaving her for Marcus to find and a bullet was in her near future. Before she could worry too much about the options, the door banged opened and the light clicked on.

Petty Officer Kevin Canton rushed into the room in a crouched position. With his head swiveling, he pointed his weapon in all directions, looking for trouble. All he saw was Mrs. Woodward sitting on the bed with panic on her face and blood on her hands.

"You okay, ma'am?" Canton asked as he holstered his weapon and advanced to the bed. He saw the handcuffs and leg binding, and pulled his handcuff key and removed the cuffs. His knife made quick work of the leg bindings, careful not to cut her legs.

"Kevin, I'm so glad it's you! Thought Vlad was coming back to kill me. Get me out of here. My legs are cramped and I'm not sure I can walk."

"No, ma'am, you need to stay here for a minute while I check on the gunfire. Just stay on the bed, please."

"Of course," Sue said as she looked at the sailor's face, recognizing a high level of concern. There was something else there, but she couldn't figure it out. As she watched Canton check outside the door and then vanish down the hall, she realized she was concerned for his safety. More than for her own.

Kevin had checked the hall before exiting the room. There were some distant voices after the shooting, but nothing else. Martinez was in position at the end of the hall watching his back. He wished that Gunny Railey had come upstairs with him rather than going off to explore the ground floor.

A noise on the stairs got his attention. He relaxed when he saw Jackson's head appear. "All clear down there, Dave?" Canton asked quietly.

Jackson nodded. "Did you find Mrs. Woodward?"

"Yea, she's safe in the room behind me. Viper found?"

SA Falla joined them and said, "Oh, yea, Mr. Colt has him secured outside. Ground floor clear. Ratfink was killed by fire from both SA Richmann and Gunny Railey after wounding Colt. Now we need to find Doctor Monroe."

Shocked by the news of Colt getting shot, Kevin demanded, "How bad is he?"

"Not sure. Gunny has him sitting up and he's talking," Dave Jackson replied.

"Okay, we need to clear these other rooms and find that guy. Dave, you go into that room and keep Mrs. Woodward secure," Kevin Canton ordered.

There were only three other rooms on the first floor. Martinez kept watch on the hall and stairs as Falla and Canton cleared the remaining rooms. The first two they checked were empty. However, they hit gold in the last.

The man was at the back of the room trying to crouch behind a cluttered desk. The sound of the gun shots had stopped his hurried packing. His open suitcase was still on the bed. He wanted to run—to escape—but new noises in the hall had forced him to take shelter in his room.

Falla was first into the room. He stepped to the right and caught sight of the man ducking down. He yelled, "Stand! Hands on your head!"

Canton entered right behind Falla and took up a position on the opposite side of the room.

"Don't shoot! I'm American!" the old man yelled as he slowly stood. Following orders, his hands were on his head, but that didn't stop their shaking.

In the harsh light of the room, Canton realized the old man actually looked older than he had on the porch. Frailness was present that he hadn't noticed before, but he was still wary of the man. "Your name Monroe?" he asked.

With a nervous smile crossing his face, the old man spit out words in rapid fire, "Yes! Monroe, Frederick. Captain, USN, retired. And I'm damn glad to see you." After that outburst, Monroe started to sob.

104

DOWN ON THE GROUND FLOOR, things had settled down a bit, but not by much. The men were still tense. It takes a while to calm down after a shooting. Marcus was on his feet, and with the help of Rattler, back into his now-ruined jacket. At least it covered the shoulder holster, and added a touch of warmth to fight the evening chill.

Marcus, Rattler, and Richmann were discussing their next move when Jackson yelled down to let them know R3 and doctor were safe. R3 had minor cuts from handcuffs, and the doctor was an emotional mess. The rest of the villa had been checked, and no one else was found. Marcus had just reached the decision to call Homestead One and have him send local law enforcement to take over the scene.

As they were starting to climb to the first floor to check on R3, Seaman Sully Eden ran into the villa and called for Mr. Colt. "Sir, Homestead One needs you on the radio immediately."

Marcus nodded to the other men and said, "Get our people down here." He pointed up to indicate R3 and the doc. "I have a call to take." And he ran to the car.

"Homestead One. R1. Over."

"R1. Just heard from your team in D.C. They discovered some interesting things you need to know. Stand by to copy. Over."

The radio conversation took several minutes. Homestead was updated on the situation and getting people moving to the villa. When Marcus signed out, he leaned back in the seat and exhaled greatly. This case had been one weird thing after another—another dead body, another crappy twist, another damn turn—and this latest one was a doozy. The pain was hampering his thought process, but he still had a job to do. As he started to exit the vehicle, the radio came alive again.

"R1. Baker. Over."

"R1 here. Go ahead Baker. Over."

"R1, we need you here ASAP. Over."

This conversation was shorter than the last, and Marcus concluded it by turning the radio over to Seaman Eden so he could take down the directions.

Marcus was happy to see that Rick Gardener had finally gotten to the villa from his sniper's nest. His sniper duties were over, and Marcus was glad to have him watching his back from a closer position.

"Heard you were hit, Mr. Colt. You okay?" Gardener asked with honest concern in his voice as he surveyed the blood-stained jacket.

"Been better, Rick, but I'll survive. Bravo Zulu on that shot," Marcus replied as he ushered Rick into the villa.

Marcus was relieved to see Sue was safe. Rattler was finishing the doctoring of the cuts on her wrists that Jackson mentioned. She gave him a small grin when he looked her over head to toe. He wanted to make sure she faced no other problems. "Glad the wrists are the only issues. They are the only issues, right?"

"Yea, and the lingering headache from the truth drug Vlad gave me. I'll be fine, but it looks like I need to buy you another jacket, Marcus. The gunny told me all about you trying to catch that bullet," Sue said.

Marcus shrugged and raised his hands in an *oh, well* gesture. He then raised his voice as he laid out the plan. "Canton. Jackson. You two take R3 to the base hospital in Eden's car—he'll be coming with me. Stay with her. Warn the hospital staff to call the CO. Tell him that I'll be along in a couple of hours. You might as well tell him why, so perhaps he'll have a chance to calm down before I get there."

The two SPs nodded and escorted Sue to the car. Marcus noted that Canton had his arm around her, and she was leaning into him.

"Adam, I know it is damn late, officially it's now tomorrow as of ten minutes ago, but I need you and Sam to stay here and work with the locals. Homestead One will be letting them know the situation in about an hour or so. First he'll be sending a couple of trucks and more personnel here. Give the villa a good going-over, load up everything you think might be important, and get the trucks out of here before the locals arrive."

Both Adam and Sam nodded their understanding.

"Jasper, I want you, Mallory, Helms, and Martinez to stay here and provide external security until the locals arrive. Keep Viper secured for about ten minutes after I leave. Legally, we can't touch him, so let him go; he'll run and complain to his embassy. When the local police take over, return to the SP HQ and type up your reports. Stay there until I show up."

Railey started to disagree, but he saw the look he remembered from 'Nam. Colt was in his zone and now was not the time to argue. He nodded and waited, feeling more was coming.

Colt turned back to Adam Richmann. "Got your cuffs handy?"

"Sure. Why?"

Marcus pointed to the old man now known as Doctor Frederick Monroe, who was standing beside Sam, and ordered, "Cuff him." He walked up to the shocked old man and announced, "Captain Monroe. You have been recalled to active duty as of 2100 hours local time today. In compliance with Article 31, you are under arrest facing the charge of treason and accessory to at least two murders. Anything you say can and will be used against you in your court martial. And after further investigation, I suspect you will be charged with other violations. Corporal Gardener, take charge of the prisoner and place him in my vehicle."

As Gardener led him away, Monroe pleaded, "No. This is all wrong. I was helping. You have to trust me."

Gardener pushed him out of the villa towards the vehicle.

Seeing all the confused faces, Marcus knew he needed to explain. He took a deep breath to gather his thoughts. "Okay, here's the deal. My team in D.C. just found evidence that Monroe has been taking money, a lot of money, from the Russians for the last several years, in exchange for information about his Rembrandt project. It looks like his 'kidnapping' might be a staged event so he could finish his project for the Russians."

Gunny Railey was the first to recover. "Damn, Marcus. Want me to shoot that traitor?"

"Not this time, Jasper. JAG will enjoy processing the case. If there is nothing else, Baker radioed and asks that I join him at a warehouse in Amalfi. He told me he has Pest under arrest, and he told Eden how to get there. I'll take Monroe with me in case there's some reason we need his input. Adam, I'll radio back to you if you need to send any more people there. Anything else?"

The men standing around all shook their heads. There was no need to ask anything else, and they all knew what had to be done.

Marcus smiled at the professionals who made up his team and said, "Sound *Boots and Saddles*."

105

MARCUS EXERCISED THE PRIVILEGE OF his rank and took charge of the driving. It was a logical choice. Corporal Gardener was guarding the doctor in the back seat and Seaman Sully Eden was the navigator needing to focus on his notes to get them to their destination. He had scribbled the hastily given directions in the dark of the vehicle, and his penmanship was sad, even under perfect conditions.

Earlier that evening, they had come to the villa from the north. Now they headed south, taking countless turns on narrow, climbing, and twisting mountain roads. In spite of the challenges of unknown roads and poor visibility due to the light rain, Sully had gotten them from the villa to the main road at Marina di Praia faster than expected.

The main road had several names: SS163, Strada Statale Amalfitana, or the Amalfi Coast Road, depending on the map being read. It was a two-lane road that hugged the Amalfi coastline all the way from Positano to Salerno. According to the travel brochures, it was a picturesque drive in the daylight—often featured in movies—but it was also dangerous. The dangerous part greatly outweighed the picturesque on a dark, rainy night.

The north side of the road frequently butted against walls of imposing sheer rock or hand-laid stone. The south side featured low, man-made stone and concrete walls—locals didn't want to hide the view—interspersed with frail-looking metal railings to keep cars from falling into the Tyrrhenian Sea. Add to that the fact that the road was one hairpin curve after another, and the chance of an accident greatly increased with each turn.

It didn't concern Marcus, who had honed his early driving skills on the narrow, convoluted back roads of West Virginia. In comparison, the Amalfi Coast Road was nearly a freeway, but with the current driving conditions, he kept the speed down to the posted 20 km/h on the turns.

Marcus was feeling pain from the overuse of his wounded arm. But he knew SA Baker had something interesting to share, so he pushed himself to ignore the throbbing and continue the drive to Amalfi. There were only a few kilometers to go, and then he could rest his arm. Seaman Sully Eden could handle the drive to the hospital.

Rick Gardener was in the back seat with Doctor—now Captain—Monroe. Rick was not too concerned, since Monroe was handcuffed and he was a really old man. Monroe kept muttering about his innocence between sobs. He looked at the prisoner with contempt, as he couldn't imagine anyone becoming a traitor to America.

The radio came to life. "Bluetick Two. R1. Over."

Eden grabbed the mike. "Go ahead, Bluetick Two. SE with R1. R1 can hear you. Over."

"Report from Rattler. Viper ranted threats against you and left ten minutes after you did. He's headed in your direction. We have eyes on Viper. Viper approaching what we believe to be your six. About three klicks back and closing, if we have you spotted correctly. Over."

"Acknowledge. Anything else? Over."

"R1, flash your lights three times so we can make sure we have you. Over."

Marcus reached for the light switch. He gave three quick flashes and waited.

"R1, we have you. No one between you and Viper. Viper still two klicks back. Rattler and friends are in pursuit about four klicks behind Viper. Over."

Marcus grabbed the mike. "Bravo Zulu, Bluetick Two. Out."

The information was disconcerting, but Marcus wasn't surprised. Viper was a killer and Marcus was his current target. As he pondered the options, Marcus knew a shootout in Amalfi with Vlad would be a bad thing. And with the turns in the road, Vlad could easily run them off the road before they got there. No time for a defensive maneuver: it was offense time.

A sharp hairpin curve to the left appeared ahead. Marcus slowed and executed the turn. Once around the curve, he did a quick three-point turn. He killed the lights and positioned his car facing the oncoming Vlad. He lowered the window to hopefully hear the following vehicle and waited.

The headlights of Vlad's car bounced off the low stone wall that protected the curve. At the moment Vlad's car eased into the turn, Marcus switched on his car's high-beam headlights and laid on the horn.

Vlad was so focused on catching Marcus that he was caught off guard when he saw headlights right in front of him. He hit the brakes and jerked the wheel to the right to avoid a collision. The rain-slicked road did the rest.

Traveling too fast for conditions, Vlad's car slammed into the stone wall and bounced up over the crumbled debris that remained.

Vlad's head slammed against something hard, and in his mind he felt the car going over the edge. It took a second or two for reality to come back to him. And with it, he realized he was not on the way to the water several hundred feet below. He was stuck with his car balanced precariously on the wall.

He tried the door, but the crash had jammed it in place. As he moved to push harder against the door, the car started to rock. Vlad realized he was teetering on the edge and any wrong move would cause his violent death.

Marcus left his car after telling the others to wait. As he approached the back of Vlad's car, Marcus noticed it seemed to be slightly rocking; the back of the car gently rose and fell and, while it was less than an inch in either direction, it was not a good sign. With his weapon drawn and the safety thumbed off, Marcus quietly moved to the driver's window. He positioned himself at the rear door so Vlad would have to turn to shoot him.

"Having a bad night, Vlad?"

"Colt, you are a hard man to kill," Vlad said through clenched teeth. He was holding his hand to his forehead, trying to stop the blood from flowing into his eyes. The blood smear on the steering wheel marked the place that had caused the facial damage.

Snickering, Marcus replied, "I needed to stay alive to see your end, Vlad. It's the least I can do for my friends that you killed."

"Hah, I have diplomatic immunity. You can't touch me." He sneered as he looked at the pistol pointed toward his head.

"You do know that immunity can be revoked. We have enough evidence on you to make your government give second thoughts to protecting you. After all, trade and treaties might have an edge over your sorry ass," Marcus said.

For what seemed like a lengthy period, the two men silently looked at each other. Contempt, disdain, hatred, or disgust, or any combination of those feelings was evident on both faces. The standoff duration was probably less than a minute, but if asked, either man would admit time stood still for an unknown period. And as fast as it started, it ended.

Vlad shifted position, leaning forward as if reaching for something under the seat. The movement caused the rocking to increase. A scraping sound came from under the car as it shifted slightly toward the dark abyss. Panic quickly overcame him, and Vlad screamed, "Help me. Get the door open and pull me out!"

"Toss out your weapon first," Marcus yelled back.

As he fumbled for his pistol, Vlad's movements caused the car to rock more. He threw his pistol out the driver's window toward Marcus.

Picking up the weapon and sliding it into his coat pocket, Marcus moved closer to the front of the open driver's window and looked at Vlad.

"Now pull me out before this thing goes over the edge," pleaded Vlad.

A small smile flickered across his face as Marcus leaned over and gently pushed down on the hood of the car. The scraping increased as gravity took over and the weight of the engine slowly pulled the front of the car farther over the wall. "Sorry, Vlad, but like you said, I can't touch you."

Gravity finally won. The engine weight took over and Vlad started his final trip. Marcus thought he heard a scream, but with all the noise of the car bouncing off the rocky cliff below, he wasn't sure. And he really didn't care.

Heat from the engine or perhaps a spark from ripped battery cables ignited the gas spilling from the ruptured fuel lines. The inverted smashed hunk of steel turned into a funeral pyre for Viper, who was probably dead already. Marcus watched the flames for a moment, then turned away.

Rattler, with his "friends" in the form of Mallory, Helms, and Martinez, arrived and stopped short of the damaged wall. Rattler exited the car and looked at Colt, waiting for a comment. None came, so Rattler simply nodded. "Not ignoring your order, Mr. Colt, but we figured with your bum arm and all, you might need some extra help. We can do reports later, right sir?"

Too tired and emotionally drained to get into a long answer, Marcus simply said, "Follow me to Amalfi."

By the time he was back at his car, Marcus's weapon was holstered. He slid into the driver's seat and gazed out the windshield for a moment. He let out a sigh as he put the car into drive, did a tight three-point turn, and headed on to Amalfi. The glow of the fire faded in the rearview mirror.

"What happened back there, Colt? Where's Vladimir?" Monroe asked between sobs.

In the dark, Monroe did not see the slight grin that covered Marcus's face as he quietly said, "He became unbalanced."

106

SULLY HAD A CHALLENGE FINDING the small warehouse that was supposed to be just a block or so off the Amalfi Coast Road in the center of Amalfi. The directions seemed simple, but proved otherwise. After giving Marcus two wrong turns, he was ready to hang up his navigator hat. Perhaps the stress of the evening was finally getting to him.

Fortunately, Monroe had calmed down some and decided to help: he provided the directions needed. They arrived a little after 0100 hrs local time.

Their destination was a small, two-story, flat-roofed building; a quick look offered an estimate of no more than two thousand square feet per floor. Like so many of the local buildings, it had been painted, some years ago, in a pastel yellow with white trim. Now it displayed a run-down, deserted look. Trash and junk littered the area around the building, and the few windows had been painted over. Only "keep out" signs adorned the walls. A small parking area was littered with more trash.

Rattler pulled in beside Marcus, and his team bailed out and assumed watchful positions. A quick glance around showed the Marine corporal standing watch in the shadows near the corner of the building. Marcus liked what he saw and turned to Rattler. "Jasper, get the men surrounding

427

the building and concealed, then join me inside. That is, if you're ready to follow orders, Gunny."

"Aw, hell, Mr. Colt. You know I try to follow orders. At least the important ones, sir," Jasper whispered with a wink.

SA Baker was standing in the light from the small industrial fixture mounted over the door. He waved to the new arrivals as Colt walked toward him. "Marcus, you are not going to believe what we have here."

Marcus had ordered the other three men to wait in the car, so he approached SA Baker alone. He waved at the Marine with his left hand and avoided SA Baker's extended hand as he pointed to the hole and bloodstain on his right arm. "Sorry, Ben, but my arm is aching like a bitch. Traditional handshakes are on hold."

"Damn! What happened?"

Marcus shrugged. "Good news is that we overpowered Viper and released Sue. I've got the missing doc with me. The bad is there was a small shootout at the villa. Ratfink fired once at me, Gunny and Adam each fired twice. Ratfink is dead and I'm out another shirt and sports jacket. Gunny said I also need a couple of stitches, so the hospital is my next stop. But first, I need to see what's got you all excited."

Shaking his head at the news, Ben said, "Damn. Too much excitement happening there. As I said before, Marcus, you are not going to believe what we have here."

"Ben, the week has been filled with too many weird twists and turns. I'm ready to believe all the animals of the Ringling Brothers Circus are in there. Or perhaps a dozen naked dancing girls, which beat elephants hands down. Show me please."

The interior was a complete opposite of the deserted image projected outside. With the exception of what might be a small office in the back corner, the entire ground floor was open. Multiple lines of ceiling fixtures bathed the entire area with a harsh white light that bounced off the white walls and light gray floor. Two rows of workbenches ran down the center of the room, and shelving lined the walls. It was immaculate.

There were several workstations on the benches that featured pieces of electronic equipment. Meters and gauges were connected to some of the pieces. Others looked to be under construction. It gave off the image of well-organized clutter.

"Damn nice shop," Rattler said as he came over to Ben and Marcus.

Mario Morelli, aka Pest, was sitting handcuffed in a chair at the back of the room. The area around his left eye was starting to darken, and some dried blood showed on his swollen lower lip. Pest did not look at all happy. SA Jerry Tomlinson from the Rome office and Staff Sergeant Mike Stump were keeping him under a watchful eye.

Nudging Ben and pointing toward the Pest, Marcus asked, "What happened there?"

"We got here just as he was unlocking the door. Pest tried to take on the corporal, who got to the door ahead of Mike and me. Pest lost the battle, as you can see."

Marcus chuckled. "Has he said anything?"

"Just a few muttered vulgarities about our family lineage."

Marcus again looked around the room. Something was not right. The pain continued interrupting his thoughts, slowing him down; nevertheless, it finally hit him. He looked back at SA Baker and quietly asked, "Don't you think this is a mighty large space for one man, our rediscovered doctor, to use as a lab? More than a few stools are at the benches, eh."

"Yea, Marcus, now that you mention it, looks like this place could handle a dozen or more people working. What gives?"

With a shrug, Marcus whispered, "Not sure. The doctor has not talked about having a team, but he hasn't said much about anything. Let's see if Mario has any answers. Y'all stand a bit behind me and put on your best 'bad cop' faces. Intimidation might work with him."

Mario stiffened as the three men approached. He had not been able to hear their comments, so he didn't know what to expect. He just knew Vladimir was going to be angry that he hadn't kept the lab secured.

Stopping about three feet in front of Mario, Marcus looked down at him and started the interrogation with a smile. "Mario Morelli, sorry about your face, but you should never disagree with a United States Marine. Lesson learned, right? Anyway, remember me from when I visited your workplace the other day?"

Mario stared at Marcus, saying nothing, but a flicker of recognition appeared.

"We know that you work for Vladimir Davidovich Kroneski and provided him with information about my visit, as well as classified data you got at our Naval Research Laboratory. He paid you fairly well, it seems, based on your Capri bank balance. But I wonder if the payments will be enough to cover your attorney fees."

Ben had stayed a couple of feet away from Marcus, to the left. He opened his jacket and placed his hand on his weapon. His facial expression was blank, but anger permeated the area around him. Gunny Railey took up a position to the right, crossing his arms to project a tough look. Mario kept glancing between the three men, nervously licking his busted lip.

Marcus continued in a friendly tone, throwing out some of his speculation as facts. "Of course, the murder charges will be the costly ones. We know you helped Vlad ram us off the Vesuvius road, where a diplomat died. And I'm gathering enough information to link you to the beating death of the NIS agent on Monday. The other charges are minor in comparison, but they are numerous. You should be able to afford it, right?"

With a slight shake of his head, Mario looked arrogant as he belted out, "I didn't kill anyone! Besides, Vladimir will protect me. He will be here soon and then you will die."

Ignoring the outburst, Marcus maintained his tone. "So tell me, Mario, how many people work here? Do you know who they are and where we can find them?"

Morelli just stared at Marcus with his jaw locked.

"Okay, Mario, I tried to help you but you're too stupid to accept it," Marcus sorrowfully said.

The all-business Lieutenant Commander Colt replaced the easygoing Marcus persona, and he turned toward SA Baker. His voice hardened to steel as he said, "Special Agent Baker, Morelli has no intention of helping himself. Since we need to have two bodies picked up, do you see any reason why we can't make it three? My official statement will be Morelli entered into an altercation with our Marine sergeant, grabbed his weapon, and you shot him twice in the chest. Work for you?"

Baker made a big show of pulling his weapon and checking that a round was in the chamber. He stared intently at Morelli and said, "Yes, sir. That will work for me. But one question, if I may."

"Shoot," Marcus replied as he glanced at Morelli. "Figuratively speaking … for now."

"You mentioned that Antonio Greco died in a shootout, but nothing about the second body. Who is that?"

Jerking his head to look at Baker, Morelli asked in panic, "Antonio is dead?"

Marcus nodded at him while Baker continued, "Like I asked, who else is dead?"

Colt grinned at Morelli and said, "Vladimir Davidovich Kroneski. He ran off a cliff a couple of kilometers back while chasing us. The fire in his wrecked car should be out by now. The morgue attendants can scrape up whatever's left."

Morelli could not control his facial expression as it turned from surprise to disbelief, and finally to resignation. He now knew that no one was coming to his rescue, and it was likely he was about to die. While he was nowhere near a genius, Morelli was smart enough to know he was out of options.

"All right, signor, I will tell you what you need to know."

It didn't take long for Morelli to blurt out all the information he possessed. Vlad had insisted they work six days a week, so there would be nine people arriving in a few hours. Usually they were all in place by 0800. Two were Russian women and one was a Russian man. Others were all Italian, except for one guy who might be German: Morelli wasn't sure. None were ever armed, as far as he knew, and he had no idea where they lived. He provided their names.

With that new information, Marcus pulled Gunny Railey and SA Baker to the front of the room. "Okay, gents, here's the plan. Corporal Gardener is going to drive me to the hospital before I fall over. Shore Patrolmen Eden, Helms, and Mallory will escort Monroe to the SP HQ where he will be confined. Ben, I need you, Jerry, and Jasper to hold down the fort here, with the help of Jasper's three Marines."

Both men nodded as Marcus continued, "Ben, please get on the phone and update Homestead One. Have him get a bus and a dozen armed men here ASAP. Let him know where I'm going and that Monroe is heading his way. Keep the bus out of sight until you have rounded up and cuffed all nine of the workers, then, keeping a strong security guard here, load the bus and bring the workers and Morelli to the SP HQ. Now, what am I forgetting?"

"Well covered, Marcus. Now get out of here before you do fall over," Ben quietly said.

107

SEAMAN SULLY EDEN DID A great job leading the two-vehicle convoy from Amalfi back to the base in Naples; he only made one wrong turn, from which he quickly recovered. Once reaching the base, Sully turned toward the Shore Patrol office complex while Corporal Rick Gardener drove Marcus to the hospital.

Marcus checked his Timex as they pulled up to the emergency room entrance; it was approaching 0300 hrs. It had been a long day. Now that the stress of the operation was past, he was starting to feel a bit woozy.

Remembering Yogi's "déjà vu all over again" comment brought a small smile to his face. After all, Marcus thought, he had limped into this place less than forty-eight hours ago from his volcano walk. He spotted Captain Smithson pacing back and forth as Marcus again limped to the door, and figured he was facing another lecture. And he knew he deserved it. Resting was not something he had done.

"Captain, sorry for getting you out of bed at this hour, sir," Marcus said as he approached Smithson.

It was hard to tell if Smithson sneered or grimaced as he stiffly responded, "Not a problem, Lieutenant Commander. I know I'll never get any decent sleep until you are off the European continent. Now, get your butt on that gurney."

The laughter caused Marcus to turn. Standing between Petty Officers Canton and Jackson were Sue Woodward and Wendy James, smiling. Both ladies looked relieved to see Marcus.

Smithson continued, "Neither of those ladies would leave until they saw you were taken care of properly. Now, off with the jacket. I'll patch you up quickly so you can dash out and save the world again … against doctor's orders."

Hoping to get on the doctor's good side, if one actually existed, Marcus complied. He passed his weapons to Canton. He then asked Captain Smithson, "Sir, is my old room still available? I could really use some sleep."

Finally Smithson smiled. "Okay, that proves we don't need to do a psych eval on you, Colt. You do have a little sense." Under his breath, Smithson muttered, "Granted, very little." Louder, he continued, "We can get you a bed, but first we need to fix this arm."

Looking at his arm for the first time in over three hours, Marcus saw that the bandage Rattler applied was soaked and leaking. Obviously, all that arm movement while driving kept the blood flowing. For sure, the bloody jacket was toast.

A quick check of his blood pressure showed it was way low, so the nurse jabbed a line into his left hand and attached a bag of Ringer's lactate to start to replace his fluids. From all indications, Marcus had probably lost a pint of blood from his gunshot wound. That, combined with his previous injuries and long day, caused his wooziness.

With Smithson carefully overseeing, the ER doctor and nurse did the manual labor. The cleaning of his wound was painful, even after a couple of pain-killing injections, but Marcus had felt that level of pain before. At least they were all complimentary about the gunny's first aid techniques. He'd try to remember to pass on their comments.

Several sutures on his nicked brachial artery finally stopped the blood flow. A couple more on the front and back of his arm closed the holes left by Antonio's 9mm round. Marcus was grateful that it wasn't as bad as it could have been. He just dreaded having to tell Kelly about it. She was keeping track of his suture count.

The new bandages were firmly in place on his right arm, and that sore arm now rested in a sling. Marcus started to sit up, but Doctor Smithson placed his hand against his chest. "Hold on, Colt. We have another task ahead of us—actually, the reason you were told to be here today. Nurse, please remove that unique cap and dressing from our patient's head. I have another wound to check before I make a few phone calls to D.C."

His head wound was healing nicely; no signs of infection were seen. The hairstyle still stunk. The nurse applied a new dressing and was ready to put a sedative into his line when Marcus asked Doctor Smithson for a small favor. "Captain, before you knock me out, I need to speak with my partner for a moment, please."

Smithson nodded and escorted the nurse out of the curtained area. He approached the small group awaiting news on Marcus, and after a quick update, told Miss James that Marcus needed to talk.

Pulling the curtain closed, Wendy hobbled over to Marcus. Leaning on her crutches, she said, "You sure make a habit of getting injured, boss. How's the arm?"

"I've had better days, and I hate having to tell Kelly there are more sutures for her to add to her list. But at least this case is coming close to ending and we can go home soon. I assume you've been with Boxer most of the evening, so you know what's happening. Right?"

Wendy nodded. "I'm completely in the loop, sir. Captain Boxer has dispatched teams to the villa and the Amalfi lab. Doctor Monroe is in lockup. And I'm so damn glad to see you, Marcus." She reached over and placed her hand on his good arm.

"Ditto, Wendy. Okay, how's this for a plan. I'm running on fumes, so they're going to knock me out for a while. I need Canton and Jackson to take you and Sue back to the consulate. Y'all need to stay there and rest until I say otherwise. Captain Boxer and Tony can handle this mess for a day or so without us."

As Marcus paused to grimace from the pain, Wendy interjected, "Sue goes to the consulate, but I'm staying with you, partner. No argument, please. Besides, you need me since I'll get your weapons from Canton."

With no energy to argue, Marcus said, "Fine. But I want you to call Admiral Chance and give him an update on the case. And since bourbon on the rocks is probably out of the question, please ask the nurse to knock me out now." Marcus closed his eyes and rubbed her hand before softly saying, "Thank you, Wendy."

The nurse responded to Wendy's call and added the sedative to Marcus's line. As he fell quietly into the arms of Morpheus, Marcus was moved, under Wendy's watchful eyes, back to the same room he had vacated the day before. Captain Boxer was again a step ahead of everyone and had two SPs ready to stand guard by his room.

Following Wendy's orders, Canton and Jackson escorted Sue back to the consulate. Sue wasn't happy about it, but understood the logic: there was nothing for her to do there except watch Marcus sleep. Frankly, she needed her own rest after her stressful ordeal. And there was a father to call. Sec State needed an update directly from his daughter.

After making sure she was secured in the consulate, the two SPs would then head to their racks for their own much needed sleep; they had been on duty for nearly twenty-four hours. Wendy had already cleared the next three days off for each man with Captain Boxer.

Needing a quiet place to call the admiral, Wendy found nurse Karen Hadley, who was again on duty on Marcus's floor. After hearing Wendy's request, Karen insisted she use a wheelchair, then took her to the same spare office Marcus had used.

The call to Chance took just under thirty minutes, but the good news was he was pleased with the results of the case. Shocked, for sure, about Monroe's alleged treason, but happy the end was near. He promised to update Admiral Gallagher immediately. His last order was for her to take care of Marcus and get some rest herself. She quickly agreed.

Wendy returned to Marcus's room and Karen helped get her settled down in the easy chair. Getting her cast-covered leg off the floor was a blessing. Her fatigue, having earlier been canceled out by adrenalin, was back in spades. But she looked at Marcus and realized that before sleep, she needed to place one more phone call.

With Marcus totally out of it, she felt a quick call from the room wouldn't be a problem. It was going on 0400 hrs in Naples, which put it not quite ten p.m. in D.C. Late, but not an unreasonable time to call. She consulted her notebook and dialed the numerous digits.

On the second ring, Doc answered, "Colt residence. SA Stevens speaking."

"Doc, Wendy James calling for Kelly. Don't panic. Marcus is okay … now. He's sleeping. I have an update for you and Kelly."

Wendy ended up talking with Kelly, then Doc, and back to Kelly for nearly an hour. Marcus was oblivious to it all.

108

WINDOW SHADES WERE DOWN. CURTAINS were closed. Overhead lights were out. Only the small nightlights near the beds prevented room 318 from being in total blackout. At the last check just before noon, the charge nurse on the third floor was pleased to see that both Lieutenant Commander Colt and Ensign James were both still in deep sleep. Doctors and medications can do many things, but sleep is often the best remedy.

A little over an hour later, Marcus was enjoying that special twilight that only exists between sleep and awake. One small part of his brain was feeling the pain from his injuries and hearing sounds of someone breathing. The rest of his gray matter was enjoying the vivid dream that was concluding. Dim lights and soft music provided the restaurant's atmosphere. Right in front of him was a large bowl of linguine laced with fresh shrimp just out of a sauté in butter and spice. Fresh chopped parsley and a drizzle of olive oil added the finishing touch. But the aroma that should be wafting up wasn't there. That missing sense brought Marcus out of the dream into a full wake state. He begrudgingly opened his eyes.

Quick bodily inventory revealed that his head still held the highest pain level inside and out—mostly inside. It was a grade A bitch. One pain level down, his knee still ached, and now his upper right arm was crying for attention. He suspected the arm would win the battle for second place as soon as he moved it.

Many of the minor aches and pains from the accident and subsequent volcano stroll had eased. Or perhaps they were just overpowered by the more intense pains. Whatever the case, Marcus knew he had to get moving. Coffee, right after a bladder relief break, was a high priority, followed by some food.

With his bladder relaxed, Marcus subdued some of the body aches with a hot shower, cautious to keep his wounds dry. He checked the locker beside his bed and found a full assortment of clothing. Obviously, Sue had ignored his order to stay at the consulate and had brought more clothing. At least his 1911 and Vlad's pistol were both in the locker. In short order, the hospital gown was ditched for his standard attire: jeans, oxford shirt, shoulder holster, and jacket. He plopped the commie cap in place to hide his butchered hairdo and slid Vlad's pistol into his jacket pocket. To keep the captain happy, he eased his right arm into the sling.

Creeping out the door to avoid waking Wendy, Marcus was surprised to see Corporal Rick Gardener in quiet conversation with the two SP guards. Rick looked up and popped to attention even while in civvies. "How are you feeling, Mr. Colt?"

With the three young men displaying short military haircuts and sports jackets, it looked like a mid-1960s fraternity dance. Lyrics about a white sports coat and a pink carnation bounced around his brain. "I'll tell ya after you help me find some coffee, Rick. Lead us on to the cafeteria, please." Turning to the sailors, Petty Officers James Dasher and Merton Fleming, Marcus said, "Miss James is still sleeping, gentlemen. Keep everyone out except Captain Smithson, okay?"

"Aye, aye, sir," said the senior man.

The cafeteria, located on the first floor, was found by following a few well-placed signs. The lunch crowd had finished, so they pretty much had the place to themselves. Marcus paid for the coffee and asked Rick to carry the tray to the table he selected in the corner. He smiled at the memory of Doc doing that chore for him just a few months ago.

After a few sips of the life-saving elixir, Marcus looked hard at Gardener, but in contrast with that look, gently said, "Thought I told you to hit the rack for a day or so. Yet you're here a mere nine hours later. Seems like a lot of people are ignoring orders around here."

Rick shook his head. "No, sir. Per your orders, I returned to the consulate after checking in with the gunny at the SP HQ. He ordered me to sleep for a few hours and then bring replacement clothes for you to the hospital. I was told to be here when you woke up. Again, he reminded me of his previous threat if I let anything happen to you, sir. You remember, sir, the one about me hanging from the flagpole by certain body parts. I got some rest, sir—honest, I'm fine. And I want to be here to help you."

It was hard for Marcus to maintain a straight face at hearing Rattler's threat or seeing Gardener's enthusiasm, so he simply nodded and took another sip of coffee. The cup helped hide his grin. "Have you had lunch, Rick?"

"Not yet, sir. I was waiting until you woke up to see where we went next."

"How about this? I'll buy if you fly. Get me two cheeseburgers with mayo and pickles, fries, and a Coke, and you get whatever you want. Eat hearty, buddy. It might be a while until dinner. Here's a twenty."

"Yes, sir," he said with enthusiasm.

As Rick headed to the food line, Marcus wasn't surprised to see Captain Smithson standing at the door looking around. He spotted Marcus and made a beeline for his table.

"Have you had lunch, sir? My treat if you haven't." Marcus gave the skipper a sheepish grin. "Least I can do for messing up your sleep … again."

Taking a chair next to Marcus, the captain said, "Best suggestion I've heard all day. I'll take you up on that free lunch, Marcus."

Having seen the back of a stranger approach Mr. Colt, Rick had stopped his walk to the food line and carefully watched. Mr. Colt's smile eased his concern, and then he saw Colt wave him back to the table.

After introductions were done, and the captain's order safely engraved in Rick's mind, he dashed off to complete his updated assignment.

Smithson turned to Marcus. "Considering your 'damn the torpedoes, full speed ahead' attitude, I'm surprised you asked for the sedative this morning." While the hospital's commanding officer formed it as a statement, it was clearly a question.

"Sir, I'm a full believer in knowing my limitations. While my body could have gone on for a few more hours or days, my mind was getting a good fog covering. Right now, I need to *think* more than *do*. I knew just trying to sleep normally with all this pain and stress from the case would fail, so I needed the shot. As folks back home say … I ain't too proud to ask for help."

"I'm happy to hear that." Smithson continued, "How's the pain level today?"

Marcus shrugged. "Headache's still nasty. The arm's not bad unless I move it too much. Knee only hurts when I walk more than a few steps. Body aches are being overpowered by the head pain."

The doctor nodded. "The head pain is to be expected, Marcus. The headache may last for a few weeks or even months. I suspect it will be short-termed, since you're not displaying the other hematoma symptoms such as nausea, confusion, or slurred speech. Unless you are hiding them from me."

"No, sir. I just have the headache." He laughed and pointed to Wendy and her entourage of the other two "frat boys" entering the cafeteria. "Of course, that lady might tell you I'm confused a lot lately." He waved them over.

"Let me know if anything changes. By the way, am I allowed to ask how the case it going?"

"Better than it was yesterday at this time, sir. We have found a missing American, uncovered what might be a treasonous situation, and I believe we have stopped the party responsible for the death of several of our people. Including the agent we saw in your morgue," Marcus offered.

The captain showed surprise. "A very productive day, it seems."

Wendy gave the captain a smile that could stop hearts and asked in her soft Virginian accent, "Got room for me?"

"Always, partner." Marcus stood and pulled out a chair for Wendy. He gestured to other chairs for the SPs. When all were settled and introductions done, he continued, "Y'all are just in time for lunch." He made the same "I'll buy if you fly" offer to James and Merton, with the caveat that they handle Wendy's order. Just as with Rick, the offer was eagerly accepted.

Captain Smithson again put on his doctor persona. He queried Wendy about the status of her leg and other aches and pains. Her positive report satisfied him.

The meal was devoured as the group discussed pleasant things like sports and local tourist attractions, with smiles all around. While Italy offers some of the best cuisine in the world, there are times when nothing tastes better than a cheeseburger and fries.

As Merton and Rick grabbed the trays to clear the table, Marcus asked, "Captain, when can I get out of here?"

Smithson laughed at that question. "Since you checked yourself in, Marcus, you are free to leave whenever you're ready. But I suggest you stop by the ER on the way out and let us do a dressing change on that arm. It should be checked daily for the next week or so. If you're ready, we can head that way now."

As they stood to leave, the public address system clicked on. "Captain Smithson, report to the ER stat. Captain Smithson, ER stat." Before they could turn toward the door, the PA system came on again. "Marcus Colt, report to the ER stat. Marcus Colt, ER stat."

A softly spoken "oh, crap" was heard as the six rushed out of the cafeteria.

109

THE EMERGENCY ROOM WAS A little more active than it was when Marcus had arrived before dawn. Though the ER was quiet, there was a feeling of intense concern. A glance out the door allowed him to see an ambulance pulling away from the entrance and several SP jeeps nearby. A small crowd clustered at the end of one of the draped exam rooms, where Captain Boxer and SSA Anthony Carter were deep in discussion.

Smithson pushed into the exam room and started speaking in hushed tones to the doctor and nurses. A man was on the table, only his head exposed. A nurse was checking his blood pressure while a doctor was using a light to check his eyes.

Marcus approached Boxer and Carter. Wendy followed as quickly as the crutches allowed. The three men assigned to their security took up positions where they could watch and protect, yet not be in the way.

"Who's hurt?" Marcus barked. No pleasantries were exchanged.

Tony answered first. "Doctor Monroe. He collapsed during the interrogation."

Boxer jumped in when Tony paused. "Things were just getting started. He seemed disoriented and rambled a bit. But Tony was gentle with him as he started the interrogation. After a couple of softball questions,

441

Monroe started yelling he was 'the good guy,' just 'following orders,' and that the 'skipper' told him to do it."

Tony nodded in agreement, then added, "Just like the Nazis on trial at Nuremburg. And after saying that crap several times over, he suddenly stopped talking, his eyes rolled back, and he fell off the chair."

"Did he mention intense pain in his head at any time?" asked Captain Smithson. He had quietly walked up behind Marcus.

Tony shook his head. "No, sir."

"What's it look like?" Marcus brusquely asked Smithson.

Smithson noticed Marcus had transitioned from friendly patient to hard investigator in charge, skipping the standard military nicety of *sir*. "We are going to do some x-rays, and blood work is underway. If you insist I make an educated guess, then it's probably a stroke. Tests will determine if it is a stroke and whether it's hemorrhagic or ischemic. More than likely it's ischemic."

Wendy asked, "What's the difference, sir? Will he survive it?"

Shifting into instructor mode, Smithson explained, "Ischemic is a blockage in a blood vessel feeding the brain. Usually it's caused by a clot. Hemorrhagic happens when a blood vessel in the brain bursts, cutting off the blood supply. Ischemic is treated with blood-thinning meds, and hemorrhagic probably means surgery. Survival? Impairment?" The captain shrugged. "Only time will tell in both cases. I'll keep you apprised. Wish I had access to his medical history."

Marcus said, "He's retired Navy and was working in the research lab in D.C. I suspect the base hospital has his records. SSA Carter has his service number, etc."

"Good. I'll give them a call." With no further questions coming, Smithson turned and headed back to the patient. Marcus called after him, "Thank you, sir."

Marcus checked his watch: almost 1500 hrs. Rubbing his forehead in a futile attempt to diminish the pain, he decided on the next plan of action. He motioned for his security team to join the group and they walked to a quiet corner.

Looking from face to face, Marcus said, "Assuming Monroe was telling the truth, we have at least one more 'bad guy' to find. I thought Vladimir was the ring leader, but last night Canton mentioned he overheard a conversation between Monroe and Vlad. Based on that, he thought perhaps they were equals. Or maybe Monroe had more power. And now with

Monroe talking about a 'skipper,' assuming he was not delirious, that points to someone else in charge."

Looking at Captain Boxer, he said, "Sir, please assign a security team to watch Monroe. Doubt he will try to escape, but he might be on a hit list."

Boxer simply said, "Already done."

"Thank you, sir." Then Marcus asked the group, "And where is the material picked up from the villa and lab?"

"Still packing up the lab, Marcus—there's a lot there," Tony answered. "But we have the stuff from the villa at NISO. Half of my guys are going through it now."

"Well, I guess we have things to see there. Petty Officer Dasher will head to the consulate and sit on Mrs. Woodward. Make sure she stays there. Okay?"

"Can do, sir."

"Wendy, give Sue a quick call to let her know we might have other players. You get to tell her she's on sort-of house arrest for her own safety."

"Yes, sir." Wendy laughed and hobbled over to the nurses' station to find a phone.

"Petty Officer Fleming. You and Corporal Gardener will come with Miss James and me to the NISO." Turning to Captain Boxer, Marcus asked, "What have I missed, Skipper?"

"Just tell me where you want me."

"Do you have a warehouse where we can store and sort the lab materials?"

"Not a problem. Secured area has been set up near my office."

"And where are we on handling the people you picked up there earlier?"

Boxer chuckled. With a sigh, he said, "You gave me a hornet's nest with those scientists. Luckily, I had several JAG lawyers on hand when the busload arrived. Based upon JAG recommendations, we will turn the Italians over to the *Carabinieri* once our lawyers and a NIS agent do an initial interrogation. That's underway now. Same thing with the one German national—he goes to the German military police, the *Feldjägers*, after interrogation. Let NATO members clean up their own mess."

Marcus nodded. "Makes sense. What about the Russians?"

"I know you'll be shocked," he said with a voice dripping in sarcasm, "but those three had diplomatic passports. They refused to get on the bus, and we had to let them go. I passed their names to the Carabinieri, and

I suspect they will be declared persona non grata in a day or so by the Italian government. Best we could do, Marcus."

"Works for me, sir. Guess the best place for you is back at your HQ. You have some evidence to wrangle, and it seems we all have a lot of reports to write," Marcus said. "Let's make it happen, people—time to sound *Boots and Saddles.*"

110

THE NORMAL SATURDAY QUIET OF the NIS office was disrupted by the slamming of boxes on conference tables, the soft crinkle of shuffled papers, the slap of closing file folders, and the frequent muttering of profanity. The agents digging into the potential evidence removed from Vlad's villa had a challenge finding something—finding anything—that could point to any other people possibly involved.

Only about seventy-two hours separated that moment from the last time Marcus Colt was in this office space, but it felt like much longer. After thanking the agents for their work on the case and getting an update on their progress, Marcus grabbed a cup of coffee. He excused himself to the front office, sat at one of the IBM Selectric typewriters, and started typing his latest ROI.

This was a needed task. In addition to updating everyone, it provided Marcus a chance to go over everything that had happened in the last couple of days. Documenting the events required deep thought, and as he remembered the events, he started typing.

Marcus pulling the twelfth and last page from the IBM machine coincided with Wendy escaping from the agents' area. A glance at his Timex showed he had been thinking and typing, mostly thinking, for the last forty-five minutes. Progress has a price.

Wendy clunked over to the desk Marcus had commandeered and dropped into the chair next to it. "Do we get compensation for paper cuts, boss? Those files are a nightmare. No organization, no logic—just dust. Some things are in Italian, but most are Russian. And no, sir, we haven't found any obvious items pointing to other people, but the guys are still digging. What are you working on?"

Tapping the sheets to get them in line, Marcus smiled with satisfaction. "Another chapter in the life of secret agent 006.5." He chuckled softly. "Actually, it is the rough draft of the ROI for our actions over the last twenty or so hours. Care to read?"

Taking the small stack of paper, Wendy replied, "Get more coffee, boss. And bring me one, please. Oh, and I do need a red pen to correct your grammar."

Marcus snickered, "Yes, ma'am," and headed to the coffee mess.

Wendy was not an officially documented speed-reader, but she came damn close. She went through the twelve pages in what most would consider record time. As she laid the last page down, she realized that even while fighting pain and fatigue, Marcus Colt was amazing. Since she had talked with many of those involved with the events overnight, it was easy to see that Marcus hadn't missed anything. The ROI was concise and complete.

"Here ya go," Marcus said as he placed the coffee mug within Wendy's reach. "So tell me, proofreading partner, how bad is that ROI?"

"Try to stay humble, okay, but I could not find a single flaw. Well done ROI, boss. You get a gold star."

Marcus shrugged. "It would be a great Report of Investigation if we knew the rest of the players in this soap opera. We're missing something, but I can't put my thumb on it."

Wendy's face twisted into a combination of concern and question. "So you're putting some credence on the pre-stroke comments?"

"Yea, I am. I suspect the doctor believed he was dying—he still might and wanted to tell us his story. Sort of a deathbed confession, but he couldn't get all the words out."

Wendy nodded. "Okay, let's run with that. His comments were something about him being 'the good guy' who was just 'following orders' from the 'skipper.' Right?" She punctuated the doctor's comments by drawing double quote marks in the air.

"True." Marcus took another sip of coffee.

"That means we need to find the skipper … whoever that is. And does he mean skipper in the true sense of the word or just the leader of the Russians? Or whoever? Or what? And why can't Vlad be the skipper?"

Avoiding any hint of sarcasm, Marcus said, "Congratulations, Wendy, you just vocalized the questions in my mind. As for Vlad, I mentioned earlier that Petty Officer Canton heard Vlad and Monroe talking before we raided the villa. He believes they're basically on the same power level, answering to a higher authority. Kevin seems sharp, so I'm inclined to go with his gut and put Vlad on the bottom of the list."

Wendy nodded. "Well, what about the commanding officer of the D.C. lab where Monroe worked? Might she be the skipper he referenced?"

"Hum, possible, but doubtful. Remember, they had a bit of a tryst in the past and weren't on the best terms. Besides, Monroe vanished a month or so before Collier took over. Without any overlapping service, I don't see them colluding on anything. He might call her 'sweetie,' but 'skipper,' probably not," Marcus said. He started to say something but halted, a quizzical look coming over his face. "What about the lab's CO before Collier?"

Wendy shrugged. "If he's the 'skipper,' then why would he be working with Vlad?"

"Yea, that 'why' thing keeps getting in the way, Wendy." Marcus took another sip of coffee, then leaned back in his chair, checking the oracles of the overhead for inspiration. After a few quiet minutes, Marcus muttered, "Why indeed."

A couple more moments of silent contemplation passed, then Marcus bolted upright. He left the chair and paced around the desks. His thoughts came out rapidly. "Okay, skip the 'why' thing for a minute. Work around it. Put yourself in this position, Wendy. You've worked for me at least a year. We're good friends. We're both dedicated officers who follow orders. One day I come to your office, close the door, and pull a chair up close to your desk. Then I tell you the CNO has secretly authorized us to infiltrate a Cuban organization by pretending to turn traitor. And we cannot tell anyone. What would you do?"

Wendy swiveled her head to keep up with Marcus as he paced. "Okay, as my friend and trusted boss, I would follow your lead."

"Yea, in that situation you would work under the assumption that me, your *skipper*, someone you trust, is on the level. Right? Time to call D.C."

III

"NAVAL INVESTIGATIVE SERVICE, INTERNAL AFFAIRS Division, Carl Freeman speaking. How may I be of assistance, sir?"

There was a slight buzz on the line, but Carl heard the voice come through loud and clear. "Good morning, Carl. Marcus calling. What are you doing in the office on a Saturday? Has war been declared?" Marcus joked.

"You might say that. Lieutenant Doty and I have declared war on the stacks of communications and files that have invaded your desk. He tries, but has trouble handling the load you do. Based on the update we got from Doc, he thought you might be home soon, and none of us want to feel your wrath if you found a messy office. How's the arm?"

Marcus chuckled. "The admiral didn't waste any time spreading that around, eh? It's just a scratch, and a gunny applied first aid, so I'll live."

"Actually, our admiral is a no-show today. I got word that he is hitting the links with your daddy-in-law admiral, and a special congressman with his chief of staff, also known as your neighbor. I suspect they will use the time spent chasing the balls by passing on the updated info. A complete update came to us lower echelon folks here from Doc when he and Victoria arrived early this morning. He told us he and Kelly had a nice chat with Ensign James last night right after she called the admiral. Therefore, sir, we're all up to speed on your latest injuries and case status."

"Wonder why Miss James didn't tell me about that call to Kelly?" Marcus glanced over at Wendy. She shrugged and gave him her best cat-ate-the-canary smile. He sighed and said, "Oh, well. Anyway, buddy, your latest info is not completely up to date. Things are changing, so take notes. Doctor Monroe had a stroke about two hours ago. Not sure if he'll make it. The best doctors are working on him. Anyway, he passed on some cryptic comments right before or probably during the stroke that we are now pursuing." Marcus provided Monroe's comments, his personal conjecture about them, and a promise that a detailed ROI was in the works.

"More of that Colt gut reasoning, right?" Carl asked.

"Yea, and that's why I called—we need some info fast. Get with Doc and find the name of the commanding officer of the research lab there in D.C. before Captain Jennifer Collier took over. Check a copy of his service record and let me know where he's stationed now. Call David Bartow if you get any grief from BUPERS on getting the records. And call over to the base hospital and see if there is a psych eval in Doctor Monroe's records. He may have had one at the time of his retirement. If so, I need it."

"Can do. Where should I call you back? Still in the hospital?"

"No, I'm at NISO Naples probably for the next couple of hours. Then Wendy and I will go back to the consulate. Unless something exciting pops, I think we've earned a quiet dinner and some recovery time. It has been a rough week."

After a few minutes of back and forth on a couple of other pressing issues at HQ, Carl hung up and went in search of Doc. No need to call BUPERS until he had a name.

Catching Lieutenant Jake Doty exiting the coffee mess, Carl gave him a quick update. Jake decided getting that new information to the admiral took precedence over the mountain of paperwork, so he left for the golf course.

Doc and Victoria were spending the day in the conference room. They were digging through the CIA files again, looking for links to Vladimir that perhaps were missed on the first pass. Victoria had shared an opinion only with Doc the day before; she was not convinced Vlad was the kingpin in the operation. Her personal knowledge of him had shown he was a very intelligent man. But he was more the type to get his hands dirty knocking heads than to plan a lot of long-range operations. With nothing else pressing for the moment, they looked for a needle in a pile of needles. Each file contained at least one bad guy, usually more, and they were looking for a bad guy. A tap on the door casing pulled their eyes off the CIA documents.

Carl said, "Sorry for the interruption, but I just got off the phone with Marcus. He needs to know ASAP the name and current location of the previous commanding officer of our research lab. He wants us to pull his service record. He's leaning toward believing that the Vlad guy was not the head honcho over there."

Hearing that, Victoria glanced at Doc with a knowing smile on her face. "Great minds usually follow the same path, Doc. You might want to make a note of that."

112

WAITING IS THE HARDEST PART of any investigation. Investigators know the bad guys are out in the world doing something evil while they sit waiting. So they try to fill that time with something productive. Marcus knew looking at the phone wouldn't make it ring—Carl and Doc would provide the info just as fast as they could—but he couldn't stop himself.

For Wendy, it was time spent keying Marcus's lengthy ROI onto the paper tape of the ASR-35. She augmented it with the latest request for information from the D.C. office before sending it, over the AUTOVON network, to NIS offices in both D.C. and Norfolk. Norfolk was included in hopes the death of Vladimir would compensate even a little for the death of Special Agent Bill Collins.

Earlier, Marcus had used part of the wait time to reread his ROI before Wendy sent it out over the wire. Her additions were perfect. He also took a couple of minutes for a call home. A chat with Kelly always perked him up. At least she didn't sound too upset about the new wound. He grabbed onto the positive and enjoyed it. Even after hanging up the phone, he sat there for a moment savoring the echoes of her voice in his head.

His headache was not getting any better from listening to Wendy key the ROI into the teletype, so he decided more coffee was in order. And with a fresh cup came the desire to relocate to a quieter place.

The three special agents in the back room, Tony, John, and Adam, were still grumbling about their task when Marcus joined them at the conference table. Tony smirked. "Thanks for joining us just when we get to the bottom of the last box."

Marcus smiled. "We all have our talents—timing's mine. Looks like you have things under complete control. Anything to share?"

Adam raised a piece of paper to his face and said, "Do you know a Peters who lives or lived in Virginia Beach? We found the name and partial address, just city and state, paperclipped to a pack of index cards. It's the return address from an envelope and based on the postmark, it has been there for a while—about five years. Perhaps it was the start of an address file. It was one of the few things in English." He laid the paper back on the smallest stack in the center of the table.

Shaking his head, Marcus looked at the four stacks. Obviously the shortest stack was all in English. Russian Cyrillic alphabet was visible on the papers in the tallest stack. Italian and German documents of lesser heights filled the other two. He touched the Italian stack and said, "Has Wendy gone through this one?"

Nodding, Tony replied, "She has, except for the last few clipped together on top. The rest consists mostly of receipts for purchases and other business docs. No mention of people beyond the known players."

Marcus pulled the English stack over and started a quick read of the twenty or so pieces of paper. Adam was right: little worthwhile information was there. Peters was the only Anglo name he saw in the stack.

John spoke up. "Marcus, we put a call in to Sue, and she is looking for Russian and German translators through her CIA contacts. She'll call back as soon as she finds one. By the way, she sounded pissed that you won't let her come over to help today." Chuckling, he continued, "You might want to send flowers."

Tony joined in the ribbing. "Or a good bottle of wine."

"Better make it both," Adam added.

Lifting his hands in a sign of surrender, Marcus said, "Okay, okay. Just so you know—keeping the harem happy is a full-time job." That provided the laughter the group needed to reduce frustration from the wait.

Rick Gardener leaned in around the door. "Mr. Colt, Miss James needs to see you out here, sir."

Giving a thumbs up, Marcus stood. "Excuse me, gents. Another potential harem member needs some help."

The laughter was still going as Marcus closed the door. "What's up, Wendy?"

"Y'all are having too much fun back there," she said, holding out a small stack of paper from the teletype. "Knowing how you feel about coincidences, you might stop laughing when you read this."

The ROI from Doc was short. Doc had written that Monroe hadn't undergone a psych exam upon retirement. Aside from the heart condition that forced his retirement, he was in good shape for his age. He retired barely over two years before he vanished. Doc added that the initial missing person's investigation noted that several lab staff members had mentioned Monroe seemed depressed and often angry after his retirement. One person recalled him being short-tempered and distant.

He read on. The second and final paragraph in the ROI was about the commanding officer of the D.C. research lab during the three years Monroe had worked on Rembrandt. The departing CO had requested his next duty station, and last one before retirement, be in the Naples, Italy area. He planned to settle in the area when retired. Captain Michael J. Peters, USN, was now the current commanding officer of the Naval Air Station Sigonella, Sicily.

"Well? What ya think, boss?" Wendy gave a *come on* hand signal. She immediately saw the Naples request as a red flag.

Marcus took a deep breath and slowly let it out through expanded cheeks. "My first thought is perhaps guilt was causing Monroe's anger and personality changes. Guilt from betraying his country. Guilt from working with the Russians."

Wendy nodded in agreement.

"As for the lab's previous CO, well, it gets wilder, partner, because the coincidences just keep a-coming. Emptying Vlad's last box, the boys in the back just found a piece of an envelope with a partial Virginia Beach return address. The name is Peters. Any wagers his first name is Michael?"

"Wow. I'll pass on that bet. Yea, it's a stretch to believe Peters' name and address just happened to turn up in a Russian-controlled villa in Naples. And Peters wanting to retire here is nothing short of a 'you gotta be kidding me' piece of info. But if Peters is the 'skipper' in Monroe's treasonous world, then I'm back to asking why?"

"I agree, Wendy," Marcus said, "but in our world the 'why' is often understood once we have the evidence, piece together the time line, and discover all the players. Hell, half the time the culprit simply tells us the why—they want to brag about it."

"So, boss, what do we do now?"

"Educate and delegate." Pointing to the hovering corporal, Marcus continued, "Rick, please ask the gentlemen in the back room to join us here."

As the agents got settled in the front office, Marcus placed a call to NISHQ. "Adam, you finding the envelope piece might be the key to busting the case wide open. Pay attention to what I tell D.C. 'cause I'm too damn tired to repeat it. Okay?"

The agents, Wendy, and the two men assigned to security all nodded.

"Hey, Carl. It's Marcus again. Get Doc and Jake on a conference call ASAP." While waiting, Marcus activated the speaker phone button and sat back.

The speaker came alive. "Marcus, I have them online. Jake just got back from updating the admirals. What's up?"

Marcus took a deep breath. "All right. You're on speakerphone here with Wendy, NISO Naples agents Tony, John, and Adam, and my two security team members. We have just discovered something potentially hot, so pay attention and take notes."

Doc said, "We're ready on this end."

After a quick sip of coffee, Marcus said, "We have a weak piece of evidence that points to Peters, the previous CO of the D.C. lab, as the one who might be running the spy ring wanting Rembrandt. I need you three to do whatever you can to quickly get any and all info on Peters. But you have to be discreet—if Peters is guilty, he will vanish if a single hint gets back to him."

Tony interrupted, "Where is Peters stationed?"

Marcus held up a single finger toward Tony, signaling him to wait one, then continued. "Doc, call my neighbor and have him get you to the right person at the FBI—we need a discreet, in-depth background check on Peters. It has to be so in-depth that it goes back to before he was conceived. Look into his parents, friends, neighbors, dogs, etc. Dig deep. Also get Victoria and Les to do the same from the CIA side. Jake, get a hold of Scott Tiller in Norfolk—he does some great magic with financial BIs. Have him dig into Peters. And I want you to go through his service record word by word, looking for anything that stands out. Carl, you're going to be the point of contact for everyone. Do your standard level of completeness and document everything, keeping everyone up to date. Help me remember who knows what and who I forgot."

Multiple words of agreement came over the line. Then Marcus asked, "Jake, where is Hank right now?"

"I kept him in Norfolk. Figured there might be more to do there with the shooting of Collins."

"Perfect, Jake. When you go through Peters' records, look for a reference to the Norfolk area about five years ago. The link we found in Vlad's villa is a return address to someone named Peters in Virginia Beach. Sorry, no street name or number. Pass the word to Hank that he needs to dig around down there. Just push the discretion part."

Never the shy one, Doc came on the line when Marcus paused. "And what are you going to do?"

Marcus smiled. "Patience, Doc. I'm getting there. Tony, please continue cleaning up the villa and the lab mess. In addition, I need y'all to keep Peters in mind as you do the clean up, and look for more of those links like the envelope. And I want you to start a discreet analysis of Peters— he's stationed in Sicily as the CO of Naval Air Station Sigonella. Y'all may have heard the word 'discreet' used multiple times. I cannot emphasize that enough."

"We hear you loud and clear, Marcus," said Jake as heads nodded around the Naples office.

"Okay, unless there's anything else, I'll hang up, Wendy will check those last few Italian pages in the conference room, and then we're heading to the consulate. You don't need us in your way while you good agents do what you do best."

113

THE EVENING INCLUDED WHAT LOOKED like a normal if somewhat fancy dinner party for a small group of people. A passerby would have the impression of college friends having a restful evening. But that wasn't the case, as the conversation at the round table in the consulate's private dining room was on murder, kidnapping, and espionage.

Sue had invited the two SP security men, Petty Officers James Dasher and Merton Fleming, to join them for dinner at the consulate. Naturally, Corporal Rick Gardener was there, making sure Marcus was protected. And much to the surprise of Marcus, PO Kevin Canton was attending. Seems Sue had been distraught the previous evening when Kevin brought her back from Vlad's villa. At her request, Kevin spent the night on the sofa in her apartment and was happy to keep her company during the day.

After telling everyone to plan on a late start in the morning, Wendy and Marcus excused themselves and headed to their rooms. With both still recovering from injuries, a quiet place and rest were called for. Marcus locked the suite door after Wendy clumped in and dropped onto one of the sofas.

She grumbled, "Tired of these crutches already. And it has only been a few days."

"When we get back to the office and you spend most of your day behind your desk, it won't be so bad. Care for a nightcap?" Marcus asked.

"Yes please, a small one, and then tell me what our next step will be."

Sue had planned ahead—a stash of ice was already on the bar. Marcus prepared two glasses with a couple of small ice cubes and a splash of bourbon and carried one to Wendy. He sat on the other sofa and took a small sip. "Again, we have to wait. We've sent the troops out to uncover the info on Peters. Until we get that from our people, the FBI, and the CIA, all we can do is sit around making a lot of speculations."

Wendy sighed. "Guess it isn't like the movies where the spies are active all the time. I'll have to work on that patience thing, boss."

"It will come, Wendy. Each agent develops his or her own way of coping. For me, I use these quiet moments to go back over the case. Sometimes I can find things we've missed, and sometimes a door will open showing me where we need to go next," Marcus said. "And sometimes I just get a headache." They both laughed.

Marcus added, "Yea, this would be an exciting movie. We would compress all the action we've had over the last few weeks into ninety minutes. That would keep you on the edge of your seat."

"So, do you have any speculations to share with this fledgling agent?"

Marcus had a grin that kicked up to the left. He casually said, "Oh, yea. But I need your promise not to talk about it to others. It's just a wild theory."

"My lips are sealed."

"Okay, try this on for size. I can't help but wonder if Peters might be a Soviet sleeper agent. This is just a gut feeling, okay, so I repeat—don't mention it to anyone."

Wendy asked, "Where the hell did you pull that from, Marcus?"

Marcus laughed. "You get the blame, Wendy. You keep asking *why*? Why would a naval officer become a traitor? Why, indeed? So the thought process runs through the possibilities. If it was for money, it's hard to hide a big influx of cash, especially with the BI that was done before he took over as the base CO. Revenge is possible, but revenge for what? Anything big would end up in his service record. And grudges don't sit well with the selection board. Until the troops find something else in their digging, this seems likely, even though it's really hard to believe. But again, it's just a gut feeling, so keep it in the back of your mind, okay?"

Wendy nodded, then a quizzical look crossed her face. "Ya know, that doesn't sound too radical. Maybe he became active when he saw the value of Rembrandt for the USSR. Granted, the backgrounds might uncover something else, but your theory seems solid ... well, as solid as speculation from a guy with a head injury can get." She giggled at the last part.

"And that, dear lady, is proof you've had enough booze. Need any help turning down your bed?"

"I'm good, but thanks. Goodnight, Marcus."

Over an hour later, slumber had yet to come to Marcus. He knew he was tired and looked forward to escaping the pain with sleep, but the case kept him awake. Part of him hoped he was wrong about Peters. Having a Russian sleeper agent reach the position of base commander was a scary thought. Yet no other reason was logical to him, unless the deep dig found something.

Marcus kept thinking of all the deceit. Doctor Monroe had deceived the Navy with his disappearing act. Probably Peters had deceived both Monroe and the Navy. Hard to think of the number of people Vlad had deceived over the years. Just a ton of deceit floating around. It was a good thing Diogenes was looking for a virtuous human and not just the honest man; he realized there was not much honesty around here. With a soft chuckle, Marcus remembered honesty is a virtue, so the pains in his head were messing with his logic.

He once more turned over and checked the clock. Right before his eyes finally closed for the night, the hands of the clock were both touching twelve.

114

BEFORE CALLING IT A DAY late the previous evening, SSA Tony Carter had finally tracked down the supervising agent of NISRA Sigonella. Like a normal person, he was out with his wife having a nice dinner. He wasn't thrilled to be called into work on late Saturday evening, but he knew Carter didn't play games. This request was obviously important and needed immediate action, so he hustled to the NISRA office to read the NIR.

Tony had gotten some rest overnight, but not enough to compensate for the week's deficiency. Starting with the death of Coleman the previous Monday, then the arrival of the Internal Affairs agents from D.C., their attack and injuries, his life had been one traumatic event after another. He needed a vacation to lift the burden of leadership off his shoulders and recharge his batteries. "But that ain't happening," he muttered under his breath.

His agents would be starting their day at the warehouse: the place Captain Boxer had acquired to house all the evidence from the Amalfi lab. This stash included multiple filing cabinets stuffed full of papers in several languages that needed a thorough review. The translators Sue had sent over the previous day, to go through the Russian and German documents from Vlad's villa, were now going to work at the warehouse. Everyone was looking for any mention of Peters or Monroe in the files. It would be a long day. And to handle the hardware, Lieutenant Commander Lane, XO of the research lab, sent a crew to catalog the equipment and various underway projects.

A quick check of the teletype showed no traffic awaited his attention. That meant he was doing what so many agents hated—waiting. He grabbed another cup of coffee and pulled out a pad of paper. It was time to put some thoughts on paper to see if they pointed toward answers.

He wrote "Travel: Naples to Sicily" across the top and started listing methods and approximate travel times. It was just over two hundred miles as the crow flies between Naples and Palermo. The fastest way was by air. Naturally, the commanding officer of a naval air station has easy access to official air travel. But what about clandestine travel? Tony wrote a couple of notes in the margin. *Is Peters a pilot? Does he own a private plane?* He pulled out another sheet of paper and started a to-do list of things to check.

The auto ferry is about a ten-hour voyage—not an efficient way for spies to travel. Train travel down the boot takes even longer. But for those who get seasick, the boat time at the end of the train trip is greatly reduced, due to the proximity of Messina, on the western edge of Sicily and Calabria, sitting on the tip of Italy's boot. In the margin, Tony scribbled another note. *"Probably not the way."*

Those realizations led him back to air travel, assuming Peters and Vladimir actually met face to face. He started wondering if Vlad was a pilot. If not, there probably were one or two in the Russian Embassy that were. He needed to find out whether the embassy had a small plane stashed around the Naples area.

Perhaps the Ministry of Transport, the Italian agency that manages aircraft registration, would provide the needed information. The need to check with them was added to the to-do list. If a Russian private plane existed, perhaps the Naples air traffic controllers could provide data on the flights. Another entry went on the list.

Tony also added the need to access NAS flight logs. He wanted to see when Peters left Sicily and when he returned. With Vladimir dead, piecing together past movements would be difficult, but he needed to try.

He leaned back in his chair and sighed. Hours had passed, and the wall clock hands were pointing to 1100, yet there were more questions and no firm answers. More things to check and more uncertainty. The cold dregs in his coffee cup forced another sigh. Or maybe it was just the frustration of the case. His eyelids closed with the hope of a bit of rest.

The single bell strike of a phone started the chain of events that disturbed his nap. Once the automatic hand-shaking between ASR-35 Teletypes concluded, the loud key clatter of the report being printed and the soft hum of the paper tape being punched brought Tony back to life. A double ding at the end of the transmission called him to the machine to investigate.

A quick read was all Tony needed to take the next step. He picked up the phone and called the suite Marcus and Wendy shared at the consulate.

115

THE BEDSIDE CLOCK SURPRISED MARCUS: it was a bit past ten. He couldn't remember the last time he slept that long, outside of being medicated in the hospital. It had to have been as a young teen, after spending a long cold day in the West Virginia woods deer hunting. As his eyes brought the rest of the room into focus and he started to move, the headache reminded him to go slow. Wounds, aches, and pain were still harassing him.

The usual hot shower relieved some of the body aches. Too bad he couldn't take a few aspirin. But getting dressed for the day improved his outlook, and with coffee in his immediate future, he walked out of his bedroom.

It looked like he was late for the party. The sitting room contained more than he expected. In addition to a small portable buffet filled with covered chafing dishes, half a dozen people were sitting around talking in hushed tones.

"About time you joined us, boss," Wendy laughed. "Hope we didn't wake you." She was taking up most of one sofa, resting her broken leg.

Corporal Gardener and Petty Officer Canton popped to attention. Fact that everyone was in civilian attire didn't matter: their senior officer was on deck. Sue Woodward and Gunny Railey maintained their seats on the other sofa and waved.

"As you were, gentlemen," Marcus said as he waved them back down. He glanced over to the buffet. "Breakfast, I hope?"

"I think they saved you a few scraps, Mr. Colt," Jasper Railey said. "Eat up and tell us what evil you have planned for us today."

Marcus was happy to find an ample supply of eggs Benedict, hash browns, and link sausage awaiting him. Two cups of coffee and a clean plate later, he pushed back from the table and finally answered. "Rattler, you know the drill. We have research underway and now we wait to see what it finds. Unless y'all know something I don't."

Wendy spoke up, "Nothing yet, sir."

As if wishing made it so, the phone rang. Sue was closest and grabbed it. After a couple of introductory comments, she held the phone toward Marcus.

"Colt speaking."

Marcus was quiet for a couple of moments, then added a few *okays* and *damns* to break the silence. His face and comments told the group things weren't good. Finally, he said, "Tony, tell your guy to hold fast. Don't do anything else until we get more info. No … I don't expect anything from D.C. until later today … local time." He concluded the call, passed the phone back to Sue, and pointed to the base. She hung it up.

"Another coincidence?" Wendy asked.

A deep inhale was followed by a seemingly longer exhale as Marcus shook his head slightly. As all eyes settled on him, he started, "Tony said—let me back up a sec. Gentlemen, I mean Rick and Kevin and not you Rattler, *Tony* is Supervising Special Agent Anthony Carter from the NISO Naples office—he said he just got an update from the NIS agent on Sicily. Captain Michael Peters unexpectedly left Sicily by air around 0100 hours Saturday morning. He flew to Brussels to attend a heretofore unannounced NATO meeting."

No one spoke for a moment. Canton said, mostly to himself, "I wonder if one of the calls Viper made that night was to Captain Peters? To warn him, maybe?" He told the rest of the team that before they raided the villa, he overheard Vlad mentioning he had several calls to make.

Marcus shrugged. "Pure speculation, Kevin, but it's probably true. No proof, of course, but it's still a good guess. Glad you saw that possible connection. Now we need to determine if he really is going to a meeting."

Rattler showed disgust or concern—it was hard to tell the difference—as he asked, "Okay to use the phone, sir?"

Marcus nodded.

After dialing the prefix Sue provided, Rattler added the number from memory. "Gunny Railey here. Sorry to bother you on a Sunday morning, Hector, but I need to know if there is a NATO meeting either yesterday, today, or this next week that requires the presence of the NAS Sigonella commanding officer."

A moment passed as Railey listened. After a couple of sighs of frustration, he added, "Yea, fine. That's not going to happen. Yea, I would owe you one, but I'm back with a new version of Colt's Crazies, and you know we both owe him big time. Ha! Yea, he sends his love, too."

Wendy's eyebrows raised in question as she glanced at Marcus. He shrugged and shook his head slightly.

Railey continued, "Man's name is Michael Peters, Captain, USN." More listening, then he said, "Okay, call me back ASAP. Hold one for the number." He passed the phone to Sue, who provided the consulate numbers.

Knowing an explanation was needed, Railey looked at Marcus and said, "Hector Ramirez was the other door gunner on the chopper that picked you guys up last year."

"Of course," Marcus said. "Short, barrel-chested guy. I don't think I ever heard his first name."

"Since you passed out after shooting that Charlie with the RPG and throwing that bleeding SEAL into the chopper, I understand your memory loss, Mr. Colt."

Marcus rolled his eyes. "Enough history, Rattler. Why did you call Ramirez and what did he say?"

Rattler's reminiscing was not to be stopped. "Well, after you dropped the guy who wanted to blow up our chopper, and we got you two back to base, Hector and me did a few more similar missions before our tours were over. I came here, and he went to a staff job at NATO. He'll check the schedules and rosters. We should know if Peters is really there for a meeting shortly."

"Thanks. Well done, Gunny," Marcus said. "Time for more coffee while we wait."

Sue turned to Railey. "I didn't know you were on that mission. Did the SEAL survive?"

"We bandaged his shoulder and two nasty leg wounds best we could. At least we stopped the bleeding. Last I saw of him was when the medics took them both off my chopper. Mr. Colt, did he make it?"

Marcus replied, "Yea, he did. He had several months of rehab, went back to his SEAL team, and through a twist of fate, is now working for me at NISHQ."

Wendy could not hide her surprise. "That was Doc? And what was going on with the RPG? A rocket propelled grenade? Really?"

Marcus realized there was no way to stop Rattler or the direction of the conversation, so he just admitted, "Yea, that was Doc."

Rattler laughed. "No disrespect intended, Mr. Colt, but for a sailor, you sure don't know how to tell a decent sea story." He turned to Sue and Wendy before continuing. Rick and Kevin were focused on him in rapt attention.

"There we were … scooting along about five hundred feet over the lovely jungles of 'Nam. We were tasked with picking up a couple of SEALs from Indian Country. We came in to the location right at dawn, saw the smoke they popped, and set down in a small open area near the smoke. The spot also happened to be near a nest of VC, and we were taking fire. Then from the bush here comes this beat-up guy—dirty, bleeding and limping ... he looked like death warmed over, ya know. He came running best he could with an M16 slung over one shoulder, a skinner guy draped over the other, and his 1911 .45 firing wildly."

Marcus rolled his eyes and poured another cup of coffee.

Rattler continued, "I was busy shooting at the bad guys that were chasing him. Hector had stopped firing to reload and was leaning down to get more ammo, so he lost visual on his side. I glanced over at the running guy, who was now about five yards away, and he points his weapon right at me and fires. I didn't know it, but he had seen a VC on the other side of the chopper stand up with an RPG aimed at us. Mr. Colt shot right past us, through both chopper doors, and dropped the VC. Then he unceremoniously dumped the SEAL into the chopper, holstered his weapon, and collapsed on the deck himself. He saved us as we tried to save him."

No one spoke for a minute as they all turned to stare at Marcus. He finally cleared his throat and shrugged. "Thing about sea stories is they get wilder each time they're told. I think we all need to get busy writing reports about the last couple of days while we wait for Ramirez to call. Sue, is there an office area we can use while we wait?"

116

SINCE MARCUS WAS FIGHTING HEADACHES, Wendy volunteered to read over the reports for accuracy. As an accountant, she was mentally geared to analyzing paperwork. And she knew she was good at it. As she expected, they were all concise and correct.

She removed her glasses and gently rubbed her eyes. A yawn followed, as did a soft sigh. Normally, paperwork would not cause this level of fatigue, but she knew that since the accident on Wednesday night, disrupted sleep, pain, and stress from the case had run her batteries down. She was looking forward to the flight home as a way to recharge.

Tapping the various files into a neat stack gave her time to think about the new information she heard from the gunny about Marcus Colt. Granted, she was more impressed by him, but it made her feel a bit inadequate. He did all that in Vietnam and carried her down a volcano, both times while wounded, and all she could do on her first assignment was pass out from the pain of a broken leg.

But she had to admit they made a good team. His strengths, both physical and mental, were many, but she possessed the ability to read people, including him. Like Doc had done in Norfolk, she was the safety valve that helped keep Marcus on an even keel. And she was damn good at paperwork … even if she did again say so herself. A smile and slight giggle escaped as she moved the stack of reports to the briefcase. With that task done, it was time to go back to waiting for the call from Ramirez.

It took longer than expected: seemed everyone had a different definition for "As Soon As Possible," aka ASAP. But Gunny Railey's NATO buddy finally called back with the information they needed. No one was surprised to officially learn that there were no pending meetings needing the base CO from Sicily. And the captain's presence had not been requested—not for a meeting and not for a private consultation. Nothing.

That information ended the frustrating wait, and things started happening. Marcus relayed the facts to SSA Carter. Discussing it for a short while, they ran over the next obvious steps: find out if Peters was actually on the flight. Tony again contacted the agent in Sicily, requesting verification that Peters was on the flight and that it actually went to Belgium.

Tony also told him that additional agents would be arriving there in a couple of hours—use them to put the captain's residence and office under tight surveillance. With that phone call over, Tony contacted SA Adam Richmann at the evidence warehouse with the message to get himself and the three temp agents over to Sicily ASAP. He gave a quick overview and said the SSA Sicily would fill them in upon arrival.

The agent in Sicily was on the ball. The tower logs had been checked. A flight did leave early Saturday morning for Brussels and, yes, Captain M. Peters was verified to be on board.

After calling Marcus with that news, Tony sat down at the ASR-35 Teletype and sent a NIR to NISRA Brussels to put the airport under watch in case he tried to fly out. He also tasked them with finding the captain and detaining him. Probably a waste of time, he considered, since it had been over thirty-some hours since Peters arrived there, but each i and t had to be dotted and crossed.

Tony copied that NIR to other NISRAs, including those in France, West Germany, and the United Kingdom. With the airports staked out, train, boat, and auto travel might sneak him under the wire to their areas. He then sent ROIs to NISHQ and NISO Norfolk.

While Tony was doing his teletype magic, Marcus called Captain Boxer. With his numerous law enforcement contacts as CO of the Shore Patrol Unit, Boxer would be the best one to ask all the European authorities to issue APBs and to get Interpol to issue a Red Notice for Peters. The All Points Bulletin would contain a note to detain Peters for questioning and to notify NISHQ and NISO Naples of his whereabouts. A wide net had been cast. And again, they had to wait for results.

Two cups of coffee later, Marcus doodled on a notepad as he ran over the parameters of the case. He was satisfied with all they'd accomplished and hoped nothing had been overlooked. A lot had been done in a short period, yet Marcus knew he had more to do. He looked at Wendy and said, "Ready to do the kill two birds with the one rock thing, partner?"

"Sure. What ya got in mind?" Wendy wouldn't admit it, but the waiting was starting to get on her nerves.

Marcus called the hospital. First, to get an update on Doctor Frederick Monroe and second, to notify the hospital's Commanding Officer Smithson that he would be in for a dressing change within the hour. Rick Gardener was standing by with keys in his hand and Wendy's crutches on his arm; he too was anxious to do something.

117

CAPTAIN SEAN SMITHSON, WELL-RESPECTED THORACIC surgeon and CO of the base hospital, was waiting in the ER when the trio arrived. He looked more relaxed than the previous visits and a touch more pleasant. Marcus got to him first and said, "Sorry to keep making you work, sir. But thanks for being here."

"Mr. Colt, you and Miss James have provided me and my staff with a few very interesting days. And it gave me a chance to see some of my emergency procedures in action. Add to that I am now just about on a first name basis with the CNO—he calls me 'Sean' and I call him 'sir.'"

Everyone laughed at the captain's expected joke.

"It's a win-win situation. Now get your butt on that gurney so they can change your dressings." He pointed to the doctor and two nurses waiting for Marcus.

Smithson chatted with Wendy about her leg while Marcus got new dressings on both his head and arm. Both were healing nicely, the young doctor said, with no signs of infection. His hairstyle still needed help, but it would wait. New dressings were applied, and Marcus was ready to go. He approached Smithson and answered all his questions about pain, etc.

"Guess you want to see Monroe now, right?" Smithson asked after the pain-level interrogation was finished.

469

"Yes, sir, but first, tell us about his condition and prognosis … assuming he has one."

Smithson raised his hands, palms up. "Well, things look better today, but he's not out of the woods yet. We determined it was a blocked vessel, probably a clot, and we used blood thinners for treatment. He has regained consciousness but has yet to talk. He has issues of some paralysis on his right side which, when combined with the speech issues, indicates a stroke in the left hemisphere of the brain."

"Can he communicate via blinking or left-hand movements?"

"Somewhat, Marcus. He gets confused, which is normal under the conditions, but we've been able to work with him."

While Marcus considered the new information, Wendy asked, "How soon can he travel?"

"We need to watch him for at least another week. Then he will need therapy. I assume you'll want him back in D.C. for legal action."

Marcus nodded. "Since he is officially under arrest, he'll remain under guard. While I doubt he'll try to escape, I'm still not sure that he is safe from harm. We keep uncovering more bad guys, Captain, as we dig deeper into this case."

"Understood. He's still in ICU for now, but as soon as his condition improves, we'll move him to a wing we have set up for higher security. That will make it easier for his keepers to watch over him."

"Okay, let's go see what he can tell us and get this task over with," Marcus said.

The visit to Monroe was anticlimactic. The only good think Marcus thought was *at least the jerk is alive*. He quickly changed his mind, dropping the *jerk* reference: from all he had discovered, Monroe believed he was doing what the Navy wanted. Marcus shook his head as he realized a smart man can also be really gullible.

After the disappointing visit, Marcus pulled Captain Smithson aside. "Sir, how soon can we be officially released from your care? I believe we have about outlived our usefulness here in Naples and we should be heading back to D.C."

Smithson smiled. "While I do hate to see you go, I understand your situation. Today's dressing change on your head should be good for a couple of days. As for the arm, just change it daily. Get to a doctor if you see it starting to show signs of infection."

Marcus nodded. "Since one of my agents is also a hospital corpsman first class, I think—scratch that—I know he will keep on top of it, sir."

Smithson laughed. "Seeing all the injuries you've received in the line of duty, I think you having a personal corpsman *is* a very good thing. As for Miss James, she is good to go. That cast will stay in place for five more weeks. She needs to check in with her doctor when she returns to D.C. I'll have a copy of your medical records sent to your office in D.C. in the next couple of days. Good enough?"

"Yes, sir, that's perfect. And Captain, I hope you'll look Kelly and me up next time you're in D.C. You have our number. We owe you at least a dinner."

"I look forward to it, Marcus. And we'll keep you updated on Monroe's condition."

118

SSA CARTER DECIDED TO WORK late—again—since so many irons were in the fire. He hoped one of the APBs would show results, but so far, nothing. The teletype was quiet. The multiple phones just sat there, taunting him with their silence. At least knowing the man who orchestrated both Collins's and Coleman's killing had been punished; that felt good.

"Marcus, what are you guys doing here at this hour?" Tony asked when Marcus and Wendy entered the office space.

Wendy dropped into the closest chair and Rick grabbed her crutches. He sat on the edge of the desk, ready to provide assistance. Marcus selected the chair next to Tony's desk and asked, "We just came from the hospital. Got any good news to share?"

Tony shook his head. "Sorry, no. All quiet on the Naples front. Well, that's not totally true. Mario has decided talking might help him with the courts, so we have confirmation that Vlad ordered the hit on you and Coleman. We suspected it, but now we hear it from him. How about you?"

"A little bit more than you, Tony, but not much," Marcus said. "Doctor Monroe is improving, but it's going to be a long, slow journey. He's paralyzed on one side and nonverbal. He was able to communicate using one finger for yes, and two for no, but he didn't provide any new earthshaking

472

info. Just that 'his skipper' said it was okay to share secrets with the Russians."

"Any confirmation on the skipper's name?"

"No, he clammed up when we asked specifics."

Wendy jumped in. "He won't be able to move for at least a week or so. You will need to work with the SP CO to make sure the protective coverage is good."

Tony said, "Done. The SPs will take good care of him. They will also escort him to D.C. when the time arrives."

Reaching around, Tony dropped the local newspaper in Marcus's lap. "While they avoided your name, I thought you might like a copy. See page three."

This issue of the daily Naples paper was in English. The large number of English-speaking residents, both civilian and military, justified two editions. The article featured a photo of a burned car upside down on the rocky shoreline. "Diplomat Dies" was the title, and it went on to explain how a member of the Russian Embassy had lost control and skidded off the highway near Amalfi early Saturday morning. Alcohol was suspected, but due to the damage from the fire, it was not certain. His body was being returned to Moscow.

"Driving local roads can be rough," Marcus said as he passed the paper to Wendy.

Marcus had picked up a pencil from the desk and was doing a one-stick drum solo on the chair arm. His mouth was twisted and brow furrowed as he looked over at Wendy. "Unless something pops soon, seems it's time for us to get back to D.C. Comments?"

She nodded her head and shrugged.

Tony watched the decision making and smiled at Wendy, "Hate to see you two leave, but you're right—this end is wrapping up. Well, with the exception of finding Peters."

"We won't find him," Marcus said under his breath.

Tony jerked his head around. "You know something you forgot to share?"

Marcus did his standard shrug. "Not really."

Wendy coughed and covered her mouth to hide her grin. "Boss, I think we can share your theory with Tony. He won't laugh too hard. Besides, he might enjoy it so much he springs for dinner."

Tony nodded. "Damn right. I'm so desperate for info that buying dinner is getting off cheap. What ya got?"

Marcus rolled his eyes and leaned back to look at the overhead. After a long moment of silence and a deep sigh, he looked at Carter. "Wild theory time. What if Peters is a Russian sleeper agent? He was planted years ago, waited, and finally came awake when he heard about Rembrandt."

Tony developed a look best described as biting into a lemon. "Where the hell did you get that?"

Again, Marcus shrugged. "Blame it on Wendy. She kept asking the 'why' question about Peters. I ran all the options multiple times and that's the only one that seemed logical."

Wendy said, "Makes sense. Come on, Tony, admit it's possible!"

Tony was holding his hands palms up in uncertainty as the phone rang.

"Naval Investigative Service Office Naples. SSA Anthony Carter speaking. How may I help you?"

He frowned as he listened to the call. He muttered a couple of "Okays" as the basically one-sided conversation rambled on. After a few words of appreciation, he hung up and shook his head as he looked at Marcus.

"What?" asked Marcus.

"That was our contact in Brussels. Interpol spotted a man matching the description of Captain Peters boarding an Aeroflot flight to Moscow early this morning. He was traveling under the name of Mikhail Petrov, a citizen of Leningrad, returning to Russia from a business trip, according to Customs records. We've lost him."

119

THE QUIET OF THE OFFICE spaces was disconcerting: made it feel like a Saturday afternoon. Most people had decided to make the long Thanksgiving weekend a bit longer and took an extra day or two off. At the moment, there was nothing pressing. There were no hot cases needing 24/7 attention. It was a rare time.

Leaving Italy two weeks ago had been bittersweet. Marcus and Wendy had completed their primary mission of clearing the NIS agent of rape. While doing that, new friendships were developed and old ones renewed. Vlad's pistol was a match for the slug pulled from SA Bill Collins, and with the death of Vlad, that case was closed. In addition, they had finished the special assignment of finding the missing scientist, Doctor Frederick Monroe, so Cold Fog was nearing an end.

The task force designed to find the doctor opened another can of worms. They had uncovered an espionage ring trying to steal U.S. military secrets that involved the doctor and the Russians. The fact that the 'skipper' of the ring was a senior U.S. Navy officer who had escaped to Russia was the sickening, bitter end of the case. At least, it was the end for now.

The mental pain of the failure was intense, but Marcus's physical pains were reducing. The constant headaches were down to just an inconvenient level. Doc had pushed him to start small exercises on his right arm, and that was going well. But the best part was being home with Kelly; that one positive made up for all the negatives.

Marcus scanned the near-empty office space and did a quick mental staff review. He had finally convinced Ensign Wendy James to go home to Richmond to spend the extended holiday with her parents. He charged it off to the convalescent leave she was due because of the broken leg. She had refused time off after the injuries and had been working extended full days in the office since their return. *She fits in well around here,* he thought.

Rita had family coming into town and needed time to prepare her feast, so she was off that day. Carl, Martin, and Diana had accepted the invitation to join the Colts for Thanksgiving dinner—and enjoy all the televised football games. Master Chief David Bartow was now spending more time with Victoria Smythe and they, along with Doc and his fiancée Ann, would make it a full house.

His two lieutenants, Jake and Hank, had decided to take a few days of earned leave; Marcus thought they had been a bit abused since they picked up his work load while he was gone for eight months, earlier that year. The long week he had in Italy and extra work on Cold Fog taxed them further. Long-standing military tradition is to sleep and eat when you can: Marcus felt that applied to leave too.

He dropped into his chair, rubbed the scars in the middle of his slowly growing crew cut, and stared at the desk. The thick package in the medium brown, government-issued, use-again extra-large envelope was lying in the center. Marcus had gotten a quick "Courier just left … it's on your desk" from Carl as he returned from lunch. Based upon Carl's grimace, Marcus was expecting a quick case of indigestion to overpower the wonderful steak sandwich lunch.

That thought was a bit of overkill, he realized. Between his neighbor Jason Wright, the guy who initiated this case, Doc, and his CNO father-in-law, he knew what information the file held. It was all frustrating stuff that he had to look at once again.

Looking at the package, he lamented that nothing lasts forever, and so it was with his break from Cold Fog. He had enjoyed the mental freedom the variety of other cases offered the previous week. Dealing with them allowed him to push Cold Fog into the dark recesses of his mind. He'd needed that break, no matter how short it was. And now back into the fog.

The previous addressee on the envelope was the FBI. He slowly untwisted the thin waxed cord that sealed the envelope with several figure-eight turns around the two riveted discs of treated cardstock. He gingerly slid the contents out onto his desk. The bright red "Top Secret" stamp had been used extensively on the front and back of the two-inch-thick folder.

"Well, that's overkill for sure. Save some ink for other files, boys," he muttered as he opened the file. The sender took time to write across the top of the cover page a bold B1, signing beneath it.

Based upon a system developed by Naval Intelligence during WWII, the sender, the director of the FBI himself, Marcus noted, rated the source and information. The B in B1 told him the director felt the source was usually reliable. Any information passed between agencies is often given a lower rate as part of the CYA–cover your ass–mentality in government. Marcus thought the source was probably completely reliable, but the FBI didn't want to say that by putting an A there.

The 1 after the B was the information rating. It had been confirmed by independent sources and considered totally legit. At least as legit as anything else in the intelligence field. Marcus was a bit surprised it wasn't a 2 rating, showing it was *probably* true. So, as his dad always said, that information was something you "could take to the bank."

Marcus read the executive summary, looking for pieces of data he may need to dig deeper into the file for clarification. It covered the main points of Captain Michael Peters' life, all of which Marcus knew, then the interesting part: his Russian background as Mikhail Petrov. It wasn't much, but it was verification.

Mikhail Nikolaevich Petrov was born in Leningrad in 1925, the only child of Nikolai Dmitrievich and Anya Romanovna Petrov. The three are documented as Jewish and emigrated to the United States in 1935 reportedly to escape the expanding Nazi regime.

Settling in eastern Virginia, they immediately changed their names to Nicholas, Anne, and Michael Peters. Nicholas worked as a commercial fisherman.

Nicholas and Anne are deceased. Both died of natural causes in 1952.

Michael was drafted into the Army in 1943 for the duration plus six months. He served in the Pacific Theater of Operation as a clerk

```
assigned to the 93rd Division Military Police.
He was released from active duty in April 1946
at Fort Indiantown Gap, Pennsylvania.
     Using the GI benefits, he attended Penn State
University graduating with a bachelor's degree
in Mechanical Engineering in May 1950.
     He married Peggy Marie Maple from State
College, Pennsylvania in 1948 and they divorced
in 1949. No children resulted from the marriage.
He never remarried.
     With the start of the Korean Police Action,
he joined the Navy and, after attending Officer
Candidate School in Pensacola, Florida, was as-
signed to the USS Bon Homme Richard CV-36 as one
of the aircraft carriers' engineering officers.
```

The file went on and on with more background information. This was information overload at its best. Marcus rubbed his aching eyes. He had read enough. The CIA file he received the previous day said the same, except with more detail on the family's time in Russia—probably due to data provided by one of the old WWII-era German spies planted in Russian intelligence that the OSS had inherited after the war.

Since his father was a history teacher, Marcus had been swamped with historical facts as he grew up. And the war years were the second most popular with his dad, right after the Roman Empire. Marcus remembered that Hitler planned to resettle the eastern area with German citizens after the war. In preparation for this, German intelligence had infiltrated the Russian intelligence agencies with their own people. It was the start of *Generalplan Ost*, General Plan East, which was never completely carried out, and died with Hitler.

The people already working undercover in Russia became part of the Gehlen Organization, an espionage network set up by the United States to focus on the Soviet Union. It was so named for *Generalleutnant* Reinhard Gehlen, the German spymaster recruited at the end of the war by the OSS. He was in charge of the unit and worked closely with the OSS, and later the CIA, until he and the organization were transferred to the West German government. They became the foundation for Germany's Federal Intelligence Service.

The CIA was positive that all members of the Petrov family had been sleeper agents. The Soviets had instructed them to come to America and wait. When activated, the Russians provided an escape plan for Michael Peters, which he successfully used when he was discovered.

Marcus again rubbed his eyes as he took a deep breath. The sigh that followed let Doc know how he felt. Marcus had been so wrapped up in the data that he failed to hear Doc call his name from the open door. He tried again. "Boss, you got a minute? I have two cups of coffee and really only need one."

Looking up, Marcus finally saw Doc and waved him in. "Have a seat. What's on your mind?" He took the extended coffee and nodded thanks.

"Gotta admit I'm a bit tired of Cold Fog paperwork today, so I figured I'd check in with my new permanent boss. Thanks again for getting me assigned to IA full time—that training gig was worse than case paperwork."

Marcus shook his head. "I've told you, it was entirely the admiral's doing. Granted I wanted you here to work with me, but for the last time, I did not fix it."

Shrugging, Doc replied, "Well, I'm happy anyway. And what are you frustrated about? I heard the forlorn sigh all the way out in the hall."

Doc always got to the heart of the matter. Marcus blew out his cheeks and said, "Just a bit of frustration about the leader of the whole deal getting away. We got the doctor back, we broke up the Russians' laboratory, the bastard Vladimir is dead, as is his second-in-command, and Mario is facing a long prison sentence, but …"

"Yea, yea, yea. 'But' my ass. Quit your pity party, sailor. You got justice for two dead agents. You found the missing doctor, and you stopped the Russians from getting Rembrandt. And you will catch Petrov … eventually."

"Doc, please change that 'you' to a 'we' since it was a team effort involving multiple agents, agencies, and offices."

Carl interrupted with a knock on the door casing. He was holding a piece of paper and grimacing. "Sorry to interrupt, Mr. Colt, but you need to see this NIR."

Marcus joked, "Sounds like your Investigation Request is about to ruin my day. Let's have it."

Marcus read it twice. Doc noticed the surprise on his face slowly turning to anger. Finally, Marcus looked at Carl and said, "Please call Kelly and let her know my favorite corpsman and I are leaving town right now.

We should be back no later than tomorrow night. Respond to the NIR— tell them we'll be on site in about three hours."

Finally Marcus turned to Doc and said, "Grab your go-bag and sound *Boots and Saddles*, partner. You and I are heading to the Philadelphia Naval Shipyard." As he stood, he passed the NIR to Doc. "Read it in the car. You won't believe this case."

Doc skimmed the sheet, smiled, and said, "At least we won't be bored."

EPILOGUE

WHEN ENTERING THE ORIGINAL CIA headquarters building lobby, the north wall grabs immediate attention. A layer of highly polished, white Vermont marble covers the middle of the wall from floor to ceiling. In the center of that attractive wall, fifty 2.25" by 2.25" stars are engraved. The stars are painted black and stand as solemn reminders.

Gold letters are engraved into the marble centered above the stars. The three lines of text read, "In honor of those members of the Central Intelligence Agency who gave their lives in the service of their country."

Mounted in wall brackets on either side of the stars are the American flag on the right and the CIA flag on the left. A book containing most of the names of the deceased rests below the stars.

Most memorials proudly display the names of those who died for a cause, but in the clandestine service, that's not the case. The memorial wall was erected in 1973 and was dedicated in 1974 with the first thirty-one stars. Just stars: no names. No fancy memorial service was done in the following years. Stars were added each year without fanfare.

However, in 1987, the decision was finally made in the executive offices to have an actual yearly memorial service starting that year. The Deputy Director of the CIA presided. The simple service was open to all CIA employees and family members of the deceased. During the service, most of the names of the deceased are read aloud by their division directors, but not all; some names will never be revealed. One of the names said aloud during that first memorial service was Gregory Walker.

In 1971, Gregory Walker was assigned to the consulate in Naples, Italy. During that assignment, while assisting with a Naval Investigative Service investigation, he was driving a car that was intentionally run off the road by a KGB operative. Gregory Walker died that night trying to control the car. His star was among the first thirty-one engraved on the wall. His parents had died while he was in college, and he was an only child. No living relatives were listed in his files.

The CIA's current ADDO, Assistant to the Deputy Director of Operations, had arranged for two people who were neither CIA employees nor relatives of a star holder to attend as surrogates for the relatives that Gregory Walker didn't have. They had a special connection to Greg: they were with him when he died.

Though the three were new friends, he called them Wendy and Marcus. And they knew Greg's dedication, even to the end, had saved their lives. Susan Woodward, who took her new husband's name of Canton two years later, had been Greg's superior in Naples when he was killed.

Marcus Colt, with his wife Dr. Kelly Anne Colt on his right side, stood to the right of Susan Canton, the current Assistant to the Deputy Director of Operations. Wendy James stood to the left of Susan. Wendy's husband was currently serving as skipper on a carrier in the Pacific Ocean and therefore unable to attend. Both Marcus and Wendy now had their arms around Susan. The gesture was for both physical support and shared sadness.

Kevin Canton, husband of ADDO Canton, stood directly behind his wife with Mrs. Victoria Smythe, Assistant to the Deputy Director of Operations, Retired, on his right. Over the years, these six people enjoyed relationships that surpassed standard friendships as they had become family.

The memorial service was short, but very moving. A few sobs were heard during the reading of the names. Soft murmuring voices, handshakes, and hugs offered consolation to attendees at the end of the service. As the bulk drifted away, Sue, Wendy, and Marcus walked to the wall and simply stared silently at the twenty-seventh star. Greg Walker would be a part of them forever.

GLOSSARY

ANGELS—Flight level, i.e., altitude given in thousands of feet.

AN/PVS-2 Starlight Scope—A night vision scope for a rifle. Weight is about six lbs and it has a range up to 3,200 feet.

APB—All Points Bulletin. A widespread notice to all law enforcement officers that a suspect or item, such as a vehicle, is being sought in connection with a crime.

ASW—Anti-Submarine Warfare.

AUTOVON—Automatic Voice Network. A worldwide American military telephone/Teletype system with high-speed switching centers.

BI—Background Information check. Used to determine eligibility for security clearances. Includes talking with friends, previous employers, and educators, looking into social memberships, and analyzing financials.

Bravo Zulu—International naval signal code for "well done."

CNO—Chief of Naval Operations. The military head of the U.S. Navy. Advisor and deputy of the Secretary of the Navy.

CO—Commanding Officer of a military unit.

Cover—Headgear. Hat.

CPO—Chief Petty Officer.

FUBAR—Navy version of SNAFU. Fouled Up Beyond All Recognition.

GS—General Schedule. GS followed by a number indicates the pay scale in the U.S. Civil Service.

Indian Country—Enemy Territory. A historical reference to the old West and the cavalry venturing into untamed areas.

Interpol—International Criminal Police Organization. An international law enforcement organization to facilitate worldwide police cooperation.

JAG—Judge Advocate General. The legal arm of the U.S. Navy.

M.E.—Medical Examiner.

Ka-Bar—USN Mark 2 Utility Knife.

Klick—Military slang for a Kilometer.

MOS—Military Occupational Specialty. A number that defines a set of skills.

NAS—Naval Air Station.

NIS—Naval Investigative Service.

NISHQ—Naval Investigative Service Headquarters, located in Washington, D.C.

NISO—Naval Investigative Service Office. Designation for the headquarters over a specific geographical area that contains multiple NISRAs. Staffed by both military and civilian personnel.

NISRA—Naval Investigative Service Resident Agency. Office that houses agents and staff that are responsible for a smaller portion of a NISO.

NTC—Naval Training Center.

Petty Officer—A noncommissioned officer that has shown skills and leadership, allowing them to advance over other enlisted personnel.

Rack—Military slang for a bunk or bed.

Red Notice—Interpol's version of an APB to locate and arrest a person pending legal action or extradition.

RPG—Rocket Propelled Grenade. A one-man, shoulder-fired missile that contains an explosive warhead.

SA—Special Agent.

SEALs—Special Warfare Operators. Acronym for Sea, Air, Land.

Sea Story—A nautical version of an urban legend or highly inflated version of an actual event. It usually starts with "This is no shit …"

SP—Shore Patrol. The police force of the Navy.

SSA—Supervisory Special Agent.

TAD—Temporary Additional Duty.

UA—Unauthorized Absence, same as Army's AWOL (Absent WithOut Leave).

UCMJ—Uniform Code of Military Justice. The foundation of military law in the United States.

VC—Viet Cong. These were the Vietnamese Communists. Often phonetically pronounced "Victor Charlie."

XO—Executive Officer of a military unit. Second-in-command.

MARINE OFFICER RANKS

1stLt—Abbreviation for the Marine rank of First Lieutenant. Second lowest level commissioned officer in the Marine Corps. Pay grade of O-2. Insignia is a collar device of a single silver bar on each shirt collar. The bar is also displayed on the shoulder boards and the right side of the garrison cover.

NAVAL OFFICER RANKS

ENS—Abbreviation for the Navy rank of Ensign. Lowest level commissioned officer in the Navy. Pay grade of O-1. Insignia is a single gold stripe around the jacket sleeve and on the shoulder board or a collar device of a single gold bar. This device is often referred to as a *butter bar.*

LTJG—Abbreviation for the Navy rank of Lieutenant Junior Grade. Second lowest level commissioned officer in the Navy. Pay grade of O-2. Insignia is a wide gold stripe and a narrow gold stripe around the jacket sleeve and on the shoulder board, or a collar device of a single silver bar.

LT—Abbreviation for the Navy rank of Lieutenant. Third lowest commissioned officer in the Navy. Pay grade of O-3. Insignia is a pair of wide gold stripes around the jacket sleeve and on the shoulder board, or a collar device of a pair of gold bars. This device is often referred to as *railroad tracks.*

LCDR—Abbreviation for the Navy rank of Lieutenant Commander. Fourth level commissioned officer in the Navy. Pay grade of O-4. Insignia is a single narrow gold stripe with a wide gold stripe above and below, around the jacket sleeve, and on the shoulder board, or a collar device of a gold leaf.

CDR—Abbreviation for the Navy rank of Commander. Fifth level commissioned officer in the Navy. Pay grade of O-5. Insignia is three wide gold stripes around the jacket sleeve and on the shoulder board, or a collar device of a silver leaf.

CAPT—Abbreviation for the Navy rank of Captain. Sixth level commissioned officer in the Navy. Pay grade of O-6. Insignia is four wide gold stripes around the jacket sleeve and on the shoulder board, or a collar device of a silver eagle.

RDML—Abbreviation for the Navy rank of Rear Admiral (lower half). Seventh level commissioned officer in the Navy. Pay grade of O-7. Insignia is a single, very wide gold stripe around the jacket sleeve. Shoulder board and collar device is a single silver star.

RDM—Abbreviation for the Navy rank of Rear Admiral. Eighth level commissioned officer in the Navy. Pay grade of O-8. Insignia is a single very wide gold stripe, below a narrower single gold stripe around the jacket sleeve. Shoulder board and collar device is a pair of silver stars.

VADM—Abbreviation for the Navy rank of Vice Admiral. Ninth level commissioned officer in the Navy. Pay grade of O-9. Insignia is a single very wide gold stripe, below a pair of narrower single gold stripes, around the jacket sleeve. Shoulder board and collar device is a trio of silver stars.

ADM—Abbreviation for the Navy rank of Admiral. Tenth level commissioned officer in the Navy. Pay grade of O-10. Insignia is a single very wide gold stripe, below a trio of narrower single gold stripes, around the jacket sleeve. Shoulder board and collar device is a set of four silver stars.

NAVAL AIRCRAFT

F-4—McDonnell Douglas Phantom. Two-seat, twin-engine long-ranger supersonic jet interceptor and fighter-bomber. Often called *Double Ugly, Flying Brick*, *Rhino*, *Old Smokey*, and a few other names.

P2V—Lockheed land-base maritime patrol aircraft. The P2V features two Wright radial piston engines, two Westinghouse turbojet engines, and a range of ASW weapons.

P-3 Orion—A Lockheed four-engine, anti-submarine and maritime surveillance aircraft introduced in the 1960s. This land-based aircraft carried a range of ASW weapons. It carried a crew of twelve.

READ HOW IT ALL STARTED FOR MARCUS COLT

FAIR WINDS OF DEATH

It's 1971, and the Naval Investigative Service, or "NIS" as it's better known, is nothing like the NCIS of present-day television. There are no cell phones, desktop computers, DNA, or the Internet. All that the Navy and civilian personnel working for this specialized unit have to rely on are their minds. Logic, investigative skills, and experience hitting the streets are all they have to get the information they need. The work is often dangerous, and sometimes, good old-fashioned luck is the real key to sending the criminals to the brig for good.

At NIS headquarters in Washington, D.C., Lieutenant Commander Marcus Colt has made a name for himself handling the country's most unusual cases. Despite his occasional short temper and hint of sarcasm coloring his attitude, Colt is intelligent and driven to succeed. And while his behavior sometimes complicates situations, as the top Internal Affairs investigator, this decorated officer is the one top Navy brass go to when no one else can handle the mission.

One such assignment is the latest in a long line of challenges to cross Colt's desk. A series of informational leaks within the NIS agency have led to the executions of at least four confidential informants on the Norfolk Naval Base, and the threat of more victims is imminent. Armed with his uncanny investigative skills and deceptively youthful looks, Colt goes undercover as a junior enlisted man in Norfolk, Virginia and works to stop the leak at its source. To accomplish this difficult task, he must build close relationships with personnel in his NIS unit, invade their privacy, and dig up their life secrets—all while keeping his true identity and mission hidden.

As straightforward as his investigative job is, nothing with this assignment is what it seems. And when the case takes unexpected twists and turns, Colt finds himself questioning everything he knows. Losing an old flame, evading assassins, meeting a high-ranking officer's daughter, and overcoming personal guilt from a Vietnam mission that nearly cost him everything—all add complexity to his assignment. But friends new and old, along with his fellow agents at the NIS, aid Colt in his mission as he works to solve the case.

He has the skills and the team, but time is quickly running out. With danger and uncertainty surrounding him, it will take everything Marcus Colt has to stop the leak before someone else dies—especially when that next someone could be him.

B. R. WADE, JR. BIO

B. R. WADE, JR., though relatively new to fiction writing, has been all too happy to add it to his list of life accomplishments. Born in Roanoke, Virginia, he spent his teen years and much of his adult life in the Tampa Bay area of Florida.

While in Tampa, Bill worked in retail management before switching to a career as a computer systems analyst for the local school system. He changed careers again and started a manufacturing company. After this last change, he made his self-proclaimed escape to the mountains of West Virginia shortly after the turn of the century where he still owns and operates a hobby kit manufacturing business.

After enlisting in the U.S. Navy Reserve in 1969, he was called to active duty and graduated top of his class from both basic training at Naval Training Center Orlando, Florida and Yeoman 'A' School at NTC Bainbridge, Maryland. Soon after, he was assigned to the Naval Investigative Service Office in Norfolk, Virginia.

Bill left active service as a Petty Officer Third Class, then spent three more years as a weekend reservist at his local Navy Reserve Center. And despite his busy work schedule, Bill obtained degrees in Business Management and Computer Science. He also studied marketing at the University of South Florida.

Happily, all of Bill's pursuits have proved quite inspiring and provide him with plenty of writing material. He is nearly finished with the third adventure for his *Fair Winds* NIS novel protagonist, Marcus Colt.